6/26/13

NEVER LOOK BACK

EMI LOST & FOUND SERIES

BOOK THREE

Cover Design by Summer Ortiz

Lori L. Otto Publications

Visit our website at: www.loriotto.com

Second Edition: January 2012

Printed in the United States of America

DEDICATION

to all of the upstanding men
i've had the pleasure of working with:
the knox street family room team

there's a little of each of you in jack

BOOK THREE
JACK

CHAPTER 1

It was a year ago yesterday that everything changed. She was almost gone just as suddenly as she had come back into my life. My memory infallible, I remember it all like it *was* yesterday.

In the hallway of the hotel, outside the ballroom, I practiced the toast I was going to deliver to my best friend and his fiancée at their New Year's Eve engagement party. I had known Chris for eleven years. He was more like a younger brother to me. We met in college when he pledged my fraternity, and we shared the same values and sense of humor, so we bonded quickly.

When we initially met, his parents were going through a messy divorce. I had little knowledge of the subject, as my parents had stayed married and shared a happy life together. But being the oldest of four children, I was looked up to by everyone in the household. My parents had instilled in me a certain sense of responsibility, and I grew up taking care of others, being there for them as needed. My father was a workaholic, so as I grew into my teen years, I was the man of the household. I would do everything to be loyal and reliable to those I cared about, and who cared about me.

So it was a good fit when Chris moved into our fraternity house. I took him under my wing and helped him through a difficult situation. I think when you meet people at such a critical time in life, you tend to keep them close.

When Chris realized that Anna was the person he wanted to marry, I was the second person he called. Emi– *oh, Emi–* was always the first he would turn to. In age, they were less than a year apart, and together they moved out of their father's home when their mother left him. They attended a new high school together and stayed close to one another, holding tight to what little bit of familiarity they had left.

I could tell that Anna was "the one" that first night he told me about her. I'd known Chris when he was in relationships with other women, but none had ever really inspired him. He was so excited, so enamored with this woman... you could just hear it in his voice. Although I knew I would lose yet another one of my bachelor friends, I was happy for him.

So that night, I felt ready to address the crowd and wish all the best to my friend and his soon-to-be wife. Focused and confident, I was ready to speak... until I saw her.

She caught my attention from the moment she stepped out of the elevator across the lobby. She was impossible to miss, her pale skin nearly glistening in a red dress that attracted the eyes of every man around. The dress was what got my attention initially, but it was her smile that really drew me in, red lipstick highlighting the most perfect lips, curled up in a way that made it seem like she had a secret that no one else could know. I immediately wanted to know that secret, know *every* secret that she kept.

I somehow managed to tear my attention from her lips as my eyes traveled up the milky skin of her soft features. Her cheeks glowed with a natural blush as her pale green eyes scanned the room around her, eventually meeting mine. Our gazes locked and her cheeks became redder. I felt my lips fall open ever so slightly, but I was as helpless to close them as I was to produce a sound from them.

I felt as if I had the wind knocked out of me in an instant. All of my confidence disappeared as I recognized those eyes. They had haunted my memories for years. My breathing shortened to shallow gasps, all of my muscles tensed at the realization. It was Emi, and I had not seen her– and rarely had spoken of her– since that one night in college. She smiled politely at me, and I returned the greeting, wondering if– *hoping that*– she recognized me. As her eyes dropped to the floor when she turned into the ballroom, I assumed she did not. *But how could she not?*

I swallowed, then inhaled deeply in an attempt to calm my nerves. Buried feelings, one-sided though they were, returned immediately, rendering me lightheaded. I needed to sit down.

When I was in my fourth year in college, Emi entered our school as a freshman and came to one of our fraternity parties. Even then, her smile was what drew me to her, but her green eyes were what held me there, captive. Once I started talking to her, I couldn't focus on anything else. She made me laugh with the animated way she recalled some of her first college experiences. She was very much my opposite, but at the time, she seemed to be exactly what I needed. To my black-and-white world, she wasn't just grey, she was every color in between. Her free spirit made me feel more alive.

At first, after having one or two drinks, she was cute and flirtatious, and after talking to her one-on-one for an extended period of time, I was getting up the courage to ask her out. As the night wore on, though, and the alcohol took its effect on her, I lost my nerve *and* my chance when at least ten guys at the party had the same idea. Eventually, she had a swarm of lonely boys at her feet, bringing her beer, each hoping for a night that would end up with her in their dorm rooms. From my conversation with her, I didn't think she was that type.

Chris, enjoying the party as much as the rest of our brothers, was naturally angry when I pointed out the crowd forming around Emi. He set out to defend her honor, slurring some threats to them, and eventually the guys backed away from his sister. Chris delivered a few choice words to her, as well, adding that she didn't belong at his party. He called a friend of theirs and asked him to come pick her up. Chris was in no shape to keep an eye on her, though, so I made it a point to do just that.

She sat outside on a picnic table, her beautiful green eyes now glazed over, tired and red. Her elbows rested on her knees, hands steadying her head. Waiting for her ride to come, a few frustrated tears escaped from her eyes as she chewed hard and deliberately on a piece of gum. Two cups and a bottle of water in hand, I walked outside to join her, wanting to comfort her. I poured each of us a drink, handing a cup to her.

"Thanks," she mumbled, taking a sip.

"You're welcome," I answered politely. I sat down next to her and fought the urge to put my arm across her shoulders, not wanting it to seem like I was coming on to her. I tried to find words to put her at ease, but I couldn't think of anything to say. In the end, we both just sat in silence, staring out into the dark night in front of us.

After a half hour or so of sitting on that table, waiting, I had accepted the fact that her friend wasn't coming.

"Emi, can I take you back to your apartment?"

"You don't have to."

"I know I don't have to, but I'd like to."

"He should be here by now," she said.

"I really don't mind."

She sat quietly for a few more minutes before conceding. "Alright, I guess," she said to me. I was happy to have the opportunity to see her home safely. I had no intention of "going back to her place," but I was relieved in knowing that no one else would be going there, either.

Just as she tried to move off the table, she stumbled. I reached out to steady her, and she laughed, embarrassed.

"It's okay," I encouraged her, trying to help her up. Her face inches from mine, she quickly leaned into me and kissed me. It took me a second to realize what was happening, as she had caught me completely off guard. But as she sat on that table, vulnerable, beautiful, her soft kiss caused a whirlwind of feelings inside of me.

Of course, my hormones raged within at her touch, but it was so much more than that. I felt numb and incredibly aware of every sensation, all at the same time. My body was alive with energy, aching to burst free from the confines of my skin, yet I could not move an inch, wouldn't move an inch away from her. Never before had I felt as if my life was missing anything, but in that moment, I felt whole.

I cradled her face in my hands. I brushed my lips against hers gently, teasing her, tentative, making sure that was what she wanted. When she pressed her mouth to mine again, I felt I had not misread her intentions.

I took in the moment with each of my senses. The lightly perfumed smell of her hair. The taste of her cinnamon gum. The warmth of her creamy skin. The music behind us, barely masking the noise of a revving car engine. The nearly translucent green color of her sad eyes... I had to open mine in an attempt to catch another glimpse. She was looking back at me with uncertainty, and we slowly moved away from one another, neither of us daring to speak.

As I helped her off the table, breathless, I noticed the addition of the dark convertible sports car parked at the curb in front of us. Without cutting the engine or the headlights, a tall, blonde, lanky kid stepped out of the car and stared directly at her. She stopped in her tracks and looked down at her feet, shrugging away from my loose grasp.

"Emi," he said to her, concern escaping with a rush of air from his lungs. He stood at the curb and surveyed the situation, only glancing briefly at me as if to warn me to stay away.

"Hey," she whimpered out unsteadily, ashamed, her eyes sparkling as she looked up to meet his gaze. She began to cry, and I couldn't tell if it was frustration, embarrassment, or just the alcohol. The tears stirred him immediately into action. He walked briskly toward her. I could see in that moment that he cared for her deeply, and it seemed she felt the same way. Although there was noise and havoc all around as the party progressed behind us, his eyes were focused only on her, as if she were the only thing in the world to him. There was something between them, some unspoken *thing*, that made it obvious that he was the one who was meant to be with her, the one meant to go back to her place. Not these drunk guys. Certainly not me.

I backed away from her and watched as they embraced one another. She looked up at him, eyebrows raised, as if she were a child looking to him for acceptance, or punishment. His eyes looked down to meet hers, and just when I thought I'd witness a kiss that I really didn't want to see, his lips barely brushed her forehead before his hand pulled her head into his chest. She sighed visibly, and he slowly guided her toward the car, her clumsy gait causing them both to trip. They laughed before he opened the door for her and helped her inside, buckled her seatbelt. He closed her door and leaned over it, staring into her needy eyes, brushing a few hairs out of her face. She put her hand on the back of his neck and pulled his face to hers, but instead of kissing her, he paused momentarily and slowly removed her hand, kissed her palm, and placed it in her lap.

He walked to his side of the car, and as Emi turned to wave goodbye, I caught the boy looking at me once again. He was no older than seventeen, still an awkward teenager. I met his gaze and held it. I imagined he was advising me to keep away from her. My stare was telling him to take good care of her. That was a battle I knew I couldn't win.

"Would you like another?" the hotel bartender asked as I swirled the ice in the glass of scotch I had ordered to calm my nerves.

"No, thank you." I had known Chris and Anna would be looking for me soon.

I was affected for months by the kiss I shared with Emi. As time went on, I expected my feelings to wane, but every time I saw the pale green color of her eyes, or smelled cinnamon, or heard the song that had been playing in the background, the feelings only intensified.

After I left college to focus on work full-time, I began dating a woman who lived in my building, creating an acceptable distraction. But in the ten years that had passed between our first encounter and this one, I had never experienced such intense feelings for any other woman, not even the one I had promised to marry. I had accepted long ago that Emi was a fantasy, not my reality. I had banished her from my thoughts.

I knew she would be at the party that night, but I had no idea what the mere sight of her would do to me. I had expected her to be different. With just one night together– and how little I knew of her– over the years, she became this vision, this ideal, this woman that I knew no *real* woman could ever come close to equalling. I expected her to be average. I expected to feel indifference toward her, to finally get closure to the questions that still lingered in my mind. Most of all, I had expected her to be unavailable to me, as she was back then.

I never expected what I saw that night.

The woman I saw in that hallway was hardly the same girl I had met. Here she was, ten years later, parading that same breathtaking smile and those green eyes in front of me, but she had an air of confidence about her that I didn't remember from before. She was beautiful back in college, but she was absolutely stunning on that particular night. No, she was *extraordinary*. And the best part? She was alone at the party.

She was alone. I was alone. I had smiled inwardly, acknowledging that there *was* something between us that night in college, even though I had since convinced myself that I had created it all in my mind. I knew then, in my heart, that there was *something there*. I had to find out.

The scotch had obviously done its job, calming my nerves *and* giving me a boost of courage. As I walked back to the ballroom, I made slight revisions to the toast in my mind.

When I made my entrance, I immediately saw Chris waving me over to him. When I reached them, Anna embraced me warmly.

"I can't believe how many people are here," Chris said. "I wasn't sure we'd be able to break away for the toast! You ready to go on?"

"I am," I said, confident.

"Let me gather the band," he said.

"Nate!" he yelled across the room. "Nate, come on!"

A tall man with disheveled, blonde hair joined the group. He looked familiar, maybe just another one of Chris's college friends, but I couldn't place him at the time.

"So, this is my best man," Chris introduced us. "You'll welcome everyone, he'll do his toast, and then you'll perform your three songs. Got it?"

"Yeah," Nate answered him, looking a little distracted before settling his eyes on me. "Nice to meet you," he said, shaking my hand. He looked at me inquisitively, almost confused.

"Likewise," I told him politely.

"Right. Are we ready?" he asked me.

"I'm ready."

"Let me get the guys, I'll be right back." He left momentarily as a waiter stopped by to hand us glasses of champagne.

"Congratulations," I told them both just before the band took the stage.

"Ladies and gentlemen," Nate addressed the crowd. "On behalf of Chris and Anna, I want to thank all of you for coming out tonight. I believe, uh..." He glanced over at me before continuing, obviously struggling over my name. "I believe Chris's best man has a few words to say."

I walked on stage, taking my place behind the microphone. I cleared my throat and scanned the room until I found the beautiful woman in the red dress– she was impossible to miss. Again, feeling more alive than ever in her presence, I was determined and confident, and I began my toast.

"It's rare that you meet someone who has the power to change the world as you know it. One day, you're alone, going about your own business, expecting that day to be the same as all the ones before. Most days happen this way. And then, out of the blue, it all changes."

I made brief eye-contact with Emi and I felt my heart jump. I looked away quickly and continued.

"You meet someone that affects you in ways you never even knew were possible. From that day on, no day you live will ever be like the ones that came before. Your future is changed with just one word or one glance... one person that stands apart from all others."

Again, I looked in her direction and noticed her cheeks flush as she averted her eyes to the floor.

"Chris called me the day that happened to him. From the moment he *literally* ran into her on Lexington Avenue, he never thought of another woman. The force of their impact caused her to spill hundreds of fabric swatches from the bags she had been carrying. The breeze on the unusually windy day took many of them into the street, and even though Anna, this woman, urged Chris to let them go, he insisted on stopping traffic to retrieve every last one."

I paused, pulling a small square of yellow corduroy out of my pocket and holding it up to show the guests.

"This is the last one." I heard a few giggles and "ahhh"s from the crowd. I glanced at Anna, who smiled at Chris before kissing him. "He kept it in his pocket, hoping to create a reason for them to meet again. He never needed it. They went out for coffee that afternoon, and never went another day without seeing each other or talking to one another.

"And that was the day he called me, the day he met her... the day he realized he had met the woman he would marry. When I had dinner with Chris and Anna a few weeks later, I knew he was right. She was warm and open, honest and sincere... a perfect compliment to his similar personality. They laughed all night together, their smiles were contagious. I couldn't help but feel happier when I was around them. In Chris's other relationships, love was hard, love was painful, love was work. But this was effortless. They made loving someone else look easy.

"So, to all of you who didn't believe in love at first sight, I hope they've made believers out of you. Anna, you're an amazing woman. And, Chris, you're a lucky man. I couldn't be happier that you found one another. May you cherish and love each other always."

I raised my glass and drank, watching the crowd follow my lead. There was a little bit of clapping as I walked off the stage to shake Chris's hand.

"Thanks," Chris said to me.

"You're welcome," I returned, patting him on the back. "Hey, I think I saw your little sister here– she's changed a lot since I last saw her."

"Yeah, Emi's here. You should say hi," he said as he and Anna took me in her direction.

"Emi, I'm Jack," I introduced myself, shaking her soft, delicate hand. "We actually met once at a party in college."

"Jack, my god!" she said laughing and nodding as the loud chorus of the first song filled the room. "That night was a little fuzzy, but I thought I knew you from somewhere," she yelled in my ear over the noise.

"Well, I recognized you," I told her, unable to hide my attraction to her. "How could I forget? You are beautiful."

"Oh... thank you..." she laughed again, waving her hand as if she always looked like she did that night. "Your toast was great," she said. "I guess I have to come up with one for the reception. I'm the maid of honor, you know."

"That's right, I forgot!" In all honesty, I didn't know, but this gave me hope of having many more opportunities to get to know Emi better. "I could give you some pointers for a speech," I added. "Or if you just need a sounding board, I'd be happy to listen."

"Thanks, I just might take you up on that. I'm not the best writer... or speaker... and I really don't like being the center of attention. It scares me."

"Really?" I asked as I allowed my eyes to leave hers briefly to travel the length of her body. I could feel my face get hot as our eyes met again and I realized she'd noticed me staring. *Very classy.* I normally had a little more self-control than that.   I just couldn't help myself.   "I'm sorry," I said, embarrassed.

"No," she smiled. "I don't normally dress like this. I was feeling a little daring tonight."

"Well... Stunning." *Speechless.*

"Stop," she blushed again as the first song died down.

"Listen, I'm going to get a drink. Would you like something?"

"I'll go with you," she said as we walked toward the bar.   "I'm a little thirsty."

"You're Emi, right?" the bartender asked her.

"I am," she smiled, looking confused.

"Your brother pointed you out to me earlier.   He stocked Bellei, your favorite wine, like you requested."   He began to pour her a glass, but she put her hand up, stopping him.

"I'm really thirsty right now," she laughed.   "Do you just have, umm, maybe a ginger ale?"

"Of course," he said, setting the wine down and filling a glass with the soda Emi had requested. "Sir?" the bartender directed his attention to me.

"Do you mind if I try your wine?" I asked her.

"Don't want it to go to waste," she shrugged, smiling. I tipped the waiter and we took our drinks to a nearby table.

I smiled, examining the pale strawberry color and inhaling its bouquet. "It's sparkling," I told her after taking a sip, surprised by its flavor and body. "A little dry... acidic... earthy."

"Don't judge me," she laughed.   "It's a Lambrusco.   It's a good one, though. The texture is a little like champagne."

"No, it's nice," I smiled as her cheeks reddened with her explanation. "Would you like a sip?" I asked, tilting the glass toward her.

"Oh, no, thank you," she said.   "Think I'll take it slow tonight.   Don't want any repeats of that night in college," she laughed.   I smiled, wishing secretly for a repeat of the kiss.

"So, I have to ask you, Emi," I began, still a little nervous. "How is it that you're here alone tonight?"

"Oh," she said, surprised. "No, I'm not." She laughed nervously as my heart fell. "Um, I'm here with Nate, my boyfriend. He's the one singing in the band." She pointed to the stage and I looked at him a little more intently. "He's actually the guy that picked me up from that party."

Of *course* he was, only he was no longer that awkward, lanky kid. He was the one I had accepted that she was meant to be with, and somehow they were still together. I knew I had seen him before, but he had grown up a lot since that first meeting. I nodded, inhaling deeply. My hopes were dashed, for a second time, by one man. I finished the glass of wine quickly as I sat silently through the rest of the second song. I sensed that she knew that I was interested, and that she could see my disappointment.

She said "boyfriend," though. They weren't married, not even engaged, by the look of her ring finger. As another song began to play, I looked up to see him focused on his guitar and decided to just take a chance.

"Would you like to dance?" The song, a jazz song I remembered playing at my junior prom. The lyrics couldn't have been more perfect.

She smiled and shrugged. "Why not?"

I took her by the hand and led her to the dance floor. It was a slow song, and as much as I wanted to pull her close to me, I was careful and deliberate about leaving space between us. I was never that guy. As soon as I felt the warm, soft skin of her back under my fingers, I adjusted my stance accordingly. If I were her boyfriend, lucky enough to hold that place in her life, I wouldn't want another man touching her.

Nate looked up from his instrument and watched as I danced with his girlfriend. I felt defiant for a second and nodded in his direction, smiling, raising my eyebrows just enough to make a statement.

I paid particular attention to the lyrics he sang, finding it strangely ironic how they described that moment in college perfectly. My heart *did* skip a beat when I had kissed her that night. My attraction to her was instantaneous.

"You two have been together a while," I commented as I stared at the singer.

"Not really," she laughed, her sparkling eyes calling out for attention. I had to oblige and got lost in her gaze. "We've been friends forever... but we've only been dating a couple of months."

"Seriously?" I asked, intrigued.

"Seriously."

"That surprises me," I admitted.

"Why?" she asked.

"I could just tell when I saw the way he looked at you that night that he loved you... deeply."

"Nuh-uh," she countered.

"Really," I said. "In fact, I had been thinking about asking you out, but when I saw you together, I just thought that you two were *supposed* to be together. That's what your brother told me way back then." I thought about the wasted years... *ten* wasted years...

"Huh," she said, glancing to the stage. "Well, maybe we were."

My heart sank, wistful. I couldn't believe it was happening. As much as I felt something between them that night, ten years ago, I was sure that I was feeling something between us as I held her in my arms. I had no doubt in my mind.

"Maybe," I smiled, my last attempt at flirting. "Maybe not." She blushed again and laughed, holding my attention with her pale green stare as we continued to dance. She took my breath away. I saw something in her eyes that gave me hope, and at that point, the thought that I was creating what I wanted with my mind, making up this strange current between us, began to diminish. Her gaze continued, and I couldn't, wouldn't, break away first. Before the music ceased to play, we had stopped dancing, and were temporarily lost in one another's eyes, neither one of us able to breathe or to speak. The need was incessant to acknowledge what had just happened between us, but my vocal chords refused to cooperate, just as they had when I first saw her before the party had begun. *What would I have said to her, anyway? Did you feel that?*

"Thank you," Nate said through the microphone as the music stopped. The sound of his voice was what finally made her look away. I was actually hopeful, my mind a flurry of ideas of things to say or do. She blushed, deeply, her eyes avoiding mine. That was a strange exchange between us, and I just felt like something was there. I watched Nate exit the stage and begin his walk toward us. The awkwardness of his earlier youth left no evidence in his self-assured stride. He was stopped by Chris and Anna, and I tried to think of some diversion, some way to get a little more time with her.

When I looked at her to speak, though, I noticed her stare was now firmly affixed on her boyfriend. She was smiling, he was staring back at her, eyes intense and intent, determined. He glanced at me, only briefly, but I saw the same look in his eyes that I saw at the fraternity party, that same warning glance. Again, just like that night, I hoped that he would take care of her, that he would be good to her. She was lost to him, again... and it was obviously meant to be. When he reached us, he touched her face softly and I was finally witness to the kiss that I had always dreaded.

And what had he said to me? "Thanks for looking after her." My stomach churns at how prophetic that statement truly is, now.

He then took her by the hand and led her out of the ballroom. She didn't even turn back to say goodbye, not even a wave this time.

Paralyzed, heart racing, I stood staring. The doorway, empty. The vision of her gone. Her perfume lingering in the air around me, I breathed deeply, taking in all that remained of her. As her scent dissipated, the crowd around me came back into focus, but I was alone.

I knew there was something between us, I knew it in the pit of my stomach, but I had to accept that there must have been something *more* between them. I didn't want to, but I had to. God, how I wished that he wasn't in the picture.

And, god, how I had regretted that sentiment from the moment it came into my head. I had no way of knowing how the events of that evening would unfold.

As I lie in bed listening to the soft patter of raindrops on my patio, Emi's head resting on my shoulder as she sleeps quietly, the horror of that night continues to play out in my mind.

After she had left with Nate, I had a few more drinks and mingled with the rest of the guests at the party. My mind was full of ideas to get more time with her. I *would* get that time with her, I just knew it. I had concocted the perfect plan, and would put it into action the next day.

Shortly before midnight, I decided I would head up to my room. Watching happy lovers greet the new year with a kiss wasn't particularly of interest to me. Chris caught me on my way out in the hallway.

"You taking off?" he had asked.

"Yeah, great party," I smiled. "Congratulations again."

"Thanks man, and thanks for the toast." His phone rang in his pocket, and he pulled it out and looked at the name on the display.

"Hey, Emi, what's up?" he asked. He was silent, putting a hand over his other ear as he struggled to hear. A look of confusion spread across his face. "Emi? Em, are you there?"

"What's going on?" I asked quietly.

"I'm guessing she didn't mean to call me... I can hear her and Nate. Hold on..." He walked farther down the hallway, away from the noise of the crowd. I followed him, curious. "I don't know, maybe I don't want to know what's going on," he joked.

"She left the ballroom with him about two hours ago," I told him. "Right after he performed." I remembered the look of desire that was exchanged between them. "You should probably hang up."

"I think she's crying... or wait... maybe not, he just told her he loved her." He strained to hear more. At the moment, I had heard enough and started to turn away. "No, she's definitely crying." He continued to walk toward the lobby as all the color drained from his face, and I followed, worried for his sister.

"Emi!" he yelled into the phone. "Emi, can you hear me? What's going on?"

"Were they staying here?" I asked. "What room are they in?"

"Emi!"

I walked to the front desk and asked the concierge to call her room. "Chris, what's his last name?"

"Wilson," he told me.

After letting the phone ring, she informed me that no one was answering.

"I don't think they're here."

"Something's happened, man," he told me. "She just keeps crying and asking for him. And I don't hear him... 'Nate, focus on me, please.' That's what she just said. I think he's hurt."

After a few minutes, he handed me the phone and asked me to try to listen. "Oh, Nate," I heard her say as my heart faltered, hearing her proclaim the name of this other man, sorrow filling her voice. I then heard her crying, confirming Chris's fears that something was wrong. *I had wished that he wasn't in the picture.*

"I'll go get your family." I handed him the phone and he nodded at me as I ran into the ballroom to find Anna.

"Chris just got a call from Emi... we think something's wrong. Can you find his parents and come to the lobby?"

"Sure," she said as a few of her friends scoured the room for Chris's family. After asking the concierge to bring my car up, I returned to my friend's side, wanting to be there for him, but wanting even more to find Emi, to help her. My heart began to race.

"I think I hear him... no, that's not him. It's a man's voice. I think I hear a

16

man's voice. I don't hear her anymore." Chris, normally cool and collected, was in full panic mode. Anna and Jen rushed past us to the elevators. His parents and their spouses stood around us.

"I'll go see if his car is here," Chris's dad said, wanting to help. After a few more minutes of silence, Chris's face looked hopeful.

"Emi!" he yelled again. "Emi!" He turned to us and told us what he had heard. "She just said, 'Wake up, Nate.' And I hear that other voice again."

Anna and Jen returned to the lobby, shaking their heads. "They don't answer the door," Anna said. "I don't think they're here."

"Nate's car isn't here," Chris's dad informed us. "The valet said they left together around eleven. Said they were holding hands, dressed casually, everything seemed normal."

"Shhh!" Chris exclaimed. "I can't hear!" He walked away from us to separate himself from the speculations of his parents.

"Yes, hello!" he said anxiously into the phone. "Who is this, what's going on?" Anna and I joined him. She took his hand while I put my arm around his shoulders. He was shaking, the fear evident in his every action. "An accident..." *Oh god.* "Where? It's my sister... Emi... I'm Chris, I'm her brother... Where are you taking her? Okay... That's her boyfriend, Nate... We're leaving right now."

"Where?" I asked him, keys in hand.

"Methodist General."

"I'll take you. Do you want to follow me?" I asked his parents, the women in tears, who nodded and rushed behind us.

"Is she okay?" his mother asked.

"I don't know," Chris said, stunned. "I didn't ask... I don't know..."

"It's okay, Chris," Anna soothed him as they both got into the backseat of my car. Chris's older sister climbed in the front seat, clutching her bag and crying.

"We'll be there in five minutes," I told them. "We may even beat them there."

She has to be okay. I'm sure she's fine. I repeated this over and over in my mind. *There was something between us. She has to be okay. I have to find out.* I drove quickly but cautiously to the emergency room. We arrived at the same time as two ambulances. My stomach sank when I saw her on the stretcher, bloody and unmoving. I wouldn't have recognized her if it hadn't been for her distinctive hair. The doctors met the EMTs at the door and rushed her inside. I stood back as Chris and his family went in after them, wanting to give them privacy, trying to wrap my head around what was happening. I watched as the other ambulance door opened, more doctors waiting. They pulled out the second stretcher, blood soaking through a white sheet that covered a body. I heard the EMTs announce a time of death.

I wanted to throw up at the sight of it. I struggled to stand upright, my body unsteady. I took a deep breath, or two or three, remembering my thoughts as he stole her away from me earlier in the night. *I had wished that he wasn't in the picture!* Did I do this?

He had died. How was she? She looked bad, really bad. I had to find her. I ran into the lobby and asked where Chris and his family had gone. They directed me to a separate waiting room down the hall. I felt the need to tell the family. I felt the need to apologize. I felt the need to confess all of my sins. I felt completely responsible.

"How is she?" I asked.

"We don't know," their step-mother said. I got Anna alone, away from the family.

"Anna, I think Nate... um... is gone. The other ambulance just carried a body. They announced what time he died."

"Oh, god," she cried, the family quickly gathering around. "Nate didn't make it," she sobbed. Everyone gasped together, cries quickly following, Chris pulling his fiancée into his chest. The family looked at me.

"I saw them bring the body in."

"Are you sure it was him?"

"I think so... but no," I said, suddenly hopeful. The thought hadn't occurred to me that it might not be him. "I'll find out." I had to know. I had to know what I had done. I hoped to God that it wasn't him. I hoped that he survived... he could have her forever... I would never interfere. I didn't mean that I wanted him to die! It was a selfish thought... it meant nothing.

In the lobby, I caught one of the EMTs as he was walking out the door.

"Was that man... that other body... was that man in the same car that the woman was in?" He nodded.

"Oh, my god..." I moaned, guilt-ridden, sick. I returned to the family and confirmed my earlier news. I had to sit down and put my head between my knees. I couldn't breathe.

"She'll be devastated," Chris's mom said. *I had done this.* A doctor finally came out to talk to the family. He explained she was in a coma, had a broken arm and leg and had some internal bleeding. She was in serious condition. There was more, but the doctor took the family aside and spoke in whispers.

Suddenly, another woman came in, who I barely recognized without her perfect hair and make-up as Donna Schraeder, a wealthy woman who sat on the board of one of the charities I was heavily involved with. I was just at her house earlier that week for a fund-raiser. Another wave of sickening revelation washed over me. I'd seen her name in print many times as Donna Wilson-Schraeder. *She was Nate's mother?* I heard her say that she thought Emi was pregnant. I saw her family deny it. I didn't believe it. Didn't want to believe it. I didn't even allow myself to consider the possibility. I never once thought about it again, until Emi confirmed it herself, months later.

Donna's sobs filled the waiting room when the news of her son was delivered to her by the attending physician. I walked to her, slowly, and held my handkerchief out to her. She looked confused, likely wondering why I was there, as she barely acknowledged me.

"Take it," I told her, pushing it into her cold hand. *It's the least I can do after wishing your son was no longer around. Oh, god...*

She finally clamped her fingers around the swatch of fabric, as she became hysterical, yelling, crying, completely inconsolable. It was too much for me to bear. I felt dizzy, as if I might faint, or throw up, or both.

"I'm... uh... Chris, call me," I told my best friend. "She has to be okay. Please let me know if she's okay."

"Can you go back to the hotel?" he asked me. "A lot of people are worried. Can you let them know?"

"Anything, Chris. I'll do anything." *I had to atone for this.*

"Anna," I pulled his fiancée in and hugged her, Emi's best friend. Her tears soaked my shirt.

"Thanks, Jack," she said, sorrow making it impossible for the words to come out in more than a whisper.

I walked out of the building, passing two more ambulances on the way to my car. The stretchers removed from both of them contained covered bodies. *I can't believe he died. I never wanted him to die.*

She can't go, too. I don't deserve her, but she can't go. Already I'm not sure I can forgive myself. If she dies, too... it was too painful to even think about.

It's still too painful to think about, a year later. For three days, Chris's family held vigil at the hospital until she came out of the coma. It felt awkward for me to be there, I really had no place there, but I stopped by every night to check in. I would relieve Chris in the middle of the night, that was my excuse for being there... but it was always for her. And on the way home from each visit, I went to a nearby church and prayed. I hadn't been to church in years, but I felt so responsible. I wasn't thinking rationally at the time. I was confused by what I felt for her that night, wondering why she had come back into my life as she did... wondering why she had the effect on me that she had.

After a few months, I finally accepted that I didn't cause the accident, but I still felt bad for thinking what I had thought. The guilt nagged me for months until I was finally able to tell Emi. I had thought all along, if she forgave me, then I knew I would be forgiven. And she had. Thankfully, she had.

I pull her body closer to mine, gently, not wanting to wake her. It had been a long night. A clap of thunder makes her jump, brings her out of her peaceful slumber.

"It's okay," I tell her, laughing. She looks up at me, her eyes tired, swollen.

"It's raining?" she asks, putting her arm across my chest and cuddling closer.

"Yes," I whisper. "Go back to sleep." I run my fingers down her bare back, her skin soft and warm to the touch.

"I'm awake," she announces, then yawns. I give her a few minutes to decide whether or not she really wants to get up. I feel her eyelashes repeatedly flutter, tickling my chest.

"How are you?" I ask, tucking her hair behind her ear.

"Slight headache," she says.

"I'll go get some aspirin," I offer.

"No, you stay here," she says, stretching her legs to get out of bed. "Where are they?"

"Medicine cabinet in the bathroom." She climbs out from under the covers, modestly covering her breasts with her arms. She smiles at me and blushes. She's wearing a pair of my flannel pants, tied as tightly as the drawstring will go around her waist, but still sagging off of her small frame. About a foot too long, the ends of the pants completely cover her feet. She is so beautiful... but still so fragile...

While she is in the bathroom, I go downstairs to get some water and heat up some chai tea for a latte. She slides into the kitchen, taking a seat on one of the barstools at the island, as I begin to pour the tea and milk into mugs. Out of all the t-shirts in my closet, she has managed to put on my most comfortable one, obscuring her feminine figure from me. I put one of the mugs of latte in front of her with a bottle of water next to it. She takes the aspirin and thanks me, looking at me apologetically.

"Don't look at me like that," I tell her with a laugh.

"Well, when you invited me here, I hadn't planned on spending half of the night crying in your bed... I had other plans..."

"I know you did," I smile. "Emi, I will give you whatever you need. You know that."

"I know. And I guess I just needed to be comforted," she says. "I didn't want the day to affect me like it did."

I had wanted to make love to her last night, had planned to, if that's what she wanted... and she did want to... but her tears made me feel like I was taking something that wasn't mine to have.

I knew I had made the right decision when she whispered his name as I held her in my arms. She was crying in her sleep. Her mind had been on him all day, but it still bothers me more than I should let it, I know. Maybe she still has nightmares about him, or dreams. We'd only slept together a handful of times, and it had never happened before. I was thinking about bringing it up, but in the end, I decide against it. I mean, of *course* her mind was on him.

When it comes right down to it, I know that she loves me. She says she does, and I don't doubt her... but it was always her concern of whether or not she could love me enough. I think she can. I think she *does*.

"So how do you feel this morning?" I ask her, testing the waters.

"I think I got closure," she says to me. "Whether I needed it or wanted it or not."

"Good," I tell her, happy with her answer and hoping it means she's just one step closer to moving on with her life, with me.

"I feel free," she says. "I haven't felt like this in ages." She motions for me to come over to her. I go around the island and stand near her, but she pulls me closer by the drawstring on my pants, then ties the ends into a bow. I lean in to kiss her, and just as the electric feeling pulses through my veins, another loud clap of thunder makes her jump again, and the electricity goes out in the house.

"This is strange weather," she says.

"Yes, it is. And it gets pretty cold in here pretty quickly... hope it doesn't stay off for too long."

"I don't mind," she tells me, her eyes flirting with me.

"I don't think you know what you're saying," I explain. "Really cold..."

She climbs onto her knees on the barstool to meet my height and puts her arms around me, kissing me. I pick her up, her legs wrapped around me, and take her back upstairs. Her lips never leave mine until I lay her down on the bed. I draw away from her when she tries to pull me down onto the bed with her.

"I'm serious, I can't keep you *that* warm." I walk to the fireplace that I haven't used in years and start a fire with some wood I had picked up a few days ago, anticipating its use, though more for ambiance than necessity.

"Nice," Emi says, smiling. When I reach the foot of the bed, I crawl onto it, feeling her feet, legs, hips, stomach on the way up to kiss her. "I love you," she says quietly, her pale green eyes cutting through me.

"I love you, too," I tell her, gently lowering my body onto hers. My lips travel from hers to her cheek to her jaw, settling on her ear. She holds the waistband of my pants tightly, her cold hands creating a numbing sensation with every touch. I put my hand up her shirt, feeling her breasts. I quickly roll over, bringing her body on top of me. Her legs immediately slide over mine.

"That's my favorite shirt," I tell her, tugging at it. "I want it back." She laughs and happily helps me to take my t-shirt off of her. The light coming through the patio door allows me a glimpse of her beautiful form. I inhale deeply to take it all in, admiring her with my eyes, letting my fingers find pleasure in her milky skin. I sit up to kiss her, her legs now wrapping around my back.

Her fingernails graze my shoulders lightly, then travel down my back, lower, lower, until her hands find their way below the waistline of my pants. I follow her lead and do the same. Soft, round... how I have longed to hold her like this. I move my arms to support her back as I pick her up and move her onto the pillows. I help to pull the blankets over us to keep us warm, just in case. She slowly, timidly, begins to lower my pants. She kisses me deeply, then allows me to pull away to kiss her neck, breasts, stomach, until I reach the drawstring that is failing at keeping her dressed. I untie it slowly, then pull the pants down deliberately, kissing areas of her along the way, areas of her body that I had newly discovered but were still not quite familiar to me. I explore slowly, learning every freckle, every scar, every imperfection that would never take away from her perfection. I touch her first, a quiet wisp of air escaping from her lips, either from surprise or from the cool touch of my fingers. My lips follow, her arousal obvious. The pace of her breathing quickens, her hands play with my hair until she closes them around my ears, angling my face to see her.

"Will you make love to me?" she requests with a desperate whisper. My lips, tongue, make their way back up her body, lingering on her breasts, but eventually finding her lips again as our bodies gently, easily connect. She gasps quietly as she wraps her limbs around me, my arms supporting our weight under her shoulders, my hands caressing her face. I watch her as she stares back at me. I kiss her, my heart racing at her eager gaze, pushing tenderly, steadily, unhurriedly, wishing this could last forever.

I want to remember this moment for all of time, need to memorize every aspect so that I can carry this feeling with me always. I feel the chill in the air on my ears, but underneath the blankets is the most comforting warmth that has ever surrounded me. The smell of freshly-washed linens mixes with the lingering scent of the lotion she had applied sometime last night, the same lotion that was causing her skin to feel like silk under my fingertips. Her soft, fine hair is messily spread out over the white pillow, the sunlight coming through the glass door highlighting the ends of it, making it appear a dark pink. Her smile, one corner of her lip higher than the other, her secrets revealed to me, one by one. And her eyes... the most mesmerizing eyes, full of love... love for me. I couldn't be a luckier man.

I've never shared a more intimate moment with anyone. Looking into those eyes, trusting, loving, confident, I don't ever want to tear my gaze away.

"I love you, Emi," I tell her again, overwhelmed. Her stare never leaving mine, she reaffirms the same. "Is this okay?"

She doesn't answer with words, her warm smile and gentle eyes telling me everything I need to know. I kiss her neck, feeling her soaring heart rate with my lips, listening to her deep breathing in my ear, in unison with mine. Her legs tighten around me as I pick her up into a seated position in my lap, forcing a deeper connection between us.

"Oh," she sighs heavily. My eyes carefully study her, her eyelids hooded over her pale green eyes. As I feel the current begin to build, her lips find mine, ravish me as her excitement grows. Her arms wrap around my back, pressing our bodies together. I caress her at the base of her neck, feeling her soft hair between my fingers as we kiss. Her eyes close as our movements quicken, still gentle and in sync. She whispers my name, repeatedly, the sound of her voice music to my ears, all of my senses heightened in these rapturous moments of passion.

"Emi," I moan, my muscles constricting before the final release alleviates all the tension, my body joining in the same blissful state that my mind has been in since our first kiss. I continue to kiss her, softly, as her breathing slows gradually, her legs loosening their grip on me only slightly. I touch her cheeks softly, and as she opens her eyes to look at me, a lone tear escapes from one of them.

"Happy tear," she whispers, sensing my concern and easing my fear. I kiss the tear away from her cheek, pressing my lips gently against her soft skin.

"I love you," I tell her so quietly I'm not sure she even hears it. Her quick smile notifies me that she did. Her hand touches my chin as another tear falls onto her blushing cheek. I catch this one with my thumb, watching her eyes in hopes that more will not come.

She had shed so many tears last night. Tears of sorrow, of guilt, punishment and need. The doubts Chris had put into her head earlier in the day stayed with her, festered in her, boiled over as the hour approached midnight. She remembered the accident while she was alone in my room. She wanted to forget the memories of that night and of all the horrible nights that followed her throughout the past year of her life.

As much as I wanted to help her forget– and as much as I knew I was able to– I couldn't. Last night wasn't about me. It wasn't about Nate, either. It was just about Emi. It was about her and her need not to escape the past, but to embrace the wonderful future we were going to have together. I had to convince her that it was okay to hold on to those elements of her past... that they were a part of her as much as her green eyes and strawberry-blonde hair. They were welcome into what we have. There was room for it all. My capacity to love her was limitless. I would love her and everything about her... eyes, hair... past included. I fell in love with those things... if not at first sight, then they were things that made me grow to love her more.

She had apologized to me, not once, but many times over the course of our night together. The last thing I wanted her to feel was sorry for being completely open and honest with me.

"Never be sorry for who you are," I had assured her. "I knew the risks I was taking when I began to pursue you last year, Emi. I knew that there was a chance you would never be able to love someone again, or so soon... much less me."

"I do," she had whispered earnestly.

"I know," I had responded with a quiet laugh. "That's why there is no need to apologize. You're here, with me. This is so much more than I could ever have hoped."

"But this night was supposed to be about me and you," she argued.

"It is. It has been. This has been a gift to me. You have bared your soul and shared with me thoughts and experiences that you could have kept locked in that pretty head of yours forever. We have our whole lives ahead of us Emi."

"But I don't want to waste a moment."

"You're not," I told her. "We aren't."

Our kisses were chaste, our touches warm and comforting, and eventually the sounds of her quiet breathing lulled me to sleep. It was an emotional night, but one that could only stand to bring us closer together.

Of course, nothing can compare to the closeness I feel to her now. Her light perspiration mixing with my own; our breaths still inhaling, exhaling in unison; the taste of her still on my lips, her smile mirroring mine. I cradle her head in my hands and kiss her once more, an assurance of my devotion to her, my mind still enjoying its euphoria. I lay her back down against the pillows, our bodies still entwined.

"I've never felt so safe... or so loved. That was..." Her quiet voice stirs me back into reality. She looks stunned as she searches for a word. "Beautiful?" she asks with a laugh. "I can't think of a better word... that sounds stupid."

"No," I assure her, disbelieving that I could be this fortunate to be with a woman like her. "It was perfect."

I move onto the bed next to her, continuing to kiss her as we listen to the rain fall and the fire crackle. Exhausted, I wrap the blanket tightly around us and pull her into my body, her head resting on my chest. I play with her hair and after she falls asleep, I close my eyes to do the same.

"Jack?" she whispers, waking me up. The sun has finally decided to come out, the brightness creating a halo affect around her head. *My angel.*

"Hey," I respond, reaching out to her. I pull her face to mine to kiss her. Her hair is wet, but she's fully dressed in tan corduroy pants and a white sweater. "How long was I asleep?"

"Two hours," she says. "And look, the electricity is back on."

"You should have woken me up," I tell her, sitting up abruptly.

"I did," she smiles.

"Earlier," I roll my eyes.

"No, you were so peaceful. And you were smiling. It was cute... to just watch you."

"Great," I tell her.

"I think I'm going to head home," she tells me.

"Wait, what?"

"Yeah, I told Jen I would have lunch with her and Clara today. I'll just get a cab."

"Absolutely not," I argue. "Give me ten minutes. I'll take you home. And you should dry your hair, you'll catch pneumonia."

"I couldn't find your hair dryer," she frowns.

I jump out of bed and go to the bathroom, getting the dryer out from the back of the cabinet.

"Okay, thanks," she smiles, taking it and plugging it in near the mirror.

I don't want her to go. I could stay in bed all day with her. I was hoping for that. I shower quickly and put on a pair of jeans and a black button-down shirt, leaving it untucked.

"Are you sure you have to go?" I ask when I find her in the kitchen after my shower. I hope she's okay, and not having any regrets.

"Yeah, I promised her we could all go," she says. "Honestly, though, I wish I hadn't. I don't want to leave you. In fact, I'd love it if you just came over to hang out with us."

"I don't want to infringe on girl-time," I offer.

"You wouldn't be. I promise."

"Then perfect. I'd love to go." We kiss again. I can't stop smiling, remembering our morning together. She seems to be happy, too, her sustained smile gleaming at me every time she looks at me. If Nate was still on her mind last night, he certainly doesn't seem to be anywhere in her periphery now.

Emi walks confidently into the lobby of her building, holding my hand. I watch her as she smiles at Marcus. Her cheeks turn a pale shade of pink. *God.*

It's the same mischievous smile she wore in the hotel hallway last year. This time, I know the secrets behind the smile. I nod at her doorman as I walk past.

In the elevator, I put my fingers through the side belt loops in her pants and pull her toward me. She smiles up at me, sighing. "Maybe we should have ditched Jen and stayed at your place today."

"We can always go back tonight." She raises her eyebrows as we exit the elevator on her floor. She unlocks the door, but can't open it.

"Jen?" Emi calls through the crack in the doorway, the chain keeping the door from opening any further.

"Coming!" she calls.

"Are you decent?" Emi asks. "Jack's here."

"Of course," her sister says, removing the chain and opening the door. "Hi, Jack."

"Jen," I greet her, smiling. "I hope I'm not intruding."

"Not at all. You're always welcome."

"Thank you," I smile.

"Why was the chain locked?" Emi asks.

"That's my doing," Brian says as he stands up, startling us both. "A little overprotective, I guess." He extends his hand to shake mine, then settles back on the couch, watching a football game.

"I guess you can't be too careful," I tell him.

"How was the rest of your New Year?" Emi asks her sister.

"Really good," she says. "I guess now I don't have to beg to let Brian go with us to lunch," she laughs, nodding in my direction.

"Ditto," Emi says.

"Did you two have a good night?"

"Yep," Emi says flippantly, avoiding eye contact with Jen, dropping her bag on her bed and sitting down. I stand in the middle of the room, hands in pockets.

"Yep?" Jen repeats, giving me a sideways glance. I can't hold back my smile. Her sister grins back at me, knowingly. I feel a bit of relief. After the discouraging conversations I had with Chris yesterday, I feel– in that moment– that Jen is going to be my biggest ally.

"The three of us are starving," Jen says as Clara peeks out from the guest bedroom. "Are you two hungry?"

Emi looks up at me and I nod. "I could definitely eat."

"Let me put a little makeup on," Emi says, standing and straightening out her sweater before crossing the room and going into the restroom. A sigh escapes my lips as I touch the stubble on my chin, still in moderate disbelief that any of this is happening.

"Wow," Jen says. "You are definitely under her spell." She laughs. "Is she okay?" Her solicitous tone makes it evident that she's talking about how Emi had coped with the anniversary of Nate's death.

"I think so," I nod, forcing the memory of her calling his name in her sleep out of my mind. "Yes, I definitely think so."

"Good," she smiles. "Just ignore Chris," she adds. "I talked to him last night. I yelled at him for butting in... it wasn't his place."

"It's fine," I tell her. "He's just worried about her."

"Well, he was an ass to say anything to you."

"Already forgiven," I tell her. "But thanks for saying so."

"Clara, are you ready?" Jen's daughter, with hair the color of Emi's, nods shyly. "Come out here then! You remember Jack, don't you?" She nods again, dashing to her mother's side, wearing a tutu over her jeans. "She won't take that off," Jen explains as I laugh. Emi comes out of the bathroom, looking perfectly put together, watching me from across the room.

"Because it's cute!" Clara contends.

I kneel down on her level. "You're just as silly as your aunt." She giggles and does a few ballet steps, still half-way hiding behind Jen. Emi laughs. "Do you get that from Clara?" I ask her, standing to meet her.

"She *is* cute..." she admits walking toward me. "Maybe."

"You look beautiful," I whisper before kissing her on the cheek.

"You're gorgeous," she says back to me, her hand lingering on my chest.

I take her head in my hands and kiss her, lightly first, knowing she'll return immediately for a deeper kiss, her warm tongue playing with mine. Jen clears her throat, but I'm ruled by Emi, not her sister, so I continue with our kiss until she breaks away.

"That wasn't exactly G-rated," Jen jokes with Emi.

"No, it wasn't," Emi brags, touching her lips and smiling, then putting her hands behind her back and taking mine in hers, walking me across the room. Brian stands and turns the television off.

"Sorry," I apologize as I pass Jen and Clara.

"Are you kidding?" her sister says. "It's about time." Emi slaps her on the arm, grabbing her keys and leading the rest of us out of the apartment.

"Clara," I ask as we settle into a large booth at the highly-rated American restaurant across Manhattan, nestled in the Upper West Side. "What did you do last night?"

"Watched a movie," she said shyly. "And I made cookies with Erin." She stares at her plate of food, the cheeseburger easily twice as big as her small hands. I cut the burger into quarters for her, and she happily picks one up and starts to eat.

Emi puts her hand on my knee, and when I look at her, she's smiling at me.

"Thank you, Jack," Jen says. "You've had practice, huh?"

"Just a tad."

"Is he your boyfriend?" Clara asks Emi with a giggle. *You have to love five-year-olds. They ask all the questions everyone else is too afraid to ask.*

I raise one eyebrow and watch Emi, letting her answer. She touches my chin lightly and kisses me, a completely unexpected move, and simply nods, her eyes engaging mine. I kiss her once more.

"Ewww!" Emi's niece exclaims. "Gross. Kissing boys is gross."

"Not this one," Emi tells her laughing.

"All of them!" Clara argues as Brian laughs at her comment.

"Clara," Jen says, "that's not a very nice thing to say to Jack. Your Anni-Emi likes him. Can you say you're sorry?"

"I'm sorry," she says with a pout.

"I forgive you," I tell her. "You know, Jacqueline told me the other day that you're in her gymnastics class now." Clara nods. "What's your favorite part?"

"The balance beam," she says, eating a french fry. "No, the trampoline!" she says with more excitement.

"I know Jackie likes the trampoline, too. That is pretty fun."

"She said she has one at home," Clara adds.

"She does," I tell her. "You know, I bet she and Maddie would love to have you over some time to play."

"Can I Mommy?" she asks.

"Don't they still live in Westchester?" Jen asks me.

"They do... I go up there every other weekend or so. Maybe we could all head up there one Saturday."

"I wouldn't want to impose."

"Kelly would love it. She loves entertaining."

"Well, that would be nice, thank you," Jen says, nodding to Brian. Emi leans into me when she's finished eating her lunch. I put my arm around her, rubbing her shoulder.

"So, Clara-bee, what do you think of Brian?" Emi asks.

"He's on her good list," Jen answers for her daughter.

"Clara," Emi starts, "do you think he is good enough for your mommy?"

"He's nice," she says, a broad smile forming on her cherub face. "He brought me a tiara!"

"A 'Happy New Year' tiara," Brian elaborates.

"Sweet, right?" Jen adds.

"That was thoughtful," Emi says, smiling, resting her head on my shoulder.

"Are you tired?" I ask her.

"I'm exhausted all of a sudden," she says. "I guess last night is catching up with me." I knew she was referring to the late night she spent crying, telling me about the conversations she had with her therapist, finally reconciling feelings she had been clinging to for months. I could tell from Jen's expression that she had interpreted Emi's comment as something else. Emi was too tired to even notice.

"Well, let's get you back home, then." We slide out of the booth after paying the waiter and begin the ten-block walk back to her apartment. Jen and Emi walk on either side of Brian, listening to the premise for his latest novel. Clara and I follow, and when we get to the crosswalk, she grabs my fingers with her small hand before we cross the street. Jen and Brian both turn around to check on her, and a thankful expression fills Emi's sister's eyes.

"I think we're going to walk over to Brian's for a little bit to watch some football," Jen announces. "You're both welcome to come."

"I'm too tired," Emi answers. "Do you want us to take Clara?"

"No," Jen answers. "That's okay."

"I've invited some friends to bring their families over. A few of them have kids about Clara's age," Brian adds. "If you change your mind, just let us know."

"Thanks," I tell him, shaking his hand again and hugging Jen goodbye while Emi kisses Clara on both cheeks. We part ways and head back to Emi's apartment, enjoying the crisp winter air.

"So what did you think?" Emi asks me after getting back to her loft.

"I think he's good for her. He seems sensible. And very secure."

"He reminds me of you," she says, "how sensible he is. He seems like a real grown up. Like you."

"Well, you and your sister can both be a little silly from time to time... sensible men are the perfect compliment to that."

"Hey!" she says, playfully slapping my arm.

"Are you not? Miss 'My Boyfriend Had To Carry Me Halfway To My

Apartment Because My Shoes Were Too Cute For My Aching Feet?'"

"Thanks for that, by the way," she laughs. "I said I'd pay for a cab, you just have that aversion to public transportation."

"It's not an aversion," I argue. "I just wanted to spend as much time touching you before bringing you here."

"What does that mean?" she asks, looking offended.

"You tend to pull away whenever we come here," I explain. "It's fine. I've come to expect it."

"No, I don't."

"Yes, Poppet, you do. We always seem to be more... *friendly*... less *intimate* when we're here. It's fine." I pour her a glass of wine and grab a beer for myself, heading to her couch.

"That's only because Jen and Clara are typically here... what do you expect *then*?"

"Like I said, I don't expect you to be intimate with me at all when we come here. And again... it's fine. I like being your friend, too."

She looks down into her glass, swirling it around thoughtfully.

"I'm sorry," she apologizes, realizing the truth in my claim. "Does it make you feel better if I tell you that you're my best friend?" She smiles.

"Much. Although I never felt bad in the first place... but this is why I like my house infinitely better than your apartment."

"I like this place."

"I know you do," I tell her with an accepting tone. "Tell me, though, what is it about it that you like so much?"

"It's peaceful, and calming... and inspiring."

"Okay." I don't press the issue any further. I know it reminds her of him. I don't know how long she'll feel the need to hold on to those memories, but it's not my place to broach the subject of letting go of them. Not now, anyway. Letting go of the memories would mean letting go of Nate, and that has to be her decision to make. If she's not ready yet, surely she will be soon. I'll continue to wait, but I'll do everything to make sure she knows I'm the best man for her. I don't need her to let go of those memories today to know that she loves me... and really, that's all that matters. She loves me.

She squeezes my hand before hitting the play button on the remote control. "What are we watching this afternoon?"

"Finding Nemo," she says as I follow with a groan.

"Sexy," I comment, glancing out of the corner of my eye. "Glad I came over with no expectations."

"You know you think Dory's hot..."

"No, not hot at all... I believe in guy-speak we would say she has a good personality. Even that would be a stretch... little annoying..."

"She's funny!" Emi argues.

"S-I-L-L-Y," I spell out to her, touching her nose lightly.

"But you L-O-V-E-M-E," she returns.

"I must if I'm going to sit through this again." She kneels on the couch next to me and kisses my cheek before pulling a pillow into my lap and laying her head down on it. I spend most of the movie watching her, how her eyes light up, how her dimples bury themselves into her cheeks when she laughs.

CHAPTER 2

"Thank you," Emi says, taking the signed Mark Messier jersey from me before letting me into her loft. She had found the sweater a week ago when she was nosing through my closet for a shirt she could sleep in. I had planned on framing it and hanging it in the game room in the basement, but I just hadn't gotten around to it yet. "You sure you don't mind me wearing it to the hockey game?"

The jersey was better suited on her than enclosed in an air-tight frame. The thought that her scent would linger on it made it that much more valuable– to me. "Not at all, Poppet. Although it will swallow you whole." She weaves her fingers between mine, pulling me toward her, brushing her soft lips against my own. "Mmmm, you keep doing that, you can have anything you want from me."

"Anything?" she mumbles, her lips now moving in sync with mine, just as needy. We hadn't made love in five agonizing days. I missed the feel of... her.

"Yes, anything," I answer, dropping my keys onto the hardwood floor and putting my arms around her, pulling her body into mine. "Where's Jen?" I whisper between breaths.

"They were staying at his apartment," she says softly back to me, the jersey now on the floor with my keys and her hands on both sides of my face, holding my lips to hers. She starts walking backwards toward the bed. Although intimacy was never a problem at my house, we had done little more than kiss at her loft since we talked about our time spent here on New Year's Day. Today, it seems she's open to trying.

"All weekend?" I ask, lifting her quickly and carrying her to the bed.

She kicks playfully as I set her down against the pillows, gently lying down beside her. "I think so," she answers, dragging her fingers through my hair as I kiss her neck. "Clara's at mom's, so I think she was going to stay with him."

"Lucky for us," I say, finding her lips again. "We can come back here after the game."

"But you don't have anything with you," she counters.

"I have everything I need for what I want to do," I inform her, positioning my legs in between hers and hovering over her body, my eyes communicating my insatiable desire for her.

"No," she says with a whine. "You'll be uncomfortable." She pushes against my chest gently, playfully.

"Not at all," I tell her with a smile, kissing her deeply to keep her from arguing with me any more. I allow the weight of my body to settle on hers and laugh silently to myself. *Uncomfortable doing this?* She pulls her arms to her side and eventually turns her head away from me. "What?" I whisper into her ear before kissing it.

"I mean, you won't have any clothes or anything."

"I don't need them." I turn her face back to mine and kiss her again, pressing against her softly.

"Jack," she pleads as I feel her begin to pull away emotionally.

So maybe she's *not* open to trying... but I'm not ready to let go of the idea so soon. I want her to feel comfortable, at home with me here, in her loft. I have lucid visions of us making love to one another here, our expression of devotion lit only by the moonlight and the expanse of the Manhattan skyline that's clearly visible from her floor-to-ceiling windows. "We can stop by my house and I'll pick up a few things after the game. How's that?"

Her eyes look away briefly and she begins to smile. "Okay."

"Okay?" I ask. She nods as she pushes me back onto the bed and climbs on top of me, sitting up.

"I have to finish getting ready," she says as she leans down and gives me a peck on the cheek before getting off the bed and heading to the dining room to pick up the jersey.

"Can you do that in here?" I ask, still turned on and wanting her back in my arms. She rolls her eyes at me, but flutters her eyelashes and moves to stand in front of her dresser. With her back to me, she slowly takes off the sweater she had been wearing. She smiles at me, watches me watching her in the mirror, her cheeks turning a darker shade of pink. Her hands go back to the hem of her t-shirt, and she takes that off next. As she turns her body around to face me, I go to the edge of the bed, grab both of her arms and pull her on top of me.

"Jack," she laughs. "We'll be late to the game!"

"What game?" I move on top of her and unfasten her bra, kiss her breasts, breathe in her scent. *I knew I missed her, but hadn't realized how badly until this very moment.*

"My brother and sister will be waiting."

"I left their tickets at will-call. Emi, let me make love to you, I have missed you."

"Tonight," she sighs, giving me a kiss, a promise, that is meant to last until then, I'm sure. "Not now. I don't want to have to shower and everything again."

"Why are you being the practical one?" I ask, pulling away abruptly.

"It's just..." she stammers. "I don't want..."

"You don't want what? You don't want to do this?"

"Of course I want to do this. I just don't want to be late," she states pertly, shoving me off of her and refastening her bra. She pulls on a long-sleeved t-shirt before dressing in the hockey jersey that completely hides her feminine figure from me. As if sensing my disappointment, which I'm trying to hide from her, she strides back over to the edge of the bed and runs her fingers through my hair. I stand up and embrace her into my body, gathering the extra fabric of the jersey in my hand so I can see her curves in the mirror. I kiss her neck, watch and feel her muscles slightly falter at the sensation.

"I hate this jersey on you," I whisper with a sly grin, dropping the shirt from my hand. The hem of it drops just above her knees.

"Well, I'll let you do the honors later," she says, unbuttoning the third button on my dress shirt and patting it gently as if to tell me to leave it that way. I glance at myself in the mirror as she goes to find her shoes. My hands move to fix the hair she has left a little unruly. "Nope," she says as she grabs my arm. "You look perfect. You're not meeting with clients, you're going to a hockey game."

"Alright, alright," I concede, facing her and away from the mirror. "It just looks like we've been fooling around."

"Well, we have been," she raises her eyebrows. "Now, you're just a reminder of what I have to look forward to after the game."

"I can give you lots of reminders," I tell her, kissing her once more as she grabs her purse and tote. She takes my hand in hers and leads me to the door. I pick up my keys along the way. "One more?" I ask, twirling her into my arms. Her palm traces my jawline, her eyes look into mine adoringly and she stands on her tiptoes to meet my lips.

Emi continues to flirt relentlessly with me as we ride down the elevator.

"You're driving me crazy, Emi," I tell her, my hands nothing short of groping her as her tongue teases mine.

"I can make it worse," she whispers.

"I don't think you can." And then, with that statement that she obviously takes as a dare, her painted lips lift to my ear and whisper the dirtiest words I have ever heard escape her pretty little mouth. I stand in amused awe as the elevator door opens, and she struts out.

"That's it," I state firmly, grabbing her quickly, still half-way in the elevator keeping the doors open, and I pull her back as she giggles and struggles to pull me into the lobby with her. "We're going back up."

"Later," she laughs with a blush and tugs on my arm. Out of the corner of my eye, I see another woman approaching the elevator, so I relent and hit the 'up' button for her as I follow Emi. I run into her back when she stops abruptly. *Has she changed her mind?* I wrap my arms around her and kiss her cheek, noticing a second too late that the woman has stopped right in front of us. I look up sheepishly.

I recognize Nate's mother immediately even though it had been over a year since I last saw her. The memory of her crying in the hospital had brought tears to my eyes for days, the guilt overtaking me. *But I was forgiven.* I take a deep breath, again reconciling those feelings.

"Donna!" Emi says, surprised, prying my already falling hands from her body. I clear my throat and stand up straight with an apologetic smile. Emi and Donna embrace tightly.

"I'm sorry I didn't call first," she says, looking at me and grinning. "It looks like you're on your way out."

"Yeah, um, Donna, this is Jack," Emi tells her with a smile. "Jack, this is Nate's mother."

"It's so good to see you again, Donna," I tell her, shaking her hand. She lets go quickly and hugs me, too.

"Likewise, Jackson, it's been a long time," she says with a thoughtful look in her eyes. "Is Emily here what's been keeping you away from the foundation? I mean, your donations are always generous and welcome, but we've missed you."

"She's part of the reason," I tell her, revealing my distraction for the second half of last year. In the first half, shortly after Nate died, I was consumed by my guilt. I couldn't bear the thought of seeing his mother, feeling somewhat responsible, even if it didn't make sense to feel that way. Using charitable work as one of the conditions of my self-imposed atonement, I focused my efforts on other organizations just to avoid her. I was a coward and I knew it.

Just seeing her now, I have a sickening feeling in my stomach.

"Well, I can forgive you for that," she says kindly. "I didn't realize you knew one another."

"I've been friends with Emi's brother, Chris, since college."

"Oh, well, did you know Nate?" she asks.

"No. I only met him last New Year's Eve, at the party..." My voice trails off to silence.

"Wait," Emi interjects, her brows furrowed in confusion. "How do *you* know one another?"

"Jackson is one of my children's hospital charity's biggest contributors," Donna informs her. "He has been for years."

Emi looks at me, confused. "Oh, okay."

"I haven't seen you since the night of the accident," Donna directs her comment to me, "at the hospital." I wasn't sure if she had even recognized me at the time. I nod as Emi cocks her head in my direction.

"I'm very sorry," I tell her. She squeezes my arm, looks at me warmly.

"Listen," Donna says, "I don't want to hold you two up. I was just in the area shopping with a friend and thought I'd stop by and say hello."

"It's no problem," I begin, looking to Emi, "if you wa–"

"Um, Donna, why don't you and I have lunch one day this week," Emi suggests.

"That sounds great. Are you free Tuesday?"

"I am. Sushi?"

"That would be perfect," Donna agrees. "Why don't we meet at 1:30?"

"I'll be there. It's so good to see you," Emi says, taking my hand again and weaving her fingers in between mine.

"You too, sweetie, and you look fantastic." Nate's mother glances at our hands.

"Thanks, so do you... I'll see you Tuesday."

"And Jackson, don't be a stranger," she says. "The kids at the hospital always loved it when you would stop by for story hour."

"I'll make it a point to schedule some time soon," I tell her.

"Good. I'll see you soon." Donna's driver helps her into a black sedan, and we watch the car drive away as we wait for the valet to bring my car around. Emi handled that very well. If she had any reservations about us, this meeting would have been rather awkward. I smile to myself.

"Okay, so that's weird that you know her... but even weirder that you never told me that."

"It just never came up," I explain. "It's not like I know her well, anyway. We would see each other once or twice a year at events, that's all."

"And you were at the hospital that night?" she asks.

"I've told you that I drove Chris, Jen and Anna there. Chris was in no shape to drive."

"Will you tell me about it?" she says as we get into my car.

"Really?" I ask, unsure that I want to get into this tonight.

"Yeah," she says as I take my seat and close the door. "I want the story from a neutral party."

I sigh heavily. "I am certainly not that," I begin. "You have no idea what that did to me."

"What do you mean?"

"In a matter of about three hours, it went from one of the best nights of my life to the worst. When I danced with you, and you looked into my eyes, that was it for me. It didn't matter that you had a boyfriend. Somehow, I wanted to be with you. And by the end of the night, I had started plotting how I was going to make that happen. You were the maid of honor, I was the best man... it was the perfect scenario, and I was going to engage you in the most intense wedding preparation known to man *or* woman. I was thinking weekly meetings, over drinks, whatever it took to get more time with you.

"And then I was there when your call came in to Chris. His account of what was happening... the fear of not knowing..." I stop talking, the memories of that night rushing back, impaling me.

"I didn't realize..." she says, "how you felt... already, back then?"

"I'm telling you, Emi," I say. "From our first kiss, I just knew... so when they brought you out on the stretcher, I just watched from a distance as your family ran in behind you. I was torn. I wanted to know every detail, but who was I? Some random guy you danced with... and kissed ten years previous. So I waited outside for bit, and I was there... when the second ambulance... God." I shake my head to make the sights of that night disappear as we get out of the car at the arena.

"I'm sorry," she whispers, taking my hand in hers.

"That vision will stay with me forever." And– forgiven or not– so, apparently, will this regret.

"Hey," she says, her hands on my cheeks. "I'm here, and I'm fine and I'm with you."

"And I'm grateful for all of that." I hug her tightly, lifting her feet off the ground and holding her momentarily. She kisses my cheek before I set her down. Hand in hand, we follow the crowd inside.

"So how did you get these tickets?" Chris asks, watching the Rangers' warm-up skate from a private box in the middle of the rink. I glance at the bleacher seats sitting in front of our suite and smile as Emi explains the rules of hockey to Jen and Brian.

"One of my clients. He has seats to all the sporting events, but he doesn't like going to the afternoon games. I had no idea your sister was *so* into hockey."

"Yeah, she loves going to games. Thanks for inviting all of us."

It was the first time Chris and I had spoken since his house-warming party nearly a month ago. That had been an awkward day. I can't remember another time when we'd had such a disagreement. It made sense, though. He had an overwhelming need to protect his sister, I got that. I was just shocked at his sudden distrust in my intentions with Emi. It was like he didn't know me at all, and I knew he did. I had always been completely respectful to everyone I met, not just the women I had dated. And it wasn't like there was a long string of women in my past. I believe in committed, monogamous relationships, and had had only a few of those over the many years I had known Chris.

And he always came to me for advice in his relationships. I knew he looked up to me. This was just about her. I couldn't blame him. I open a couple of beers and take one to him, sitting down next to him to watch the game.

"Listen, I'm sorry about New Year's Eve," Chris says. I was never worried about our friendship, and didn't even think it needed to be discussed, but it was nice that he brought it up.

"Water under the bridge," I tell him. "No need to apologize."

"Well, I had no right to interfere. I was worried about her. I felt like she was using you as a distraction. Not *using* you, not intentionally, you know."

"I knew she was really vulnerable that day."

"I knew that, too," I remind him.

"What I didn't know is how close you two had become. When we had dinner a few months ago, you two seemed intentionally distanced from each other. I wasn't sure it was going anywhere, if you were just friends, what was going on. And she didn't talk to me about you."

"It was all intentional. She wanted to be sure of her feelings."

I never talked to Chris about Emi, either. Before I had asked her out the first time, I ran it by him... but that was pretty much the first and last time I talked to him about her. Emi had wanted to keep it private, so I did. I normally would anyway. Sure, Chris was my best friend, but I wasn't one to kiss and tell. Well, the one time I did– when I confessed that Emi had kissed me in college– I paid dearly for it with a black eye that lasted a few weeks. I had anticipated that reaction from him then, actually, even though he wasn't a violent person. He was just that protective of her. And maybe a little drunk. He felt horrible immediately after.

"She seems pretty sure of them now. Emi came over last week, and I have to admit... I hadn't seen her that happy... since him... she was glowing."

"I love her, Chris," I tell him.

"So I have to ask..." her brother hesitates. "Have you changed your mind about what you told me a few years ago?"

"Which was..."

"That you were never going to ask another woman to marry you after Caroline..."

"Yes," I tell him. "I was hurt then, and angry. But Emi changes everything."

"Because I know she wants a husband... and children... if she can't have that with you..."

"It's kind of soon to be talking about that, isn't it?" I ask.

"Is it? You don't take these things lightly. I know you, Jack. I know you've considered the possibility."

"I have."

"I just don't want to ever see her hurt again." I nod in understanding, having no intention of ever causing Emi any pain. "Have you told her about Caroline?"

"Not yet," I tell him. "Is it even relevant?" It has never seemed important for me to bring her up to Emi. Although the relationship ended poorly, and wrecked me in some ways in the end, it is all insignificant in hindsight. Emi was all I ever wanted.

"You've seen all of her baggage," he says, his undertones telling me I should tell Emi about that painful part of my life. "You should probably show her a little of yours."

"Noted," I tell him without looking at him, my response clipped, signaling the end of this conversation.

The lights in the arena dim slightly, a spotlight shining on an American flag hanging from the rafters. Chris and I move to the row behind the rest of our group in the bleacher seats as the national anthem is sung. I rub Emi's shoulders, surprising her with my touch at first, as the hockey game begins.

"Refills?" I ask everyone, the group nodding in unison.

"Let's go into the suite and toast," Anna says as she holds Chris's hand. They smile lovingly at one another. We all get up and go back into the box as I hand out fresh beverages to everyone. Chris and Anna stand in front of us, hands poised for a toast. Jen and Brian have a seat on a leather couch across from the chair Emi has chosen to sit in. When I hand her a glass of wine, she stands up, offering the chair to me. I sit down and she settles into my lap, putting her arm around my shoulder and planting a chaste kiss on my lips. *She's already tipsy.*

"What are we toasting to?" Brian asks.

"A Rangers win!" Emi exclaims.

"Have you had anything to eat today?" I whisper in her ear. She shakes her head.

"Sure," Anna laughs. "To a Rangers win," she adds, holding her bottled water and taking a sip.

"Anna... water?" I ask, knowing how much of a wine connoisseur Chris's wife is.

"Well, that was really what I wanted to toast to. We're pregnant," she announces, placing her hand on her stomach. Even with her petite frame, I can already see a small bump under her form-fitting shirt.

Emi just smiles, seemingly in on the secret. Jen and Brian stand up to congratulate them.

"Did you know?" I ask, nudging her off my lap. She nods as I stand up to shake Chris's hand and hug Anna tightly. "You didn't waste any time," I say to them, smiling.

"How far along?" Jen asks.

"About twelve weeks," Chris says. "She just told me yesterday."

"I just wanted to make sure everything was okay before telling everyone," Anna sighed. "The doctors say everything looks good."

"I saw the sonogram," Emi says, small tears barely noticeable in the corners of her eyes. "It's beautiful." I move behind her and wrap my arms around her, kissing her cheek. I can feel her sigh heavily against my body.

"Clara is going to be so excited!" Emi's sister says. "*I'm* so excited. I'm *finally* going to be an aunt!" Everyone gets quiet, all eyes go to Emi. "I mean–" she stutters.

"No," Emi says as I hear the brave smile in her voice. "Being an aunt is the best. You get to spoil them and do all the fun things you want... and then when they get cranky or angry, you just send them back to their parents."

"It's true," Chris agrees. "Same for uncles. I guess now I'll get to deal with the consequences of too much sugar and too little sleep."

Jen still looks remorsefully at Emi. Brian massages her neck slowly, his eyes diverted to the floor, obviously sensing her discomfort and likely knowing the reason why.

"Jen, it's fine," Emi says as she removes my arms and walks over to her sister.

"I'm sorry, Em," she whispers, hugging her tightly.

"Don't make me cry," Anna says, weepy. "I'm already so hormonal." She joins the other two women in an embrace and they all sniffle quietly before laughing together.

A horn sounds in the arena, signaling a home-team goal. Emi perks up immediately and runs back out to the bleachers, Chris following behind her quickly to cheer on the team. He puts his arm across her shoulder and kisses the top of her head. She pulls him closer as the celebratory song plays over the loud speakers. Eventually, Anna goes to join them.

"Brian, do you like any other sports?"

"Baseball," he says. "I played in college before I hurt my arm."

"What position?"

"Catcher."

"Pitcher," I smile. "State champions in high school."

"What year?"

"1993," I tell him. "In Jersey."

"Nice. 1991 champs. New York."

"Do you still play?"

"Yeah, for fun."

"When my brothers come to town, we get a group of our old friends together to play. I'll have to invite you next time. We need a good catcher."

"I'm in," Brian answers.

An arena employee enters the suite with a cart of food. He sets up a small buffet on a table near the back of the room. I tip him before he leaves, then walk to the bleachers to let Emi know.

"The food is here," I tell her, Chris and Anna. "And you, my dear, need to eat something."

"I'm fine," she grumbles playfully, stumbling a little on her way back into the suite.

In the second period, I get a phone call from Kelly's husband, Thomas. Ducking into the hallway to hear a little better, I answer the phone.

"Hey, Jacks... I just got your message about Colorado. Is everyone in?" he asks me.

"Yeah, I think so," I tell him. Every year in March, the whole family gets together for a week-long vacation. I had treated my parents and siblings to a vacation the spring after I sold my company. We had such a great time that I decided to make it a yearly tradition, even though the size of the family has nearly doubled since that first time. It's a small price to pay to get everyone together at least once a year.

"The kids can't wait... is Emi coming?"

"I haven't asked yet," I explain.

"Too soon for the parents to meet her?"

"Oh, no, not at all. I definitely want them to meet her," I tell him quietly.

"It's just been a crazy couple of months." I say months, and even though I've been committed to her for those months, she really wasn't sure about us until a few weeks ago. I don't want to rush her into anything she's not ready for, so I was trying to give us some time before telling her about the yearly tradition.

"Your brothers are in, too?"

"They are. I talked to Matthew yesterday. He and Lucas are flying in on Saturday. I think he said Steven and Renee are doing the same. She's going to bring her daughter this time."

"Oh, that's good. Maddie and Jackie will be happy to hear that. They had a lot of fun the last time they all came up from Texas."

"Was Brandon going to bring a friend?" My nephew had been the odd man out last year, too old for the kids activities and too young for the adult ones. I had told him he could invite a friend if he wanted to.

"I think he is."

"Well, let me know. I'm booking this week." I guess I should invite Emi soon.

After the game, I barely have the door closed to my house before Emi pulls my head to hers and wraps her arms around my neck, kissing me. I can still taste the fruity wine that she *may* have drank too much of on her lips and tongue. "What are you doing, Poppet?" I mumble.

"Trying to seduce you..."

"We're going to your place, remember?"

"I know, but I can't wait," she says.

"Well, you have to," I state, pulling away from her and prying her arms from my neck. An adorable pout spreads across her lips. I have to look away to keep from capturing that bottom lip with mine. *God, what she does to me.* "I need to check a few voicemails and emails. I'll make quick work of it. Do you want to go put some things together for me?"

"Okay," she says, frowning and crossing her arms in front of her chest.

"Ten minutes, tops," I assure her. She nods before going upstairs as I dial

50

into my voicemail. I head into my office, looking for a pen and paper to make some notes. After booting up the computer, one message stands out from all the others. It's from Nate's mother, with the subject "Story-time Schedule at Children's Hospital."

Jackson, it begins. *It was a pleasure running into you and Emily today. I must say I was a little surprised to see the two of you together, but pleasantly so. She is very important to me and deserves to be happy. Anyway, the point of this message is to send you a schedule of story-hour at the hospital. It's changed a little over the past year– Mondays and Fridays instead of Tuesdays and Thursdays– but I hope you can still work us into your busy schedule. You can even bring Emily if you'd like. Her smile was always as contagious as yours. Let me know when you can come by! And, Jackson, please... take care...*

I re-read the last line. *Of her?* I'm probably reading too much into it. But of course I'll take care of her. I'll spend my life doing whatever it takes to see that contagious smile. My lips curl up at the thought.

Seconds after I click on the next message from a client overseas, my chair is whirled around to face Emi. She's grinning mischievously, holding my suitcase in one hand and something else in the other. I scan her from head to bare foot. She seems to only be wearing the jersey. My eyes glance up to meet hers.

"You have a choice to make."

"Do I?" I ask, leaning back into the chair.

"Yes."

"Emi, why are you wearing that?"

"Because I said you could do the honors. Remember?"

"I meant why aren't you wearing anything *else*," I clarify, suspicious.

"That goes back to your choice."

"And the options are..."

"I've packed your suitcase with everything you need," she says as she sets the suitcase down on the floor. "So we can go over to my place whenever you're finished."

"Or..." I urge her to continue.

"Or we stay here and you can have me, right now."

I look away from her, my heart set on going to her loft. I don't know why I'm so decided on this. I feel like I'm trying to prove something to myself by staying there instead of here. I want her to feel comfortable being intimate with me over there. Until she is, I'll always feel like she's still holding on to a piece of him.

"Thanks for packing," I tell her, sounding detached and standing up. "And I'm finished here, so let's go to the loft." .

"Oh, one thing," she says, stopping me as I begin to walk past.

"Yes?"

"You have to dress me first. Starting here." She holds my hands in hers, placing whatever else she was holding into my palms and folding my fingers around it. I look more closely as she drops her hands to her side. *Her silk panties... that she's no longer wearing.* I sigh heavily, conceding defeat when she begins to raise the hem of the jersey up her thighs. "Go on," she teases.

"You're a little minx, you know that?"

"A little minx who thinks five days is too long to wait for her boyfriend to make love to her... and I don't want to wait a second longer."

"Well, I won't make you wait, Poppet. Let's go." She takes me by the hand and drags me up the stairs with her, undressing me quickly, frantically, on the way up. By the time we make it to the bedroom, the jersey is the only article of clothing left between the two of us.

"Okay, take it off," she says as she anxiously bounces on the tips of her toes.

"Where did my sweet and patient girlfriend go?" I ask her as I kneel in front of her. Very slowly, I lift the hem of the shirt up, planting thoughtful kisses up her body, inch by inch.

"I think the wine had its way with her. You're left with me." She kneels in front of me and takes the jersey from my hands, pulling it over her head and tossing it across the room.

"That was my job," I argue playfully, pulling her naked chest into mine.

"You were taking too long," she says as she kisses me. "And you said you wouldn't make me wait." She lies back on the carpet and pulls me down with her. "Make love to me, please?" she whispers desperately.

"You don't want to move up to the bed?"

"Why are you stalling?" she asks with a smile, her eyes pleading with me, her body pushing against mine. "I want you."

"Just one second," I laugh, kneeling up. She tugs on my arm, barely giving me enough time to open up the night stand and pull out the last– *the last?*– foil packet from the drawer.

"So, who looks better in the jersey? Me or Messier?" Emi asks after we make love, pulling the sweater back on to keep her warm. My chest acts as a pillow for her head as we continue to lie on the floor of my bedroom.

"Messier, no question," I answer, staring up at the ceiling, avoiding her gaze when she snaps her head in my direction.

"Really?" she asks with a disbelieving tone in her voice.

"Really," I tell her, now looking into her eyes. "What?" She kneels up, putting one leg on either side of my body, crossing her arms in front of her. "You look better *out* of the jersey. In fact," I uncross her arms, "let me take another look." I sit up to remove the jersey from her body. "Thanks for letting me do it that time." I ball up the shirt and throw it far across the room, hoping she won't put it back on again. She holds on to the waistband of my boxers as I lie back down to look at her. "Yes, definitely better out of the jersey," I mumble quietly.

"I'm cold," she shivers. I tug the comforter off the bed and wrap it around her shoulders.

"Come lie back down," I encourage her by pulling her shoulders down. She kisses my lips once before resting her head on my shoulder, shifting her body next to mine. I kiss the top of her head and we both sigh contentedly together.

"This is nice, Jack," she says.

"It is," I agree. I stroke her soft hair gently, listening to the hum of the heater. "You know, Em," I begin. "As much as I like having you here, I think the loft deserves a little love, too."

"I know," she says.

"Is there any particular reason you didn't want to go over there tonight?"

"It just..." I stay quiet in hopes she'll continue. "It just didn't feel right earlier."

"I just wish you could try. It would mean a lot to me."

"I will. I promise. I mean, I packed your bag, we could have gone. You chose–"

"Emi," I stop her. "You knew what you were doing."

"I know," she admits again. "But I really like your house."

"Thank you," I say after a brief silence. "I kind of like it, too. And I like it even better when you're here, with me." This may be as good a time as any... "So, remember when you asked me why I decided to get this house?"

"Yes, it was on our first date."

"Remember when I said there was a story behind it?"

"Yes..."

"Would you like to hear it?"

"Of course I would." I move slightly so I can face her, and offer half of the pillow to her. After kissing the tip of her nose, I settle in for the uncomfortable conversation.

"So why did I decide to get this house?" I sigh. Her smile encourages me. "It was actually a gift."

"A gift?" Her eyes widen with curiosity. "From who?"

"Me."

"Oh. Well, then, *for* whom?"

"Uhhh..." I hesitate only slightly, but it's still too long. "For my fiancée." I search her eyes for her reaction. She looks confused, her eyes squinting.

"Fiancée. You were engaged? I mean, I feel like I should have known that already."

"I know, but it just never came up." I take her hand in mine, entwine her fingers and kiss the back of her hand.

"Wait, was she ever your wife?"

"No," I confirm quickly. "And it was so far in the past, I jus–"

"How far in the past?" she interrupts.

"We broke up a little over three years ago."

"Huh." She nods and bites her lip before diverting her eyes to our hands. "How long did she live here?" she asks, her face slightly cringing as if she may not want to know the answer.

"Only a month... not even... Emi, look at me."

"Tell me about her." Her eyes challenge mine. "What happened?"

"I love you," I assure her. "I always have."

"What's her name?"

"Caroline."

"And when did you meet Caroline?"

"I guess it was about five and a half years ago. At Harvard, she was a friend of a friend."

"You dated a long time."

"We did. We dated about two years before I asked her to marry me. It was more like a business proposition. She and I were very much alike... very rational, very career-minded."

"So you had a lot in common?"

"I guess you could say that," I respond. "But not the important things."

"Like..."

"Well... as soon as she said yes to my proposal, I started seriously considering a family... and I wanted children. Kelly had just given birth to Andrew, and he had some health issues when he was born. She and Thomas were visiting doctors all over the country, and I spent a lot of time watching the other three kids while they were gone.

55

"I got pretty attached. Caroline spent a little time with them, too; never as much as I would have liked her to. But her job was pretty demanding so I never forced the issue. She was stressed out a lot."

Emi sits up and pulls part of the comforter with her, her back against the bed. She rests her arms on her knees, her head on her arms. Contemplative, her pale green eyes stay on mine as she listens.

"I didn't want to put any extra pressure on her, but the time I spent with those kids made me feel whole. No matter what I was going through, work-wise, they put everything into perspective. I looked forward to my time with them. Instead of stressing me out, they calmed me down. They brought me balance. I figured if Caroline just gave them some time, she would find the same thing.

"I mean, we had talked about kids many times, casually." I roll over on my back and close my eyes, remembering the dull but familiar pain. "I knew I wanted them... she would always just say that she wasn't ready yet. I thought she just needed time to adjust to the idea."

"So the house..." Emi interjects impatiently. I again roll onto my side to see her.

"The house," I smile at her, touching her toes playfully under the blanket. She not-so-subtly kicks my hand away. "Em..." I plead. "Don't do this, please."

"The house?" she repeats.

I stare at her, unblinking, my jaw locked. I swallow and sigh before continuing, resigned. "I had this grand idea to surprise her with this house for Christmas. She had always loved the neighborhood, the brownstones, so I bought this house in the fall and worked with an architect to create this haven for us. Big kitchen, nice living area for entertaining, peaceful bedroom, spa-like bathroom, state-of-the-art office...

"And she loved it all... and then I took her downstairs. As soon as she saw the bedrooms down there, which I had decorated for my nieces and nephews, knowing they'd make perfect rooms for our own children someday in the future, she freaked out." I couldn't help but notice how Emi flinched when I said *our own children.*

"She told me she never wanted to have kids. After much persuading, she agreed to stay for awhile. We tried to work through it, but in the end, I wasn't going to give in... and she wasn't willing to, either. So she left."

Emi puts her head down, her face now hidden from me. I sit up to watch her. "How did that make you feel?" she asks.

"It was hard," I tell her, "at the time... but it never really felt right."

I reach across to touch her arm and take her hand into mine. She lets it lay in my palm, limp. "Emi, listen to me."

"I'm listening," she says, her voice annoyed.

"Em, I missed the spark, too. I searched for it over the years, as well. I was just settling for her." I move closer to her and lift her head up. She looks hurt. "Believe me when I tell you this, Em, I couldn't be happier that she left. I've got what I *always* wanted now... you..."

"Why have you never told me this?" she asks in a hushed voice.

"Because it wasn't important. *She* wasn't important."

"You were going to marry someone who wasn't even *important* to you?"

"Emi, don't twist my words around. She was important then. But she's not now. And she's not you. You are the only thing that matters to me now, you know that."

"Do I?"

"Don't," I warn her, my tone serious. "Don't question my feelings for you because of this. Caroline has nothing to do with me and you."

"It's not Caroline. It's just the fact that you've been hiding this from me."

"I have not," I argue. "This is the first time it's come up, Emi, that's all."

"The second time. You could have told me when I first asked."

"Like I didn't mess up that night enough with my honesty," I remind her. "Are you going to storm out tonight, too?"

She rolls her eyes at me. "I'm going to storm out of your bedroom... I just want some time alone."

"Emi, come on, this is no big deal."

"I think it is," she says as she pulls the entire comforter off of me while standing up. She wraps it around her body tightly and walks out of the room, the edges of the blanket following her like a train.

Emi is lying on my bed, her back to me, when I come out of the shower. She makes no motion to face me, and I watch her from across the room. *She's still here.* That's progress. I walk to the edge of the bed, leaning over and whispering into her ear. "I know you just need to process this, and it's fine. But it really is nothing. You must know, it's always been you."

She blinks twice and sighs. "I just don't know why you kept it from me," she mumbles.

"I don't think I did." I sit down on the edge of the bed. "I never brought it up because I don't see how it affects you and me at all. How I acquired this house shouldn't matter. My past relationship with a woman who could never make me as happy as you do shouldn't matter. Dwelling on the past is something you and I don't need to do. Our lives exist in the present, and in the future."

"But you wanted to marry her."

"It was just the natural progression of things. I'm so glad it didn't work out, though, Emi."

"What if it gets to that point with us?"

"What do you mean?"

"If you propose to me someday, how will I know it really means something, and isn't just the next logical step in *our* relationship?"

"You're not listening to me, Emi." I push her hair out of her face. "*You* mean something to me. And I think it's safe to say I toss all logic aside when it comes to you. If this relationship was based on logic, I'm not so sure we would have one. A logical man doesn't pursue a woman because of a single kiss. A logical man has needs and doesn't abstain from sex for months and months on end while subjecting himself to regular meetings with the one woman he can't keep his mind– or his hands– off of." It looks like she's trying to withhold a smile. I kiss her cheek.

"I... *feel*... things with you, Em, that I've never felt with anyone else. I don't know why you doubt me... but whatever the reasons, just rest assured that I'll keep doing whatever I have to do to erase those doubts."

She still doesn't respond, just keeps staring toward the sliding glass door that leads to the patio overlooking the backyard. "I'm going to get dinner started. Are you hungry?"

"I don't know," she mumbles.

"Well, if you decide you are, I'll make enough for both of us."

After finishing cooking dinner and setting the table, I go back upstairs to ask Emi to join me. She's no longer in the bedroom. I begin to worry that she left when I finally find her in the girl's room in the basement. She's still wrapped up in my comforter, sitting on the edge of one of the daybeds and holding a stuffed monkey in her hands.

"Emi?" I ask from the doorway, not wanting to startle her.

"Come here," she says softly. I kneel on the floor in front of her, and she pulls me in for a kiss. "Personally, I like these rooms."

"Thank you." I smile earnestly.

"I like what they represent. And I think you will be an incredible father."

"Again, thank you." She kisses me again.

"I love you," she tells me, and before I can return the sentiment, her lips are on mine again. When we part, she continues. "If we end up, you know, together..." she blushes, "I want to have your children."

"Is that what you want?"

"What?"

"To end up together?" Her eyes search mine as a small smile forms. Without blinking or wavering, she nods.

Marry me, Emi. I remember back to the first time I wanted to whisper those words to her as we danced at the engagement party. The urge to attempt to steal her away from Nate was almost too great as I held her in my arms that night. I can definitely see myself marrying her someday.

"I love you, Emi." As soon as our lips meet again, she's pulling me on top of her, opening up the comforter and inviting me in to join her.

"I'm sorry I was upset," she says as she removes my t-shirt.

"I'm sorry I didn't tell you earlier. I have no more surprises, I promise."

"It's okay." She starts to unfasten my pants and I begin to get lost in my desire for her. A sliver of sanity brings me back into reality, and I stop her from going any further.

"What's wrong?" she asks as I still her hands with my own.

"Emi," I laugh quietly, "as much as I want to do this with you, I don't really think it's a good idea to start a family now. I don't have any protection."

"Oh, I'll go upstairs and get it." She nudges my shoulder and moves out from under me. I turn over on my back and hold her hand tightly before she can walk away.

"No, you'd have to go to the store. We used the last one earlier." She climbs back onto the bed, putting one leg on either side of my body, and lies down on my chest with a look of consternation.

"Well, that's not very like you. You're always so prepared." Her finger traces my lips that ache to find hers once again.

I kiss her hand, finger by finger, my eyes burning with need. "As I would have been if we had followed our earlier plans."

"There aren't any at my place," she says, her head shaking.

"There sure as hell better be. Or else I'll have to ask what man you *will* allow to sleep with you at your loft." I turn her hand over and kiss her palm.

"Huh?"

"You don't look in your nightstand often... although I could see how you could miss them in the mess of whatever you cram in that drawer."

"You went through my *nightstand*?" Her cheeks blush a dark shade of pink, her eyes wide with recognition.

"No. I just pushed everything over to carve out a tiny square for my stash.

Call it wishful thinking... but speaking of what's in that nightstand–"

"Jack!" she slaps my chest playfully.

"Not judging," I smile. "Whatever makes you happy."

"*You* make me happy. Whatever's in that drawer just placates me when you're not around."

"Mm-hmm."

"Hey," she whispers as she kisses my chest. "Back to the whole reason we got off track with this conversation." She begins to move her body back, kissing my stomach. "You know there are other ways... for me to make *you* happy." She grips the waistband of my pants and looks up at me.

"Emi, you don't have to do *that*." She pulls my pants off, leaving my boxers.

"But I don't want to leave you like *this*..." I inhale sharply as she brushes her fingers against me, and I pull her body back up so her lips can meet mine once more. Her hips move against me, slowly at first. As her actions come quicker, so does her breathing.

"Jack, please make love to me. Please," she begs. I turn her over, less gently than I'd hoped but desperate to be with her. I push against her, listening to her soft moans. "Please, Jack," she pleads again as she tries to remove my boxers.

"Emi, we can't." *But god how I want to...* My words say one thing, but my movements say something completely different as I allow her to push the waistband of my underwear down. "Oh, god," I exhale as I feel her skin touching mine. She pulls my face to hers, her eyes reflecting the same passion I'm feeling. Her hands grasp my back, needy, as I kiss her cheek, her neck, her ear, ravenous, wanting to taste every inch of her.

"I've been on the pill for a few weeks," she breathes into my ear.

"Are you sure?" I ask, barely assigning meaning to what she just said to me as I kiss her soft breasts.

"Yes," she whispers. Without any further thought, she shifts slightly and I feel the most all-encompassing pleasure I have ever felt in my entire life. We move together slowly, without reservations, wholly committed to each other's total satisfaction.

Emi's arms are clasped tightly around me, holding me to her, as I feel the familiar stirring in the pit of my stomach. "Let go," I tell her.

"I am," she says.

"No, I'm coming," I caution her as I kiss her cheek. She pulls me even closer to her.

"Oh, Jack," her voice is sexy, sultry, and I can't contain myself any longer. "I am, too."

We continue to kiss softly as we both come down. The reality of what just happened keeps the exhaustion I normally feel at bay.

"That was unbelievable, Emi," I tell her.

"Thank you," she blushes. I move to her side and she nuzzles into my chest, tracing figures on my stomach with her fingernail. She pulls the blanket around us when she feels me shiver.

"Can I talk to you about something?" I ask, kissing the top of her head.

"Of course," she says as she brings her eyes to mine.

"About tonight. You have my word that I will be better prepared from now on."

"You worry too much, Jack," she smiles. "It's fine."

"No, it's not. I'm not entirely comfortable with what happened here. I didn't mean for... *that*... to happen."

"Why not?"

"Because the pill isn't a 100% guarantee."

"You're so freaking practical!" she groans. "I'm sure it's fine."

"Please don't get frustrated with me. I just want to make sure we're taking precautions. I know for a fact your dad owns a shotgun," I try to lighten the mood.

"Are you implying he'd have to strong-arm you into marrying me?" she laughs.

"Definitely not. But I would like to marry someone on my own terms. That's all." She nods and continues to lightly scrape my chest.

"Can I ask you a question?" I begin again after a few minutes of comfortable silence.

"Sure."

"Were you on the pill when it happened... before?"

She looks back up at me, smiles and pauses. "No. Is that why you're worried?" Her hand moves a few strands of hair from my forehead.

"No, I'm not worried, Emi. I trust you." She kisses my chest and pulls her leg over my thighs. I rub her back lightly. "Was that common?" I ask quietly.

She sighs. "It was our first time– my only time– to ever have sex without contraception."

"Wow."

"Wow?"

"Yeah, wow. That doesn't exactly put my mind at ease."

"I'm on the pill," she reminds me.

"I know, but still."

"What, you think I'm easily... impregnatable?"

I laugh lightly. "Is that a word, Emi?"

"I just said it," she says with a determined look on her face. "That makes it a word."

"I think you're thinking 'impregnable–'"

"Well, then that," she shrugs.

"But it doesn't mean what you think it does. And no, I'm not saying you're easy to impregnate. I don't know one way or the other."

"Then why 'wow?'"

"Emi," I sigh as I wrap both of my arms around her. "The only woman I want to get pregnant is my wife." I hear a quiet gasp escape her lips as I kiss her forehead. She moves up slightly so I can kiss her lips.

"That's very idealistic for a realist," she mumbles against me.

"I have my moments." Our kisses grow deeper, more tender. "Wait," I stop her, pulling back to see her eyes. "It's idealist for me to want to only get my wife pregnant? Would you just let any old man get you pregnant?"

"You're not any old man. You're *my* old man," she says as she jabs me in the side.

"You're asking for it," I warn her, leaning over her until her back is pressed against the mattress. I lean into her and kiss her again.

"I know I am," she says flirtatiously.

"Wouldn't you rather it be your husband?"

"If *you* were my husband," she blushes.

"Listen, I have one more question." She groans. "Well, if you don't want to go on a vacation with me, that's fine."

"Wait, vacation?"

"No, never mind."

"Jack," she sighs and tries to tickle me.

"You don't want to start that," I warn her, tickling her back and finding the sensitive spot. Laughing, she finally grabs my hand and weaves her fingers between mine. "I love you," I tell her again. I can't tell her enough.

"Tell me about this vacation."

"Well, there's this resort... Mirabella, in Vail, Colorado, and I would like you to come with me... for a week, in March."

"Skiing?"

"Yes."

"I've never been skiing... do you think we can just stay in the room and make love all day?"

"Mmmm..." I ponder her request. "Probably not. There is a catch," I tell her.

"What, is this a business trip? Because I can just spend my days in the spa and then make love to you all night. That's fine, too."

"No, not a business trip," I explain. "It's a, uh... *family* thing."

"Family, like, who?"

"Dad, Mom, Kelly, Thomas, Matthew, Lucas, Steven, Renee... and about six kids."

"Holy..." she says, apprehensive. "Everyone, huh?"

"My grandmother isn't coming this year," I tell her.

"Of course, Grandma can't make it." She laughs.

"Are you still in?" I poke her playfully in the side.

"A week?"

"Leave on Saturday, come back the next Sunday."

"I don't know, you tell me. Is your family tolerable for a week?"

"I think they are," I tell her. "My parents spoil the grandkids and the rest of us just catch up with each other. We're all really close... we always have a great time. We only all get together once a year, really... when the kids are out for Spring Break. Christmases are impossible with all the spouses, girlfriends, partners..."

"Will I be the only outsider?" Emi asks. "You've told me about Lucas and Matthew, I know they've been together forever... What about this Renee girl, is she a first-timer?"

"Uh, no. This will be her third trip. First one for her daughter, though... but we've all met her at some point..."

She exhales deeply, but her dimples can't hide her evident excitement. "Let's do it."

"Seriously?"

"Of course, I want to go! The trip sounds amazing... I'd like to meet the rest of your family... and I assume we'll have our own room... we will, right?"

"We'll have our own private cabin," I tell her.

"The whole family?"

"No. You and I will have our own. All the couples will have their own. And Mom and Dad have bravely accepted the responsibility of the kids."

"Wow." She claps her hands together. "I can't wait."

CHAPTER 3

"This is an insane amount of luggage," I tell Emi, eyeing the four large suitcases and two duffel bags at baggage claim. I begin to load our things onto a cart.

"It's the ski clothes, I swear," she laughs.

"And not your need to have 'choices?'" I smile.

"Pretty sure it's the ski clothes... and you're the one who made me buy them in New York. We could have rented them or something once we got here." She shrugs her shoulders playfully.

"I told you," I explain, "I don't think this will be your last trip to the mountains. I hope not anyway." She picks up both duffel bags, putting one on her shoulder and one on mine, then kisses me.

"Thank you for this," she says.

"Jacks!" my brother's familiar voice calls from across the room.

"Matty," I say, walking toward him and meeting him halfway. I hug him and his partner Lucas.

"Is that her?" Matthew asks me, nodding at Emi, waiting with our luggage about twenty feet away.

"She's beautiful, right?" I ask him.

"Gorgeous," he says, outpacing my stride to meet her first. "Even prettier than she was when we rescued her on the streets of New York."

"Emi," I call out to her, "Matthew." She extends her hand to him.

"Uh-uh," my brother says. "This is *not* a handshake family." He pulls her into a bear hug, her smile growing into a laugh. "Sweetie, you are breathtaking." Her cheeks turn bright pink.

"You're not too bad yourself," she says. Growing up, before my brother came out to the family, he was always the most popular with girls. Kelly used to share with us the opinions of her friends. "Handsome" and "boy next door," she would call me. "Rugged, gorgeous, and sexy" were Matthew's words. Steven, six years younger than us, was forever pigeon-holed in the "cute" category, even as he grew into a man. At twenty-nine, he still had a baby face, his wide-eyed optimism adding to the perception.

"Lucas," Matthew jokes, "watch out for this one." Lucas hugs Emi, kissing her on the cheek.

"Are you ready for this?" he asks her. "I know all the family secrets, just stay close to me."

"Okay," she sighs.

"Honestly, I look forward to this every year," he confesses. "I was an only child so I've got years of sibling rivalry to catch up on."

"Emi, how much of this luggage is yours?" my brother asks.

"Um... three of those... and this bag..."

"Love her," Matthew says to me. "She can stay."

"Where are your things?" I ask him.

"Already loaded in the SUV. You ready to go?"

"Lead the way." I push the cart behind Emi, Matthew and Lucas flanking her sides, engaging her in lively conversation. She laughs easily, my brother and his partner always charming and entertaining.

Once our bags are loaded, Lucas takes the driver's seat and Matthew offers the front seat to Emi, but she chooses to sit close to me in the back seat, holding my hand.

"When will Kelly be here?" she asks.

"Kelly and the girls are coming later on today," I tell her. "And Thomas is bringing the boys Monday. Brandon and his friend have a basketball tournament this weekend."

"Stevie and Renee will be here this evening, though," Matthew adds. "Now what's her daughter's name again?"

"Lexi," I remind him.

"That's right. Renee got pregnant in high school," my brother tells Emi, a scandalous tone in his voice.

"Matty..." I warn him.

"What?" he says. "It's true." He shrugs quickly.

"Yes, it's true," I tell Emi. "She was apparently pretty wild in her younger years. She lost both of her parents when she was a teenager and finished her high school days with a distant aunt. Motherhood has mellowed her, though. She's different... very smart, very honest... very good for Steven."

"She's still pretty wild, Jacks," Lucas laughs. He's right. She could drink us all under the table, and had many times before. "She and I click. She was an only child, too."

"And they've been dating how long?" Emi asks.

"Two and a half years."

"Cool," she says. "And your parents came on Thursday?"

"Yes," I answer her. "I flew them up early so they could have some peace and quiet before the circus comes to town."

"You're a good son," she says, laughing, squeezing my hand. I pick it up and kiss it, then lean over to kiss her.

"I'm watching you," Lucas says, eyeing us through the review mirror.

"So, is there anything on the agenda I need to know about?" I ask them. "You guys are still staying until next Sunday?"

"That's the plan," my brother says.

"I think Steven's up to something," I tell him. "He wanted me to book his cabin through next Wednesday... said he's going to pay for it and everything." Matthew and Lucas exchange glances, then shrug in unison. "What do you guys know?"

"Nothing..." Matthew answers. "Yet..."

"Is he proposing?"

"Possibly... at this very moment..."

"Matthew, you promised him."

"Well, it's about time," I tell them.

"Matty," Lucas warns. "He'll be pissed."

"Yeah, just forget I said anything."

"Damn it, Matthew. I hate it when you do that." After sitting in silence, I accept that my brother isn't going to say anything more.

"So, what do you think about Colorado?" I ask Emi.

"It's beautiful. Pictures don't do it justice."

"See that mountain up there? That's where we're going skiing."

"Do they have, like, baby slopes?"

"Bunny slopes," I laugh. "And yes..."

"Can everyone ski but me?"

"Yes." She crinkles her nose at me. "I won't abandon you, though. I can't wait to teach you. I promise you'll love it."

The in-car navigation system guides us to the main hotel. "I'm going to get us checked in. Em, you want to come?"

"Sure," she says, excitedly hopping out of the car. "This is incredible."

"It's not bad," I smile, knowing that what's to come is so much better. The manager had sent me pictures of each available cabin and their views, letting me select which ones I wanted to book since I was a preferred member of their hotel group. I was confident we would get VIP treatment for the whole trip.

The manager is waiting for me when we walk in.

"Bill?" I ask after seeing his name tag.

"Mr. Holland?" He extends his hand. "It's a pleasure to meet you."

"Likewise. This is Emi." He graciously shakes her hand as well, then guides Emi and me to the check-in desk.

"I've got everything ready for you."

"My parents are doing okay?" I ask him.

"I believe they're enjoying their stay."

"Excellent. Thanks for taking care of everything, this has been pretty hassle-free so far."

"Our pleasure, Mr. Holland." Emi looks up at me and smiles, a look of confusion on her face. Bill pulls out a map of the property and circles the cabins that the families will be staying in. "Your parents are here... and then your sister's cabin is next to the main one. We've got one brother over here... and another here... and then yours is right here. The best view of the mountain on the entire property."

"Thank you. This is Emi's first time to Colorado. She's never been skiing... so I wanted her to get the full experience."

"Well, we hope you enjoy your stay," Bill says to Emi. "You have reservations for twelve tomorrow night at eight in the main dining room," he informs us. Emi's legs are bouncing, obviously anxious to check out more.

"Shall we go see our cabin?" I ask her. She stares into my eyes, a small, sexy smile on her face, and nods. Bill hands us the keys for our cabin and for Matthew's, and we head back to the SUV.

"Just let me know if you need anything," Bill says as we walk away.

"Mr. Holland, huh?" Emi teases me. "So formal."

"Here's the map," I tell Lucas. "We're in fifteen. You guys are in eleven... so if you can drop us off, we'll get settled and meet up with you in about an hour at Mom and Dad's. They're in eighteen." Lucas navigates through the winding snow-covered roads until he reaches our cabin. Matthew helps me unload our things, setting them on the patio, the air crisp and chilled.

Emi stands by the car, eyeing the cabin from the outside.

"Wow," she mouths to me, and I motion for her to join me. After Lucas drives away, I open the door for her, allowing her to enter first.

Emi looks stunned as she walks around the cabin. She touches the suede couch, running her fingers along the back of it. Her eyes wander to the large stone fireplace, which is actually shared with the bedroom, a fluid fire already crackling, warming the rooms. She peeks through the opening to see the bed, then turns around and smiles at me. She catches sight of a few dozen gerber daisies of all colors overtaking a small dining room table and walks over to them, smelling them and removing the card from the envelope.

"I love you, too," she says after reading it, taking her coat off and hanging it on the back of a chair.

"Would you like a glass of champagne?" I ask her, noticing a bottle chilling on the coffee table next to a tray of chocolates and fruit. She nods her head and continues her exploration of the cabin as I pop the cork and pour two glasses.

The bedroom is richly decorated, the bed large and plush with a fluffy down comforter on top. Three large windows on the back wall look out to the mountain, the view breathtaking... miles of beautiful Colorado land spread out before us. She pulls the curtains back all the way, letting the sun soak the room. She wanders into the bathroom, which has a walk-in shower and a large jacuzzi tub. Two robes hang on hooks by the closet, house shoes positioned neatly below them. I hand her the drink as she looks more closely at the smaller robe. She takes it off the hook and turns it around to show me.

"My name is embroidered on this," she tells me.

"Is it?" I ask her coyly. "Just something they offered to do." I take the robe from her and hang it back on the hook, taking her in my arm and kissing her. "To us," I tell her, holding out my glass. She taps hers against mine and we both drink.

She is quiet, taking it all in, eventually sitting down on the edge of the tub. Her eyebrows inquisitive, she says simply, "Your parents must be doing really well to pay for all of this." The statement sounds more like a question.

I look at her curiously. "This is *my* treat to the family."

"Huh." She nods slowly, looking confused. "*Your* treat."

"Yes," I smile slightly.

She's silent for a few more seconds before continuing. "So, um, do they even make tax brackets to contain people like you?"

I laugh. "What do you mean?"

"Well... I mean, first class airline tickets, *again*," she begins. "The penthouse suite at the Ritz on Christmas.... I know the coat you gave me wasn't cheap... And then, like, you know how when you visit a website for a hotel or a resort– say, the Mirabella, which I may have peeked at once before coming? They feature their best room on their website the day the interior designer finished styling it... and when you get to your actual room, it's never anything like it... it's always decorated differently, gaudy, never looks as big. They use the wide-angled lens to make it look bigger..."

"Okay, yes..." I stop her rambling.

"Have you seen this place?" she asks, astounded.

"Yes," I laugh. "It's pretty nice."

She shakes her head as if trying to organize her thoughts. "Who *are* you?" she asks.

"I'm not following you."

"This place is incredible. I expected rugged log cabin... cozy... This place is huge. Do we have, like, the special deluxe cabin or something? Does everyone else have a place like this?"

"Yes," I tell her. "We just have the best view."

"I don't mean to be... rude... or nosy... but how wealthy *are* you, actually?" Her question catches me off guard. I had just assumed Chris had filled her in on the details of the Internet start-up I founded in college. He was there when it all happened. I had actually offered him a position when I quit school, but he thought finishing college was more important. He had regretted that decision over and over again when we went public, when the stock split...

and especially when I sold the company.

I look at her confused. "Your brother doesn't really keep you in the loop very much."

"I told him early on I didn't want him to tell me everything about you. I wanted to draw my own conclusions.." She sets her empty glass down on the edge of the jacuzzi and holds on to the edges. "What are we talking here?"

"Is it important?"

"It's important if you're living beyond your means... if you've charged this vacation to your Visa or taken out a second mortgage on your house."

I laugh... *close... AmEx Centurion...* "And if I did..."

"I don't have the money to help pay this off," she jokes. "I'm just a meager graphic designer. I'm about three paychecks away from being homeless. I think you've got the wrong girl."

"I know I don't have the 'wrong girl,'" I tell her, leaning against the large vanity, crossing my legs casually. "And let's just say you'll never have to help pay anything off."

"That's comforting," she tells me. "So you earned all this money by selling your company?"

"That and some good investments," I tell her.

"Your parents, *were* they wealthy?"

"No, but they live comfortably now." I smile at her.

"So you made all this money... yourself?"

"Self-made," I admit.

"Wow," she says. "That's impressive. It must have been a good company."

"I got in at the beginning of the Internet boom," I tell her. "I loved the company, and the work... but the offer on the table was just too much to turn down. I knew it would afford me a different life... I could volunteer more, travel more... choose my own projects... and never have to worry about money."

"So," she asks, looking at her feet. "Are we talking millionaire?"

"Kind of," I tell her.

"Okay," she sighs, still looking confused. "What's that mean?"

"I would be in the 'multi' category."

She's quiet for another second. "And out of all the women in the world..."

"You're the only one that matters," I finish her sentence.

"Holy shit," she mumbles. "Can I get a refill?"

"Sure."

I take her by the hand and lead her back into the main living area. She sits down, reclining in the plush cushions of the couch, and I pour her another glass of champagne. "Chocolate?"

"No," she says, a distant gaze filling her eyes. "I don't like chocolate."

"That's right." I remember her telling me about the craving she had for it the night Nate died... that her craving was the reason they left the hotel. I immediately feel bad for not recalling that before now. "I'm sorry." She shakes her head, her smile returning.

"I love fruit, though." She picks up a strawberry and takes a bite, a small amount of juice from the plump fruit pooling in the corner of her mouth. I lean over and kiss it from her lips. She feeds me the second bite of the strawberry, and then kisses me back.

"Your house is nice," she starts talking abruptly, "but it's nothing, like, palatial, you know? And you drive a Volvo... not even a fully loaded one... And you dress pretty, you know, normal. There is nothing flashy, nothing that warns people of the oncoming millionaire."

"So?"

"I don't know," she says. "I don't know why it matters. Nate had money... but his was inheritance... he didn't really respect it, I don't think. I just feel like you're in a different class of people. Like, how could I fit in to that?"

"That's crazy, Em," I tell her. "Do you really ever feel like I'm in a different *class*?"

"No," she admits. "You're so down-to-earth. And relatable."

"Well, the fact that you now know about me shouldn't change any of that. I'm still the same person."

"I know," she says. "I feel like I should be more proper, or something," she laughs. "And not say things like 'holy shit.'"

"You better not change a damn thing," I pull her into my lap, kissing her cheek. "Let's get unpacked... and if you need to freshen up or something, we have time."

"Is it wrong that I just want to stay here and make love right over there, by the fireplace?"

"Not the bed?" I ask.

"*And* the bed," she says. "*And* the jacuzzi... this couch is pretty nice, too..." She angles her body to face me, kneeling over me on the couch. I pull up her sweater and tank top and kiss her stomach, running my fingers up and down her back. She takes the sweater off as I begin to unbutton her jeans when we're interrupted with a knock on the door.

"Jacks?" a familiar voice calls through the door.

"This would be a good 'holy shit' moment, Em," I joke with her, fastening her jeans and helping her to put her sweater back on. "It's my mother." She giggles and kisses me quickly, then takes a deep breath.

"Ready?" I ask her.

"Thank God for champagne," she smiles.

"It'll be fine." I open the door for my mother as Emi stands next to the couch. Mom hugs me tightly, then notices my beautiful girlfriend.

"This must be Emi," my mother happily states. "It is so good to meet you. Jacks has told us so much about you."

"Mrs. Holland," Emi begins toward her. "It's a pleasure." Again, she tries to shake the hand of another of my family members, but my mother reiterates to Emi that we are a 'hugging family' and embraces her.

"I hope I'm not intruding," she says.

"Not at all," Emi says hurriedly. "We were just checking out this amazing cabin. I've never seen anything quite like it." Her blushing cheeks betray her.

"Mom, have you and Dad had a good time so far?"

"It's so beautiful here," she says. "Thank you so much. And that Bill, the manager, he's very attentive. We don't want for anything!"

"Good," I tell her. "Where's Dad?"

"Matty and Lucas came over. They were showing him their new video camera, and I just couldn't wait to see you!" She hugs me again. "Looks like you two have some unpacking to do... that's a lot of stuff!"

"Yeah..." Emi says shyly.

"Emi likes options," I tell her. "But speaking of unpacking, we should probably do that and then we'll be over in a bit. We were thinking about grabbing something to eat before we head over." I exchange a knowing glance with Emi.

"Yeah, I didn't eat before we left," Emi confirms.

"Oh, no, we have a fully stocked kitchen, I'll fix something for you two."

"That's okay, Mom, rea–"

"I insist," she says.

"Alright," Emi nods, agreeing to my mother's request. "We'll see you shortly."

"Okay, Emi, I can't wait to spend more time with you," she says.

"You, too, Mrs. Holland."

"Sharon," she corrects Emi. "I'll see you in a few minutes!" My mom exits the cabin and I lock the door behind her.

"She's totally on to us," Emi says.

"I think so." Emi blushes a deep crimson color. I walk over to feel the warmth of her cheeks and tease her with my lips.

"When can we come back?" she whispers softly, her gaze serious, wanting.

"This evening," I tell her.

"An hour?" she asks, her hand guiding mine up her body.

"Definitely a little longer than an hour," I admit. She lifts up her shirt and puts my hand on her chest. I unfasten her bra so I can feel her supple breasts, flawless skin. I kiss her deeper, but she pulls away to ask another question.

"Two hours?"

"Probably a little longer than two hours," I tell her as she unzips my jeans, putting her hand through the opening. "Oh, god, Emi," I sigh as I take her hand in mine and pick her up, carrying her to the bedroom. I lay her down on the bed, and as I begin to lie down next to her, she climbs off the bed and refastens her bra. "What are you...?"

"Well, we certainly don't have time for this right now," she says, shrugging her shoulders and retrieving a few of her suitcases, placing them on the king-sized bed. "But I wanted to remind you what's waiting for you."

"Really?" I ask her, hopeful.

"I promise I'll make it up to you," she says, unzipping a suitcase and taking out a sheer black lace corset and panties, holding them up briefly, deliberately teasing me again.

"What are those?" I ask her. Emi's taste in undergarments is typically anything that's comfortable, so the lingerie is a bit of a shock.

"Oh nothing," she says, putting the items in a drawer.

"Wait, was that cute-but-impractical sleep wear?"

"Cute?" she asks.

"You're right, those were not cute. Sorry. Incredibly sexy..."

"Maybe," she says. "Whatever they are, I don't intend to sleep in them, *Mr. Holland*," she tells me.

"What else is in there?" I ask, reaching into her suitcase, which she shuts on my hand.

"It's a surprise," she says. "Don't ruin it, okay?"

I grab her forearm and pull her back on the bed with me. She crawls right up to me and kisses me, sweetly. "This trip is going to be so much fun," she says, her legs on either side of my right one. She raises her knee and strokes me slowly, but instead of allowing her to continue, I take her leg, put it on the other side of my body and roll over on top of her, teasing her in the same manner. She starts to breathe faster and closes her eyes, allowing her desire to take over.

"But," she says between breaths, "your mom... is waiting."

I immediately roll off of her, off of the bed, crossing the room to begin unpacking my things.

"Are you getting even with me?" she asks, her eyes expectant.

"There's a law somewhere that states that sex *cannot* happen when a parent is mentioned in the midst of foreplay. I believe it's a law of nature," I explain, smiling through gritted teeth.

"No, I'm sorry," she whines. "Forget about your mom."

"You just said it again. It's over." I continue hanging things in the closet and putting things in the dresser.

"Damn it," she pouts.

"We definitely have something to look forward to," I smile. "Where are your ski clothes? I'll hang them up."

"In that one, I think," she says, pointing to the one suitcase left over in the living room.

"Are there any surprises in there that I shouldn't see?" I ask.

"No, it's safe, I think. Is this okay to wear, or should I change?" she asks.

"These are my parents, not the president and first lady," I tease her. "Stop worrying. You look perfect."

"Thank you," she smiles as she bites her bottom lip, her gaze lingering. "Where's your camera?"

"On the dresser, why?"

"Let's get a picture of us," she says. "Come over here." She pats the bed.

"Is this a trick to lure me back?" I ask.

"Maybe," she says. "No, we just don't really have any pictures of us. And I just don't think I could feel any happier than I do right now."

I grab the camera and sit next to her on the bed, putting my arm around her and holding the camera at arms-length. I lean my head into hers, and she does the same before I snap the picture. She takes the camera and looks at the display.

"That one's cute," she says. "Let's do one more, though."

I hold the camera out again and count down. On three, she leans in to kiss me on the cheek. I turn the camera over and preview the second shot. "I like that one," I tell her. "Third time's a charm?" I ask.

We both have the same idea with the third picture, leaning in to kiss one another. After the camera clicks, I toss it on the bed and take her head in my hands, kissing her deeply, slowly.

"That will never get old," she says when we separate. I run my hand down her arm, goosebumps breaking out across her skin, as I get off the bed.

"I know." I sigh heavily, wanting nothing more than to stay here with her but knowing that my family is waiting. "Are you about ready to go?" I go into the kitchen to see if they had stocked Emi's wine, and find a few bottles of it on the counter. I grab one to take with us to my parent's cabin.

"I just need to do one thing," she calls to me. "Just a minute." She goes into the bathroom and comes out a few minutes later, her hair brushed and lipstick freshly applied. "Ready," she says, scanning the living room. She picks up the tray of fruit and puts it in the refrigerator. "Do you think your mom would like the chocolates, or did you want them?"

"I think Mom would appreciate them. That's a good idea." She picks them up, then her purse, and after we put on our coats, she takes my hand.

My dad answers the door quickly when we knock. He hugs me swiftly, then takes Emi in his arms.

"Welcome, Emi," he says. Dad has mellowed since retirement. He used to be rigid, all business, a little unsentimental and cold, but with his free time– and maybe with a little influence from the grandkids– he has been able to finally focus on his family and has become a very warm and sensitive man.

"Thank you, Mr. Holland," Emi says.

"It's Jack, to you, my dear," he says.

"So *this* is why they call you Jacks," Emi says to me with a smile. "I suddenly see the need in calling you something else." My mom comes to us and hugs us both again, thanking Emi when she hands her the box of chocolates. Matthew is pointing a video camera at us, narrating our every move. I nudge Emi, pointing it out to her, and we both wave and say hello. My brother continues filming, following my mother and Emi into the kitchen.

"Jacks, this is the best place we've ever stayed," my father says. "It seems a little exorbitant," he whispers to me. "Are you doing okay, financially?" He always worries about money. Needlessly.

"Yes, Dad. I can afford this... and I'll still be able to scrounge up enough money to pay for your nursing home," I joke with him. He pats me on the shoulder and nods. I catch up with Emi in the kitchen.

"Jackson," she says, playing up the formality, "would you like something to drink?"

"I'll grab a beer. Did you want a glass of wine?" I offer.

"Yes, please," she says, handing me a wine glass. Emi and I take a seat on the floor by the fireplace, surrounded by Matthew, Lucas and my parents.

"Emi, tell us about yourself," my mom says. She shifts uncomfortably, takes a sip of wine, and begins to answer her question.

"Well," she says. "I went to NYU and got a Fine Arts degree... I'm a graphic designer and illustrator... mainly freelance jobs for books and magazines."

"That sounds very fun," my mom says. "Very creative."

"Yes," Emi continues. "I really enjoy it."

"I know your brother, Chris," my dad says. "Any other siblings?"

"Yes, we also have an older sister, Jennifer. She and her daughter, Clara, live with me."

"And how did you meet Jacks?" Lucas asks her.

We both laugh a little. "When, the first time?" I ask.

"This sounds like a story," he settles in to the couch, ready to listen.

"Oh, it is," Matthew says.

"We met in college," I tell Lucas. "Her brother– he's the one whose wedding I was in last September– he was one of my fraternity brothers... and Emi came to one of our parties."

"My memories of that night weren't crystal clear," Emi blushes. "But I remember Jack being the only gentleman there."

"The only gentleman... but the only one who got to kiss you."

"I remember that," my mother says. "He was crazy about you."

"So you've known each other all this time?" Lucas asks.

"Not exactly," I explain. "We didn't see each other, for many years. But we got reacquainted, um... at her brother's engagement party." I stop myself, swallowing back any additional words. I don't really know how to tell our story without getting into the sad reality of it. I am afraid to look at Emi, afraid to see her sorrow– it's been awhile since I've seen it– so her voice startles me when she continues.

"I was dating someone else at the time, though," she says. My eyes meet hers, and she smiles warmly, sensing my struggle.

"But later in the year, after seeing each other around the city a few times, I just decided to ask her out," I say, encouraged to continue.

"We spent a lot of time getting to know each other, just as friends," Emi says. "Jack was very patient with me... but I think we both knew all along we'd end up together."

"I'd hoped for that since that day in college," I lament. She squeezes my hand. I'm grateful that she guided that conversation. I feel like what has happened in her life is her business. I had only told one person: Kelly.

I had called my twin sister as I left the hospital early in the morning. It only took one ring for her to pick up. She told me she had just awoken a few moments earlier with a sinking feeling in her stomach. She knew something had happened with me immediately. I felt completely destroyed in that moment as I recounted the entire night to her. Normally able to control my emotions, I had no idea how to deal with what had happened. Kelly had been so worried about me that she had driven to my house to stay with me– for two days.

Emi's history affects me directly, but it really doesn't affect anyone else. I have deliberately chosen not to tell anyone else about Nate's death. If she decides to share that, it will be her decision.

"And so," Matthew interjects, "does that take one of Manhattan's most eligible bachelors off the market?"

"You had to go there?" I ask.

"She doesn't know?" he laughs. I shake my head and roll my eyes, then look at Emi.

"Know what?"

My mom answers, proudly. "Jack was featured in Gotham magazine as one of the most eligible bachelors in the city last year."

"Shut up!" Emi laughs. "Really?"

"Yes," Mom says. "I'm sure he has a copy at home he could show you."

"No, I don't," I assure her.

"Oh, I have to see that," Emi starts, "why didn't–"

"Thanks, Matty," I interrupt. "But to answer your question, yes. I think it's safe to say I'm off the market."

Emi looks at me, eyes wide, smile even wider. She leans in to kiss me, never afraid of little PDAs, apparently in front of my family, either. I have to admit, I've never really been comfortable displaying my feelings in front of other people... but with Emi, it's different. I feel like a different person around her. I want to kiss her, touch her– whatever it takes to make her smile or laugh. I don't even think about it, worry about what anyone else thinks. I want people to see how happy she makes me. I feel my face get hot for once, though, as I realize my family is staring, a bit taken by surprise by my actions.

"Does anyone need a refill?" my dad says, standing up, seemingly uncomfortable. My mother is just smiling, and couldn't look more pleased.

I eye Emi's nearly-full glass and tell him no.

"Oh, you two were hungry, weren't you?" my mom asks. Honestly, we had eaten on the plane.

"You know," Emi says, "I'm just going to wait for dinner."

"Yeah, me, too."

"Well let me know if you change your mind," she follows up.

My sister and her daughters show up a short while later. Mom and Dad immediately get reacquainted with their granddaughters, leaving the rest of us to talk in the living room.

"Do you dance, Emi?" my brother asks.

"After a drink or two, yes," she admits.

"Excellent, so, are we hitting the clubs tonight?" Matthew asks.

"No," Kelly whines. "Can't we wait until Monday, when Thomas gets in?"

"We can't do both?" Lucas asks.

"I don't know," my sister answers. "I kind of want to relax tonight, don't you guys?"

"Let's just go tomorrow night, or Monday, so Thomas can join us," I suggest. "Emi and I had an early morning."

"Whatever," Lucas argues. "We were up a good three hours before you two, so you can't use that as an excuse."

"I could go for a little bit," Emi says with pleading eyes. "It'll be fun," she shrugs in my direction.

"I thought you were tired," I look at her, questioning. "Didn't you say you just wanted to go to bed? Early, I mean?"

"I'll still be plenty tired later," she blushes as my brother and his partner look at her skeptically. "Please?"

"Whatever you want to do, Em," I tell her, secretly just wanting to be alone with her.

"Thank you," she says, squeezing my hand.

"Hey," Matthew interjects. "Steven just texted. He and Renee and Lex are here. They said they could be ready in an hour... so I'll come by and pick you all up in the SUV then. Sound good?"

"Perfect," Emi says, standing excitedly and helping me up. We tell my parents and nieces goodbye before walking back to our cabin.

Forty-five minutes later, Emi is still undecided, standing in front of a full-length mirror.

"I think this is the right one," Emi says to herself, staring at her tight leather pants and fitted shimmery silver top. I glance away quickly, unable to look at her without getting turned on. I hate my brother for suggesting we all go out. Especially now that she's dressed like this.

"I can't believe you wasted this much time picking out an outfit, Em," I say as I thumb through the resort's brochure, looking at anything to keep my eyes off of her. "We could have done so many other things in that hour."

"Okay, Grumpy," she argues. "There will be plenty of time for *so many other things* later. I think it's important that I spend some time with your siblings, so they can get to know me. I think this sounds like fun."

"It does," I tell her. "I'm just jealous that you'd rather spend time with them and not me."

"You'll be there."

"I want you to myself, though." I snake my arms through hers and hold her body tightly next to mine, placing an unexpected kiss on the corner of her lips as I run my hands over her behind tentatively. "Especially with you dressed like this."

"So you *do* like this outfit? Because you haven't said anything about it yet..."

"I'm trying not to acknowledge that you're really going out in public looking like that."

"What's that supposed to mean?" she asks, offended.

"It's too sexy, Emi," I tell her, kissing her ear. "Do you have any idea what I want to do to you right now?"

"No," she whispers. "Tell me."

"Absolutely not," I tell her, letting her go. "I'll just show you later tonight. Are you wearing that black thing?" I ask.

"Are you kidding?" she asks. "Like anything would fit under this." She flutters her lashes at me as she turns to walk away, grabbing her coat on the way to the door.

I close my eyes and count to ten before following her out of the cabin when we hear the SUV's horn, unable to remove the smile from my lips or the many thoughts of her from my head.

Lucas orders a round of shots as soon as we get to the club in central Vail. My sister passes, having agreed to be the designated driver tonight. We pull together a few tables in the bar to accommodate my family.

Steven and Renee show up about a half hour later.

"We had to get Lexi settled with the girls," Renee explains, hugging everyone warmly with Steven following behind her. I introduce Emi to my brother and his girlfriend, and when Renee reaches Kelly, a loud squeal erupts from my sister's lips.

"Yeah," Steven says loudly, addressing all of us. "We would like to invite you all to a wedding next summer."

"No way," I say to him, walking over to Renee again to give her a kiss on the cheek. I find my brother and do the same. "Congratulations. We thought this day would never come."

"When did this happen?" Kelly asks.

"On the plane," Renee says. "He asked me over the loud speaker on the airplane!"

"Let's have another round for the newly engaged couple," Matty announces, passing out more shot glasses. I find a menu and take a look at their food options, pulling Emi to my side.

"You should probably eat something, Em," I encourage her. "I think I'm going to get a chicken sandwich, do you want me to order something for you?"

"Sure," she says, already a little giddy, her feet tapping anxiously to the loud music. "Just get me whatever you're getting." I order the sandwiches and a beer for myself, a glass of wine for her.

"Hey, Jacks," Lucas says over the crowd noise. "Can I borrow your girl for a dance?"

"Come with me," Emi adds, pulling me by my arm.

"I think Lucas will be enough for you," I tell her, planting myself in a seat. "He's a much better dancer."

"You lie, you're a great dancer," she pleads.

"I don't dance to this, Emi. I need to catch up with my brother, anyway."

"You don't mind?" she asks.

"Not at all, go have fun," I smile. I glare at Matty as he hands her another shot before his partner takes her to the dance floor. "Matthew, she hasn't had much to eat today. Go easy on the shots, okay?"

"You're such a worrier. We won't get her too drunk."

"Yeah. Thanks," I roll my eyes at him as Steven sits down next to me. Renee, Matty and Kelly all join Lucas and Emi. My youngest brother and I have similar temperaments, both a little too reserved to feel comfortable letting loose on the dance floor. I don't mind slow dancing, but I just feel like an idiot dancing to faster songs.

"Congratulations, Stevie," I tell him again, patting him on the back. "I'm really glad you're making it official."

"Yeah, I think it's time." Steven and Renee had been living together for about a year. Renee thought it was best for Lexi, wanting her to grow up in a household that had two parents. "How is it going with Emi?"

"Great," I tell him. "I couldn't be happier."

"Now, she's the girl from college, right? The one that you were crazy about."

"I guess, yeah," I admit. I could remember going home for Christmas that year. It was just a few weeks after I had met her, and I had a difficult time getting my mind off of her. My family noticed the evidence of the black eye immediately, so I had to tell them the story. My brothers teased me relentlessly about her.

"How'd you get back in touch?" Steven asks.

"I was the best man in her brother's wedding. She was the maid of honor. It just sort of happened from there," I tell him simply. It's an easier story to tell.

I watch Emi dancing with the rest of my family. It's hard for me to not be jealous of my brother and his partner. Matty is free with his hands, pulling her body to his as he dances seductively with her. She looks at me and blushes, shrugging her shoulders at me but laughing at the same time. If it were anyone other than my flirtatious brother...

Renee hands her yet another shot as I fight the urge to go to her, take it from her and ask her to eat something before she drinks anything more. I'm being overprotective. I take a drink of my beer and force myself to stay seated, watching her from afar until the food comes. Then I'll ask her to join me.

"She's very pretty," he says. "She seems to be having fun out there. Will she be here the whole week?" he asks.

"Yeah. She doesn't have to report to work or anything, so she can take off at a moment's notice. Kind of nice, really. Fits my schedule."

"That's convenient," my brother comments. "Does she have a house, or rent an apartment?"

"She and her sister share an apartment that she kind of inherited."

"Interesting." The waiter brings the food to the table. Emi looks over a few seconds later and I signal for her to join me. Lucas tries to hold on to her as she stumbles away from him. I stand up to pull the chair out for her. As soon as I sit down, though, she stands up and moves to my lap, putting her arm around my shoulder and tilting my head up to kiss her.

"Are you having fun?" I ask her. She nods, taking a baby carrot from the plate and eating it. I brush a few errant strands of hair from her eyes and kiss her once more. My brother stands abruptly and moves to the bar, taking a seat.

"Did I make him uncomfortable?" she giggles.

"Maybe," I tell her. "But I'm comfortable." I run my hand down her thigh as she takes another carrot and feeds it to me. "You are so sexy, Emi. I can barely stand to watch you dance out there like that."

"Really?" she smiles innocently, batting her eyelashes.

"Really. Here, eat something substantial," I tell her, picking up one of the sandwiches and offering it to her. She takes a small bite before setting it down on the plate, then sees the wine and takes a drink. After setting the glass back down, she kisses my cheek, then my earlobe. "I can't wait to get back to the cabin," I tell her.

"Come dance with me," she says excitedly.

"Emi, eat something, please," I beg.

"Dance with me first," she barters as a more down-tempo song begins to play.

"One dance, then you'll eat?" She smiles seductively and nods. I nudge her off my lap as she takes my hand and leads me to the floor, leaving our food behind.

Emi pulls me close to her, gripping my shirt tightly as we dance to the slower song. I clasp my hands behind her and lean down to kiss her.

"I'm not wearing anything under this," she reminds me.

"Yes, I know. You mentioned that in the cabin," I laugh.

"Did I?" she blushes.

"You're a little drunk, Em."

"I know," she giggles. "I like your family."

"I think they like you, too. Not as much as I do..."

Her hands move from my shirt to my hair, her eyes searching mine. "Do you love me?"

"That's a silly question. You know I do." I brush her cheek with my thumb, smiling assuredly.

"Why?"

"Why what?"

"Why do you love me? You could love anyone in the world."

"Why are you asking me this? Are these the shots talking?"

"No," she says. "I just don't... what's so..." she stammers.

"What is it, Emi?"

"Why am I so special?"

I laugh quietly at her question. "I have a list at the cabin," I tease her. "Shall we go back and read it?"

"Jack," she pleads, as if she's really curious... as if she really doesn't know why she is so special to me. The drum beat of a new song interrupts us.

"My turn!" Matthew says as he takes her from my arms. "I got the DJ to play your song!"

"Emi, come eat something."

"No, it's my favorite!" she yells over the music. "One more dance." I nod and roll my eyes, just wanting her to come back to the table with me... or actually, wanting her to come back to the cabin with me. I assume it's the alcohol that's causing her insecure questions. Surely I've told her a million times why I love her, shown her how I love her.

One song turns into six plus, and I have the food sent back, accepting that she's not going to have dinner. Emi's question eats away at me for some reason, and I can't figure out what has changed... what has brought on her uncertainty in my feelings. Exhausted and no longer in the mood to be among the growing crowd in the club, I call my sister over.

"I'm going to get a cab back to the resort," I tell her. "I'll let Emi know, but she seems to be having fun."

"She's a blast, Jacks," Kelly says. "Oh, my god, she's so funny."

"She's so *drunk*," I tell her disapprovingly. "Will you promise to keep an eye on her?"

"Of course," my sister assures me. I sign the ticket for the food and drinks we've consumed so far, and walk to the middle of the dance floor where Emi, Renee, Matthew and Lucas are all dancing.

"Can I interrupt for a second?" I ask her. Her eyes are glazed over, but she smiles shyly and nods, following me to the side of the room. "I'm exhausted, so I'm getting a cab back to the hotel."

"Do you want me to come?" she asks, but I can tell she is not ready to go back yet.

"No, stay and have some fun," I encourage her.

"Are you sure?"

"Of course I'm sure." By the time she gets back to the hotel, I have no doubt it will take her only mere seconds to pass out. I gave up on being intimate with her a good hour and a half ago. "Take this," I say, handing her the card that will grant her entrance into our cabin. She looks at it curiously before putting it in her small purse.

"Okay," she says with a nod. "Will you be ready for me when I come home?" Her finger scratches lightly down my chest.

"Oh, yes, my dear," I laugh. "I'll be ready for you... to crash. I'll pull the sheets down for you."

"I'm fine," she argues.

"I know you are." My words are filled with sarcasm. "I'll be ready, don't worry."

"Okay," she sighs. "I'll see you soon."

"Be careful. I wouldn't be upset if you ate something."

"You worry too much," she tells me, brows furrowed, as she leans in to kiss my cheek. "You can feed me some fruit later."

"Right, okay," I agree, simply to appease her.

"Like ya," she tells me, biting her bottom lip. I cock my head curiously at her strange choice of words. Her smile falls slightly as she shakes her head. "I mean, I love you," she corrects herself, swallowing hard.

"I love you, too." I kiss her forehead before leaving the club. When I get back to the cabin, I settle in to make a list prior to turning in for the night.

I wake up to the sound of Emi throwing up in the bathroom. A brief glimpse at the pillow next to me confirms that she did come to bed at some point, and I'm surprised I didn't wake up to greet her. A dim orange glow signals the impending sunrise, but it's obvious my sweet girlfriend will not be ready to start the day any time soon. I trip over Emi's shoes on my way to the bathroom, her leather pants and silver shirt laying nearby.

"Em, you okay?" I ask after knocking on the locked door.

"Make the room stop spinning."

"Open up, sweetie."

"No," she whines. I leave her alone to get her some sparkling water.

She is sitting on the bed with her robe on, legs crossed, eyes closed when I come back into the room. "I hate your family," she moans.

"You loved them last night," I smile, setting the water on the nightstand and sitting down next to her, pulling her head into my shoulder.

"Oh, don't move me," she says, then leans into me on her own accord. "I feel so sick."

"I can tell. You're clammy... and you smell like liquor."

"I'm sorry."

"You should be," I joke with her. "What time did you get in?"

"Two-thirty, I think. I don't really remember. What time is it now?" she asks.

"Six-fifteen. You ready to hit the slopes?" She finally opens her eyes as she looks at me with disdain.

"Tell me you're joking."

"Of course I'm joking, Drunky." I try to smooth down her wild, matted hair, but there's no use. "How many more shots did they force you to drink, anyway?"

"God, who knows?" she says with a frown. "Although I can't blame them entirely. I think I bought a round or two at some point. Your brothers sure can drink. And Renee, too. Ugh, I don't even want to think about it anymore." She falls back into my chest. I wrap my arms around her as her body shudders quickly.

"Are you cold?"

"I don't even know," she says. Her ice-cold feet touch my thigh as she shifts uncomfortably.

"I think you are. Lie back," I suggest, helping her under the covers. "Do you think you'll be okay if I go work out for a bit?"

"I'm just going to try to sleep," she mumbles.

"Okay. I'll take my phone. Call me if you need anything, the workout center is nearby." I move her phone to the nightstand, next to the list I had made last night. "There's some water here for you, too."

"Thank you," she says, her eyes closed again as she cuddles under the blankets.

After my workout, I head back to the cabin and quietly boot up my laptop in the living area. Careful not to wake her, I catch up on some email correspondence with one of my bigger clients in Europe. As I start working on the proposal I'm set to present to them in a couple of months, I hear the faucet turn on in the bathroom. *I hope she's feeling better.*

She doesn't meet me on the couch after her shower. Instead, she calls my name from the bedroom. Putting my work aside, I go in to see if she needs anything.

"Hey, Poppet," I say to her from the doorway. "How are you?"

"A little better now," she smiles as she crawls back under the blankets dressed in one of the t-shirts I had brought along. She holds up the piece of paper I had left on the nightstand. "Top Ten Reasons Why You're So Special," she reads the heading. "You really made a list?"

"I don't want you to have any doubt. I sensed that you did. I just didn't know why."

"I think I was just overwhelmed at all the new information. You're a tra-zillionaire–"

"Not quite–"

"And," she says loudly, cutting me off, "you're one of Manhattan's most eligible bachelors–"

"Not so much now," I assure her, walking toward the bed.

"And," she continues, "you have this perfect family that adores you–"

"I pay them to," I tease, my expression deadpan.

"And then there's me. Some ragged, hungover lush who has given you nothing but trouble."

"Right," I laugh as I sit down on my side of the bed. "And what was number... seven, I think it was?" I take the paper from her and read it to myself. "What does it say you've given me?"

"Was that the *hope for your future* one or the *best sex* one?"

"Neither. *You've given me the chance to see the world in an entirely new light*," I tell her. "Did you read the list at all?"

"Yes!" she squeals, grabbing the paper back and laughing.

"Well, then you'd know *best sex* was number three." I lie down next to her and lean over her.

"Three," she repeats as she shifts to her side, her face inches from mine. "How can we put that at the top of the list?" she whispers.

"First," I tell her as I run my fingers through her damp hair, "you can't sneak into bed, drunk, in the middle of the night."

"Sorry about that," she blushes. "Next time I'll wake you up."

"That's a start," I smile as we meet in the middle of the bed with a kiss. "We could work on that now," I suggest.

"Ummm..." she hesitates. "Ragged hungover lush here," she states, pointing to herself. "I think I need a little more sleep. Raincheck? Tonight, maybe?"

"Definitely. You took some aspirin?" I ask. She answers with a nod. "You'll let me know if you need anything else?" Again, she nods. I kiss her forehead before leaving her, getting back to my work in the adjoining room.

Early in the evening, we finally make it out of the cabin to meet my family in the resort's casual dining room. The day Emi spent in bed must have been exactly what she needed, because from the looks of her now, I can't even tell she was feeling bad at all. She looks stunning, her cheeks naturally rosy, eyes bright. Over dinner, my family gets caught up on the happenings of one another's lives, and they get to know her a little better.

Matthew insists on sitting on the other side of her, and has stolen her attention for most of the meal. Even if it means less time with me, I'm happy she's connecting and having a good time with him and Lucas, Kelly and Renee, and I can tell they're all getting along well. Steven shifts uncomfortably as I try to engage him in some business conversation.

"Excuse me," Emi interrupts as dessert is served, getting up from the table

94

abruptly and heading toward the door. I start to get up, but Kelly motions for me to stay as she follows her. I look at Matthew, who looks a little stunned.

"I was just telling her how smitten you were with her after that kiss in college," he says. "I told her that you thought she was 'the one' after that night. I asked her if she felt the same thing...

"She said she did," he continues. "And then I asked her what took her so damn long... but then she just teared up... and left..."

"Okay," I say to my brother, taking the napkin from my lap and putting it on the table. "It's alright."

"What did I say?" he asks.

"Nothing, Matty, don't worry about it. She'll be okay." I take Emi's coat with me and walk out the front door. My sister and Emi are embracing tightly.

"I'm fine," Emi says to me, looking up, smiling at me with tear-streaked cheeks, sniffling.

"I know, Em," I tell her, smiling, draping her coat around her shoulders, not too worried about her tears, almost expecting them on occasion.

"We are guessing you haven't told anyone else about what happened," Kelly says. "I tried to get Matty to stop, but he wasn't reading my signals."

"I don't want people to be afraid to talk to me about it," Emi says. "It's not some big secret. It's a part of who I am... I just figured they all knew."

"No, I told Kelly, that's it," I tell her. "I can tell the rest of them, if you'd like... if that will make it easier."

"I'd rather that than tiptoe around the subject," she says. "I could probably tell them," she offers, "but when people look at me, like they feel sorry for me, it just makes me sad." She smiles.

"Got it," I tell her. "I'll take care of it."

"I think I'll drive her back to the cabin," Kelly says.

"Is that okay?" Emi asks.

"It's fine, love." She walks over to me and kisses me as I hand her the key. "I'll be there in a bit."

The entire family is looking at me as I walk toward them across the restaurant. I take Emi's seat and pat Matthew on the back.

"Is she okay?" he says, his eyes apologetic. The family stares expectantly.

"Yes." I clear my throat. "I don't know if you guys picked up on my hesitation yesterday when I was talking about the night Emi and I got reacquainted..."

"At the engagement party..." Lucas adds.

"Yes. Well, Emi was there with someone else that night. She was with her boyfriend, Nate, who had been her best friend since high school. They hadn't been dating very long, but they were about as close as two people could be."

I swallow, remembering the look in his eyes as he walked toward her that night, taking her away from me. I avoid the eyes of my family members, succumbing to the guilt again, trying to compose myself.

"They left the party shortly before midnight, and his car was hit by some drunk kids. Nate died at the scene. Emi was hurt, she was in a coma for three days. She missed his funeral... never really got to say goodbye to him," I explain. "Sometimes she just gets a little sad."

"That's awful," my mother says. Renee and Matthew just look shocked.

"I'm sorry," Lucas says.

"Where does that leave you?" Steven asks. I look at him, curious.

"What do you mean?"

"She's still upset about him," he says. "I know you've laid everything out there for her. I know you're completely in love with her. How does she feel about you?"

"She loves me," I tell him confidently. I don't have a doubt in my mind, even though I see it in his eyes. "You'll see."

"I see," Matthew chimes in. "And I think she's amazing."

"Me, too," Lucas says.

"That's a hard thing to go through," my mother adds, and I sense some concern in her, too.

"It's been really hard for her," I agree. "We took things very slowly. I thought I knew her, inside and out, just by my intense feelings for her... but she is so much more than I could ever have hoped for. As I got to know her, I just loved her more.

"She asked me to tell you all about Nate," I explain, "because she wants you all to know her, and understand her. She didn't want to have to see these sorrowful looks. So do me a favor, and when you see her tomorrow, don't look at her like this.

"Yes, she still gets sad occasionally, but we really are happy together. You don't have to avoid talking to her about her past, either, she can handle it. She thought you all knew already, so she was kind of caught off-guard. That's my fault."

"Okay," my dad says. "Tomorrow's a new day. I think she's a very sweet girl."

"Thanks, Dad." When Kelly comes back in, I thank her for being there for Emi.

"She feels bad for leaving like that," my sister says. "But she's fine."

"I'm on my way there," I tell her. "Thanks again." I tell my family good night and put my coat on. I decline my brother's offer to drive me back to the cabin, choosing to walk back to give Emi a little more time by herself– and to enjoy the crisp mountain breeze, such a departure from Manhattan air.

It begins to snow when I'm about half-way to the cabin. My ski jacket would be nice right now, instead of the trench coat I brought with me. A hat would be even nicer, my hair becoming moist, cold as the snowflakes fall.

When I reach the cabin, the door is locked. I knock quietly and wait, but when she doesn't answer, I knock harder and call her name. Suddenly, she swings the door open to reveal herself, wearing only a thong and the corset I had gotten a peek of the day before. The winter air freezing, blowing into the cabin, I wanted nothing more than to pick her up, but I was cold and wet from the snow and only wanted to stay away.

"My god, Emi," I laugh, helpless. "I can't even warm you up!"

"I think you can," she says, kissing me while taking my wet coat off, hanging it on a hook by the door. "You are cold," she laughs, sounding a bit more sensible. She leads me into the bedroom, where she has pulled the down comforter and pillows off of the bed and laid them on the floor in front of the fireplace. "Get comfortable," she says, going into the bathroom and bringing out a towel. She attempts to dry my hair with it, but I decide to take over that task and let her begin to undress me. Once she has both of my shirts off, I stop her from going any further.

"Let me see this," I tell her. She takes a few steps back and allows me to admire her body. The smell of soap still lingers from her recent bath. I walk toward her, and turn her around, taking in the other side. I kiss her neck, then her shoulders, my hand feeling her behind... then I shiver from the cold, my head actually feeling a little numb. "Okay, I'm going to have to take a shower or something," I tell her.

"Really?" she asks.

"I'm freezing, Em," I tell her. "You could join me."

"I just took a bath," she explains.

"I don't see how that has anything to do with my invitation."

"But I just put this on," she says, smiling, eager.

"And you look so incredibly sexy in it... but it's going to come off sooner or later," I tell her, unfastening the top hook in the middle of her back. I sit on the edge of the bed, pulling her toward me so I can work my way down the rest of the hooks. I kiss her back with each one, watching her expression in the large mirror on the wall facing us. Her eyes meet mine with each glance.

Once I finish with the last hook, I slowly lower the corset to reveal her breasts, eventually dropping it to the floor. I take her by the waist, pulling her closer, as she shyly covers herself with her arms, our gaze never breaking. My hands travel to meet hers, and she gives way to my touch, my fingers likely uncomfortably cold, but she doesn't flinch. I stand up to kiss her neck again, and she turns around, pressing her warm torso against me, kissing my chest, her hands fumbling with my belt until she manages to unfasten it, then my pants, letting them fall. I step out of them and pick Emi up, carrying her toward the bathroom. When I set her down, she again perches on the edge of the tub, as she had yesterday, putting her nearly naked body on display. I turn on the shower and allow the water to heat up.

She shifts her body slightly when I go to her to remove her delicate lingerie. I kiss her softly, my tongue exploring her intimately. When she lets out a long sigh, I give one last kiss, then stand up in front of her. She pulls down my briefs and touches me gently, the warmth spreading quickly throughout my body. I take her hands in mine and lead her into the large walk-in shower, three separate shower-heads trickling hot water down our bodies.

Hours later, after Emi falls asleep, I get up to stoke the fire and add some more wood. The warm orange glow of the flames dances in her hair, making it even redder. Her expression is peaceful, content. I could sit here and continue to admire her body from afar, or I could go to her and feel her soft curves in hopes of rousing her from her sleep.

I lie down on the comforter next to her, matching the angles of her body with my own, and put my arm across her body, pulling her into me. Small drops of perspiration dot her forehead, and I wonder if they linger from the night's activities or if she's too hot in the blanket, so close to the fire. I kiss her bare shoulder, then move her hair from obstructing my view of her soft neck. Her hair has really grown out. I hadn't realized how much, subtle differences from day to day, but it's inches below her shoulders. I comb my fingers through it, gently working out a few knots, eventually allowing my tongue to trace up her neck, jawline, settling on her ear lobe. This awakens her. I should have let her sleep, I know.

She rolls over onto her back, smiling. "How are you not exhausted?" she asks me, running her fingers through my undoubtedly messy hair. I slowly, lightly tease her lips with mine, and she responds with a deeper kiss and a soft moan. "I love you," she whispers to me. My heart full, I return her sentiment in both words and gentle, attentive actions.

"Jack!" Emi says in a panic the following morning, sitting up hurriedly.

"What?" I open my eyes, the sun pouring into the room through the large windows.

"Weren't we supposed to meet everyone for breakfast at nine?"

"What time is it?"

"Nine."

"Mmmm," I respond, pulling her back down to kiss her.

"You don't seem very concerned."

"I am always on time. Always the one who waits on everyone else. It's someone else's turn today," I smile. "I just want to take my time with you... take in every second."

"Well, if you're *always* on time, then they're going to blame me. I already bailed on dinner last night. The cards are already stacking against me. The goal is for them to like me, right?"

"Are you worried that they don't?" I ask.

"I'm worried that they *won't*," she corrects me. "They don't know me yet." She stands up and holds her hand out to help me up.

"They're going to love you," I assure her. "Matthew is the biggest critic, and it was love at first sight with him. Just like it was with me."

"Awww," she says, mockingly. "Come on! We have to get ready! I'm going to take a shower."

"That's all you had to say. I'm coming," I tell her. She glares at me, but can't keep from laughing.

"Sorry, we missed the alarm," I announce to the family flippantly as we sit down. Emi's beautiful blushing cheeks, averted eyes, give our earlier activities away, though. *God, I love her.*

"Did you sleep well?" my mother asks.

I pour coffee for both of us and let Emi answer.

"Very well, thank you," she politely states, and my mother smiles and nods.

"You just lied to my mother," I whisper in her ear. "We've never had a more sleepless night." She slaps my thigh and laughs.

"No, Mrs. Holland," Emi says quietly, leaning in to me, so only I can hear. "Your son and I fooled around in the shower first... and then shortly after I dozed off, he woke me up, and we did it again a little later on the floor, by the fireplace. Eventually, we did go to bed, but only to make love one more time... and this one was crazy, we tried some new things... you should have seen it, Mrs. Holland. I think we both passed out from sheer exhaustion around four this morning. And *then*, in the shower this *morning...*"

I tuck an errant strand of hair back under her pink knitted cap and kiss her. "I had an amazing night, Em."

"Me, too." She blushes again.

"I'd forego sleep any night for you."

"I'm sure you would," she laughs.

"You two better eat something, we've got a long day of skiing ahead of us," Matthew says, passing a basket of muffins and giving us a knowing glance. "Might need to keep your strength up," he says under his breath, lifting a brow. Emi's mouth falls open before a quick laugh escapes. I put my fingers below her chin and pull her toward me, kissing her lips softly.

"Mr. Holland," Bill calls to me from across the dining room. "How are you enjoying your stay so far?"

"It's been incredible, thank you."

"Does anyone have any special requests for today?" I look around the table, and everyone shakes their head.

"Nothing more than what we discussed," I tell him.

"And dinner for sixteen tonight in the formal dining area?" he confirms.

"Yes, everyone will be here for dinner. My brother-in-law and nephews should be arriving in the early afternoon."

"Right, there will be a car waiting for them at the airport."

"Thanks, Bill."

"Anything, Mr. Holland. You have my number if you need anything." I nod as he walks to talk to the guests at the next table.

"What did you discuss?" Emi asks me.

"Oh, just, you know, about the car for Thomas and stuff."

"And stuff?" she asks. "Stuff?" That word really isn't in my vocabulary... and she knows that.

"Just eat your breakfast, Poppet," I say to her playfully, obviously dodging her questions.

"Emi, are you a good skier?" Renee asks.

"I have no idea," she says. "I've never tried."

"I hadn't either when I first came," Steven's fiancée admits. "I stayed on the beginner slopes the first time. But the second time, I got out there with all the adults. It takes some skill, but it's more about confidence."

"But by now, even all the kids are probably pros, right?" Emi asks.

"Not the little ones," Steven says. "They'll need a chaperone." I notice sarcasm or something in my brother's voice, and begin to pay more attention to his attitude toward Emi.

"I'm great with kids," Emi smiles, undeterred.

"Lexi's never skied before, either," Renee says. "She's a little scared."

"Well, we can learn together, right Lex?" The child nods her head enthusiastically.

"It's Lexi," Steven says, and Renee and I both glare at my brother.

Emi looks surprised, but quickly apologizes to Renee's daughter. "I'm sorry, Lexi. I thought I heard someone call you that earlier."

"I don't mind," she returns, taking a bite of her cereal and smiling.

"If you'll excuse me," Emi says, "I'm just going to go to the ladies room." I study her face, and she seems fine.

"I'll go with you," Renee offers, and both women make their way to the restrooms.

"What's up, Stevie?" I ask my brother, kicking him under the table. "You're never like this. Why in the world are you being like this to her?"

"I just don't trust her," he says. "I don't think she's over that other guy...

which makes me wonder why she's with you..."

"And why do you think she's with me?" Matthew and Kelly slide into the seats left by our girlfriends, noticing the heated conversation.

"I would guess money," he says. "Seems pretty obvious."

"What's going on?" Kelly asks.

"Stevie's being an ass," I tell her.

"Jacks is being a fool," Steven counters.

"How so?" Lucas asks, joining the conversation, standing behind Matthew and me.

"I think she's still in love with that other guy. Nobody gets that upset over someone that they don't care about anymore."

"Of course she still *cares* about him," my sister chimes in. "He died. Her best friend and lover *died*. She'd be inhuman if she didn't care about him."

"Well, how does that work?" Steven asks. "She lost her best friend, lover, her *soulmate*. What does that make you, Jacks?"

Soulmate. Such an odd word. I hadn't– for the longest time– considered I had one... mainly because the one I thought was mine belonged to someone else for so long. But isn't she mine? Am I hers? Can people have more than one?

"It makes me the man that she loves now. That's all I want from her. That's enough for me... it should certainly be enough for you."

"She makes him really happy," Kelly says. "You're not around to see it, but I am. Jacks has always been considerate and generous and giving... he's always been about doing things for other people. And I know it's always made you happy," she says, looking at me. "But there was always a sort of emptiness, something missing, some sadness inside of you. And it's gone, with her."

"It seems like she makes you someone you're not," Steven says. "Kissing in front of us, you were an hour late to breakfast... that's not you."

"I'm finished with this conversation," I tell him. "I don't have to justify myself or explain myself to you."

"Give her a chance, Stevie," Matthew says. "She seems really genuine, and if nothing else... have you ever seen Jacks so happy?"

"I just don't buy it." I feel my heart rate rise, anger welling inside of me, which is pretty hard to evoke in me.

"Boys," my mother says, far enough away from the conversation to be unable to hear, but close enough to feel the tension between us.

"This is really uncalled for," I mutter to Steven.

"Hey, I'm just looking out for you."

"Well, don't," I tell him.

When Renee and Emi return to the table, Steven stands up and asks if anyone is ready to ski. Everyone begins to gather their things.

"Black Diamond this way," he says, gesturing to one side of the table. "Bunny hills over there." He points to Emi, who shrugs her shoulders and smiles. Renee crosses the table to stand next to me and Emi.

"What are you doing?" Steven asks her.

"Lexi's never skied before," she says. "I'm going to help teach her. Come on, kids," she calls to my nieces.

"You can go with them," Emi encourages me. "I'll be fine."

"Absolutely not," I tell her, wanting to avoid my little brother just as much as I want to spend time with her.

"You guys have fun," my father says. "Your mother and I will be in the lodge, so if the kids need a break, just send them in."

"I'll check in when Thomas and the boys get here," Kelly says, joining Steven, Matthew and Lucas as they leave the dining area.

"Jacks, I'm sorry," Renee says after we've partnered the little girls up with a ski instructor. I wasn't going to talk about it any more. "I don't know what's gotten into him."

"Don't worry about it," I tell her. "I'm not."

"He has no right to be that way to you," Renee tells Emi. "I'm kind of embarrassed by him right now."

"It's okay," Emi says. "One out of twelve ain't so bad," she jokes.

"It's really one out of sixteen," I correct her. "Thomas and the boys like you, too."

"Right. I'm not sure what I did... but oh, well."

"You didn't do anything," I assure her. "Sometimes, I think he's just a little naïve."

"He can be," Renee says. "Understanding the complexities of love is not his forte. He broke up with me after our first couple of arguments," she goes on, "before I explained that it's normal for people to fight... even people in love."

"He believes there's one woman made for every man, and vice versa. Very idealistic," she explains. "I like that he thinks that I'm the one for him. I love that everything's pretty simple with him.

"But he has a hard time understanding how people can love– really love– more than one person... not necessarily at once, but in a lifetime. He's never felt anything like what he feels with me, with any other woman. He can't fathom that he could.

"I've loved pretty deeply before, though," she explains. "I really did love Lexi's dad, with all my heart... but the timing was all wrong for us. We were both addicts when I first got pregnant. When I found out, I stopped using, cold turkey. I never gave it another thought. He quit with me, too, but eventually, he couldn't stay away. It broke my heart to leave him, but I couldn't bring her up in that environment.

"He's clean now," she adds, an almost bittersweet smile on her face. "He's married and has another little girl. I still care about him a lot... but Steven and I don't really talk about him. He just doesn't understand. And I love Stevie very much, too much to make that an issue.

"So it's nothing you did, Emi," she says. "And he'll like you, when he gets past that. I mean, *I* already can't wait to be your sister-in-law." She smiles, then her eyes get wide at her faux-pas. "I mean, if you two ever decide to... shit."

Emi laughs nervously, avoiding eye contact with me. *Of course it's my intention to marry her.*

"Show me what I'm supposed to do, *Jackson*," she says to me, gesturing toward the small hills and beginning to hobble into the snow.

"I'm going to go watch the kids," Renee says as she easily skis away.

"Alright, Poppet." I help her out into a clear patch and begin to show her the basics.

I soon find that Emi's not really a natural at skiing, but we have a fun time nonetheless in our own private lesson. I may have been too much of a distraction for her, but I couldn't get the image of her from last night– this morning– out of my head, and I had a hard time keeping my hands off her. She didn't seem to mind. She seemed to be having the same problem.

"If I'm this sore after bunny hills, I don't think I'll survive anything bigger," Emi says as we enter the lodge.

"Are you sure it's just the bunny hills?" I ask.

She glares at me through a smile. "Actually, no."

"Go grab a seat on the couch, I'll go get something warm to drink." I watch Emi greet my parents as she takes a seat next to my dad. The girls and my youngest nephew sit on the floor around the coffee table, playing a board game. After I order a chai tea latte for Emi and a hot chocolate for myself, I wander to the small sundries shop while the barista prepares the drinks to get some ibuprofen and water.

I set down the pain reliever and water in front of Emi. She smiles and thanks me, quickly taking the pills. I return to the barista and pick up our hot beverages and take them back to the couch.

As soon as I sit down, my nephew runs to me and jumps in my lap. "Andy, you're getting so big! How are you?"

"Fine," he smiles.

"Where's your brother?"

"Skiing." He pushes out his lower lip.

"Oh, did you want to go?"

"All the adults are on the big slopes," my mother says.

"I tell you what," I suggest. "Let me drink this hot chocolate and then I'll take you skiing. Is that okay?"

Andrew nods enthusiastically.

"Can we go, too, Uncle Jacks?" Maddie asks.

"You can all go," I tell them. "And you can stay right here... or go back to the cabin, if you want," I tell Emi.

"I'm good here," she smiles. "Gives me some alone time with your mom and dad. Too bad they didn't bring photo albums of you when you were a baby."

"But we have tons of stories," my dad says.

"I'm not sure I should leave," I hesitate, joking with her.

"Oh, no, you've promised the kids," Emi says. "You can't back out now."

"No, Uncle Jacks!" Maddie and Andy both cry.

"Alright," I feign frustration, taking a sip of my drink. "Andy, do you remember Emi?" He nods and gives her a hug.

"Oh, thank you, Andy," she says. "Lexi, how did you do out there?"

"I only fell once," she says proudly. "I can't wait to do it again."

"You did better than me," she tells Lexi. "I fell three times."

"The secret is bending your knees," Maddie tells Emi, as her friend nods.

"That's what I told her," I tell them. "She just kept standing like this." I pass Andy off to Emi, who happily sits in her lap, and exaggerate a stance, sticking my butt out, making the kids laugh.

"It wasn't that bad," Emi argues, glaring, bouncing my nephew on her lap as he giggles.

"No, it was cute," I tell her, kissing her forehead.

"Why didn't Clara come?" Jackie asks.

"Clara's home with her mommy," she tells them. "She was really jealous, though. She even knows how to ski better than I do."

"Maybe she can come next year," I suggest. "Get Jen to come out, too.

Chris and Anna will probably be too busy with the baby."

"Is Chris having a baby?" my mother asks.

"Yes, Anna's about half-way through the pregnancy," Emi tells her. "They got pregnant right away... it was planned, though, or so they say."

"Is he so excited?"

"They both are. We all are. We just found out it's a boy."

"That's wonderful," my dad says.

"Okay, kids," I announce. "Who's ready?"

"Me!" Maddie, Lexi and Andy all say in unison.

"Is it okay if I stay here?" Jackie asks.

"Sure, sweetie," Emi says. "Come keep me company." Jackie takes Andy's place in Emi's lap and plays with a doll she has with her. "What's your baby's name?" she asks my niece, raising her eyebrows and smiling at me as I put my coat back on. My mom helps to get the other three kids bundled up.

"Love you," I tell Emi.

"You, too," she returns.

After an hour and a half, the kids are tired and hungry, so we head back to the lodge. Emi and my parents are still seated around the coffee table, talking to another couple. Jackie is lying down on the couch, her head in Emi's lap. Emi strokes her hair as she sleeps. She looks so beautiful, the scene perfect. I stare from across the room, taking it in, knowing now, more than ever, that I want her to be the mother of our children.

I can't wait to have children with her. Her eyes meet mine and she signals for me to come to her. The other kids wake Jackie up and my parents take them all to get drinks.

I kiss her slowly, touching her soft cheekbone, before taking a seat next to her.

"That was nice," she says.

"I couldn't help myself," I tell her. "Do you have any idea what an amazing mother you will be someday?"

"I hope I am," she says. "If our kids are as sweet as Jackie, it will be easy." *Our* kids. My smile grows wider at the thought. "You know, if we have them someday," she adds, her cheeks getting red.

"I hope we do," I tell her, kissing her one more time. "How was the chat with my parents? What did you talk about?"

"It was good. We just talked about, you know, things."

"What 'things?'"

"Well, I tried to dig up some dirt about you, but there is none," she says. "You were apparently a model child... sounds like your brothers were the hellions."

"They were," I tell her. "But I had my moments, I just hid my indiscretions well... and they trusted me a lot– more than they should have when I was a teenager. My sister, too. We covered for each other."

"Really?"

"Uh, yeah," I laugh, remembering one particular night when I was a junior in high school. My parents had gone out, and I had a girlfriend over. I expected them to be out much later, but they came home early. Kelly knew my date. They were in different cliques in school, but my twin sister and girlfriend pretended to be best friends when my parents came in. Kelly convinced my parents to let her stay over. I lost my virginity that night... and I owed Kelly dearly for her help.

I remember I had to pay off Matthew when he saw her sneak out of my bedroom early the next morning.

"In time," I tell her, "you'll hear them all, I'm sure... just not in front of the parents. I have a reputation to protect."

"I can't wait," she smiles.

"Have you seen any of my siblings, by the way?"

"Thomas and Kelly went to their cabin for awhile."

"Sans kids, huh?"

"Yes, Brandon and his friend stayed on the slopes with the others."

"Are you getting hungry?" I ask her. "I'm starving. We have reservations in an hour, so they should all be getting back soon."

"Hope Steven's mellowed," she says.

"If he's not, I'll take him outside and rough him up a bit."

"Right," she says. "I'm pretty sure he could take you."

"He does play dirty... and, yeah, I'm not a fighter," I admit.

"No," Emi says. "Lover, though..." We kiss again. "Do we have time to go change before dinner?" she asks.

"Sure." We wave goodbye to my parents from across the lodge and begin the walk back to our cabin. "We could have hitched a ride on a shuttle," I tell her, remembering how sore she was earlier.

"I'll be fine," she says. "I just need to walk it off."

"I could carry you," I suggest, but she scoffs and glares at me. When we reach our cabin, Emi immediately lies down on the couch.

"I'm not getting up," she moans after I get out of the shower.

"Yes, you are," I suggest. "I'll help."

"Just give me a second," she sighs. "We're dressing up tonight?"

"Whatever you like," I tell her.

"Okay," she says, excited, popping off the couch and running into the bathroom, closing the door behind her.

"Um, can you at least hand me some clothes out of the closet?" I ask, laughing.

"I'll pick," she says, eventually handing me my grey suit, an off-white shirt and a matching grey tie.

I sit down in the living room, checking my watch periodically, anxiously waiting for her to come out so we can go to the restaurant... I don't want her to find out the surprise...

"Okay, I'm ready," she says, walking out of the bedroom. She's wearing a sleeveless off-white silk dress that falls to her ankles, accentuating each of her delicate curves. Her red hair falls in curls on her shoulders, her makeup highlighting her natural beauty. Around her neck is the beautiful necklace given to her by Nate, and I realize part of the surprise shouldn't wait until we get back.

"You look incredible," she tells me quietly.

"And you are an angel, Emi," I tell her, nearly unable to breathe. Her cheeks turn red as she picks up her coat. "Just a second," I tell her. "We're not quite ready." I walk into the bedroom and pull the suitcase out from under the bed. "Come in here for a minute," I tell her, setting the rectangular turquoise box in the middle of the bed.

She stops in the doorway as soon as she sees the gift that awaits her. She looks at me, unsure at first, then smiles. "Come sit down," I encourage her. She sits on the opposite side of the bed, the box directly between us. She swallows hard, then touches her necklace slowly. She makes no move toward it, so I pick it up and untie the bow.

"Wait," she says before I pry the box open.

"Why?" I ask, ignoring her request and slowly lifting the lid.

"Oh," she says softly. She touches the bracelet, double strands of pearls that match the necklace. "Jack, it's perfect," she says, her eyes tearing up.

"I know how much the necklace means to you, Em... and it's exquisite and you're gorgeous in it, and I can tell it makes you feel beautiful, and I don't want to take that away from you. I would never want to take that away from you.

"But I wanted to give you something that would remind you of me." I take the bracelet out and fasten it around her wrist. She takes my hands in hers and holds them tightly.

"I *have* you," she says, her eyes demanding the attention of my own. "You don't have to buy me gifts, Jack. I think of you constantly. You don't have to worry about my commitment to you, not for a second. I feel so lucky every single day we are together. There was a time that I truly believed that I would never feel happiness or love again... and to be honest, what you and I have surpasses anything that I had ever hoped for."

"I love you so much, Emi," I tell her. I touch her soft cheek and we lean in to kiss each other. I glance at my watch again. "We need to go," I tell her hurriedly.

"Okay," she smiles, standing up gracefully and straightening her dress. "Thank you," she adds. "I love it."

"I'm glad." I help her with her coat, and as soon as she picks up her cell phone to put it in her pocket, it rings.

"It's Jen," she says, then answers the phone. *We have to go...* I guide her to the SUV that Lucas has left for us, locking the door behind us, as she talks to her sister.

"Really? No, it's fine, but why?" I help her into the car and make my way to the other side. She continues her conversation as I drive to the restaurant. "Alone? Where? No, really, it's fine. I'll be fine. It's just... sudden, I don't know... I had no idea you were considering moving out. Well, yeah, of course. No, I know... Well, when? Seriously? It's nothing I did, though... okay. Well, of course, I'll help when I get home. Late Sunday night. Okay. Alright, well how's Clara? Oh, well, I miss her, too. Yeah, give her a kiss from me. Okay. Love you, too. Bye."

"She's moving out?" I ask her.

"Yeah," she says, a little stunned. "She wants her own place. She found a townhouse in Astoria, two bedroom. They're moving out in three weeks."

"Wow, well, what do you think about that?"

"I don't know what to think," she says. "I've never lived alone."

"Ever?"

"No, never." As much as I would love to just move her into my house, I want to prolong our courtship a little longer.

"You can stay at my place anytime," I offer. "Or if you want company, I'll come there... watch Disney movies with you... or just watch you sleep like I did the first night you were there."

"I forgot about that," she laughs. "Yeah," she adds.

"You know, I do have a confession to make about that night," I tell her. She looks at me, curious. "Chris actually asked me to stay there... to keep you company that night."

"Really?"

"Yeah," I smile. "He was really worried about you. But, of course, I was happy to oblige him. I was looking forward to spending a little time with you. But honestly, I kept thinking, *she's got to be wondering why this creepy guy she really doesn't know is lingering in her apartment.* I was waiting for you to kick me out."

"Well, I have a confession, too. I saw the message come in. I liked having you there. I needed someone there, but it was just... comfortable... with you there. I mean, the idea of us in a relationship was the farthest thing from my mind at that point... so you were safe... pretty harmless... plus, I fell asleep."

"Yes, you did. And I watched you for the longest time before I dozed off as well. You looked peaceful."

"Well, I would definitely like for you to stay over again... but I might need to do some redecorating first."

"Redecorating?"

"Yeah," she says. "I think the bed's a little uncomfortable."

"It is, isn't it?" I agree, considering the memories more than the lack of a pillow top or its firmness. "I'll help you pick something out," I suggest.

"Okay," she says, smiling. "I'd like that." Maybe we're finally making some progress.

At dinner, all eyes are on Emi when I remove her coat and hand it to Bill. Matty whistles at her, making her blush. She smiles sheepishly before sitting down next to Renee.

"I don't think we're in Kansas anymore, Toto..." my brother says.

"That dress is stunning," Renee adds.

"Thanks," Emi says.

"Wait, I think I saw that in Cosmo a few months ago. That's from that new designer from... Philadelphia, wasn't it?"

"Wow, you're good. A fashionista," Emi says, nodding to Renee.

"I actually looked into some of his dresses, but they were so expensive! I could never afford one."

Steven coughs from across the table, glaring at me.

"That's why New York is so fabulous," Emi says. "Resale shop. I got it for 75% off the designer's price. Worn once. Well, twice now."

I glare back at my brother.

"You have to take me shopping next time I go to New York," Renee gushes.

"My sister-in-law is the shopper. She just drags me around and tells me what looks good most of the time. But I'd love for you to come," Emi offers.

"So, are you, like, a socialite?" Steven asks. "What do you do with your time? Get your hair and nails done with trophy wives in your circle of friends?"

"Steven," I admonish my brother. Emi puts her hand on mine.

"No," she answers, composed. "I work. I'm a graphic designer. I guess you missed that conversation."

"Starving artist kind of thing?" he digs further. "Needed a little extra bank?"

"What are you implying?" Emi counters.

"I think it's obvious. What do you aspire to be? What do you hope to gain from being with my brother?"

"Steven!" my mother joins in the conversation. Renee blushes, removing herself from the table.

Emi just smiles her brilliant smile across the table. "It's okay," she says to my mom, then turns her attention back on Steven. "You think I'm with Jack for his money." He raises his eyebrows. The table is quiet.

"She didn't even know–" I begin.

"No, Jack, that's really irrelevant," she says. "Steven? Can I ask you something?"

"What?"

"Have you met your brother Jack? Do you know him at all?"

"Of course," he mutters, defensive. "I've known him a lot longer than you."

"Well, apparently, I know him a lot *better* than you. The Jack I know has a lot more to offer me than his money. It's true, I had no idea about his wealth when we began talking, as friends. He was generous with his time, with his attention... his patience with me. He didn't have to be. Our love for each other was there from the start, but grew deeper over time as we got to know each other... as we peeled beneath the layers, went beyond the people we are to the outside world. That outer persona is not what he's about, nor what I'm about. You act like I'm with him so that he can elevate my social status... but in actuality, he grounds me. He's my stability... my security–"

"Security. Financial security," Steven spits out. "Did you or did you not charge two bottles of champagne to my brother's credit card the other night at the club?"

"What?" Emi and I both say in unison, looking at each other.

"And did you not flippantly say, 'I'm not worried, Jack will take care of me,' when we tried to stop you?"

"That's not what happened," Emi says, shaking her head vigorously. "That's not what I meant."

"Then, please, *do tell us* what you meant," Steven pushes. "I saw him hand you his credit card before he left, ten minutes before you ordered the best champagne in the bar."

"That's it," I say, standing up. "Get up." I can't believe I'm about to fight my youngest brother. We haven't done this in twenty years.

"Jackson, sit down," my father pleads.

"Steven, shut up," Matthew adds.

"What don't you like about me?" Emi asks.

"I don't see how you can love Jacks when you still love someone else. You don't cry like that, don't become an emotional wreck over someone you're over. You're not over that other guy... and then you go and drink away

Jacks's money."

"Now," I demand of my brother. "Let's take this outside."

"Jack, please stop," Emi requests, pulling on my arm in an attempt to make me sit down. When I don't, she stands up next to me, holding on to my forearm tightly. "Steven," she begins. "You don't know me at all. But when you're ready to give me a chance, I'll be here. And I forgive you."

"I'm not sorry," he scoffs.

"You will be," I answer him, staring him down.

"Boys," my mother whispers harshly, looking around the restaurant that has become deafeningly silent.

"I'm leaving," Steven says, his face red. He pushes away from the table quickly, knocking down the chair next to his. I look around and notice a few of the other diners have been watching us. Embarrassed, I pick up the chair across from me before sitting down and adjusting my tie.

"Are you okay?" I ask Emi. "Do you want to leave?"

"I'm fine," she continues to smile but begins to lose a little composure, her cheeks flushing red. "I'm sorry," she says to the rest of my family, standing up abruptly and walking quickly toward the ladies room.

"Emi, you didn't do anything," Kelly says as she starts after her. I hold my sister back.

"I've got this." I follow Emi to a small lounge area in between the restrooms. She's sitting on the edge of a couch, looking frantically through her purse.

"Jack, did you give me your credit card? Because I swear I didn't charge that to your card. I put it on mine," she stammers. "In fact, I went over my limit, the bank called yesterday, I *know* it was on my card."

"I didn't give you my credit card, I gave you the room key, remember?" I rub the back of her neck, attempting to calm her.

"Oh," she sighs, then looks up at me again with pleading eyes, speaking quickly and shaking her head. "And when they tried to stop me from ordering the champagne, I thought they just didn't want me to drink anymore... so I was

assuring them that you would take care of me if I came back to the cabin...
drunk..."

"It's okay," I smile assuringly. "You don't have to explain anything to me,
ever."

"I can see why Steven might think what he does. It did look that way..."
She looks into my eyes, unsure. "I swear, I meant nothing by what I said," she
says again. We both look up at my mother abruptly when she announces her
presence with a soft cough. "I'm really sorry..." Emi explains.

"I am, too," my mother cuts her off. "I'm sorry he's being like that to
you. He's protective, like his older brother... he's just looking out for Jacks..."

"Don't stand u–" I begin to argue, but Emi, again, squeezes my hand to
quiet me.

"I hope so, Sharon. Over time, I just hope you can all trust that I just want
what's best for him, too."

After our eventful dinner, I drive the SUV back to our cabin. On the way,
I ask Emi about the night at the club.

"Did you really max your card on champagne?"

"Apparently," she frowns. "I already made a payment, though. It's fine.
I had no idea how much champagne could cost... and apparently it wasn't even
the best they had."

"Emi..."

"If it makes you feel any better, we were toasting how great you are. It
was in your honor."

"Actually, no, it doesn't make me feel better knowing you spent your
paycheck on champagne you probably don't even remember drinking. Let me
pay for some of it... my family got you drunk, I can take the blame for that."

"I can take on some extra freelance jobs this month, it's really okay." She
shrugs and shakes it off.

"We can talk about it later," I smile as I pull up to the cabin, a warm glow
emanating from the windows.

"Did we have a fire going?" she asks.

"I don't remember," I lie, opening the door.

"Holy shit, Jack," she says, covering her mouth. "What have you done?" The cabin is filled with literally hundreds of candles of all sizes, a light scent perfuming the air. Interspersed among them are small bouquets of white daisies. Her favorite artist plays quietly through small speakers scattered around both rooms. "Is this the 'stuff?' Is this Bill's work?" she asks.

"Let's just say I couldn't have done it without him. Come here." I hold her hand and lead her into the bedroom, where they've set up a massage table replete with lotions and oils. "To alleviate your soreness."

"Are you going to give me a massage?" she asks.

"I am. I didn't realize how much you'd really need one after our dinner tonight, but I'm glad it worked out like this."

"Please, don't worry about dinner," she says. "It's behind us, and I have a feeling Renee will talk some sense into Steven. I'm going to put on my robe," she smiles. "You should do the same." She pulls me with her into the closet and begins to take off my tie and unbutton my shirt. As I finish undressing, she moves to a corner of the room, her back to me, and pulls on the zipper that runs down her back, the dress easily falling to the ground. I just watch in awe, biting my bottom lip and inhaling deeply. She reaches her arms behind her back, a poor attempt at unfastening her bra, then turns her head around, blinking her lashes and smiling.

"Can you help?" she asks.

"Of course." I unhook the undergarment, and she pulls herself up on the vanity, her bare legs dangling, her arms outstretched to me. I put my arms around her and kiss her, pulling her body into mine. She wraps her legs around me tightly and I lean her back gently to kiss her breasts... if I continue on this course, there will be no massage in the near future, and this is something I've been wanting to do for her... and for myself, wanting the chance to explore every inch of her milky skin with my hands. I remove her legs from my body and help her off the counter. "We can pick that back up later," I tell her. "Come lie down on the table."

~ * ~

At the end of our stay in Colorado, it's safe to say that both Emi and I are completely exhausted, but not anywhere near tired of each other. If anything, our time spent together just makes me want to be with her more. I'm not looking forward to going back to our separate lives and homes in New York, but I look forward to the possibility of another trip together in the near future.

After breakfast on our final day, Emi excuses herself from the table to finish packing, leaving me alone with my parents for the first time.

"Jacks, we had such a good time with everyone," my dad says. "Thank you so much for doing this for us. You've always had such a good sense of family."

"I get that from you two," I tell them. "I love doing it. I love seeing everyone together."

"Well, I'm sorry Steven's been so distant," my mother says. "I just don't know what's gotten into him."

"I'm not worried about it, Mom, so please, don't you worry, either. We'll work it out. We always do."

"I'm not worried about you at all, Jacks. Emi is simply precious. She's beautiful, and she's so sweet, too, and polite and open... and she's *genuine*. The kids seem to adore her. That has to make you happy. She wants kids?"

"Yes, she wants kids. We won't see a replay of Caroline with this one."

"Most of all, Jacks, I can just see how happy she makes you. I don't think I've ever seen you this happy."

"She's everything I've ever wanted. I couldn't ask for more."

"Do you think you'll marry her?" my dad asks.

"God, I hope so," I laugh. "I don't see it ending any other way. I can't imagine my life without her... and I'm pretty sure she feels the same way."

"Have you talked about it?"

"A little, maybe," I tell them. "We have alluded to kids, and I've been thinking about it. But I like where we're at right now. I mean, I feel like I've known her all my adult life. I've known of her... I've known this woman I thought she was, but I am still learning new things about her every day. And everything takes me one step closer to marrying her. But at this point, I want to enjoy this. I don't want to rush anything. And I don't feel like we're missing out on anything."

"She did say something to me that made me think," my mom tells me. "She said that, every day, she experiences a little bit of fear that it will all be over tomorrow. I think anyone that has lost someone so beloved, that it really makes you cherish every day... makes you not want to waste a second."

"She knows I love her," I tell my parents. "She knows I would do anything for her. I would marry her tomorrow if she wanted it."

"If it were me," my dad says, "I just wouldn't let this one get away. Don't wait too long."

"Don't worry, I won't let her get away... and I won't wait too long, but I've got to figure out how I'm going to do it, anyway... and I haven't the slightest idea on that one."

"Well, I know you'll think of something perfect."

"I hope."

"Well, Jacks, we love you. Will you come see us before Christmas?"

"I'll do my best. I've got a trip to Europe next month that could lead to a little more travel, but I'll try."

"Well, bring Emi when you come."

"I'll let her know she's invited."

"Anytime," my father says.

"Have a safe trip back to Wyoming," I tell them. "Call me when you get home so I know you made it safely."

"Okay, Jacks. You take care."

CHAPTER   4

Four weeks later, Emi and I survey her half-empty apartment. "I can't believe she's gone," she says, closing the door behind Jen after she had picked up the last of her things. "It's going to be weird, being alone."

"You'll be fine," I tell her. "I think you'll actually like it. You can drink out of the milk carton, play your music as loudly as you like, walk around naked..."

"It's so quiet," she says. "We're alone."

"Yes, we are... and there's a brand new bed right over there. What do you think?" The new bed she picked out was delivered yesterday, and she and I had spent a few hours last night arranging the room around it. She wanted it to feel completely different in the space... after all, it was his home for many years, and the memories attached to it were still fresh enough to keep Emi from feeling comfortable being intimate with someone else in it. Last night, we were so tired after helping Jen with the move that we both just collapsed on her couch, the bed not even made up with sheets.

"I'm not sure," she says, contemplative.

"Alright, then," I say, smiling, understanding. "Not a problem. I've got some errands to run today, so can I pick you up tonight? We can go out, whatever you like."

"That sounds good. But, hey, can we talk about Europe really quick?" she says.

"Of course."

"You really want me to go with you?"

"I would love for you to, Em. You've never been and it would be a great opportunity for you. Lots of museums and beautiful old places... I'll be busy during the week, but we could do whatever you wanted on the weekends. It's a week in Paris, a week in Rome, and then a week in Madrid..."

"I would love to just go photograph things over there," she says. "And I've got some freelance to do, too, but I can do that anywhere."

"Well then come," I encourage her. "You have the opportunity to spend your birthday in Madrid... come on... I don't know why you're even wavering."

"Because it's three weeks. Aren't you sick of me yet?"

"God, no. Are you tired of me?"

"No way," she smiles. "Never."

"Does that mean you'll come?"

"Ummm..." she says, deliberately teasing me. "Yes."

"Great." I kiss her quickly. "So, tonight... I'll pick you up at eight?"

"Sounds perfect... hey, one last thing."

"Yeah?" I ask.

"Jen left this... I thought you might like it... you know, just in case." She drops a key into my open hand.

"Really? To your loft?"

"Yeah, you know. It's not like we're over here much anyway, but I want you to know that you're welcome here anytime, any day..."

"I'll take it. Thanks, Emi."

"Love you," she says with a slight bit of crimson pooling on her cheeks, her hands clasped behind her back.

"Love you." I put my hands on her waist and pull her into me for a longer, more passionate kiss.

"Can't wait until eight." I kiss the top of her head before leaving.

Onto the errands. She's in for Europe. Now the question is where... Paris, Rome or Madrid. Paris is the City of Love, but is it too cliché? Will she see it coming? I think it's too cliché. And if she did think I was going to propose, she would suspect it would be there... so if I don't ask her to marry me in Paris, she'll probably think I'm not going to.

I'm not sure she'll think that I would do this anyway. It has only been a few months. She knows I'm pretty practical and traditional. In a normal relationship, I would think it was too soon. But our relationship isn't traditional, isn't really normal, per se. And I wasn't going to do it now, but after talking to my parents, it has really made me think. Why am I waiting, making her wait? Why am I putting this off? I want to start my life with her as my wife as soon as possible.

And I do remember her saying one of her regrets with Nate was that they didn't have more time together. Sure, we're together now, but I want to show her my level of commitment to her... and I want to start a family with her.

This trip to Europe is the perfect time and place.

"I'm here to meet with Adrienne," I tell the associate who greets me at the Harry Winston shop in Midtown. I hold in my hand a ring I took from Emi's jewelry box that I've seen her wear from time to time, but not often enough to miss it.

"Mr. Holland, it's a pleasure to meet you."

"Thank you."

"Adrienne has been expecting you. Right this way." He leads me to the back of the store and offers me a seat at a desk. "She should be right over."

"Thank you." All of a sudden, I feel nervous excitement, my hands actually shaking, my stomach jittery.

"Mr. Holland? I'm Adrienne."

"It's Jack," I tell her, standing up, shaking her hand before she takes a seat across from me.

"Well, Jack, what can I help you with today?" she asks.

"I want to ask my girlfriend to marry me," I tell her. "So I guess I need a ring."

"Well, congratulations," she says. "Lucky girl." She flashes a smile at me.

"Thank you."

"What is her name?"

"Emi. Short for Emily."

"Well, tell me about Emi," she encourages. "It'll give me an idea of where to start."

"She is beautiful," I begin. "Strawberry blonde hair; these amazing green eyes; soft, porcelain skin." I feel my heart rate quicken just thinking about her. My palms begin to sweat. "But she's so much more than beautiful," I add. "She's funny... a little silly, at times. And so creative. She's a graphic designer, very hard-working and driven. She would want something unique, I think, you know, because she's a designer. I don't think she would want an every day diamond solitaire, you know? And her eyes, they're captivating... this beautiful green color..."

"You *are* at Harry Winston," Adrienne says. "And you keep mentioning her eyes."

"They're incredible," I laugh, feeling my face heat up.

"Tell me a little more about her. Is she, say, very feminine, or does she play sports? What does she like to wear when she goes out?"

"She's pretty casual," I continue, "comfortable in jeans... but she does like to get dressed up every once in awhile. And she looks amazing when she does. She's confident and self-assured... she's the strongest woman I've ever known. She's a survivor...

"And she's very affectionate, very romantic. She... loves... like no one else can. I just feel it whenever I'm with her."

"Wow," the sales associate says, "I hope some man says things like that about me someday."

"She's everything to me. Hence the reason I need to marry her."

"I think I have the perfect ring," Adrienne says, walking over to a locked cabinet and pulling out a few different boxes.

"Now, I need you to have an open mind here. I've got a few options. I think this is really nice and distinctive, has a sort of vintage-feel to it." She opens the box where a conservative, cushion-cut diamond ring sits atop a delicate platinum band. Two small, curved "V"s flank either side, each filled with diamonds.

"It's beautiful," I agree, taking it and pushing it on the tip of my smallest finger. "Pretty traditional..."

"I said to keep an open mind, right?" Adrienne asks. "You said unique... you mentioned she's a designer. And she's a survivor." She smiles. "And something about green eyes?" She holds out a stunning platinum ring with a large, round, green stone, just a shade or two darker than her eyes. On the side is a small butterfly made of eight diamonds.

"Wow," I say, stunned at the sight of this unusual ring. I pick it up and hold it in my hands. The setting is unique. The stone is flawless, the facets glistening in the light. I slide the ring on the end of my finger to get a better idea of what it would look like on.

"You're good," I tell her. "Is it too non-traditional?"

"Is it her?" she asks the only question she needs to ask.

"It is. This is perfect."

"You like it? Is the stone too large? We can do something custom, go smaller."

"No, it's perfect. Now, what sort of wedding bands do you have that go with this?"

"We would have to design something. This isn't part of a set. But I've got a sketch," she smiles. "I always loved this ring." She returns to the cabinet and pulls out three more boxes and a small pad of paper. One band is just a matching platinum ring. The second has a few diamonds, spaced out strategically. The third is the one. It's completely encircled in smaller round diamonds.

"See, we could take a ring like this, and curve it here, to tuck into the engagement ring." She traces along the sketch she had made.

"Is it too much?" I ask for her advice.

"It makes a statement," she says. "I don't know of a single woman that would turn down a proposal with that."

I exhale deeply, anxious, wondering how I won't just pop the question the next time I see her. I can't wait to give it to her, can't wait to be engaged to her, to marry her...

"Let's do it," I smile.

When I get home, I look at the ring one more time before placing it in the safe. Next on the agenda... decide how I'm going to propose. We'll be in Madrid on her birthday. Would she expect it on her birthday? I just want this to be a complete surprise.

So, not on her birthday... I'll get her something else, something really nice for her birthday... something that will certainly throw her off. Art. I'll buy her a piece of art. There are tons of small galleries all over Europe. We can check them out on the weekends and I'll just pay close attention to what she likes. It's perfect.

Still, where? Definitely in Spain, after her birthday. She will never see it coming. We'll have a weekend there after my work is finished, so I'll do it that weekend. I jump online and start looking at hotels, famous sites, good scenery...

The Canary Islands. Tenerife. Perfect. Calling immediately for reservations. The only thing left to do is talk to her parents.

Full of energy, I rap quickly on her door at five till eight.

"You didn't have to knock," Emi says when she answers. "I gave you a key for a reason."

"Well, if you're here, I might as well be polite, and knock."

"But you don't have to," she instructs me.

"Alright, maybe next time I won't. Maybe."

I pull her into me and embrace her tightly, overflowing with excitement that I cannot contain.

"Kiss me, Em," I tell her, leaning in to steal a kiss from her willing lips. Without separating, I pick her up and cradle her in my arms, carrying her over to the new bed, now made up with new linens, and laying her down gently.

"What's gotten into you?" she laughs.

"What do you mean?" I ask, lying down on my side, next to her, my hand on her stomach, barely lifting her shirt to touch her skin. "Can't a man be excited to see the woman he loves?"

"I guess so," she smiles.

I move closer to her, slide my hand up the back of her shirt, put my leg in between hers. A deeper kiss ensues. Thoughts of us together, engaged, on a foreign beach under the warm sun play in my head. I cannot wait.

"What would you like to do tonight?" I ask her. "Are you hungry?"

"I could eat," she says. "This is nice, too, though." She kisses me again.

"Is it okay?" I whisper in her ear before taking her lobe gently between my teeth. "Here, I mean?"

"I don't know," she says. "Maybe?"

"Maybe?" I ask.

"It still feels a little weird, I guess."

"Alright," I sigh. "Let's go get some dinner. And pack some things, you're coming over tonight."

"I'm going to stay at your place on the first night I'm alone?"

"I hope so," I encourage her. "I'd like to be with you tonight... and if this place still feels strange, I'd like to go somewhere that feels... normal. Comfortable, even."

"Jack," she says. "I know this should be fine. I know I should be okay with this. I'm sorry."

"It's okay," I explain. "But one day... I think we may just have to, you know... try. It's *your* place, Poppet. It deserves some love, too."

"I know."

"I have a key now, you know. I could use it some night when I'm missing you horribly. Then what are you going to do?"

"I'll try," she commits. "Maybe we can just start out with sleeping only."

I roll my eyes at her. "Really?" She nods, an uncertain expression covers her face. "Well, not tonight." I kiss her again. "I'm already missing you horribly."

"That's fine with me," she agrees.

The restaurant is bustling with people by the time we are seated. We peruse the wine list and move closer together in order to hear one another while we wait for our orders to be served.

"Did you check your schedule for the 25th?" Emi asks as the waiter sets down our entrees.

"What was the 25th?"

"The couples baby shower for Chris and Anna, remember?" I had completely forgotten, the preparation of my trip taking up most of my free time these days.

"Right. Couples baby shower, huh? Is this some new trend or something?"

"A little," Emi admits as she takes a small piece of chicken from my plate with her fork, popping the food in her mouth playfully. "The baby always gets tons of things, the mom always gets pampered... but I think it's important that Daddy Chris gets some presents, too."

This may be the perfect opportunity. "Who's going to be there?"

"Chris and Anna... your friend, Russell, and his girlfriend. Mae and Andy. Jen and Brian. Some friends from their respective offices. Her parents. My parents and steps. That's about it."

Yes, it's perfect for the last part of the plan. "Of course, I'm free." All I
have to do is get her parents alone for a few minutes to let them know of my
intentions. She won't suspect a thing.

"Great..." she pauses momentarily. "Is your house free, too?"

"Oh, I forgot. You wanted to host it at my place, didn't you?"

"If that's okay. You just have a lot more room."

"That's fine, Emi."

"Good, because I sort of already put it on the invitations."

I laugh as she cringes sheepishly. "Am I cooking, as well?"

"Oh, god, no," she says. "But I was wondering if we could ask Kelly to
make a cake for it..."

"Consider it done," I tell her. "She loves doing baby shower cakes."

"Thanks, Jack," she says, moistening her lips slowly with her tongue
before leaning closer to kiss me. "I love you," she adds.

"You're just using me," I tease her. She kicks my shin under the table,
glaring at me playfully.

The following morning, my cell phone alerts me of a text message before
I'm actually awake. I reach across the bed, wanting to greet Emi before
checking the phone. I open my eyes when I find her side of the bed is empty.
Suddenly roused, I pick up the phone and see the message from Chris.

"Anna just showed me the paper."

"What's going on?" I text back.

"Where's Emi?" he responds.

I listen intently and hear music playing in the kitchen downstairs. I
recognize the smell of coffee, too, as I become more coherent. *"She's in the
kitchen downstairs, I think. Why?"*

*"Page Six reports on one of NYC's most eligible bachelors... coming out
of Harry Winston in Midtown with an engagement ring."*

"Shit. Does it mention me by name?"

"There's a picture of you, mighty dashing, I might add. And yes, Jackson Holland, II. You're mentioned by name."

Shit! I get out of bed hurriedly, pulling on some pants and running my fingers through my hair before heading downstairs. Emi doesn't really read the paper. She's never one to be up on the latest news. But the one thing she checks on a regular basis is Page Six.

The phone beeps one last time. *"Congratulations!"* I toss the phone back on the bed.

Shit shit shit!! I run down the stairs, consciously slowing myself as I round the corner into the kitchen, not wanting to needlessly raise any suspicions on the off-chance that she hasn't heard the news from someone. I take a deep breath as I watch her from across the room.

Emi's sitting at the dining room table, legs bouncing, coffee in hand, wide smile on her face... newspaper spread out in front of her.

"Hey, baby," I start cautiously, syrupy. Her smile grows bigger. "There's no way you didn't actually *read* the paper today... is there?"

She looks up at me, doe-eyed, looking guilty. "I don't know how to answer that." Her green eyes begin to water, her beautiful smile hidden when she bites her bottom lip.

"Let me see it," I sigh, frustrated and slightly perturbed at whatever ass clown leaked this story, this picture, to the press. "Maybe it's a pair of earrings for my mother," I mumble as I scan the brief article. *Another customer in the store said she heard him say he wanted to ask his girlfriend to marry him.* I knew I should have requested a private meeting... I just really didn't think I was newsworthy– at all.

"Jack," Emi sighs, putting her arms around my waist as I stand beside her.

"No, Em," I caution her as I try to stifle my annoyance. "Please. Don't say anything, okay?"

She nods in acceptance.

"Just listen to me." I squat down to meet her watery eyes, kissing her on the cheek and taking her hands into mine. "Okay, so I'm sure it doesn't come as a surprise to you that I want to marry you," I begin softly. When she blinks, a tear falls.

"Stop crying, I'm not proposing right now, okay? Let me get that out of the way." She looks confused, sniffles, but nods again. "It's not out of principle or anything... or maybe it is, I don't know. I wanted to surprise you with the proposal... okay, you know it's coming now. But will you please let me do it at my own pace, as I've planned to do it? And do me a favor and not try to figure it out?"

She nods again.

"You can say something now," I encourage her.

"You know I'll say y–"

I cover her mouth quickly with my hand. "Anything but *that*. Please do not ruin this for me, Emi," I tell her through gritted teeth before a smile breaks out on my face. She nods and kisses my palm before I replace my hand with my lips and kiss her back. "We are not engaged," I mumble into her mouth. She giggles sweetly, a few more tears falling quickly.

~ * ~

Emi has been obliging over the last couple of weeks, 'forgetting' the upcoming proposal as best as she could. She was positively giddy for the first couple of days, seemingly anticipating the question any time we were alone, but over time she's gotten back to a place where I don't feel like I'm disappointing her every night by not asking.

Pacing the foyer at the baby shower, I have a difficult time playing it cool. I don't think that anyone has informed Emi's parents of the Page Six article. If they know, they aren't letting on that they do, but Emi would have probably asked them not to say anything. Regardless, it doesn't make me any less nervous to talk to them about my intentions.

On my second beer, my heart starts to beat faster as I open the door for Emi's father and his wife. Her mother called to say she was running a little late. I was hoping to give them a tour of the house together while Emi was being a good hostess to the shower guests. I decide to postpone the tour and offer her dad and stepmom a drink first, instead.

"I'll take a beer," her dad says. "I've never been to a baby shower," he mutters. "What do men do at these things?" he asks me.

"Honestly, Mr. Hennigan, I'm not sure myself... but I have a nice deck and some cigars on hand if we need a break."

"Excellent. And it's Robert."

"Elaine, what would you like to drink?" Emi asks.

"A glass of white wine, if you have it." I take a beer out of the refrigerator for Emi's dad as Emi pours a glass of wine for her stepmom, Jen and Anna's friend, Mae. The doorbell rings again.

"I've got it, Em," I tell her.

"Jack," Russell says as he enters the house, Nicole following closely behind and hugging me. I see another car pulling up and recognize Emi's mother in the passenger seat.

"Russ, Emi's in the kitchen getting drinks for everyone. Why don't you two join them." Russ stops on his way to shake hands with Andy and introduce himself to Jen's boyfriend, Brian. I walk outside to greet Emi's mom and stepdad.

"Karen, Don," I say, hugging them both. I've spent more time with this set of parents and feel much more comfortable with them... Chris was always closer to his mother. "Come in."

"Are they here yet?" Karen asks.

"Not yet. And Anna's parents aren't here, either."

"Chris said they were going to follow them here."

"Oh, good, okay. Would you two like something to drink?"

"No, thank you," they both answer, politely.

Emi and Jen are both arranging trays of food and talking to the women in the kitchen. The men are all sitting around the living room, talking about last night's baseball game.

"Karen," I begin, taking a deep breath. "Since you've never been here before, I thought I'd give you two a tour of the house."

"That would be nice, Jack," she says, taking her husband's hand. I tap Robert on the shoulder and ask if he'd like to see the house, as well. I debate going to get Emi's step-mother, too, but she's with Emi and I don't want to raise her suspicions or even let her know that I'm with her parents at all.

I take them immediately down to the basement.

"Listen," I say to them, my throat suddenly dry. "I'd like to talk to you about something. Um, would you like to have a seat?" They exchange worried glances and then sit down on the couches. I pace the floor in front of them.

"Is everything okay, Jack?" her father asks.

"Everything's fine. No, great. Everything is great." My palms sweaty, I inhale and exhale deeply once more before taking a seat on the coffee table, facing the stairs so I can make sure no one comes down them.

"I guess you know that I'm going to Europe on business next weekend, and that Emi's coming with me."

"Yes, and she's so excited," Karen says. "She has always wanted to go to Europe."

"I'm glad she's excited. I am, too." I smile at them, their expectant eyes giving me courage. "Well, after my business trip is over with, I'm taking Emi to the Canary Islands for a few days. She doesn't know, though."

"Wow," her step-dad says. "I hear it's nice there."

"It looks amazing, I've never been myself... but I found this amazing place... and... well, I just wanted to let you know that I bought a ring and I intend to propose to Emi while we're there."

Her mother gasps, a smile spreading across her face and tears forming in her eyes. I guess she hasn't heard about the article... or she'll be up for an Oscar at next year's Academy Awards with her convincing performance. Emi's step-father looks at Robert, as if waiting for him to speak. When he doesn't, his gaze fixed on me, I continue.

133

"Mr. Hennigan– Robert, I'm sorry– I have been in love with your daughter since the day I met her. It was idle infatuation back then, I'll admit it, but over the past year and a half, I have had the opportunity to learn more about her, and to fall more in love with her each and every day. You have raised an amazing woman, and I want her to be my wife... to be the mother of my children..."

Her mother sighs audibly, the tears beginning to stream down her rosy cheeks.

"You two haven't been together very long," her father says.

"You're right, we haven't, sir," I say, nervous. "Four months, but we had been building a friendship for months before. She makes me feel whole. I hope I do the same for her."

"Why the rush?" he asks.

"I want to start my life with her as soon as possible. I want her to know that I'm here for her, for good... that I'm not leaving her. I want her to feel that assurance... to feel safe with me. I want there to be permanence. I don't want there to be any doubt of my feelings for her... and I don't want her to have any regret, that we've wasted time... I know she had regrets about him... about Nate..."

Her dad bows his head to the floor at the mention of his name. "I know he was a part of your family. I respect that... and that he was a part of Emi's life, that he always will be. I don't want to change her... I would never ask that of her.

"I promise to take care of her, to be a friend to her, and a good husband and father to our children. I love her very much."

"And she loves you?" Robert asks the question that catches me completely off-guard.

"I know she does," I tell him, a tinge of defiance coming out in my voice. I clear my throat. "Chris told me about their relationship. I didn't know Emi and Nate, together... and I don't know the woman she was with him. I only know the woman that he left behind. I saw her mourn for him, many times. I saw her broken. I cried for her. And as she began to heal, I encouraged her as best as I could. I was strong for her when she felt weak. I gave her love when she felt there was no more. And in return, she made me laugh... made me love like I never thought I would have the chance to do. She and I share something incredible. I know it's hard for you all to envision her with someone other than him, but we are in love. And I'd like your blessing."

"You have mine," Karen cries. "I always thought you were such a catch," she says. "I always secretly hoped you'd end up with one of my girls."

"Thank you so much." I stand up to hug her, and she embraces me tightly. Don shakes my hand, giving me his silent blessing.

"I promise to cherish her, every day of my life, Robert. And I'll take care of her, you'll never have to worry about that."

"Jack," her father says, "I don't doubt how you feel about her. I see how you look at her. It's obvious. I just worry that not enough time has passed since..."

"I understand. But I just ask you to trust that we are both ready to move forward with our lives, together. I know this... I have no doubts."

"Well, of course you have my blessing, then," he says, standing to shake my hand. "Good luck," he smiles.

"Thank you, sir."

"We should get upstairs," her mother says.

She blots her eyes with a tissue and breathes in deeply.

Chris, Anna and her parents make their entrance just as we come upstairs, so the welcoming of the guests of honor take any eyes off of us.

"Emi, can I help with anything?" I ask, walking into the kitchen to help carry food out. She kisses me, gazing into my eyes, her hand lingering on my cheek, before handing me a tray. I catch a glimpse of her mother and father watching her, smiling.

~ * ~

A few nights after the party, my cell phone, vibrating, wakes me from a rather immodest dream. The clock tells me it's two-thirty in the morning. The caller ID shows it's Emi.

"I was just dreaming about you," I answer, not completely awake. She doesn't respond. "Emi?" I say, sitting up, alert, "is everything okay?"

"Yeah, um, Jack, um..." she stammers, her voice strained. "I just got an email from my editor."

"At this hour?" I ask.

"Yeah, I know, but he says that this job I'm working on is going to require me to be at a bunch of meetings over the next couple of weeks."

"What?"

"Yeah."

"But we're leaving on Saturday, Em. In two days, we're leaving for Europe."

"I can't go," she states. "I'm sorry."

She has to go. The proposal. *She has to go.*

"Surely you can work something out with him," I encourage her.

"No, he made it very clear. There are three planning meetings a week for the next two weeks. He says I have to be there."

"Really? Emi, but..."

"I can't help it, Jack," she says, her voice distant, final. I sit, silent, waiting for her to continue. Instead, I hear her sniffle, the first sign in her demeanor that she might actually be sad about missing the trip.

"Are you crying?"

"I'm just upset that I can't go," she says. "I wanted to go. But now I'm going to be really busy. He added about seven illustrations, too, so even if I didn't have to be in New York for the meetings, I'd be so busy that I probably wouldn't be able to enjoy myself anyway."

"Emi, are you serious?"

"Yes, Jack," she says curtly.

"What about when you finish? Can you come meet me when the job's done?"

"I'm not sure it will be finished before you come back," she says.

"I thought it was due the day before your birthday." I remembered her telling me that.

"Well, they may have to extend it since he added more work, I'm not sure."

"God, Emi," I sigh.

"I feel bad enough as it is," she cries. "I'm sorry." Her voice is weary, faint.

"No, I'm sorry," I tell her. "Please don't cry. It's okay. Hell, we can go to Europe any time," I say, trying to lighten the mood. She, again, doesn't answer. "Emi, really, sweetie, it's okay. Why don't I just change your ticket so you can join me that last weekend?"

"I really don't think I'll be done," she says.

"If you're not, you're not. So what? But let's just hope you are and you can come spend a few days with me in Spain." It will be fine if I can just get her to Tenerife with me. Everything will go as planned.

"I don't know," she wavers.

"Don't worry about it. I'll just book it and if you can come, great. If not, well, we'll have a lot of catching up to do when I get back."

After another few seconds of silence, I grow more concerned. "It's okay, really, Emi. I'm disappointed but I understand. Listen, why don't I come over?"

"No," she says abruptly. "No, it's late. I need to just go to bed. I've got a lot to do."

"Are you sure?"

"I'm sure."

"Are you okay?"

"I'm fine," she answers. "I just need to go."

"Okay, sweetie... but it's really okay, alright?"

"Alright," she says, her voice strained again. "Good night, Jack."

"Good night, love," I say to her, unsure. Something doesn't seem right. And this proposal... I don't want to wait. Maybe I should do it before I go. She would never expect that, and it may put her in a better mood. But it would just be rushed, and unmemorable. It has to be memorable.

And her birthday... shit. I don't want to be away for her birthday. I'll fly home for her birthday. I'll propose that night. I have time to figure out the details. She won't see it coming, whatever I decide to do.

Having spent most of the night tossing and turning, mind racing, I decide to get up at six and go for a jog. I just feel uneasy about our conversation. Something else seems wrong. I don't mean to doubt her, don't want to doubt her, but I'm not sure I believe her story. Why would she call in the middle of the night to tell me this? Why would her editor email her in the middle of the night? It doesn't really make sense.

Throughout the day, I call Emi, leave her a few voicemails, but I can't get in touch with her. As the day wears on, I get increasingly worried. Sure, the whole story could be true, and she could just be really busy. I have no reason to believe she's lying to me. I don't think she ever has.

I finally just decide to send her a text at ten o'clock, letting her know I'm coming over. She has never not returned my phone calls. Busy or not, it's not like her.

"Okay," she answers. I grab the keys and head over to her loft.

She answers after the second knock and leans on the edge of the open door as I walk in. She's wearing plaid flannel sleep shorts and a v-neck t-shirt that sets off her tired green eyes that show evidence of recent tears. Her smile is sad.

"What's wrong?" I ask immediately. She nods her head at me as her eyes well up. We both walk toward one another and end up in a tight embrace.

"I'm fine," she says quietly. "I don't know why I'm so emotional today. I think I'm just exhausted. I was up most of the night."

"Working?"

"For the most part."

"And the other part?"

"I'm just upset," she says, following with a sniffle. When she steps back slightly, I take advantage of the distance to finally kiss her. When I pull away, her beautiful green eyes are hidden behind her tightly shut lids, two tears sliding down her cheeks.

"About this job?" I sweep my thumbs across her cheeks before she has a chance. She nods again. "Then screw it, Emi, just forget the work. Just come with me."

"Jack," she huffs as she walks into the empty guest room and looks out the side window. A few boxes and shopping bags are scattered along the wall. Her arms cross in front of her chest. "This is my livelihood."

I move to stand behind her and wrap my arms around her, kissing her cheek. "I understand, Emi," I whisper in her ear, "but if it's making you this upset, it's not worth it."

"If I quit this job, I may have no work to come back to." She turns around and looks up at me, holding onto my belt. "He's my biggest client."

I take her head in my hands and look at her intently. "You don't have to work, you know," I remind her.

She laughs briefly as she rolls her eyes at me. "I don't want to be some kept woman. If that's what you're looking for–"

"You know that's not what I'm looking for–"

"Well, then don't say things like that."

"I'm just trying to help."

"I don't want to be *beholden* to you, Jack. I don't *need* your money," she mumbles as she pushes against my chest and walks out of the guest room, clearly annoyed with my suggestion. She picks up a glass of wine that had been sitting on the kitchen island and takes it into the living room with her. She sits down on the couch with her back to me. I move into the kitchen and look over the two open bottles of wine sitting out. One is empty, the other is about half full.

"I know you don't need my money, Emi, but it's here, and I want to share it with you. You know you would never owe me anything. Why be miserable when you don't have to be?"

"Money can't buy happiness," she recites abruptly. "Isn't that what they say?"

"I'm not trying to buy your happiness," I mutter as I start toward her.

"Can you bring that bottle with you?" she asks. I grab it from the island and take it into the living room. She holds out her now-empty glass, her hand a little unsteady. I take the glass and pour a half-serving. Again, she rolls her eyes at me when I hand her back the smaller portion.

"Is this your happiness today?" I hold up the bottle to her before setting it on the coffee table behind me. She blinks twice, looking me in the eye, before drinking all that I just poured for her. She sets the glass down on a side table and spreads out across the couch, laying her head on the armrest. She diverts her attention to the far wall, away from me. "Emi, what is going on?"

"I've told you already. I just had a rough night."

"Are you sure nothing else is wrong here?"

"I'm sure."

"So this is all about your work?"

"Work... and not being able to..." she sighs heavily, her attention still focused elsewhere, "go with you to Europe." Another tear escapes, but she swats this one away herself.

"Don't worry about that, we can go any time. It's certainly not worth crying over."

"I know you'll resent me for it," she says quietly as she closes her eyes. I sit down next to her on the edge of the couch, taking her hand in mine.

"What the... Emi, when have I ever *resented* you? For *anything*? *Ever*?" I push an errant strand of hair behind her ear.

She shakes her head before answering softly. "You will, this." She finally opens her eyes to meet mine. She stares and nods her head slightly.

"No, Poppet, I won't. This is... kind of crazy, Emi. I'm going there on business anyway." Her lips part as she inhales, as if getting ready to speak. After a second, she closes her mouth again and smiles warmly. "Sure, it would have been nice for you to go with me, but it's one trip. Three weeks. There will be many others."

"I know," she says as she sits up a little and squeezes my hand, repositioning to give me a little more room on the sofa. She takes a deep breath and swallows.

"If you want, we can make arrangements for something else now... maybe give you something to look forward to..."

"Okay," she breathes.

"Where would you like to go? Anywhere in the world?"

"Honestly... I just want to be with you," she says quietly. "It's not that you're going on a trip without me. It's that we'll be apart all that time. I don't know what I'll do without you."

"Well, what if you finish early? I could fly you out when you do."

"I doubt that will happen," she says.

"But if it does, I will." She shrugs and smiles again. "We'll have a few days to ourselves in a foreign country... we can do whatever you like. You could plan the days."

"It wouldn't matter, as long as you were still with me."

"Of course I'll still be with you... what are you afraid will happen?" I laugh.

"I'm afraid you'll leave me," she says shyly, looking down at our hands in our laps.

"Leave... like Nate... left?" I ask cautiously, wondering if she's envisioning the worst.

"No," she says. "Leave... like you would *choose* to leave me."

"Hey," I tell her softly, picking up her chin, not at all understanding where this is coming from. "I'm not going to leave you."

"Why would you leave me?"

"I just said–"

"No, I mean... what sort of thing would drive you to leave me?"

"Nothing," I tell her as worry begins to seep in. "Is something more going on here?"

"No," she laughs. "Just hypothetically. I just think about these things sometimes."

"I apologize, but that seems like a waste of your time, to worry about things like that. I can't imagine a single thing that would make me want to leave you, Emi, not a one. We could work through anything." My mind wanders, gauging different scenarios.

"But there has to be *something*," she urges me.

"This is a pointless conversation to have in a hypothetical sense. If you've done something, Emi, then lets talk about it."

"I haven't *done* anything."

"Well, have *I*?" I ask, wondering where this is heading.

"No," she assures me. "I'm just wondering."

"Well, I'll just go with the obvious three. Lying, cheating, stealing... those things would be hard to overcome... but I can't say I would definitively leave you for any reason. I'm a fair person, Emi, and I would want to hear you out."

"Okay," she says. "Thank you."

"For?"

"For answering honestly."

"You said you haven't done anything... are you *planning* to do something?"

"No, Jack," she insists. "I would never plan to hurt you, in any way. I love you, you know that. You *do* know that, right?"

"Of course I do. And you know I love you," I tell her with conviction. "I can't imagine my life without you."

"Me, neither," she says as her voice wavers and her eyes begin to water once more.

"You don't have to," I tell her, my eyes confirming every bit of my devotion to her. "I am here to stay, no matter what. Now, no more tears over this, Emi," I smile as I try to comfort her. She nods and wipes her eyes as a sigh escapes her lips. "Do you need to work some more tonight, or do you think you could get some rest?"

"I think I can take the night off," she says. "I just need to sleep."

"Can I tuck you in?" I ask as I run my finger down her leg, watching the goosebumps break out under her pale skin.

"You won't stay?"

"Would you like me to?"

She nods. "I have a headache, though."

"Is that code?"

"No," she laughs. "I really do."

"Too much *happiness*?" I say, standing up and picking up the wine bottle and glass, motioning it toward her.

"Maybe a little too much *happiness*. But, hey, that's what you do to me. You make me happy."

"I don't ever want to drive you to drink. Just talk to me next time. I'm a pretty understanding guy." I put the glass in the dishwasher and put a stopper in the bottle before setting it back in her wine rack.

"I hope so," she says as she stands up and walks toward her bed.

After undressing to my boxers and undershirt, I grab some aspirin and water and take it to her. She turns off the lamp after taking the medicine and curls into my side, giving me a kiss before settling her head on my chest.

"I love you," she whispers, sliding her arm up the front of my shirt and clutching tightly to my side.

"You too, Emi," I say softly back, kissing the top of her head.

By the time my phone vibrates softly against the pillow in the morning to wake me up, Emi finally seems to be sleeping soundly, her body curled around a pillow. She had slept very restlessly throughout the night, tossing and turning more than she ever had before. I dress quietly, careful not to wake her, and leave a note on her nightstand for when she wakes up.

Hope you finally got some rest. Would love to take you to dinner if you're up for it. I love you.

I'm disappointed when she calls me later in the day to tell me she really needs to catch up on her work since she took the night before off. I had wanted to see her once more before I left, but she insists that her work needs to take priority tonight. What's more disappointing than not seeing her, though, is that she doesn't even seem very upset by it. Her voice is distant, even as she reaffirms her feelings for me.

CHAPTER 5

Pick up the phone, Emi...

"Hey, it's Emi. Leave a message."

"Em... I know you said you'd be really busy, but come on... it's been three days since I last talked to you. We've never gone this long without talking. I miss you. It's bad enough I can't see you... but to not hear your voice, either... I'm going through withdrawal. Please call me... I'm starting to worry."

Even the conversation on Wednesday had been strange. She'd been distant ever since I left. We'd spoken three times while I was in Paris. She still wasn't feeling well the night I got in... and the other two times, she said she was too busy to talk. The phone call on Wednesday only lasted five minutes. She sounded upset and said she needed to get off the phone to work. She said she'd call the next day, but never did.

I would have called Chris to go check on her, but she was still sending me text messages every now and then, updating me on her work progress, asking me how I was doing. I appreciate that she's thinking of me, but I want nothing more than to talk to her.

As I settle into the hotel room in Rome, I try to distract myself with a little television. It's pointless. I can't stop thinking about her. At the beginning of last week, all I wanted to do was nail down plans for the proposal. I'm still planning on flying home to surprise her on her birthday. I want to propose... but I can't even talk to her long enough to figure out what her plans are at this point.

Her phone call wakes me up.

"Emi," I say, relieved.

"Hey," she says with little enthusiasm.

"How are you?" I ask.

"Fine," she says, but she still sounds so different. There's no life in her voice.

"You don't seem fine."

"I'm just busy, Jack," she says, annoyed.

"Okay, I'm sorry." I can no longer mask the frustration I'm feeling with her. The tension builds through the silence. Sensing she's not going to be the first to talk, I continue. "How's the project going?"

"Fine, I guess."

"Do you think you'll be finished early enough to come out for that last weekend?"

"I doubt it," she says.

"Really?"

"Yes, really," she says curtly.

"Emi, what is wrong?"

"I told you, I'm busy. I'm stressed, okay?"

"Something else is clearly going on," I suggest. "I don't know what it is, but I really wish you'd enlighten me. You're obviously angry with me. I'd like a chance to apologize for whatever it is."

"It's nothing," she says, her tone softening. She swallows audibly. "You didn't do anything. This is just hard."

146

"What, being apart?"

"Yeah, I guess."

"Well, I feel the same way... but that doesn't make me want to fight with you across the Atlantic."

"I know, I'm sorry," she says.

"I miss you."

"You'll be home in two and a half weeks."

"And I can't wait to see you." She doesn't respond. "Do you miss me?" I'm honestly not sure she does.

"Of course," she answers. More silence.

"So, do you have any plans for your birthday next week?" I ask, wishing I had been less direct. I don't want her to have any idea that I'm coming home.

"Yeah, we're having a party or something."

"That's great," I say. "Who's throwing it?"

"Teresa," she says.

"At her place? Or yours?"

"Mine," she responds.

"Oh, okay. Well that sounds like fun. I hope you have the project done by then so you can relax and have a little time for yourself."

"Me, too."

"I really wish I could be there."

"Me, too." Her tone isn't very convincing. I sigh in defeat.

"I really wish I was there right now, Em. I feel so disconnected from you. I don't feel like we're communicating very well."

"Well, I'm just distracted by work," she explains.

"I hope that's all," I tell her. I can't stand the silence any more. "Listen, Em, I've got to get ready for my meetings. Will you call me tomorrow?"

"If I get home from my brainstorming session at a reasonable hour, I will. If nothing else, I'll text you."

"I hope you'll call... I love you, Emi."

"You, too," she says, spiritless. I feel my heart break a little.

147

When she doesn't call the next day, just sends some generic text message, I decide to focus all my efforts on work. That's why I'm here, anyway. I can't continue to worry about her when I'm halfway across the world. I do decide to call Chris, though, and ask him to check in with her to make sure she really is okay.

"Hey, Chris, how's it going?"

"Fine, man, where are you?"

"In Rome."

"I bet Emi is so jealous," he says.

"I don't think she is, Chris," I begin. "Something's wrong with her, I think. She says she's really busy, but I just get the feeling something's up."

"I thought you didn't want me interfering with your relationship... sounds like you're wanting me to get involved."

"I wouldn't ask if I wasn't genuinely worried about her... and if I wasn't an ocean away."

"Alright, man, okay. What would you like me to do?"

"I don't know, just call her and make sure she's okay... and what do you know about this birthday party next week?"

"Nothing," he says. "She told me she was going out with friends."

"Really..."

"Yeah, what did she say to you?"

"She said Teresa was organizing a party at her loft. I would have thought you and Anna would be at the top of the list of invitees."

"Yeah, me, too... that's kind of odd."

"Well, if she's going out, that sort of throws a wrench in things. I'm planning to fly home for her birthday, to surprise her."

"I'm sure she'd welcome a visit from you, no matter where she is."

"You'd think that," I tell him, "but she's been really distant... I feel like I've done something wrong, but I can't figure out what it could possibly be. She just seems... angry."

"Well, let me make a call or two. I might get Anna to do it. If she's mad at you, she's more likely to tell her."

"Thanks, Chris. Again, I wouldn't ask if I didn't suspect that something was very wrong."

"I know. I'll give you a call as soon as I know something."

"Thank you."

I hear from Chris the following afternoon.

"She asked to talk to me right away," Chris said. "Anna called her, but she immediately assumed you asked us to call."

"Was she mad?"

"No," Chris said. "She wanted to know what you said... wanted to know how you were doing."

"Really? That's odd. I'd be happy to tell her if she'd speak to me." None of this makes any sense.

"Yeah, she didn't seem normal to me, either. Maybe she is stressed out, I don't know. I'm used to hearing happy Emi, not this one. She seems... depressed. The way she's acting reminds me of how she was most of last year."

"Yeah," I agree.

"Anna and I are going to stop by tomorrow. Maybe we'll get a little more info then. I did ask about her birthday, though, and she said again that her friends were taking her out. She told me she didn't know where... that they told her it was a surprise."

"That's just weird."

"I know," he says. "I told her Anna and I might like to meet up with them, and she said she'd text us when she knew where they would be."

"God," I sigh. "I hate that I have to be here. I wish I could just rearrange things and come back sooner, but I can't. I guess I'll just plan on coming home next Tuesday on her birthday. When you see her tomorrow, will you call me? Let me know what you think is going on?"

"Of course. I'll keep an eye on her until you can make it home, don't worry about her. I'll call Jen, too. Maybe she can take Clara over. She can always cheer her up."

"Okay. Thanks, Chris. I appreciate your help."

~ * ~

Emi continues to withdraw over the following days. As if the physical distance wasn't enough, she proceeds to pull away emotionally. On her birthday, I find the quietest part of the airport to call her from. I don't want her to be suspicious. I still can't figure out what's going on with her. We've spoken three times, and although our text messaging picked up, it just feels like she's hiding something from me.

I pull the phone out of my left jacket pocket and the Harry Winston box out of the other. I'm not sure I'm going to propose tonight, but I want to be ready. I have a feeling we will be having a serious conversation about our relationship, either way.

I turn the ring over in my fingers and sit down on a bench in a far corner of the airport, waiting for Emi to answer.

"Hello?"

"Happy Birthday, Poppet." I hope the nickname makes her smile like it typically does.

"Thanks, Jack," she says... still depressed.

"How are you doing today?"

"I'm not feeling great," she says.

"What's wrong?"

"I don't know, just generally blah."

"Are you going to be okay?" I ask her, concerned.

"I'm sure I'll be fine," she answers.

"I miss you... I really wish I could be there."

"Ditto," she says, and follows with a sniffle.

"Is it a cold, do you think?" I ask her.

"I don't know. Maybe allergies or something."

"Are you still doing something tonight for your birthday?"

"Probably," she says. "I guess it just depends on if I feel any better."

"Well, did you finish the job?" I ask.

"No. I'm not going to be able to come out this weekend." I sigh, rubbing my forehead. "Sorry."

"No, it's alright," I tell her through gritted teeth. Sure, I'm disappointed... but I just want to see her at this point. I just want to be with her, feel close to her. I hope she is excited to see me tonight. I begin to fear what she will be like when I show up at her doorstep, if she's even there. "Hey, can I call you tonight?" I ask.

"Sure," she says. "If I don't answer, just leave a message. I'll call you when I get a chance."

"Okay. I love you, Emi. I hope you have a good day."

"You, too."

I watch the city disappear as the plane ascends over the Atlantic. My palms are sweating, my nerves shot, thinking about this proposal. I try to play out possible scenarios in my head.

What if she isn't home? I'll call her until she answers, find out where she is. Maybe she'll be out with Teresa and her friends. I'll go to her. I want this moment to be just between the two of us. I'll ask her to accompany me outside. We'll walk, catch up with one another, until I find the right spot to propose. I'll remember that exact location for the rest of my life. I'll get down on one knee. She'll cry. She'll say yes. This would be ideal.

And if there's a party at her apartment? I'll join in, wait until the last guest leaves. Maybe I'll help her clean up, "find" the ring... ask if someone may have left something behind. She would never see it coming.

And if she's home, alone... which I suspect she will be, based on her mood and the tone of our recent conversations. I'll kneel in front of her door and knock. The words "Will you marry me?" will be the first words she hears from me. I wonder if they'll bring back the smile I have missed since I left...

151

since *before* I left...

I struggle to figure out what has upset her so badly. She's never been so stressed out about work. It has always been something she has enjoyed. I can understand unrealistic deadlines, and her disappointment in not being able to go to Europe with me, but still... stress or sadness over these things should be fleeting. I would think she would get over it relatively quickly, especially as she makes progress on the job... or gets reassurances from me. Something isn't adding up.

As I ponder asking her to be my wife, a traitorous thought creeps into my head. What if this is about him again? Could she be upset about Nate... still? Is there an anniversary I don't know about? Did something set her off? What if it *is* him? Then what?

Then what?

I fight. I fight for her. I fight with this figure from her past and I show her that I love her with all of my heart. That I accept her for who she is, understand the issues she brings with her into our relationship. I show her that I am here to help her through it, through everything. She just has to trust me. She just has to love me...

An uneasy feeling overwhelms me, and stays with me through the entire flight. It only gets worse once we land.

As I step off the elevator, I touch the ring box one last time to make sure it's still in my jacket. I just have to be conscious of it until I can take my jacket off. I don't want her to know it's there, in case this doesn't happen tonight. I just don't have a good feeling about this at all.

When I get to her door, I adjust my tie and take a deep breath... and I'm pretty sure I hear her crying. I knock loudly, calling her name from the hallway.

"Jack?" she calls back to me, sounding confused.

"Yeah, it's me, Em, open up."

"Just a second," she says. I wait in the hallway, and after a minute, I knock again. I get my keys out of my pocket and slowly open the door myself.

"What are you doing here?" she says, her eyes red, face flushed. She stands five feet in front of me in sweat pants and a t-shirt, her hair messy, no makeup. She makes no move to welcome me home, no hug, no kiss. She barely moves out of the walkway to let me in.

"Emi, what's wrong?" I walk past her into the loft and put the bouquet of daisies on the cabinet before taking my jacket off and hanging it on the back of a chair. She closes the door and stands with her back against it. "Emi?"

"What are you doing here?" she repeats her earlier question.

"I wanted to see you, for your birthday."

"But I just talked to you a few hours ago..." She looks confused. Just as I did last time, I find two wine bottles on the kitchen island.

"I wanted to surprise you." She walks over to me quickly, throwing her arms around me, and pulls my head to hers for a kiss. I taste the wine on her lips and tongue but am more caught up simply in her presence and embrace. It amazes me, what a single kiss from her can do to me.

"Oh, Jack," she whispers, a tear falling from one of her eyes.

"Emi, what is the matter?"

"I'm just not feeling well."

"Why?" I ask. "What doesn't feel well?"

"Just me." She starts to cry.

"Come sit down, sweetie," I encourage her, taking her hand and leading her to the couch. "Please, talk to me. Tell me what's going on." When she doesn't answer, I continue with my questions. "Where are your friends? I thought you were doing something with them tonight."

"I cancelled," she says. "Jack, I missed you so much."

"Really?" She interrupts me with another kiss. "I didn't get that from our conversations."

"I know, I'm sorry," she cries and takes a sip of the wine that had been sitting on the table beside her.

"Shhh, Em, it's okay. Whatever is wrong, I'm here. We'll figure it out together. What hurts?"

She holds her hand over her stomach. A jolt goes through my system as I take the glass from her hand and set it on the coffee table. "Are you pregnant?" I didn't even have time to consider the words before they escaped my lips. My heart begins to pound.

She ducks her head and cries more.

"Emi, are you?" I can't help but smile at the thought and take her hands into mine. Is this why she's so upset? She looks into my eyes and shakes her head.

"Stop," she says. "Don't do that."

"Don't do what?"

"Smile. Don't smile at me. I'm not pregnant."

"Okay, I was just wondering. All the signs were there... are you sure?" I laugh sympathetically.

"It's impossible," she answers with a sigh. I reach for a tissue and wipe her eyes for her. She takes it from me and blots her nose.

"Not impossible," I laugh again. "Highly *improbable*, because we've been careful, but not impossible. That time–"

"No, impossible," she says, sitting up straight, her stare piercing directly into me, into my soul.

"Not likely," I correct her tentatively, gauging her reaction, my smile quickly fading.

"Impossible," she responds tersely. Silence overtakes the room as she swallows hard. She clears her throat before continuing in a voice so soft I barely hear the words. "It would be impossible."

"What do you mean?" I squeeze her hands tighter, anxiously awaiting her response.

"I had a doctors appointment... just my yearly exam." Her eyes are unsure, scared.

"And..."

"Jack, I can't have children." My heart sinks at the news as I involuntarily let out a heavy sigh. "I can't look at you," she says, burying her head into my chest. I pull her into me tightly, hold her close, trying to process the information. I have to fight off my own tears as I try to comprehend what she's said. Nausea fills me from the pit of my stomach to my head as the news hits me like a punch in the gut... chest... arm... head... it's all-encompassing, the shock and despair. I look for hope, grasp to anything that might give us hope.

It takes me a few seconds to realize I'm not breathing.

"Wait... what do you mean? You were pregnant once before..."

"There's scar tissue," she says, pulling away. "There's too much damage, left from the accident. I could never get pregnant now."

"Can't they remove it? The scar tissue?"

"It's too much," she says.

"Says who? Let's get a second opinion."

"I already did," she cries.

"A third, then."

"Jack, I *did*. It's too late. If I had caught it early on–"

"Emi, we can afford the best doctors in the world. Let me–"

"Stop," she says to silence me. "I talked to Donna."

"Why Donna?"

"Because she's not really family, and I trust her."

"You don't trust me?"

"Of course I do. But I didn't want to have this conversation with you if I could do anything to avoid it. But apparently there's nothing more I can do."

"What did Donna do?"

"She knows a doctor from all of her charity work. He's apparently the best OB-GYN in the country. Some sort of fertility specialist. He's booked months in advance, but she got me in to see him. He ran a bunch of tests... I even had a procedure done–"

"God, Emi, you should have told me! When?"

"Last week."

"Are you okay?"

She looks at me with consternation. "No, I'm not. I can never have children. I can never *give you* children. I'm devastated. I'm scared."

"Maybe there's another doctor... another way..."

Tears drip down her cheek quickly. "Believe me, I exhausted all of my resources before telling you this. The last thing I wanted to see was *that face*." She points at me. "The last thing I wanted to see was your disappointment. I can't stand it."

I'm sure she's right. I can't hide my reaction to such news. "I'm sorry, Emi. When did you find out?"

"My first appointment was the Wednesday before you left," she says.

"God damn it, Emi!" I stand up and begin to pace around her living area. "This is what's been going on all this time? You've known this for almost three weeks? Why wouldn't you talk to me about this before? When I could help you through this?"

"I don't know," she says.

"There is no freelance job, is there?"

She just shakes her head. "Well, there was. But I finished it before you left."

"Emi..."

"I'm sorry," she sobs. "I wanted to find out for certain before I told you. And I didn't think I could bear to see your reaction. I wanted to tell you before you left, but I thought maybe there was still a chance... and my heart was already so broken... I couldn't bear the thought of you leaving me forever. I know it was selfish."

"I can take just about anything you throw at me, Em," I tell her. "But not this."

"That's why I've been distancing myself from you. I wanted to make it easier for you to leave... before we got in too deep."

"What? You don't think we're already in too deep?" I ask, incredulous.

"I don't know," she cries, looking so small on the couch. "We aren't engaged... you could still love someone else..."

"Right." As I nod my head, a tear escapes. I can't pick an emotion and stick with it. Shock, anger, disappointment, sadness... love. Love. My love. Emi. My love for her is stronger than all the rest, combined. "Emi, please listen to me. Please stop crying." I kneel down on the floor in front of her and put my hands on her legs.

"I don't want you to leave, but it's not fair to make you stay with me."

"Emi, what I was going to say, is that I can take anything you throw my way, except for you pulling away from me. You can't force this distance between us, not now, not when you are hurting... not when you are dealing with something this monumental."

"Why has everything been taken from me? What did I do to deserve this?"

"Not everything, Em. I'm still here."

"But I don't *want* you to be," she says. "I can't give you what you want anymore... and I don't want you to feel like you have to stay with me under these circumstances."

"Stop saying that," I tell her. "I'm not leaving you. I told you I wouldn't leave you. I *couldn't* leave you." I put my hands behind her and pull her body into mine, embracing her, untangling her hair gently.

"But you want a family... you can't have that with me."

"Of course I can. We'll figure it out."

"I want you to think about it," she says. "I don't want you to commit to this life without thinking about everything you'd be losing."

"I don't see myself losing if I end up with you," I explain.

"Jack, I'm serious. I don't want you to resent me in ten years."

"Do you love me, Emi?"

"More than anything," she cries.

"Do you trust me?"

"I do."

"Well, I'm not leaving you. Ever. Trust that. Why don't you come back to my place tonight and we can talk about it some more."

"I'm a mess," she says. "I don't want to go anywhere."

"Okay, well, I'll stay here."

"No, Jack," she says. "I want to be alone."

"You've apparently been alone for weeks. I don't want you to be here, alone, any longer."

"Please, Jack. Please give this some thought. Tonight. For me. I don't want you to make any impulsive decisions because you feel sorry for me, or feel put on the spot... or whatever." Her voice is soft and pleading.

"You're not thinking clearly, Emi. I'm not. I don't."

"Really, Jack. Please go."

"Emi," I plead. "I'm not leaving you alone. I don't need time to think about this. You're being ridiculous."

She stands up and walks to the door, stumbling to it before opening it. "Please, go. This is your out," she explains. "I want you to leave right now. Do it for me. When you come back, I'll know it's for good. But you have to digest this... and figure out if I'm worth all the sacrifices."

"I told you–"

"Please? Go." When she reaches for my jacket, I immediately get up and take it from her, not wanting the ring to expose itself to her now. I know there's a "yes" in our future... but this isn't the right time. I put the jacket on and reluctantly give in.

"I'll be back," I tell her. "Don't doubt that for a second." I kiss her softly, anticipating her more eager kiss in return, which she graciously gives. "I love you."

"Thank you," she says.

I drive home, angry, hurt that she thinks I would leave her now. I drive faster than I should, careless. I shouldn't, I know. I shouldn't for her. *Breathe.*

I take the ring out of my jacket pocket when I get home and throw the jacket on the back of the couch. I want a drink... something numbing.

She can't have children. How is it that the woman I love can't have children? How can someone so perfectly intentioned to be a mother not be able to bear children?

She's right. What did she do to deserve this?

What did I do? This is punishment. This is karma.

The scotch burns on its way down. I stare at the ring, still secured in its small box. This changes nothing about the way I feel about her. It can't.

I remember how her skin glowed the night of the engagement party. She had been pregnant... she was radiant that night. I would never see that glow again. I wouldn't get to watch her stomach slowly swell. I wouldn't be able to hold her hand when we found out the sex of the baby. I wouldn't get to feel our child kick, move inside of her. I wouldn't get to run to the store in the middle of the night to fulfill her midnight cravings. I wouldn't get to remind her to breathe, try to take away her fear and pain, as she delivered our baby. These are all things I had looked forward to.

And what about her? All the things she will miss... all the times she will see her friends and family members getting pregnant, their dreams realized while hers never can be. Will she ever be happy? Will I ever be able to make her happy? *Would anyone?*

The losses just keep piling up for Emi... but I will not be one of them. I am here for her, to love her. I love her more than the ideas of what we could have over a nine-month span of time... such a short amount of time, when it comes right down to it. We can still raise children. Plenty of children need good homes.

Emi alone is the only person I would ever need, though. If she didn't want to adopt, she would be enough... wouldn't she? We already have a plethora of nieces and nephews and more on the way. We could see them as often as we wanted. Could that be enough for us? For me?

For years, I've wanted to hear the sound of children playing in the house... to be able to play with them in the backyard... I bought this house knowing that I would raise a family here.

Why wouldn't she want to adopt? Would children– other people's children– just be a constant reminder of her inability to conceive? Would the presence of children in her life just make her unhappy? Make her feel inadequate?

Would I resent her? Could I ever? In ten years, like she said, would I regret marrying someone who couldn't give me Jackson Andrew Holland the third? Biologically?

I imagine the looks of sorrow our families would display when we gave them the news. I consider how difficult it would be... I imagine Steven's reaction; this, just one more reason why I shouldn't be with her. Everyone would be disappointed.

No one more so than Emi, though, and she is the one that matters to me most. I could face a million people looking at me, feeling sorry for us, before I could face Emi as she watched me walk out of her life. I could never– *would* never– do that to her. For anything. The thought of her not in my life makes me feel sick.

When I finish my glass of scotch, I take off my tie and untuck my dress shirt before going for a walk. My body feels exhausted from the long day, the jet lag, the devastating news, but I know that I won't sleep if I go to bed now. I wander, briefly, around my neighborhood before taking a turn east.

I'll be damned if I'm going to fly back to Spain tomorrow without spending this night with her, without reassuring her that I am here, for good. If I could cancel this week's meetings, I would. I don't want to leave her alone. Maybe I can convince her to come with me.

"Is everything okay, Mr. Holland?" Marcus asks as I briskly walk into Emi's building.

"Just anxious to see her," I answer, forcing a smile, as I breeze past him.

I debate knocking when I get to her door, but decide to use the key again. She has welcomed me here and I belong here. Wherever she is... that's where I want to be. I quietly unlock the door in case she is sleeping. It's obvious that she hasn't been getting enough sleep over the past few weeks, and I would hate to wake her if she was actually able to escape into pleasant dreams.

The light from the hallway floods her apartment, and I immediately see Emi, lying in bed and clutching the stuffed dog I had won for her on one of our early dates, her sorrowful eyes on mine. She doesn't move. My eyes adjust to the darkness once I close the door. I take off my dress shirt and slacks, setting them on the love seat, and climb into the bed behind her. Putting my arm around her, I pull her body, gently, next to mine. She holds on to my hand tightly with both of hers. I outline her lips with my thumb, and she kisses it lightly. She sniffles quietly.

"Don't cry," I whisper, choked up. In the same moment, a tear falls from my own eye. She rolls over to face me, wiping the tear from my jaw. Her eyes shift back and forth, looking for something in mine. "I'm here for you, Emi. For us. Try to sleep." I touch her cheek and lean in to kiss her. Our legs entwined, she cuddles closely into my chest as I run my fingers through her hair. She puts her hand up my t-shirt and lightly scratches my back with her nails.

Once I know she is asleep, I close my eyes, allow a few more tears to escape.

Her soft lips wake me up sometime during the night. I thought I was dreaming, until I open my eyes to see pale green, lit only by the bright moonlight, staring back at me. She continues to kiss me, slowly, our gaze never breaking.

"Make love to me," she whispers. I consider her request, my heart racing.

"Are you sure–"

"Yes," she cuts me off.

We separate just long enough to help one another undress. Kneeling, facing me in bed, her naked body is a faint silhouette in the night. I touch her gently between her thighs, and she lies back, pulling me on top of her. I kiss her slowly, my lips traveling to her neck as she tilts her head back with her eyes closed.

I look at her, analyzing the moment, wondering how to approach the subject without upsetting her. Out of respect for her, I make no assumptions with Emi. Sensing my hesitation, she opens her eyes and looks at me, wondering.

I smile as I lean over to her nightstand and pull out the small box I had placed there months before. I start to open the package as she wraps her hand around it.

"We don't need those," she says as she takes the box from me and sets it back on the night stand. It's the response I didn't want.

If she had wanted me to wear one, I could believe that there was at least the slightest bit of hope that she *could* get pregnant, regardless of what the doctors have told her. I stare into her eyes as she smiles, hopeful. I bite back tears and force a smile of my own.

"There is no way that it can happen, Jack." I nod in understanding as she pushes the hair out of my eyes. "It is impossible. If you're thinking we can prove them all wrong... don't. We can't."

I swallow back a lump in my throat as I come to terms with the fact that there will be no children with her soft red hair, her entrancing pale green eyes.

I stroke her ears, her hair, with my thumbs, holding her face close to mine as I kiss her deeper. I cling to her, desperately, needing her. Eventually, my tears mix with hers, the saline flavoring our kiss.

I pull away briefly for air, and kneel in the bed in front of her. As her legs press warmly against my body, her knees bent at my sides, I admire her elegant form. My hands slide down her body, from her shoulders, to her breasts, settling on her hips, gripping firmly. I lean down to kiss her navel and linger, feeling a strange sense of loss. She sniffles, one last time, and lifts my chin up with her hand. Her soft smile is warm, concerned, loving. I follow as she leads me back to her wanting lips.

"Are *you* sure?" she asks me, her matted eyelashes fluttering.

Life without her is no longer an option.

"I am," I tell her. "I love you."

"I love you, Jack."

"Emi, *you* are all I that ever wanted."

She stares at me and smiles. "You can have me," she whispers.

She tenses and gasps as I pull myself into her, her smile widening as her body relaxes beneath mine.

The woman I love, the feel of her skin against mine, the intensity of our lovemaking... I've never felt closer to any woman, emotionally or physically. Without a shred of doubt, I know she was made for me... and I know that– somehow– we'll have a family together.

I hit the snooze button within seconds of the alarm going off, cursing myself for not remembering to turn it off before I went to bed last night. We both need *a lot* more sleep. I roll back over and put my arm back around Emi, the same place it had been since we both fell asleep, exhausted and completely spent in every way.

"You're still here," she whispers groggily, stretching slightly.

"I am. Go back to sleep."

"Okay." She moves onto her side and presses her back into my chest, pulling my arm closer to her body. I kiss her neck and sigh, my eyelids heavy and adamant to keep the sunlight out. "Mmmm..." she sighs, and I can tell she's smiling.

"What was that for?"

"I just remembered last night..."

"Yeah," I agree. "Last night was..." There is no word to adequately describe our night– and morning– together.

"Last night meant more to me than... than... any other night in my life," she says reverently. "I've never felt more... cherished, or loved."

"You are," I remind her as I plant a kiss behind her ear. She sighs again and snuggles closer into me, if that was even possible.

Just as I begin to doze off, she sits up quickly in bed, pushing my chest. "You have to get up, you have a flight to catch!"

"I'm postponing it," I mumble, trying to pull her back to me.

"No, you can't. You said the meeting was important."

"It is, and it will still be important the next day."

"I'm okay," she says as she lies back down, this time facing me. "You don't have to stay for me."

"I'm not," I tell her, smoothing her wild hair. "I'm staying for us. I think we need a day together, just me and you. And then I want you to come meet me in Spain."

"Really?" she says. "I'd love to." She kisses me softly.

"Good. My flight is at noon tomorrow and I have meetings the next day. I can get you on the evening flight on Thursday and we can spend the weekend there... fly back on Monday? Would that be okay?"

"Yes, of course," she smiles. "But you shouldn't miss your meetings because of me, Jack."

"Hush," I tell her. "I am still spending today with you." I press my finger to her lips before she can argue. "Unless you had other plans."

"My only plans were to meet my family for dinner. They wanted to celebrate my birthday, so we settled on tonight."

"Would I be intruding?"

"Absolutely not... but it may be a little uncomfortable."

"Have you told them yet?"

"No. I wanted to tell you first. I didn't know if I'd also be delivering break-up news, as well."

"It doesn't make sense to me that you would ever think that I would break up with you for this." I kiss her again, a reassurance.

"But I lied," she says, mumbling against my lips. "I lied about the freelance... and if you think about it, I'm kind of stealing from you, too. I'm taking away the opportunity for us to have children of our own."

"You lied for good reason... and *you're* stealing *nothing* from me. We'll make this work, Emi. Somehow, we'll figure it all out."

"Okay," she smiles.

"So we can tell your parents together tonight."

"Right. And then escape to Madrid for the weekend."

"Mmmm..." I hesitate. "Pack for some place a little more... tropical," I tell her. "We won't be staying in Madrid."

"Oh? Where?"

"Just be at the airport with your passport when I tell you to be. I want it to be a surprise."

"Please tell me," she begs with a wide grin spread across her face.

"I'll tell you if you let me go back to sleep."

"Really?" she asks.

"No, not really. But let's go back to sleep anyway. And just dream of the most perfect place on earth... because that's where we're going."

I had debated bringing the ring with me to dinner, but I decided in the end that I didn't want it to seem like I was simply reacting to her bad news. Hopefully she understands fully that I am here to stay... after our day together, I believe she does.

At Emi's mother's house, her family is already gathered and waiting when we arrive. She clutches my hand tightly; even as we hug her parents and siblings, she refuses to let go. She said very little on the drive upstate, undoubtedly trying to find the right words.

After dinner, Jen puts Clara to bed in their parents bedroom while everyone gathers around to talk over drinks. When Emi's sister reappears, Emi decides it's time.

"I have some news," she says, swallowing hard. She looks at our hands, still clasped, as I meet the eyes of all of her family members. They all wait patiently for Emi to continue, but she doesn't.

"*We* have some news," I clarify after clearing my throat. Emi nods her head before leaning into my shoulder. I switch hands with her so I can put my arm around her, rubbing her arm.

Emi's mother claps her hands together and stands up. "Congrat–"

"Mom," Chris says, holding her back, sensing immediately that it is not good news we're bringing to his family. I smile politely at her mother, meeting her questioning eyes and shaking my head minutely.

"I can't have children," Emi announces abruptly as she starts to cry. Anna doesn't hesitate as she crosses the room to grab a box of tissues and brings them to us. She kneels down in front of her sister-in-law, setting the box on my knees, and then hugs us both.

"Thank you, Anna."

"I'm so sorry, Emi. You're sure?" she whispers. Emi wipes her eyes and nose with a tissue before pulling back and nodding. She scans the room to see the reaction of the rest of her family. They all look stunned and ready with questions.

"Why?" Jen asks first.

"There's apparently a lot of scar tissue. Too much," Emi explains in one quick breath.

"From the accident?" her father asks. We both nod.

"Emi, baby," her mom cries and comes to hug her daughter.

"Get a second opinion," Chris says from across the room.

"She did," I tell him as Emi and her mom cry together. "She had a procedure done at the urging of the best OB-GYN in the country. She saw two other specialists, as well. They all had the same findings." As I look around the room, seeing the looks of sadness and disappointment, I recoil at the thought of telling my own parents.

They knew what the deciding factor was in my failed relationship with Caroline. They knew that everything hinged on the fact that she didn't want children, and on my unfaltering decision to have them someday. I remember how they took the news when I told her she had decided to leave. They were sad, but they all knew that I had made the right decision to stand firm on my future plans. They all agreed that the only woman for me was one who would be a mother to our children. They knew that I would be a father someday... they knew it was the one goal in my life I had yet to achieve.

Now, I hope my family won't see this as a hopeless situation. I hope they can see the difference. After all, it's not that Emi doesn't want children, it's that she can't have them. But together, we can still raise them... and that's the difference. Still, the disappointment they're all sure to feel... the looks on *their* faces...

"Right?" Emi asks me with a hopeful smile. All eyes are on me.

"I'm sorry, what was the question?" I laugh, feeling my cheeks get hot as I realize they had continued the conversation without me.

"Are you alright?" she asks. "You look flushed."

"I'm fine, what did you ask?"

"I told them that I was going to meet you in Spain this weekend."

"Right," I clear my throat and see the expectant looks of her parents. "Yes, Spain, I'm very excited."

"So everything's still on track?" Emi's father asks me. I clearly hear the underlying question: if I still intend to propose.

"This changes nothing between us," I assure her family, and Emi. I fully intend to propose. I'm just not sure this weekend will be the right time. I want... *us*... to be normal... and *happy*... and *whole*... again.

CHAPTER 6

I fix a drink before settling in to the hotel room in Madrid. I only have five hours until the meetings begin at nine. Going to sleep now would be pointless, so I hope the brief nap on the plane tides me over. I had a hard time sleeping, my mind racing with possible options for Emi and me. When I see our future together, I still see children. I can't imagine our life without them... but I'm trying to come to terms with this possibility.

It's probably the perfect time to call Kelly back in New York, though. I pull out the phone and dial her number, taking a long sip before she answers.

"Hey, Jacks, what's up?"

"Hi, Kell. Is this a bad time?"

"Not at all... kids are all in bed."

"Good. How are they?"

"They miss you," she tells me. "They're demanding you come out to the house the second you get back."

"Well, I miss them, too."

"So, how's business?" she asks.

"Good. The meetings have been great. Very productive. This will probably be a yearly thing, so that's cool. Not a bad business expense."

"Maybe you can take me next year," she laughs. "But Emi couldn't make it, I heard?"

"No, but actually, I just got back from a short stay with her in New York."

"What?" she asks. "Why?"

"I surprised her for her birthday," I tell her, sighing.

"Uh-oh," she responds, sensing my mood. "Is everything okay?"

"It will be." I hesitate, taking another sip.

"What's going on?"

"Well... while I was there, she told me she can't have children," I tell her, an audible gasp escaping her lips.

"What?" she asks, surprised. "How long has she known that?"

"She just had a doctor's appointment right before I left."

"What's wrong?"

"There's apparently a lot of scar tissue from the accident... she said three different doctors confirmed the diagnosis. Too much damage was done, apparently."

"What? I can't believe it... Jacks..." she sounds so disappointed... and it hurts to hear it. My stomach quivers at the lingering thought of telling my parents... still not looking forward to that conversation.

"Yeah," I concur. "I don't want anyone else to know, Kell, but she was actually pregnant when the accident happened. She lost the baby... she just told me about that right when we started seeing each other more seriously... she wanted kids very badly... especially since she lost that one."

"Jacks..." she lingers again.

"I know, Kell, I know."

"What are you going to do?"

"The only thing I can do," I tell her. "I'm in this, for better or worse..."

"Well, this is pretty bad. And for the record, you haven't exchanged those vows yet," she tells me.

"But we will. I love her, more than anything. You know that."

"I guess there are options," she adds. "You can adopt, right?"

"That's the plan. We'll work through it."

"Jacks, I'm so sorry," my sister says, attempting to comfort me. "You are going to be the greatest father. You have to be. It would be such a waste if you didn't have children, raise some on your own."

"Please don't say that... that it would be a waste... I would never consider my life with Emi to be a waste, children or not."

"I didn't mean it like that. I'm sorry..."

"We always have your kids, and her niece and soon-to-be nephew... we've got a great extended family, so if nothing else..."

"Will that really be enough for you, Jacks?"

"It has to be," I sigh. "It may be all we have. Honestly, Kell, a life without children is still a better option than a life without her," I tell my twin, the thought of Emi making my stomach flip. "She's everything. Twice, I lost her, by no fault of my own, and it crushed me. I would never make the choice to lose her a third time. That simply will not happen."

"You sound pretty certain of that."

"I am. I love her."

"Okay," she says, her smile audible. "Jacks, she is so lucky to have you. I hope she knows that."

"I think we both feel that way about each other. But I'll make sure I remind her." We both laugh.

"If there's anything I can do for you, you know I'm here for you... for you both. If she needs anything while you're gone, let her know she can call me anytime."

"Thanks, Kell. She's supposed to fly out Thursday. We're going to the Canary Islands on Friday morning."

"Wow, that sounds nice... was this already planned?"

"Elaborately, actually," I admit. "I was going to propose."

"You *were* going to?"

"Yeah... I'm not sure now's the time."

"So you *are* having second thoughts..."

"Not at all," I assure her. "I just think she may think I'm just reacting to the news... or overreacting... overcompensating, I don't know. I just don't know how she'd take it right now."

"It might reassure her," she encourages.

"Yeah, maybe..." My thoughts linger. "But I just want the proposal to be happy, to be what it is, a proposal of marriage, a request to spend the rest of my life with her... and not a band-aid to patch what's not perfect right now... I don't want her to have any doubts of what it is... and I don't think now's the time. But I'm going to play it by ear..."

"Okay," she says.

"I just want us to be in better frames of mind when the time comes. I want to be back to where we were before we found out this news."

"Do you ever think you'll get back there?"

"I think we'll get close," I tell her, confident. "With time."

"I hope you do, Jacks. And you can borrow the kids anytime. In fact, I'll just bring them with me when we pick you up from the airport on Monday and drop them off at your place, okay?"

"Uh, no," I laugh. "I'll need a few days to get back to my regularly scheduled life... but I'll let you know."

"Alright," she says. "Anything you need, Jacks, I'm here."

"I know, Kell. Thanks. I'm going to call Matty now... probably too late to call Mom and Dad."

"Have you talked to Stevie?"

"I have not... I tried to call him before I left, but he hasn't returned the call."

"He's probably wrapped up in his new fiancé role, you know..."

"I'm sure. We'll be fine, I'm sure."

"I know. Well, call me this weekend, if you have time."

"I will."

"And if you do decide to propose, get down on one knee..."

"Alright, thanks for the tip."

"Love you, Jacks."

"You, too, Kell. Bye." I grab a bottle of water before dialing my oldest brother. His partner answers.

"Hey, Lucas, is Matty there?"

"Well, hi to you too, Jacks. No 'how are you?' No nothing?"

"I'm sorry, Luc... a lot on my mind. How are you?"

"I'm fine, is everything okay?"

"Yeah," I sigh. "Can you put Matty on speaker or something? I want to just let you both in on something."

"Are you proposing?" he excitedly jumps to conclusions.

"Someday, but that's not what this is about... speaker? Matty?"

"Sorry, Jacks, sure." He yells out to my brother to join him and puts the phone on speaker mode.

"So, guys. I just wanted to let you know that Em and I got some bad news the other day."

"What?" my brother asks.

"Because of the amount of scar tissue left by the accident, she can't have children." They're both silent. "Say something."

"I don't even know what to say, Jacks," Matty responds. "I am so sorry. How is she?"

"She's pretty upset... she's known for weeks, but she just told me yesterday when I flew in to surprise her for her birthday."

"Oh, my god, that poor thing!" Lucas exclaims.

"Yeah, it's going to be hard... but this doesn't change anything between us... but I wanted you two to know."

"Well, you know, Renee works for an agency that helps pregnant teenagers," Matthew says. "We've talked to her before about adoption... she would be a good resource, if that's what you decide to do."

"I forgot about that," I tell him. "Maybe we'll give her a call after we sort through things a little more... get used to the idea."

"I know you two will be fine," Lucas says. "You're meant to be with each other. She is so in love with you, Jacks. One night in Vail, she just went on and on..."

"That was the night you got her drunk..."

"Well, yes, but that's when the *real* truth comes out," he laughs.

"We're here to support you, Jacks," my brother says. "We love you both. You know that. She's already family... make it official soon, okay?"

"I will, I promise. Listen, it's too late to call Mom and Dad, so don't say anything if you talk to them before I do."

"We won't," they assure me.

"Bring us back something from Spain!" Lucas calls out.

"Alright. Have a good night, guys. I'll call you when I get back."

"Good night, Jacks."

I call Emi next, hoping she's still awake.

"Hello?" she answers.

"Hey, love."

"Hi, Jack." I can tell she's smiling, her voice much less nasally than it's been in weeks.

"How are you feeling?"

"Relieved," she says. "Jack, I am so sorry I didn't tell you before you left... I was just so worried... and I should have known... should have known you better than that."

"Yes, you should have," I agree. "But, Emi, it's okay. In the future, though... just out with it, okay? Don't be afraid to tell me anything... anything at all. No more secrets."

"Okay, then, where am I going on Thursday?"

"Madrid," I tell her.

"You said we weren't staying there."

"Oh, that. It's a secret."

"But you said–"

"Now, Em... I get one, okay? Let's be fair," I reason with her, joking. "This is it. No more after this one."

"Yeah, that doesn't seem fair. What if I pack wrong? Then what?"

"It would be tragic, yes, dear," I tell her, "but they do have stores where we're going."

"So no deserted island?"

"Mmmmmm... no."

"Island?" she asks.

"I'm not talking about this anymore with you."

"It *is* an island," she taunts me playfully.

"Emi, I... stop... I'm changing the subject."

She giggles. "You suck at secrets."

"Well, that should please you, then. It's an island, that's all I'm saying."

"Very nice. But we're meeting in Spain?"

"Yes, I'll be waiting for you at the airport."

"Awesome. I cannot wait."

"Me, neither. I can't wait to see you."

"Did you talk to your parents?" she asks me.

"No, it was too late to call. I told Kelly and Matty today, though... it wasn't easy, but they're supportive of us."

"I knew they would be," she says. "You have a great family."

"We both do. Listen, I need to go get ready for my meetings. You'll be okay?"

"I'm great," she says.

"Good. Go get some sleep. You'll need it."

"Will I?" she asks flirtatiously. I laugh out loud.

"Jet lag, Emi, is what I was talking about."

"Oh," she laughs back. "Just jet lag?"

"Emi, go to sleep."

"Good night, Jacks."

"Good night, Poppet. I'll see you... tomorrow morning."

After the meetings, I call Stevie back before settling in for a nap. Emi will be here in a little over twelve hours. I can't wait. My youngest brother has left two messages during the day. I can only assume he has spoken with one of our siblings.

"Steven, what's going on?"

"Jacks, hey, man. You still in Spain?"

"Yeah... what's up?"

"I, uh, man, I just want to apologize..." he stutters.

"For?"

"For Vail... you know, for being an ass to Emi... and you... I know it was uncalled for."

"Yes, it was, but it's already forgotten. Don't worry about it."

"Man... I talked to Matty this morning." I wait silently for him to continue. "He told me about her... that she can't have children."

"Yeah, well, we're working through that."

"I'm really sorry."

"It's alright. It's all going to work out," I assure him.

"You know, Renee has some connections to adoption agencies and things like that. She works with a lot of pregnant girls who want to have their babies adopted by good parents."

"Yeah, Matty reminded me of that. If that's the route we decide to take, we may call on her to–"

"Well, I just thought you guys might want to come down and talk to her. Why don't you make a trip to Texas? Come spend a few days with us... you can talk to Renee... I can show your girlfriend I'm not a complete jerk."

"She knows you're not," I tell him. "But we'd both appreciate a little groveling."

"Whatever," he laughs. "Will you come?"

"I'm a little anxious to be home for awhile, but sure... we'll plan a trip to come down there. I'll see her tonight, so we'll talk about it this weekend. I mean, it's too soon to start looking into adoption, but I think it would be nice if we could see what the options are beforehand."

"Yeah, and Renee would just like to see you guys anyway."

"Well, I appreciate the invitation. And the apology."

"Are you going to propose soon?"

"Jeez," I joke. "You are an impatient bunch!"

"I just assumed... didn't you plan some elaborate getaway?"

"I did, but I'm not sure this is the right time."

"Sure it is!" he encourages. "Just go for it."

"Alright, Stevie, I need to get some sleep. My schedule's all messed up this week."

"Okay. Call me when you get back to New York. We can figure out the details."

"Sounds good. Tell Renee I said hello... and thank you."

"I will. Bye."

"Bye."

I go to bed shortly after Emi calls from the airport in New York. The alarm goes off at six o'clock local time, and I anxiously get up, get ready, grab my luggage and take a cab to the airport.

She looks tired when she gets off of the plane, but grins widely at first sight of me across the room. We meet halfway in the middle.

"You look amazing," she tells me.

"Thanks, you, too. I'm so glad you decided to come, Emi."

She hugs me tightly before I can remember to adjust the ring box in my pocket, which is now jabbing me in the rib cage. Instinctively, I pull back and laugh nervously. I try to defer her attention with a kiss instead, hoping that she didn't feel the trinket. It seems to have worked.

"Where are your things?" she asks.

"Already on the plane. Let's go get yours," I suggest.

We hold hands on the way to baggage claim, and as we wait for her bags around the turnstile, she leans sleepily into my body. I pull her into me, enveloping her in both arms.

"Those are mine," she mumbles, pointing at her luggage. "The green tapestry ones." The man standing next to me, unbeknownst to Emi, picks up her bags. She becomes alert. "No, those are mine," she says louder.

"That's Javier... he's with us, Em," I tell her. "It's okay. Are those the only two?"

She looks up at me and smiles, a self-satisfied grin. "I did my best to not overpack."

"Four days, two bags... not bad." She hits my chest playfully.

The man takes her bags and leads us out a side door at the airport to a small runway.

"You're kidding me," Emi says as she sees a smaller plane waiting for us.

"What, the jet? No. It's just easiest... and I didn't have to worry about any flight delays, the threat of us missing a flight, you know..."

"Right, okay."

"Plus, I figured you'd need some room to spread out, coming off that eight-hour flight... I promise, it's exceedingly practical. Take it from someone who's missed a few important flights."

"But this is a pleasure trip," she says.

"But it's an important flight to me," I counter.

She is quiet as she ascends the stairs, and turns around before letting me on the plane behind her. "Me, too," she states.

"Good. Go pick your seat."

"Or bed," she comments, seeing a bedroom through a door just beyond the leather seating area.

"If you'd like," I offer.

"Yeah, that's about right. My first flight on a private jet and I'm just going to sleep it away."

"Who said anything about sleeping?" That comment earns me another playful slap, this time across my arm. "I'm just kidding. No mile-high club today." She raises her eyebrows as if considering the idea. "Kidding, Em... have a seat."

I take off my jacket and drape it over the chair closest to the door, out of the way but in constant view so I can keep an eye on it. God, I hope she didn't feel it. I just want it to be a surprise.

She wanders around the plane, and I decide to sit down on the couch, waiting for her to settle in next to me. The pilot comes to introduce himself shortly after Emi curls up on the couch, leaning into me.

"Yo soy el capitán Suárez," he says, extending his hand to me.

"Soy Jack, y esta es mi novia, Emi." The captain takes her hand and kisses the back of it, causing her to blush.

"El tiempo de vuelo será de aproximadamente dos horas y cuarenta y cinco minutos," he tells me. "Si necesitas algo, Javier puede conseguirlo para usted. ¿Quieres algo para desayunar esta mañana?"

Emi looks at me, confused, as the captain returns to the cockpit.

"He says the flight will take about two hours and forty-five minutes," I tell her. "He'd like to know if you want anything for breakfast."

"Is there toast?" Emi asks.

"¿Tiene usted alguna pan tostadas con mantequilla?" I ask when Javier comes into the room. Emi looks at me, stunned. "What?" I ask her with a smile, knowing exactly why she looks so perplexed.

"Puedo preparar pan tostadas, si lo desea. ¿Hay algo más que te gustaría? Los huevos o tocino?"

"He can make toast," I tell Emi, "and wants to know would you like any eggs or bacon?"

She nods, bewildered. "Maybe some fruit?"

"No, pero nos gustaría un poco de fruta, también. Y mimosas."

"I got mimosas..." she says. "I'll be fast asleep in no time," she mumbles.

"Café, también," I add. "Gracias." Emi smiles as Javier goes into a small kitchen area.

"You speak Spanish?"

"Ummm, yes, it's kind of necessary. The businessmen here take you more seriously if you're fluent in their languages and aware of their customs. It's a sign of respect."

"Well what did you do in France? And Italy?"

"I spoke their languages, as well."

"You speak French and Italian, too?"

"And German."

"How..."

"I learned some in college, in my International studies... and the rest with language software and a few trips."

"Say something in French," she encourages me.

"Dans l'histoire du monde, aucun homme n'a aimé une femme comme Je t'aime."

"And Italian?"

"Il colore dei tuoi occhi è come una scintillante piscina, che riflette la profondità del mare."

"Wow, I hope you didn't just say something completely insulting, because it sounded beautiful..."

"Only complementary, I promise." I lean in closer, kissing her right cheek and whispering the English translation of the French phrase in her ear. I then repeat the action with the Italian phrase in her left.

"And how do you say, 'I can't wait to make love to you... how much longer is this flight?'"

"Which language?" I laugh.

"I don't care," she breathes before running one hand down my cheek and kissing me, the fingers of her other hand tangling in my hair.

"Speaking of sleeping with you," I say quietly, interrupting the sentence with a kiss, "did you sleep on the flight over?"

"Not at all," she admits. "I was just so excited... I tried to sleep, but my mind was just racing. I watched three movies on my iPod. One was really boring and I *still* couldn't sleep!"

"That's not good," I tell her. "Maybe you should nap a little now."

"No, my mind's still racing."

"Maybe after you eat something..." She nods. "Did you talk to your family any more?"

"Just Anna and Chris. I needed to assure them that I wanted to know every little thing about their baby. I didn't want them to feel awkward talking to me about him... and I wanted them to know how important he– and Clara, too– will always be to me. They may be the closest things to kids I have..."

"And my nieces and nephews," I add.

"If..." she says.

"If I don't leave you?" I scoff. "Em, you're my future. You have to know that I'm not leaving you."

"I don't know, but I hope. It's not official, you know."

I shake my head at her and roll my eyes playfully.

"Chris said my mom's worried you'll leave, too."

"Seriously?"

"That's just how her mind works... woman can't give man what he wants, man leaves woman... I have my dad to thank for that," she jokes. "Only it wasn't kids, it was... ew, you know what, never mind, I don't want to talk about that."

"So I need to win over your mother then..." I ponder. "Easy enough. I'm not leaving. I guess it will just take some time for her to see that."

"Time, yeah..." she lingers. "Or a commitment..."

"A commitment, huh?" She blushes as she shrugs her shoulders. "I love you, Emi." I lean in to kiss her gently first, then deeper. "You know I'm committed. Did you mean a proposal?"

"I didn't say that," she denies as Javier brings our food out. "Yum. Perfect, thank you." She smiles, obviously not wanting to venture further in this conversation right now. I am positive that she thinks it's happening this weekend.

"Este pan es *increíble*. Gracias, Javier." He laughs at us and leaves us alone in the sitting area. "So, we didn't really get to hear from Anna much the other night. How is she doing?"

"She's great," Emi says. "She says he's kicking a lot. She invited me over so I could feel it... I told her I'd come when we got back." Her eyes water. "It's hard now, but it's a beautiful thing. I want to be there for her."

"I know, Poppet." We kiss again. I pick up both of the drinks, handing one glass to her. "To *our* life together." One corner of her lip turns up as she searches for something in my eyes. She sighs before taking a drink.

At the hotel cabana in Tenerife, I read through a copy of USA Today, the only link to America I can find... I've been so out of touch recently that I feel like I'm missing out on all the news from back home.

Emi was so tired by the time we got here that she only took the time to give a cursory glance around our villa before she lay down on the bed and fell asleep. I guess that's what being awake for twenty-four hours straight will do to a person. She kicked her shoes off, and that was it. Didn't even bother to change clothes.

Before she dozed off, she did let me know it was okay to unpack her bags. No surprises for me this time around... although the bathing suits are new to me, and I can't wait to see her in them. I put away her things neatly before taking a tour of the resort.

If I do decide to propose here, I need to find a perfect place. I was sure I would find that place somewhere near our hotel, but after an hour of wandering around, I haven't found it yet.

Overall, the resort is perfect, though. The grounds are beautiful, just as amazing in person as they were in the brochure, and the weather is gorgeous. Any place would be acceptable for a proposal... I just haven't felt the right one yet.

Inside our private villa, there are two separate living rooms, a kitchen, a bedroom and a bathroom with a tub that could almost be a second private pool.

The bedroom has a large canopy bed in the center with wood accents all over the room. The living areas are each tastefully decorated with comfortable furniture and Spanish artwork. Windows look out onto the deck, overseeing an infinite pool which appears to flow straight into the distant ocean.

The pool and deck are both enclosed on two sides by tall stone walls, our own private paradise. The deck outside is home to its own table and chairs... and bed. I guess if it only rains five days out of the year, you don't need to worry so much about all-weather furniture.

The hotel itself is palatial, unbelievable. When you look one way, you see the vast expanse of the ocean; the other way, a volcanic mountain. It's like nothing I've seen before. Akin to Hawaii, maybe, but there's something a little more exotic here. Maybe it's just the Spanish influence.

The bartender sets down two glasses of sangria in front of me, and then hands me a napkin with a message scrawled on it in black marker.

I think I'm still dreaming. Pinch me? I look around for Emi, but don't see her anywhere.

"Ella dice que se reunirá con usted en su habitación," the server says with a smile. *In the room.* I tip him and take the two glasses with me to the villa, just a short stroll away.

I enter the quiet room and immediately spot Emi through the windows, looking over the poolside into the ocean, wearing a blue bikini that seems to blend in with the water. Already in my swim shorts, I quietly walk out onto the patio.

"It's real," I tell her, setting the drinks down at the edge of the pool. "Good evening."

"I slept through the entire day," she says apologetically.

"You needed it. You got up in time to see the sunset... I think you made it for the best part of the day."

"This is so pretty," she says, wading through the water and picking up a glass. "Thank you," she smiles.

"Thank you." I get into the warm water and sit down on the top step leading into the pool. Emi joins me on the second step, sitting in between my legs. I begin to rub her shoulders, watching the tips of her hair become enveloped by the water. She takes my hands in hers, pulling them across her chest, holding them there. In silence, we watch as the sun slowly drifts lower until it is hiding beyond the horizon.

"Are you hungry? There's a restaurant on the beach." She turns around on the step and kneels in front of me, her eyes even with mine. She kisses me, her hands scraping my back lightly, before she whispers in my ear.

"I'm starving," she says seductively.

"Uh... for?" I ask, unsure.

"Well, of course, for you... but food, really," she smiles. "I just ate toast and fruit, remember?"

"Then come on, let's get dressed to go eat, silly." She takes my hand and we walk into the villa together. I put on some khakis and a white button down shirt. Emi is wearing a thin, long, light blue sundress and white sandals. She pulls her hair back into a low ponytail and puts on a modest amount of makeup.

"Do you think we'll need our jackets?" she asks, motioning toward mine.

"Poppet, it's eighty-four degrees outside... I think we'll be okay," I tell her, suspicious. *She knows.*

"I didn't know if it would be breezy or something by the water, that's all," she says innocently.

"Well, I don't know... I'm pretty sure I'll be fine, but you might want to bring something, I guess." She nods and grabs a wrap, folding it neatly over her arm.

"I'm ready, then."

Once we're seated, the table lit only by a small candle and the moon, we look over the menu and decide on our meals. After we place our orders, Emi folds her hands into her lap as her gaze settles on me.

"Okay, so how long have you been planning this trip?" she asks.

"For a while," I admit. "I think I thought of it the weekend that Jen moved out."

"The weekend Jen moved out... isn't that the same weekend that a certain article was in the paper?"

"I don't know what you're talking about," I lie.

"Right, so the trip... what was the occasion you planned this trip for?"

"Your birthday," I tell her with a sideways glance, knowing what she's insinuating. "I thought you would like to get away from everything. Was I wrong?"

"No, it's great. It's incredibly romantic. Easily the most romantic place I've ever been." *Is she really fishing for a proposal?*

"I'm glad," I smile, taking a sip of water. "Happy birthday, Em."

"Thank you... pretty elaborate for a birthday..."

"What are you getting at, Emi?"

"Nothing!" she laughs. "I'm just sayin'..."

"Alright. Next year, we can stay in and I'll order pizza and beer."

"That would be fine," she says.

"Is this just too much for you?"

"I just don't deserve all this fuss... for a birthday... it's not even an important one. Thirty-one... big deal..."

"Well, I've missed all your other birthdays, so can't this count for all the past ones, too?"

"You didn't miss last year."

"That's right," I recall. "I gave you a bottle of wine."

"You made my day!" she says. "That was very sweet. But I wasn't even on your radar... You were dating Marie at the time... "

I scoff at the idea. "You're kidding, right? I drove my date out to New Rochelle to hand deliver a bottle of wine to you. A forty-minute-out-of-the-way-drive, just to see you."

"Right..."

"I'm serious, Em. Laugh if you want, but I was just biding my time with her. She's a great girl, she is, don't get me wrong... I wouldn't have dated her if she wasn't... but I only wanted to be with you. As soon as I felt the time was right, I broke it off with her. You remember..."

"And when did you feel the time was right?"

"It was that one dance, at the club. Just holding you... it felt right... you changed that night. You seemed open, when for months you had completely shut down. You had been unrecognizable as the woman I thought I knew before. But that evening, you let your guard down. You allowed yourself to be vulnerable with me. I saw that as my opportunity." I recall the events of the night, remembering the pain I felt when she exited the club.

"But then after you left with that other guy, I was doubting myself."

"Nothing happened, by the way," she interjects. I laugh a little.

"Well, regardless, how was I to know? First, all I could think was 'Why can't that be me?' I'd watched you walk out on me time and again, and it was a habit I was wanting to break. I can remember feeling guilty for thinking that I wanted to take you home, especially since I *was* on a date with another woman...

"And then I thought maybe you were just lonely... that maybe the time you and I spent talking was just a friend-to-friend thing. That's why I called you, wanted to meet you the following day. I wanted to see if I still felt something between us... and more particularly, I wanted to see if it seemed like *you* did."

"And you thought I did by that meeting in Grand Central?"

"No," I laugh. "I didn't get that at all. You were out of sorts again. But I knew *I* felt something, and that was enough for me to go on. I broke it off with Marie that evening.

"I knew it was a matter of time at that point. I just had to be patient... I knew you'd come around."

"Took me long enough," she says.

"It took as long as you needed it to take. You are worth the wait."

"I don't deserve you, Jack." Her eyes water.

"Wait, no! Where did those tears come from? They were not invited to this dinner. No crying, no way... I mean it, Em. Whatever sad thing you're thinking about right now, just banish it from your mind."

She sniffles and wipes her tears with her napkin, setting it down on her plate of half-eaten food. "Let's go for a walk on the beach."

The seaside is relatively quiet, the calm ocean surf the only noise except for some tropical music playing in the distance. I roll up my pants and we both take off our shoes before wading in the shallow water. Emi takes my left hand into hers and starts playing with my ring finger.

"What are you thinking about, Emi?"

"Just about how perfect this night is... that's all."

"Is that all?"

"Do you still want to marry me, Jack?"

"Is that a proposal?" I laugh, taken by surprise.

"Oh, no, that's... no... not what I meant. I mean, since all this came up... are you having second thoughts about me?"

"Absolutely not."

"Well... this would be the perfect opportunity..."

"For..."

"Don't make me say it."

"I don't have the slightest idea what you're talking about... so you'll have to say it."

"I felt the box... in your pocket... I thought maybe that's why you invited me here... so?"

"I still don't know what you're talking about."

"Jack!" she yells, frustrated, hitting my arm. "We're on a romantic island, there's not a cloud in the sky, there's not a soul around us..."

"I will not be pressured into this," I state adamantly, smiling at her. "Okay, we've established that I'm no good at keeping secrets, but I want it to be a surprise. I certainly don't want you expecting me to do it. How romantic would that be?"

"Perfectly romantic," she pleads. "Really?" She hangs onto my arm, looking at me, hopeful. She lightly pats the pocket on my shirt, then moves her hands down to the pockets on the back of my pants, then brings them around to the front.

"I don't have it with me," I tell her. "I'm serious, Emi. Half of the surprise is already gone... please, let me redeem myself by making it somewhat unexpected."

"You don't have to go to that trouble."

"Em, I'm *going* to go to that trouble. This isn't all about you, you know. I'm part of this equation, too. What story will we pass down to future generations? *Kids, your mom figured it out and pressured me into giving her the ring.*"

Her face falls immediately, before I even realize what I said. She tries to force a smile, watching the look of shock in my eyes turn into sorrow... into an apology.

"Emi..."

"No, I know," she says quietly, her head hanging low. "It's hard to completely reorganize your thoughts around it, I know."

"I'm sorry," I whisper, holding her head in my hands, forcing her gaze to meet mine, my heart racing, sinking. "I'm so sorry." I catch her tears with my thumbs before pulling her into my chest, wrapping my arms tightly around her.

I guide her farther up the beach, and we find a dry spot in the soft sand, facing the dark, vast ocean. She sits in between my legs, my arms still holding her.

"You haven't given up on children," she finally breaks the silence.

"We don't have to, Emi. I think we should look at all the options."

"Am I not enough?" she barely manages to ask. Her words break my heart into pieces.

"I don't even know how to begin to answer that," I tell her honestly. "Of course you're *enough*. If it ends up just being me and you, Emi, I'll still be happier than most people. But I think you and I would be *better*... with children... when I see our future together, I don't see us alone. Do you?"

"Honestly, yes," she cries. "Some adoption agency is probably going to look at my string of misfortunes and tell me I'm not fit to adopt a child, I don't know."

"You're talking nonsense right now... be serious."

"I am," she argues.

"Emi, we would– no, we will– make extraordinary parents."

"Do you really think we could love someone else's children like they were our own?"

"Of course I do. Look at Kelly's kids, and Clara... don't we love them like they're our own?"

"They're blood relatives, it's different."

"Not really, Em. They're not our children," I explain.

"But we were there through the whole thing, the whole pregnancy. We were a part of their family before they were even conceived."

"So? We could try an open adoption, you know... where we get to know the mother before she gives birth... there are a lot of women who prefer that."

"I don't know that I want that. I hear that ends badly a lot... where the mothers just can't give up their baby."

"I know this won't be easy, Emi. Nothing we do ever seems to be easy. But I know one thing... with every challenge we face, we become closer. And just when I think I couldn't possibly love you more... I do."

"I just don't want you to get your hopes up," she pleads. "I don't want you to go into this thinking that children are a given. There is a possibility that we may never have them... and you have to be okay with that."

"Anything is possible," I contend. "And I am hopeful. You want children. I want children. The mere fact that we, together, can't conceive a child does not mean that we won't have one... or many..."

"Jack, I just can't bear to see that look of disappointment again."

"You won't," I assure her, "because I will be grateful for every day we're together. Having lived without you before, I can truly appreciate how amazing each day *with* you really is." She turns slightly so she can see my smile. Her hand touches the stubble on my jaw as I lean down to kiss her.

"But don't think for a second that I won't do everything in my power to find a child for us, if that's what you want. I will do anything to make you happy."

"But you already make me happy," she says. "And I want you to know that I will be the happiest woman in the world the day I become your wife. Anything beyond that is just icing on the cake."

"So you won't be the happiest woman until then?"

"Well..."

"I bet I could make you pretty happy tonight. And *no*, I don't mean by proposing."

"I didn't think so," she smiles, standing up and offering her hand to me. "Let's see what you can do." We race each other back to our shoes. I pick up hers when I beat her to them and slip mine on my feet.

"Mine," she says, holding her hand out.

"No, nuh-uh," I argue. "Mine." I sweep her into my arms as a quiet squeal escapes her lips. She kicks her feet briefly, but succumbs to my grasp quickly, kissing me deeply before I carry her back to the villa. "The pool?" I ask.

"Yes, please," she answers playfully. Once on the deck, she pulls her dress over her head, revealing her naked body underneath. She takes out the clip that holds her hair back, and shakes it out, allowing it to fall softly on her breasts. She takes cautious steps into the water.

"Is it cold?" I ask, turning off all the exterior lights and lighting a few candles that sit on the edge of the pool.

"Just a little." After undressing, I dive into the pool, the ripples of the water climbing up her torso. Eventually she meets me in the middle of the pool, shivering.

"It's not *that* cold," I joke with her.

"Warm me up," she whispers in my ear before tracing it lightly with her tongue.

I pick her up and wrap her legs around my torso, carrying her to the edge of the pool where a bench juts out from the side of the wall, waist-high. I sit on the bench, pulling her onto my lap. She gasps quietly.

"Are you okay?" I ask.

"Better than okay," she sighs.

"Is this comfortable?" She nods, rocking slowly against my body, guided by my tight grasp against her, as she gazes out into the ocean. "Oh, wow. I'm on sensory overload, I think." She tucks her head into her chest briefly, then continues to moan softly as I tilt her head back up, my lips finding hers. "Oh, Jack," she murmurs between kisses. "Deeper," she whispers, pushing her body more forcefully against mine. "Oh," she sighs with a smile. We move together, the sounds of the waves lapping over the pool the only other noise around us.

"I'm coming," I say quietly, my tongue now tracing her lobe and the hollow below her ear. She holds on to me tightly, gasping quickly and repeatedly. As I'm climaxing, she yells out my name, then slows her movements to a near-stop, covering her mouth with her hand, a look of surprise in her eyes. Once the headiness clears my mind, I laugh and move her hand so that I can kiss her.

"You outed us," I joke with her.

"Shut up!" she blushes. "I was trying to be so quiet!"

"You were, I was quite impressed, actually."

"Years of living with Teresa... no walls..."

"Oh, I see. Well, did you want to go inside?"

"Eventually," she says. "Let's just sit here and enjoy this for awhile. It's beautiful out here." She kisses me before climbing off the bench and standing against the wall, overlooking the town below and the ocean in the distance. I follow her, standing behind her, kissing her neck and ears in hopes of arousing her again.

"You know," she says. "It would be unexpected right now."

"You don't give up!" I tell her, tickling her before picking her up and carrying her toward the villa. She shrieks again, and I put my thumb over her lips in a failed attempt to keep her quiet. She takes my finger into her mouth and bites gently first, then closes her lips and begins to fondle it with her tongue. I push it in, a little deeper, as her eyes lock onto mine, a smile forming across my lips.

"Bedroom?" she asks around my thumb.

"Yes, please," I answer coyly.

CHAPTER 7

"Jack, it hurts to wake up," she whines from her first-class seat.

"Em, I know, but we're home. Just a little longer and you can ache in private... no clothes, or however you want to be."

"Oh, god, I can't wait." She takes a deep breath and stands up, careful not to bump anything.

"I've got your things. Just go ahead." She slowly makes her way off of the plane and into the terminal. I follow closely behind her, carrying her purse, carry-on and my own duffel bag.

Kelly and Thomas meet us at the baggage claim carousel.

"Oh, my god, Emi, you're... *crispy!*" my sister exclaims, and I can't help but laugh quietly behind her. "No sunscreen?"

"I swear, I wore it, but not enough, I guess. And not in all the right places, apparently," she mumbles under her breath. The daytime skinny-dipping exposed some delicate skin on her, skin that had probably never seen the light of day before. I feel bad for her, but it *is* a little humorous. She'll laugh once the pain subsides... I hope.

"You poor thing," Kelly says. "Yeah, you're so fair-skinned... you probably do burn easily."

"Apparently," she mumbles again, forcing a smile.

"She's in a lot of pain," I tell my sister and brother-in-law. "Some ibuprofen would probably help."

"I have some right here," Kelly says. "I'll go get some water."

Emi swallows the pills quickly. I take the water bottle from her and press it gently against her shoulders and back. Even her loose-fitting tank top is painful next to her skin.

"Thank you," she tells both Kelly and me.

"Jacks, do you have any aloe at home?" my sister asks.

"Yes, plenty." Thomas and I grab our bags and carry them all to their SUV.

"Use that, and a cool bath would probably be good. Or cool compresses, maybe," Kelly adds as we get into the car.

"Thanks, mom," I murmur to her.

"Well, you did bring her home in this condition. I have to make sure someone can take care of her."

"She was fine until yesterday. It just seemed to get worse throughout the night."

"Sunburns will do that," Thomas says, fair-skinned like Emi. "I've been there, Emi, I know what you're going through."

"Oh, I'm not sure you do," she responds. I imagine she is blushing underneath the burned skin of her cheeks.

"Trust her," I add.

"I just want to be home," she whines.

"We'll be there before you know it."

"Aside from the burn," Kelly begins, "did you two have a good time? What was Tenerife like?"

Emi manages to smile, then looks over at me and puts her hand on mine.

"It was amazing," she says. "I'd happily get this sunburn again if it meant I could go back there."

"Thank God," I sigh. "I was beginning to wonder if you were regretting the whole thing."

"Of course I'm not!" she exclaims. "Jack, I wish we could have stayed a lot longer. I hope we can go back there someday. I'll just be a little smarter... stick to the indoor pools or something."

"Well, and now I know how fragile you are," I smile. "I'm sorry you got so burned, Em." I kiss her and I'm taken with her, oblivious of my surroundings for the briefest of moments.

"I'll be as good as new in a few days, I'm sure," she whispers.

"I hope. I don't want this to be the main thing we remember from this trip."

"It doesn't even make the top five," Emi says. "Promise." We exchange mischievous glances.

"Okay," I say, satisfied, as Thomas pulls into my driveway.

Emi slowly pries herself off of the leather seat, grimacing with pain, as the rest of us unload the SUV and take the luggage into the house. Kelly immediately goes upstairs and starts running water for a bath. I don't know what I would do without my sister sometimes.

"We did some grocery shopping for you," Thomas tells me. "Just some things to get you through the next few days so you don't have to hassle with that."

"You guys didn't have to do that, but thank you. Em, can I get you something?" I ask her as she hobbles into the kitchen.

"Diet soda?" she requests.

Kelly comes back downstairs. "Emi, I ran a cool bath for you. You'll feel better after that."

"Wow, thanks, Kelly," she says, surprised.

"Jacks, do you want me to fix you two something to eat?"

"No, Kell, I've got it. Thank you both. We'll be fine."

"Alright, then," my sister says. "Let us know if you need anything."

"I will. And let the kids know I'll be by this weekend. And I'm not coming empty-handed."

"You spoil them, Jacks."

"I know. Just indulge me."

"Alright. Hey, Emi, why don't you see if Jen and Clara want to come out, too. She could bring Brian, if she wants... and Chris and Anna, too, if you'd like."

"Thanks, Kelly, I'll ask them," she says, smiling.

"Okay... Well, have a good night. Emi, get some rest... and get better."

"I'll be fine," she says.

"Thank you... good night." I close the door behind my sister and brother-in-law. "Come on, Crispy," I laugh. "Let's get you into that bath."

"You're not allowed to be turned on by this, you know," she warns me. "I'm in way too much pain for anything."

"I can't *not* be turned on, but I promise I'll be on my best behavior. I won't lay a hand on you."

She frowns before thanking me. "That's a weird thing to thank you for."

Upstairs, I carefully take her shirt off, over her head. Her yoga pants slide easily down her legs. "Was that okay?" I ask.

She nods, then puts her hands on my face and kisses me. "Thank you." I hold her hand as she carefully steps into the bathtub. She grits her teeth at the temperature of the water.

"Cold?"

"Very."

"It will probably feel good. Just settle in. We can add some warm water gradually." After she sits in the tub for a few minutes she relaxes and says that the bath is soothing on her skin. I sit on the step outside the tub and lightly sprinkle water on her shoulders, the only really sunburned part not completely submerged in the water, hiding under the mound of bubbles.

"Why do you do this?" she asks me.

"What?"

"Take care of me like this... why are you so attentive?"

"I don't think I understand the question, Em."

"Do you ever think, *'Man! She's a lot of trouble!'*"

"Of course I do," I laugh. "I'm just constantly thinking, *'Wow, what have I gotten myself into?'*" She splashes me softly with water. "That is cold... can I add a little warm water for you?" She nods and smiles. "Tell me if it gets too hot."

"Seriously... you don't ever feel burdened by my 'crazy'?"

"Never once have I felt burdened, Em. Taking care of you would never be a burden. I've committed myself to this."

"That sounds like a sentence... like prison time..."

"Not at all," I smile. "I promised to take care of you. Does that sound better?"

"Promised who?"

I purse my lips, briefly but undoubtedly noticeably, before answering. "Myself... and Nate, actually."

"Nate?" she asks. "How did... when?"

"I guess it started in the hospital, I was making deals left and right, hoping you'd come out of the coma... at the time, I was feeling responsible. I had just found out he had died. I had just realized that the person 'meant for you' would no longer be there for you. I felt like I needed to do something about it.

"I've told you this before."

"I know, but you made it sound like some sort of vow you took."

"I guess it kind of was. A silent vow that I made with him. I guess I continued going over things in my mind at his funeral, too."

"I didn't know you went to that..."

"I learned so much about him, from his friends and his mother, and your family... The one thing that stood out, no matter what anyone said, was just how much he loved you... and the lengths he would have gone to in order to make you happy.

197

"I still felt like it was my wish that took him from you... I hate to keep bringing it up, really... I hate that I ever thought it."

"Jack, I never, for one second, believed that you meant anything malicious by it. You don't have a mean-spirited bone in your body."

"Thank you... but anyway... I sat in the back of the church and listened... prayed... and I stayed behind when everyone went to the gravesite. I prayed to God, sure, but I felt like I really owed Nate something. I can remember thinking that I would just never pursue you, for him. That was my sacrifice. If he couldn't have you, neither could I. I thought he would be happy with that...

"But then I started thinking– and I was in that church for hours after everyone left– no... he would go to great lengths to make you happy, they said. They said he only wanted you to be happy... and I started thinking and *really believing* that I could make you happy. I remembered the kiss in college, the spark that was ignited there. And I remembered the dance at the party, the way you looked into my eyes... how you seemed to stop breathing for a second, the same second I did... and I knew that the best way to honor him was to keep his dreams of making you happy alive and well.

"That, and I knew I couldn't stay away from you. I didn't want to make him a promise I couldn't keep."

"I'm glad you didn't stay away," she says. "I really think he would have liked you, if he had gotten to know you. I know he would have."

"I think we're pretty good together," I admit. "Do you feel any better?"

"Yeah... I'm just cold now." I help her out of the tub and gently pat her down with a soft towel. I grab the aloe from the medicine cabinet.

"This will have to tide me over, I guess."

"What do you mean?"

"Well... this is probably all the touching I'll get to do for a few days. Think I'll take my time... make sure I do the job right."

"Hey, now, I'm not happy about that, either. I kind of got spoiled over the weekend... it was really the perfect weekend, Jack. Thank you. It really was what I needed."

"You feel like I'm committed enough?"

"For now," she smiles. "I don't think you're going anywhere."

"Definitely not." She tells me she loves me before leaning in to kiss me.

"Okay, stand still... and I think this will feel cold, too."

I suggest that Emi try to take a nap, and she willingly climbs into bed, naked, carefully pulling up the sheet to cover her body.

"Why don't you just plan on staying here for a few days, until you feel a little better? I'll go pick up some things from the loft, if you'd like."

"Are you sure you don't mind?" she asks. "I really feel like a burden right now."

"Stop, Emi. I'd love to for you to stay here with me. Then I'll know the second you're better..."

"As long as you're getting something out of this," she jokes.

"If you're going to wander around naked for days, I definitely want you to stay here." She rolls her eyes at me and names a few things she needs from her apartment.

"Do you want anything else, while I'm out?"

"No. Just hurry back."

"If you change your mind, just call me." I bring her cell phone to her with a bottle of water. "Just try to nap for a bit."

The air in Emi's apartment is warm and somewhat stagnant. I check the window unit to make sure it's working, but notice she's just left it off while she was out of town. No lights, no sounds. It just feels deserted. I get chills as I think of this being his place, imagine him watching me wander around his loft. It almost feels... creepy. I wonder if this is how she normally feels, when she is uncomfortable being intimate with me, here. Does she feel his presence, too?

Surely, she does. It has to affect her. I wonder how I can convince her to move in with me.

How things have changed in the past couple of months. When I found out

Jen was moving out, I didn't feel the time was right for us to move in together. But now, so much has been forever altered. We are different people now. My desire to take care of her has become a need. I don't ever want her to be alone again. I don't ever want her to go to that sad place, the place where she feels abandoned, depressed, inadequate, unworthy of love.

I have no idea how she would feel about leaving this loft. I'm unsure how to bring it up. Is she holding onto it... for him? There are so many things to consider.

I find her computer and her silk robe, the only two things on her wish list, and put them in a piece of luggage left behind on her bed. I find some lounge pants and soft shirts in her lingerie drawer and pack them, too. A paperback book sits on her nightstand, a bookmark in the first half of the book, and I decide to bring that to her, as well.

Before I leave, I throw out the daisies I brought her last week for her birthday, sadly wilted and shriveling in a vase. I decide to stop and get her some fresh flowers and wine before heading home.

Traffic is particularly bad today, so it takes a lot longer to get home than I had anticipated. Chris's car is in the driveway when I reach the brownstone. Anna greets me with a smile from the kitchen when I walk in.

"Hey, Anna, what are you doing here?" I say to her warmly, happy to see her.

"Jack, welcome home! Did you have a nice trip?"

"I did. I especially enjoyed the weekend with Emi," I tell her, setting the suitcase in the living room and carrying the flowers and wine into the kitchen.

"She looks pretty bad," Anna says, cringing.

"I know, I know. You look beautiful, though," I tell her, hugging her and kissing her on the cheek. "Is she still in bed?"

"Oh, no," she says. "She and Chris are on the patio catching up... in the shade, don't worry."

"Okay. Are you cooking?" I ask her, noticing some ingredients set out on the counter in front of her.

"She was hungry... I thought I'd make spaghetti. You don't mind, do you?"

"I only mind that a woman in your condition is slaving away, alone in the kitchen," I laugh. "Let me help you."

"Thanks," she smiles. "You know," she begins, filling a large pot with water, "I half-expected a ring on her finger when she got home. Is she just not wearing it because of the sunburn? Because she hasn't said anything."

"She doesn't have it," I confess as I take the pot from the sink and carry it to the stove for Anna. "I didn't ask her. Maybe I should have done it there... she knows it's coming. She discovered the box... but I want it to be a surprise. I don't want her to expect it.

"Maybe that's just stupid at this point, I don't know," I lament.

"No, it's not stupid," Anna assures me. "It's your decision... but it is still coming, right?"

"Of course, Anna," I laugh. "Nothing has changed."

"It seems a lot has changed." Her eyes look concerned.

"Okay, a lot has changed. But nothing has changed the way I feel about Emi. Nothing can change that. I want to be with her. She's all I've ever wanted."

Anna quickly grabs her swollen stomach.

"Are you alright?"

She smiles softly, rubbing her belly. "He's very active these days." She notices my curiosity without me having to say a word. "Would you like to feel?"

"That's not weird?" I ask.

"Jack, perfect strangers come up to me and touch my stomach. You're family." She grabs my hand and presses it against her, moving it slightly to find the right spot. "There, do you feel him?"

I pull my hand away slowly after feeling two distinct kicks. Anna and I exchange glances, and my eyes begin to water. "That's amazing." I turn around and blink away the tears before they have a chance to fully form. She grabs my arm before I can walk away.

"Hey," she says, spinning me around. "You can't be sad around her," she warns me. "I know you're sad, but you can't let her know that."

"I don't," I tell her. "I know we'll have children someday. We'll adopt... these things, though... it's just hard to get used to. I'm fine."

"You were saying she's all you ever wanted..."

"And she is," I confirm. "I can't wait to marry her, and start our life together."

"We can't wait, either," Anna responds. "And Jack," she adds, "we want you to be the baby's godfather."

"And Emi?"

"Well, of course she's going to be the godmother. That's what she and Chris are talking about right now."

"Oh," I comment.

"Chris had already decided he wanted her to be the godmother and you to be the godfather, whether you end up together or not. But if something happens to us, I want our son to be with two people who love each other and have a home together. So I wanted to see where your mind was... for my own peace of mind, you know?"

"God, don't say things like that, Anna. Nothing's going to happen to you two."

"If we've learned anything in the past couple of years, it's that life is short. And we just want to have a plan, that's all."

"I don't even want to consider such a thing," I tell her, "but of course you can count on us... together."

"Thank you. Now make it official!" she laughs. I roll my eyes at her, feeling the pressure of so many people on my shoulders.

"Patience does not run in *either* of our families," I mutter.

"Here, make a salad," Anna says, handing me a head of lettuce.

"Patience, I said." I smile at her, putting the vegetable down. "Let me see if they need anything." As I go out to the patio, Anna puts the flowers in a large glass of water.

"Chris, how's it going?" I ask, interrupting their conversation. Emi's brother stands up to shake my hand and pat me on the back.

"Good to see ya," he returns. Emi squints up at me, the sun peeking in between the two umbrellas they set up on the deck. Her short pajama shorts barely hang beneath one of my t-shirts as she pulls her knees into her chest. I adjust one of the umbrellas to keep the sun off of her.

"How are you feeling, Emi?"

"Still hurting," she says, "but less, I think."

"That's good. Why don't you come inside? The sun can still find you in the shade, you know..."

"I'm fine, Jack," she says. "We're just talking. We're going to be godparents, did you hear?"

"I did. I can't wait... thanks, Chris, I'm honored."

"You guys were the obvious choice," he says. Emi extends her hand to me and I take it as I move in closer to her. She wraps her fingers in between mine and kisses the back of my hand. I squat down next to her and gently kiss her lips.

"Think I'll go help Anna," Chris says.

"We'll be right in," I return. "How do you feel?" I ask Emi again.

"I told you, I hurt less," she smiles, pushing a few hairs off of my forehead.

"I mean about the godparent thing..."

"Uh..." she wavers. "Consolation prize?" she asks, warily.

"You know that's not it," I tell her. "You know they would have chosen us, regardless of what's happened."

"Yeah, I know," she says, her expression anxious. "I'm sure it was hard to ask me," she adds. "But I'm glad he did."

"Life goes on," I tell her.

"It does," she agrees. "Did Anna tell you the name?"

"Of..."

"Of the baby..."

"No, she didn't. What is it?"

"Elliott Nathaniel. Eli for short." She smiles, unsure.

"What do you think about that?" I ask softly.

"I think it's perfect," she laughs, a quick tear falling from her eye.

"It is perfect," I agree, wiping the tear away and kissing her again. "Are you hungry yet?"

"Starving," she says.

"Alright, then. Let's go help with dinner."

~ * ~

By the following Saturday, Emi's burn has turned into a peeling tan. She puts on the most protective sunscreen before we leave for Kelly's house.

"You don't even have to stay outside," I remind her.

"But if everyone else is out there, I want to be," she responds. We both grab a bag of food from the counter and carry them to the car. I arrange the trunk– the souvenirs, the cooler, the food– while Emi climbs into the front seat.

After we pick up Chris and Anna, the forty-five minute drive goes by quickly with lively conversation.

Brian and Jen are unloading their car as we pull up the driveway. Clara bounds out of the backseat, dolls in hand, and runs up to the front door.

"She seems excited to be here," I laugh. When I put the car in park, Clara turns around to see her aunt and uncle get out and runs toward them.

"Anni-Emi! Uncle Chris! Anni-Anna!" she cries, hugging them each equally. "Hi, Jack," she waves, shyly standing behind Emi.

"Hey, sweetie. I hear Jacqueline has been on the trampoline all morning... I can hear them in the backyard, if you want to go meet her..." I point to the gate and follow her as she runs over, opening it for her and then closing it softly behind her as I head back to the car to help unload. I shake Brian's hand and give Jen a hug on the way.

"Thank you so much for inviting us to come," Jen says. "Clara has been chatting about it all week."

Once inside, Jen and Kelly get reacquainted as they watch their girls try to out-jump one another on the trampoline.

After lunch, the adults sit around the back yard while the exhausted kids go inside to watch TV. Emi and Anna have apparently gone inside, too, likely to escape the warm summer heat.

"Jen," I ask Emi's sister as the others are engaged in conversation, "how do you think Emi would feel about moving out of the loft?"

"Like, to move in with you?" she asks.

"Something like that, yes."

"I'm not sure," she ponders. "Something about that place has always inspired her, creatively. I think she enjoys the view..."

"And the sentimental value?"

"There's probably some of that, too. It's a great loft... in a great spot... and it's free, of course. I had a hard time giving it up... but then again, giving it up meant I could have guests over again, so that was the selling point for me." She laughs. "Why do you ask?"

"I don't know. She's been staying with me all week with this sunburn, and it's been awesome having her around... and I was just over at the loft the other day picking up some things. I swear I felt his presence there. It was a little weird... and it's just obvious she still doesn't consider it her place, wholly."

"It makes *you* uncomfortable, so *she* should move out?" she smiles, her eyebrows challenging me.

"That's not it. I think it makes her uncomfortable. And honestly, it makes me more comfortable when she's with me... I like to think it's the other way around, too."

"I'm pretty sure it is, Jack. She missed you so much when you were in

Europe without her. She needed you... she didn't want to admit it, but she did."

"I wish I had been here..." I lament. "I would have been here, if she had asked... or at least filled me in."

"I know. I know you'd do anything for her." Anna walks out onto the patio and takes a seat next to Jen.

"What are we talking about?" she asks.

"Jack wants Em to move in with him. What do you think?"

"You know what I think," Anna says. "R-I-N-G."

"Yes, Anna, I know."

Jen laughs. "I'm sure she'd say yes with a ring. To moving in, marriage, having her wisdom teeth pulled, whatever."

"But without the ring?" I ask. "Where is she, by the way?"

"I assumed she was out here with you," Anna says. "I was lying down on the couch." We exchange curious glances and I decide to get up and go inside the house.

I search in the obvious places: kitchen, living room, dining room... no Emi. The two guest bathrooms are empty, so I keep walking down the hallway to the kids playroom, where I hear laughter, and eventually her voice. I watch her from the doorway.

"Your turn, Andy," she says, my nephew in her lap. "What do you want me to draw for you?"

"Batman!" he exclaims.

"Batman," she repeats. "I'll try." She pulls out a piece of white construction paper and a black marker and draws a cartoon version of his favorite superhero.

"He has a bat on his belt," Andrew instructs.

"Of course he does," she smiles. "His utility belt... should we draw the Bat-mobile, too?"

"Yes!" he squeals. Once she's finished, he climbs off her lap and joins the other kids, gathered around the coffee table coloring the drawings she's made for them. Still unbeknownst to her, I admire her, leaning against the door frame as she crawls over to them and inspects their work.

"What color should that be?" Clara asks, pointing to part of the dress on her princess artwork.

"It can be anything you want, Clara-bee," Emi answers. "But red would be pretty." Clara takes her advice and snaps the red crayon out of Jackie's hand.

"Hey!" Jackie says, grabbing it back. I start to step in but Emi kneels down next to Clara and talks to her, one-on-one.

"Clara," she begins, "that wasn't a nice thing to do to your friend. Say you're sorr–"

"But she has the red!" Clara pouts.

"We share the crayons," Emi reminds her. "Her flowers need red, too. You know, you could make the sash purple, instead," she suggests.

"I want red!" Clara whines.

"Well, you'll just have to wait, then," Emi says. "Why don't you color her shoes first?" Not a second later, I watch as my always-thoughtful niece breaks her red crayon in half and gives one of the pieces to Clara.

"Oh, now Jacqueline, you didn't have to break the crayon," Emi says. "Clara could have waited."

"But I don't want her to be sad," Jackie responds. "See, she's happy now!"

"Thank you, Jackie," Clara says, coloring her picture again.

"Yes, thank you, Jackie," Emi repeats.

"Hey, um, hey," Andy says, tugging on Emi's sleeve.

"It's Emi," I tell my nephew, startling Emi. "Her name is Emi, remember? We don't call people 'hey,'" I remind him. She looks up at me and smiles, her eyes locked on mine.

"Sorry, Uncle Jacks," he mumbles. "Emi?" he asks.

"Yes, Andrew," she answers, her attention shifting back to him.

"What color are Batman's boots?"

"Ummm..." She looks at me curiously. "Black?"

I nod.

"Black," she repeats. I sit down on the edge of the sofa behind Emi, inspecting their artwork.

"Maddie, what are you working on?" I ask my oldest niece.

"It's the solar system," she says, rolling her eyes.

"Is it?" I ask, looking at Emi curiously. Maddie hands me her drawing and I count the orbs on the picture.

"Seven... planets... Em?" I ask, laughing.

"Yes, seven," she states confidently, blushing, knowing she's wrong. "Maybe I took some artistic license..."

"Name them," I tell her, smiling.

"Earth, Saturn–"

"In order?"

"Alphabetical?" she challenges me.

"Distance from the sun."

"Mmmm..." she begins.

"Mercury," Maddie answers.

"I know Earth is third," Emi states.

"Earth, the third one, would that be the biggest planet on your drawing here?"

"Well, it *is* Earth," she says. "It's the biggest to me..."

"Just name what you can, then," I sigh.

"Mercury, Earth... Saturn... Venus, Mars... Uranus... Neptune. There. Seven."

"Jupiter, maybe?" I suggest. "The largest of the *nine* planets... and Pluto, the smallest."

"I thought they took that one out," she argues.

"Depends on who you believe, I guess," I tell her.

She shrugs her shoulders. "Science was not my forte. I did the best I could... I was running out of space."

"I think it's pretty," Maddie defends Emi, taking her paper back and continuing to color the planets she *did* draw.

"It's pretty," Emi says, satisfied, squinting her eyes at me. "That's what matters." She then crosses her arms, her brows furrowed, and sticks her tongue out at me.

"Do that again," I challenge her, moving closer, making sure all the kids are engaged in their artwork. She slowly sticks her tongue back out at me, unable to hide her smile, and I meet her with a kiss. "Are you having fun?" I ask.

"Tons," she whispers. "I think you have a family of artists. Jackie's sense of color is amazing... and Maddie has this thing with patterns... see how none of the planets have the same texture?

"And then Andy... you see, he has this wild style... lines be damn– oops," she says, covering her mouth, catching her slip-up. The children just continue to color and talk amongst themselves, oblivious to our conversation. "He'll be like Nate," she smiles. "He was never a fan of staying in the lines.

"I lost Brandon, though," she says. "He was down here for awhile. He can draw some menacing-looking creatures," she says of my teenaged nephew. "He's very good... draws better than me, by hand, for sure. But I guess he got bored."

"Well, the rest seem perfectly content," I comment.

"What have you guys been talking about outside?"

"Nothing in particular. Sports, weather, the loft, summer vacation..."

"What about the loft?" she asks, pulling herself onto the sofa next to me. "Why were you talking about the loft?"

"I was just telling Jen how nice it was having you stay with me, at the house, this week... I was kind of thinking... you know, maybe we should move in together."

Her face is expressionless as she stands up and takes my hand, leading me into the hallway. She stops, pushes me against the wall, and with her hand on my chest, she tells me she loves me.

"You know that, right?" she adds.

"Yes, of course."

"I can't give it up," she states, then puts her hand behind my neck and pulls my head toward hers for a kiss. I stare at her, my lips pursed, unmoving.

"Why not?" I say, teeth clenched, avoiding her kiss.

"It's my haven," she says. "The creative spirit is alive and well there. It's inspiring... artistically, you know?"

"Spirit," I murmur. "Interesting choice of words."

"What do you mean?" she asks.

"When I was there the other day... I just... felt him, there..."

"That's silly," she says. "Plus, I didn't think you believed in ghosts."

"I hadn't met any yet." I wait for her to respond, but continue when she doesn't. "Don't tell me you don't," I argue. "... feel him there, I mean. You can't even be intimate with me over there."

"Yes I can," she says. "We were."

"Once... and I'm not sure that counts."

"Of course it counts," she contends.

"Let's stay there tonight, then," I challenge her.

"Fine. I want to go home anyway."

"You do?"

"Yeah, I kind of do. I want to do things for myself. You've been waiting on me hand and foot for a week now."

"I'm so sorry, I didn't know it bothered you," I tell her, frustrated.

"It doesn't bother me, stop that," she says. "I don't like feeling helpless, that's all."

"Do you want to be alone, then?" I ask. "Would you rather go there alone?

"No," she sighs. "Not at all. Let's just reverse the roles. *I'll* take care of *you* tonight." Her seductive tone piques my attention.

"Really?" I whisper in her ear, then kiss her earlobe gently.

"Yes, really," she answers, her hand lingering on my belt buckle, then slipping to the front of my pants, slowly.

"Oh, god, sorry!" Anna says, shocked and turning around.

"Anna!" Emi yells, blushing, putting her hand in her pocket and taking a step away from me. "It's okay, come back!"

"No, no, I'll just go this way," she laughs.

"Anna..." Emi calls to her, and eventually her sister-in-law turns around. "What?"

"Well," Anna says sheepishly, staring at Emi, not looking me in the eye. "Kelly said that Clara could spend the night here, so Jen and Brian and Chris and I were going to go out to dinner in Manhattan... we just wanted to see if you two were in."

I run my hand through my hair, looking at Emi. "It's up to you."

"No, Anna, see, I have this headache..." she lies, and Anna knows.

"Sure you do. You don't look so good..."

"In fact, Jack, here, was just offering to take me home."

"I'm sure he was," Anna says, her cheeks now becoming red.

"Oh, don't judge me," Emi jokes with her. "I've been sunburned all week and–"

"Please! Say no more!" Anna pleads. "Go home. Have your 'headache.'" She walks toward us and hugs Emi. "Love you."

"You, too, Anna. I'll call you tomorrow?"

"Okay. Bye, Jack." She hugs me, too.

"Good night, Anna." We tell all the nieces and nephews goodbye before collecting our things and saying farewell to our siblings.

"Can you drop me off at the loft first?" Emi says as she closes the door to the Volvo. "I want to straighten up a bit before you come over... maybe you can go get our things and meet me a little later?"

"If you want," I tell her. "It looked fine to me, though."

"Just give me an hour and a half."

"Okay. What's on the agenda? Do you want to go out? Or stay in?"

"Let's play it by ear," she says. "We'll figure it out, okay?"

"Okay." After dropping Emi off at her loft, I slowly drive home, wondering what she's planning for the evening. Before gathering some things to take to her apartment, I decide to shower and change clothes. Unsure of whether or not we'll go out– or to where, if we do– I put on some pants and a nice button down shirt. After a short debate, I decide to add a tie, loosely tied around my neck.

I check off all the things I needed to bring... my overnight bag, Emi's computer, her clothes, book... I'm torn, conflicted, unsure, but decide to leave the small burgundy box behind, my mind made up.

"Would you like help carrying that up?" Marcus asks as I unload the bags from my car.

"No," I smile. "Thanks. I've got it." I hand him the key to the Volvo as he opens the lobby door for me and head toward the elevator.

"*Just come on in,*" Emi tells me in a text message.

I slowly open the door to her loft as a warm glow emanates from candles in the guest bedroom, now empty since Jen moved out. All the other lights are out. The moonlight peeks in from the windows in the main room. Music softly plays throughout the loft. I set down the bags on the kitchen table and close the door softly, locking it behind me.

She stands in the doorway of the second bedroom, the candlelight behind her creating a beautiful silhouette. She's wearing a strapless taupe satin dress covered in a thin layer of black lace that falls just below her knees with tall, black heels.

"Wow," I say, inhaling slowly. "So we're going out?"

She shakes her head.

"Staying in, then?"

She nods.

"You've never looked more beautiful."

She smiles softly, then turns around and enters the room. Her slow steps echo on the hardwood floors. I take it as my cue to follow her, which I gladly do. The music is slow and romantic.

"Will you dance with me?" she asks.

"Of course," I tell her, taking her in my arms, kissing her slowly. "This is different."

"Good," she says. "That's what I was going for."

"Harry Connick, Jr.," I comment.

"Yes," she says.

"This came out when I was in high school."

"Yeah," she laughs. "I was a little too young to appreciate it back then... *fully* appreciate it."

"You were what, twelve?"

"Thirteen," she corrects me.

"I do believe this song is a little too sexy for thirteen."

"Thank God I'm thirty-one," she smiles.

"Thank God, indeed," I whisper, kissing her cheek, ear. I rub her shoulders, feel the peeling, healing skin on her back. "Are you going to let me put some lotion on that tonight?"

"No," she states, adamant. "You're not allowed to do anything for me all night. That was the arrangement."

I inhale through gritted teeth. "All night?"

A blush sweeps across her cheeks. "Until midnight."

I check my watch. "Midnight, then... So, this room makes a nice dance floor," I laugh. "I guess that would be one advantage to keeping this place."

"I don't think I'm ready to leave yet," she says after a brief pause.

"Why not?" She's silent, contemplative. "What can this place give you that mine can't?"

"Aside from a dance floor?" she jests.

"I can build you a dance floor, Emi," I counter.

"I know. You could build me anything," she says.

"I could... I *would*."

"I know," she tells me as we continue to dance slowly. I pull her closer to me, wrapping my arm tighter around her waist. She puts her head on my chest, her hand caressing my biceps. "It's just, I don't know... I always felt more creative here... around him..."

"So you *do* feel his presence..."

"Ummm..." she hedges. "I wouldn't say that. But I don't know. It's all I have left of him, you know? He wanted me to have it... Donna was insistent on me taking it. I don't want to let them down." She looks up at me. "Let *her* down, I guess."

"I don't think she expects you to stay here forever."

"No, but still, it doesn't change the fact that I work better here."

"And you don't think we could create something like this in my house?" I question her.

"No," she answers. "I'm not sure that we could."

"Alright. Well, then, we keep this as your studio. Problem solved."

"I don't know," she wavers. "You know I work best at night... so I'd still be spending a lot of nights here."

"Hmmm," I murmur into her ear. "So you'll just stay here forever, then," I state, shrugging my shoulders, nodding my head.

"Not forever," she says. "I'll move out when there's a reason."

"A reason... like a commitment?" I laugh.

"Is that old-fashioned?" she asks. "I don't know. Maybe."

"Alright, we don't have to decide anything tonight." I kiss her again as the music breaks. I recognize the next song immediately when I hear the drumbeat intro. "Wow," I say, stopping our movement.

"What?"

"This song."

"What about it?"

"Well, maybe it's not a bad thing that you don't remember. It probably wouldn't remind you of me..."

"What do you mean?"

"This is the song that we danced to at the engagement party," I tell her, leaning back slightly to see her expression.

She raises her eyes to the ceiling, in thought. "I don't remember the song," she says shaking her head. "There are still details I don't remember from that night."

"Well, this was my favorite part of the night," I tell her.

She smiles and swallows hard.

"I'll change it. I don't want to upset you, Em," I say, starting toward the iPod.

"No," she stops me, pulling me back to her swiftly. "You'll dance with me," she says, taking me into her arms. "I don't remember it. I'm not upset about it."

"Are you sure?"

"Of course," she says. "Tell me why it was your favorite part."

"It's this part right here," I tell her softly in her ear, my head leaning down against hers. "Listen." I whisper over the words that come through the speakers, vowing my love to her just as Harry Connick, Jr. did to his muse in song.

"That's exactly how I felt," I tell her. "And Nate," I say cautiously, but she doesn't flinch, "he and I had a little stare-off while he played with his band, far away on that stage, and I held you in my arms, danced with you." It all seems a little bittersweet...

"Really?" she laughs.

"Really."

"Hmmm..." She looks up at me suddenly. "I love you, Jack." It's a statement, a reassurance.

"I know, Emi." We dance silently through the rest of the song. I remember the look we exchanged that night and smile to myself. I knew back then that there was something between us. I knew from our first kiss that she would be mine someday. I couldn't be happier.

Another song on the CD begins to play, undoubtedly the most romantic one on the album. I reach into my pocket, adjusting the small piece of metal on my thumb. I lock her hand into mine and, distracting her with a kiss, slip the ring on her delicate finger, closing my hand around hers in one swift movement, holding it firmly as she struggles to pull away, curious.

"Marry me, Emi," I whisper, my eyes piercing into her hers.

"What?" she looks at me, shocked.

I move the ring slightly on her finger. "Marry me."

She pulls her hand away, staring at it, at the large green stone on her finger. I study her reaction cautiously.

"I can get you a diamond ring, if you'd prefer it, but something about this ring said... Emi..."

"God, no, it's beautiful," she gasps. "I've never seen anything like it. Oh, my..."

I've clearly caught her by surprise. I smile as I read her changing expressions, my throat dry, my heart pounding harder than I thought it would, could.

"I have to sit down," she says, then realizing there is no furniture in the room, falls quickly but gracefully to her knees. I kneel on one leg in front of her, holding her hand to steady her shaking legs as she inspects the ring, touching the diamond butterfly.

"Emi," I tell her, "until I met you, I never really considered myself to be someone who could be swept away by love."

A tear drops quickly from her eye. She stares at me, speechless.

"But you were unlike any woman I had ever met... and the second I looked into your pale green eyes, and the moment I felt your lips on mine, I was doomed to a lifetime of not just wanting love... but wanting *your* love... and *only* your love."

"Oh, my god," she chokes out, her hand now shaking in my unsteady grasp. "Jack," she smiles, pulling my face to hers and kissing me.

"You said you'd be the happiest woman in the world the day you became my wife," I remind her. "I want to make you that. I want you to be the happiest woman in the world. I want you to be my wife.

"So, um... Emily Clara Hennigan," I clear my throat. "I have cherished every second that I've known you. I want to learn everything about you... and I never want to be without you... so marry me, Emi."

"Jack," she cries again.

"You've already said that," I laugh, impatient.

"Of course I'm the happiest woman in the world!" she exclaims.

"So yes?"

"Of course, yes," she says. I slide toward her, closing the gap between us, and cradle her head in my hands, teasing her lips with mine first, then returning for that second, deep kiss. Her tears continue to fall, begin to stream, and she sniffles quietly, but her lips don't leave mine. "I love you I love you I love you," she says quickly into my mouth with a soft giggle.

"I love you, Em," I return. "Your heart is racing."

"So is yours," she says, her hands on my neck, thumbs rubbing my earlobes gently as our kiss continues. Minutes pass as the song plays on until the end, my lips never leaving hers. Silence eventually takes over the room, the only remaining sounds coming from our passionate kiss.

"Thank you," I tell her.

"For?"

"For reminding me of what's important. I cannot wait to start our life together. I want to make love to you."

"Here?" she asks, eyeing the hardwood floor beneath us.

"I don't care where," I tell her, feeling the desire she must see in my eyes. "Wherever you want. I am yours."

"Not here," she says. "And not now."

"No?" *How can she not be as turned on as I am?* Her smile grows into a goofy grin, and I can't help but laugh. "What?"

"We're engaged!" I nod as my lips connect with her neck, move to her delicate shoulder, my kisses making a trail down her arm to her wrist, and finally settling on the finger that wears my promise to her.

"Hold on," she says, getting up and turning on the lights. As she looks at the ring, I stand up and cross the room to look at it with her. "It's so beautiful," she says. "Amazing... breathtaking..."

"So you do like it?"

"It's perfect," she says. "Absolutely perfect. Oh, Jack, thank you so much." I wipe the tears from her eyes and kiss her again. Suddenly full of energy, she quickly jumps up and down. "I have to call Anna," she says. "And Jen! I have to call Anna and Chris and Jen."

"One call, they're all together... call away," I laugh after a frustrated sigh escapes my lungs. "And your mom, Em." Seeing her this excited, this happy... everything is worth it. I would sacrifice anything to watch her in these moments, such a stark contrast to the sadness I've watched her live for too long. *I knew I could make her happy.*

"Wait, did you ask–"

"No," I tell her. "I didn't ask your parents' permission... a 'yes' from you is the only one I needed. But I told them I was going to ask you... and we have their blessing."

"I love you I love you I love you," she says again, still giddy. She pauses just long enough to kiss me once more. "Champagne," she says. "There's some in the fridge... we should have some."

"I'll get it. Go make your calls."

"No, wait," she says. "You're not supposed to do anything for me tonight, though! Not until midnight. What are you doing?" she whines.

"Call them, Em. We'll get back to that. I won't forget." She bites her bottom lip, smiling at me before running to her phone. As I pour the champagne, Emi climbs onto a barstool and hops up onto the island. Her legs kick, feet dangling as she talks to her family.

"Hold on," she says to Anna when I hand her a glass. "To us," she says, clinking my glass and kissing me before we both take a drink. The drink burns, but soothes my dry throat. I finish two glasses before Emi gets through half of hers. I hadn't expected to be so nervous. I text my siblings with the good news. I receive congratulatory messages from each of them within seconds.

"Have you told Mom and Dad?" Kelly adds. In truth, I haven't spoken to my parents in a few weeks. I had planned to call them after my trip to Europe, but I decided to put it off a little longer. Hearing my mother's disappointment at the news of Emi's inability to have children was about the last thing I wanted to hear. For years, she's been hoping I would find the right woman so we could start a family. She always said she knew I would be the perfect father. I just kept ignoring the nagging feeling, the necessity of calling her. Emi never asked what my parents' reaction was. I was grateful. I didn't want to lie, but I couldn't tell her the truth, either.

Quickly, I text my brothers and sister back. *"Don't say anything to Mom and Dad. I'll deliver the news."*

Kelly responds again. *"But you did tell them about Emi... right?"*

"Just don't say anything." I turn the phone off and shove it in my pocket. Emi looks at me, concerned, but just seeing her smile makes me forget everything else. She is all that matters. I pour another glass of champagne for me and top off her glass. After another drink, I stand in front of her. She moves her knees apart, allowing me to stand in between her legs as she talks to her sister. I slide her body into mine, her dress now hiked up to reveal the slightly tanned skin of her thighs.

My hands travel up her legs slowly, cautiously, my eyes never leaving hers. I push up against her gently, pulling her closer. The height of the island couldn't have been more perfect.

She struggles to pull the dress down to cover her skin and smiles. I shake my head, my hands thwarting her efforts. As she listens to the person on the other end of the phone, my lips are drawn to hers.

"Jen, I need to go," she says, taking a breath. "Bye." She puts the phone down quickly and holds my face to hers, kissing me deeply. "We're getting married," she tells me.

"Yes, we are... and I can't wait."

"Okay, time's up," Emi says. "Let me do something nice for you." I help her off the kitchen island, and she stands in front of me, holding both of my hands in hers, staring up at me. "What would you like?"

"I have what I want now, Emi," I tell her. "You're all I need."

"There has to be something else," she says.

"Of course, I'd like to make love to you."

"You would?" she asks coyly.

"I definitely would." She guides me to her bed and motions for me to sit down. Bending over to kiss me, she loosens the tie and takes it off completely, examining it for a second before folding it and putting it on the nightstand.

She kneels down in front of me and ceremoniously unbuttons my shirt, then untucks it. She removes my belt and sets it on the floor.

"Move back," she instructs me. I arrange myself on the billowing pillows and watch her every move. Standing up next to the bed, she puts her right foot on the edge and unbuckles her heel, removing her shoe. I run my hand up her calf muscle. She does the same with her left foot. "Now stay here," she orders me, walking to her dresser and taking something out of the top drawer. "I'll be right back."

While she's gone, I put my watch, phone and wallet on her night stand, crossing my ankles as I wonder what she is plotting. After a few minutes, the iPod starts playing her playlist from earlier, and as I look in the direction of her guest room, I catch sight of the most beautiful woman in the world: my *fiancée*... and soon she will be my *wife*. I'm sure she can hear my slow intake of breath as I drink her in with my eyes. I am not modest with my stare, but neither is she with her choice of clothing.

Her pale skin blushes against the light blue lace of her lingerie. The top has small sleeves that almost fall off her shoulders. It comes together at the front in a bow between her breasts, which are covered by the sheer fabric. The material hangs open loosely over her stomach, her firm stomach begging to be touched. A string bikini peeks out below the top. I hold my hand out to her, beckoning her to me. She smiles and takes my hand, crawling on the bed and kneeling over me.

"My god, Em, you are a vision tonight." I hold the material of the lingerie in my hands.

"Thank you," she says, her voice genuine. "This color reminded me of your eyes."

"Really? That outfit just reminds me of what I'd like to do to you..." She bites her bottom lip and bows her head bashfully. I lean up so I can kiss her, freeing her lip from her teeth.

"Not yet," she says as she looks into my eyes.

"No?" I tuck her hair behind her ears to have a better look.

She nods her head, pushing my dress shirt from my shoulders. "It's a foregone conclusion that we will be making love tonight. Now, what would you *really* like?"

"That's all," I tell her, shaking my head. I would never ask her... *is she suggesting that?*

"Really?" she asks as she pulls my undershirt over my head. I take the shirt from her and throw it to the end of the bed, studying her eyes intently as I nod. She pushes me back into the pillows, then slowly moves back until her knees are even with mine and begins to pull my slacks down my legs. I adjust my body to help her, leaning up on my elbows to watch her.

"Did you have something else in mind?" I ask, hopeful, but not too eager. She stands back off the bed to remove my pants entirely, then gets back on the bed on her hands and knees. Nodding her head, she crawls up my body– painfully slowly and sensually– until her lips press against mine, desperate, taking. I pull her hair lightly as she does the same to mine, leaning over me on her elbows. My hands move all the way down her back as I try to press her body against mine. She doesn't comply. "What?" I ask between kisses before she moves her lips to my jaw, then to my neck, not answering me. *You've got to be kidding me.*

Her body moves with her lips as she begins to kiss my chest... stomach... *lower*... abs... She grips the waistband of my briefs and pulls them down a few inches, covering the newly exposed skin with soft, fluttering kisses, her attention focused on each movement. I swallow hard as my breathing quickens in anticipation. She pulls the underwear down my legs and sets them on my shirt, finally looking into my eyes through her own eyelashes, blinking innocently. A sweet smile spreads across her face as I stare at her in awe.

"Now," she says again softly. "Are you going to tell me what you'd like?"

"Ummm..." I stammer, unable to answer before she leans over me and brushes her lips against me lightly. I feel her tongue next and grip the bed linens rigidly. I quickly inhale, overwhelmed by her touch, blurting out my response in one breath. "Emi, if you find that demeaning, you don't–"

"Demeaning?" she says, not looking up and not moving her lips far enough away to keep the vibrations from shooting wild impulses throughout my entire body.

"Oh, god," I exhale.

She pulls her lips away briefly to respond, but her hands glide unhurriedly over my lower abdomen. "What's *demeaning* about *this*? About a woman wanting to drive her fiancé crazy with desire for her?"

"Nothing," I answer quickly when our eyes meet. "Nothing at all."

"I like *this*," she declares. "In fact, I love *this*. I love that I do this to you." She touches me faintly– *god, more, please!*– shifting her focus away from my gaze once more.

"I love *you*." I release the sheets from my hand and run my fingers through her soft hair.

"I know you do," she replies playfully. "It's quite obvious."

CHAPTER 8

"She's in labor!" Emi yells happily through the phone. "Chris just called me. They're at Memorial."

"Would you like for me to come get you?"

"No," she says, "I'm in a cab already. Can you meet us at the hospital?"

"Of course. I'll be right there."

"Hey," she adds.

"Yes?"

"Can you stop and get some flowers for her?"

"Sure."

"Love you," she tells me.

"Love you, too."

After stopping by the florist, I quickly drive to the hospital. The nurses in the labor and delivery wing direct me to Anna's room. The door is closed, and Jen, Clara, Anna's mother and father, and all of Emi's parents are waiting outside.

"Has anyone seen Em?" I ask, a bit concerned, knowing she had plenty of time to get to the hospital.

"She's in the room with them. Anna wanted her there."

"Wow," I smile, greeting all of her family members with handshakes, hugs or kisses. "That's... surprising..."

"Emi was on top of the world," Jen says.

"Do they know how long it will be?" I ask.

"She's pushing... any time now," Emi's mother answers.

"Clara, how are you?" I ask Emi's niece.

"Good," she says, stretching her arms out for a hug.

"Are you excited to meet your cousin?"

"Yes!" she exclaims. "I can't wait to meet Eli!"

"She is full of energy," Jen says. Clara runs around the waiting area while the rest of us find seats and drink coffee. The families are nervous and anxious. "So, it's been two months, Jack," Jen smiles. "When are you two going to set a date?"

"We're working on it," I assure her... assure myself...

Eventually, the door opens and the doctor announces that it's a healthy baby boy, and that everyone is doing fine. He tells us that they'll be taking the baby down to the nursery soon so everyone can see him. A few minutes after he goes back into the room, Emi comes out, tears streaming down her face.

"What's wrong, baby?" her father asks. She walks past him, her eyes locked with mine, and nearly collapses in my arms.

"Oh, Em," I tell her, hugging her strongly as she seems to hold onto me for dear life. She sniffles softly in my shirt. I tilt her head up by her chin and smile, kissing her. "It's okay," I whisper, wiping away tears.

"I didn't know that would be so hard," she says.

"But was it amazing?" I ask, leading her to the corner of the room.

"It was," she smiles. "But to see Chris... and to think you'll never get to see that." She cries harder still.

"Shhh," I tell her. "Emi, it's okay, sweetie. I'm okay with that. Stop crying. Stop being sad. This is a happy day, remember? Eli's here. Your nephew is here and healthy... our godson."

She begins to calm down again as her mom and dad stand on either side of her, rubbing her arms.

"I'm okay," she says, breathing deeply. "He's so cute."

"Who does he look like?" her father asks.

"He has Anna's skin tone and hair. Chris's nose, I think. He's adorable."

A few minutes later, the doctor invites the parents in to see Anna and Chris. Shortly after, a nurse comes and lets us know that Eli is in the nursery. While her family takes turns going to see the baby, I take Emi to the cafeteria and get her a latte.

"What made you decide to go in there with Anna and Chris?" I ask.

"She asked if I wanted to be in there... so I could experience it with them... I was just so excited, I didn't even think. I was fine until I saw Chris crying." She swallows hard. "The way he looked at Eli... just pure awe and adoration. It was beautiful... and I thought about you... and then it hit me."

"Will it make you feel any better if I tell you I was in the room with Kelly when Jacqueline was born?"

"Really?"

"Yeah, Tom was on a business trip. Jackie came about two weeks early, and Kelly didn't want to do it alone. I was on standby for all the births... the back-up plan. But Jackie's is the only one Tom missed."

"Was that weird?"

"No," I laugh. "I stood away from the action and just coached Kelly through the breathing and pushing. And she nearly broke my hand, but that was fine. I did get to cut the cord, though."

"You did?"

"I did. That was pretty amazing."

"Still..." she says, sipping her drink.

"Still nothing," I say. "We'll have so many other moments to share, Em. And I remember how much pain Kelly was in. The thought of seeing you like that... well, that's one thing I won't really miss.

"Listen," I tell her. "Steven invited us out to talk to Renee. She works with some placement agencies and deals with pregnant teens all the time. I thought maybe you and I could take a trip down to Texas just to talk to her about options.

"Of course, we don't need to do anything now. Just figure out what the processes involved are. Just so we're better informed and kind of know where we need to start... how long it might take... those sort of things.

"I booked a flight for early September."

She doesn't respond. "Emi?"

"I'm going to go see Eli," she says as she stands and walks away from me. I stare after her for a few seconds, confused, but eventually follow her to meet our godson.

When we get home, Emi heads straight to the kitchen to pour herself a glass of wine. She hadn't spoken to me since we left the hospital, just stared out the window, her eyes glazed over and seemingly focused on nothing in particular.

"Did I say something?" I ask for the third time.

She doesn't seem angry... just distant. More distant than I've ever seen her. Her line of sight looks beyond me as I sit on a barstool in the kitchen.

She hops up onto the counter across from me and rocks back and forth, her arms crossed. "I'm not going to Texas," she says, still avoiding my curious stare.

"Is that what this is about?"

"Yes, that's what *this* is about."

"Okay," I start cautiously. "Can we talk about it?"

"Yes, Jack, and *thank* you for asking me." Her response drips with sarcasm, and she follows it with a long sip of wine.

"What's the matter? I thought you'd be happy about this..."

"Why?" she whispers. "I thought we agreed that children... just weren't an option."

"No," I tell her, taken aback. "We never agreed to that."

"In Tenerife," she reminds me. "You said I was enough." She swallows hard. "For you."

"Of course you are, Emi, but that doesn't mean I'm giving up hope of raising a family with you."

"You need to."

"What?"

"If you want to be with me, you need to." My heart stops beating. My breath, gone. I open my mouth, hoping some words will come out, but none can find their way. "We're not going to be parents," she says.

I can't believe what I'm hearing. "Yes, we are," I argue, raising my voice. "I'm not having this argument with you." I walk out of the kitchen and upstairs to the bedroom to change clothes.

"You wanted to talk about this," she says, following me into the closet. "So let's talk about it."

"I don't want to talk to you when you're not making any sense, Emi. What you're saying is ludicrous."

"Ludicrous, huh?"

"Yeah, Emi, it's complete nonsense. We will have kids if we want kids, and last time I checked, we were both on the same page with this."

She shakes her head slowly at me. "No, we're not."

I pull on a pair of sweatpants and stand up straight, unmoving, staring into her sad eyes, completely bewildered. My heart is about to pound out of my chest.

"Who said I wanted to go to Texas?"

"I thought we wanted to check out our options."

"*You!*" she yells. "*You* wanted to check out our options!"

"Why are you saying that?" I say softly, controlling the anger in my voice as best as I can.

"I never said I wanted to adopt. I've been thinking about it, Jack..." She picks at her fingernails, avoiding me. "I don't think–"

"God, don't do this to me, Emi. You can't do this to me." After putting on my running shoes, I walk briskly out of the closet, but she pulls me back in.

"What exactly am I doing to you?" she asks. "*I* can't have kids. This news is not new to you."

"We can't conceive children, Emi, but we can still have them."

"We can't," she hisses at me. "And what gives you the right to plan my life?"

"Wow... I'm not planning your life, Emi, I'm doing what we talked about doing!" I shake loose of her and start to go back downstairs to escape the conversation.

"Don't walk away from me!" she yells from the top of the stairs. I turn around, holding on to the railing to steady myself. "You're making decisions about what I want without consulting me! How is that not planning my *life*? How is that not trying to *control* me?"

"Are you *kidding* me? I'm *controlling*? I waited for four months for you to tell me when you were ready to commit to me. Four months! What man in their right mind would do that for any woman? My entire future hung in the balance, waiting for *you* to make the decision to move forward," I state furiously.

"That was a decision we made together. You agreed to that."

"I agreed to it because it was a condition I *had* to follow if I wanted to be with you. Period."

"Still," she says. "I gave you a choice. I even told you that you could date other women. You weren't trapped. And even then, once we decided to hang out more, you still made all the decisions... where we went, what we did... I didn't have a choice back then."

"You never acted like you wanted a choice. I was just trying to pull you out of that dark place you had been living in... I just wanted to distract you from that, to show you that your life could be better, even *good*, with me. I would have given you options if I had known you wanted them."

"I shouldn't have had to say anything," she says.

"My god," I sigh. "This all happened eight months ago, Emi!"

"No, it continues to happen to this day. We do everything you want, the way you want it. You meticulously planned both trips we've been on this year... you always decide on our dates–"

"You've never protested anything! How can you be mad at me for things I never knew I was doing wrong? When I met you, Emi, you were in a very bad place. You didn't have an opinion on anything. You could barely take care of yourself. All I've ever tried to do is take care of you, the best way I've known how. I have opinions when you don't. I make decisions when you can't... or won't. Don't hold that against me."

"I'm not that girl anymore," she says. "I have an opinion now. And I'm trying to tell you what it is. And instead of *listening* to me and *hearing me out*, you're shutting me down and just making assumptions about what I want–"

"You wanted *this*!"

"No, *you* wanted this! I *never* said I wanted this!"

"Emi, you *did*, we both want children. We've talked about this."

"Things have changed, Jack, or hadn't you noticed?"

"I'm not going through this shit again," I tell her, continuing down the stairs and opening the door. "What kind of fool am I?" I quietly mutter to myself.

"So you're leaving? Really? You're leaving me *now*?"

"I'm going for a run, Emi. I can't go through this again. I won't."

"You can't run away from this!" she calls to me as I walk out and close the door. I don't even walk ten paces before turning back around and going back into the house. She meets me in the foyer.

"When did things change? When did *this* change?"

"When I found out I couldn't have children!" she says loudly as she turns away from me and goes into the living room. Frustrated tears stream quickly down her cheeks as she sits in the leather chair.

"That doesn't make sense, Emi!" I walk over to her and grasp her by the shoulders, kneeling in front of her. "You don't *want* kids because you can't *have* them?"

"I'm not supposed to have them," she cries softly.

"What?" I ask her.

"I mean it," she says. "I'm obviously not meant to have children."

"Why would you think such a thing?" I ask her, taking a seat on the coffee table across from her, holding her small hands in mine.

"Because," she sobs.

"Because why, Emi?"

"Because he took her from me..."

"Who did?" I struggle to follow her thoughts. "Nate?"

"No. God."

"God?"

"Yes. He took away my baby and he took away my ability to have any more. I did something, somewhere, sometime... and I'm obviously being punished for it. He's obviously telling me I wouldn't make a good mother." She cries harder.

"My god, Emi," I squeeze her hands tightly, trying to get her to look at me. "You will make a wonderful mother. What happened to you was an accident. It wasn't divine intervention."

"How do you know?" she asks, weeping.

"Your child and your boyfriend were killed by a drunk driver... and you were hurt so badly by that accident that you can't carry a child. The poor decisions that stupid kid made that night did this to you. *God* did not do this to you."

"You can believe what you want. But I think He did."

"No, Emi, no. You can't believe that. Please, don't..."

"I don't understand why this is happening," she cries. "I thought when you came back to me that night that you were okay with it just being me and you. And now you're going back on that."

"Emi, I never abandoned the idea of us adopting children. You know I

230

want kids. Yes," I say to her, trying to be as convincing as possible, "you are enough for me. But there is no reason why we have to close the door on the possibility of having kids."

"There is if I'm going to be a horrible mom."

"You're not, damn it." I drop her hands in frustration and put my head in my hands, trying my best to stay composed. "You can't do this."

"I *am* doing this, Jack. If you want to be with me, you have to be okay with... just... me. Look at the signs. This is not meant to be."

"Don't give me this ultimatum now," I beg her. "I can't do this."

"It's the same thing I asked of you the night I told you. You had to decide if I was worth the sacrifice of the family you've envisioned. You came back to me."

"I came back to you because I knew there were solutions... that this situation was easily rectified. I don't care that you can't bare our children. But we can still raise children."

"No. Maybe you can, but I can't. Stop telling me what *I* can and can't do."

"But you *can*! God, Emi, stop being so stubborn!"

"I'm not stubborn," she argues. "I'm decided. It was decided for me. I am not meant to be a mother. And if you need a wife who is, you need to..." She sighs heavily. "You need to find someone else."

I shake my head at her and go into the kitchen, pulling out groceries to start making dinner. I refuse to continue this conversation with her.

"What are you doing?" she asks me, standing in the midst of the kitchen, her hands on her hips.

"I'm making us dinner," I mumble.

"I don't fucking *want* dinner!"

"God damn it, Emi!" I yell, carelessly throwing the knife I was using into the sink. "You don't want kids now. You don't want dinner. What *do* you want from me?" I lean over the island with an aggressive posture that she mirrors back to me.

"I want you to stop making all the decisions here!"

"What decisions have I made? We're having chicken tonight, is that okay?" I say loudly, sarcastic.

"As a matter of fact, no! I don't want chicken." She crosses her arms at me in defiance. "All I want is for you to try and understand where I'm coming from!"

"I can't understand. I don't want to understand. I won't. You have to realize how completely unreasonable you're being."

"*Me?* How is what I'm doing any different from what you're doing?"

"I'm exploring options. You're leaving us with none."

"You have options. Stay or go."

"What, stay in New York or go to Texas?" I know what she's saying to me. I don't want to hear it, turn around to face the sink to avoid seeing her mouth say the words.

"Stay with me, just the two of us... or go find someone else who can give you what you really want."

I bite my lip, incredulous, brimming with anger, hurt, betrayal.

"Alright, I'll cancel the trip to Texas, but I'm not giving up on the idea of adoption. I'll put it aside for now," I tell her, offering the best compromise I can make. I turn around abruptly to drive my next point home. "But I'll be *damned* if you think I'm going to walk away from this. Make *me* the bad guy. How's this?" I ask her forcefully. "You want to make decisions? This one is yours to make. If you want to leave... if you don't think this can work... it'll be your choice to walk away from what we have. I won't do it.

"But I'll tell you right now, Emi. You do that? You choose to leave me? It will be the last time. There will be no coming back. I have seen you walk away from me too many times. I have... *hurt*... too much for you already. And I have already lived this fight." A lump in my throat nearly destroys all my resolve. I swallow hard, afraid that she will decide to leave me. I don't know what I would do without her.

She stands across from me, still defiant, holding back more tears.

"It's your choice to make," I finish. "Take your time."

"I guess I have a lot to think about," she says quietly.

"I guess you do."

"I'm going home." She grabs her purse. "Goodbye, Jack."

Is this what it will feel like? "Goodbye."

A few hours later, I hear the phone ring as I'm crawling into bed.

"Hello?"

"I just wanted you to know that I love you," Emi says, her voice heavy with sadness. "I didn't want to go to sleep without you knowing that."

"I love you, too, Em."

"Good night."

"Good night."

~ * ~

A week later, I take Emi's hand into mine as we walk back from the subway station to my house. "You were really good with him tonight," I tell her with a smile. Chris and Anna had invited us to see Eli and have dinner, and we put on a good show, acting as the happy couple to Emi's brother and sister-in-law. They had outlined for us what we would be doing at the end of the month at our godson's christening.

"I don't want to talk about this tonight," she warns me, not angry, but clearly not happy, either.

"How much longer are you going to drag this out?" I ask.

"I'm not deciding on what color *shirt* to wear, Jack," she says sarcastically, letting go of my hand. Her following statement was much softer. "I don't know what to do."

"Well, just so you know, Anna only wants me to be Eli's godfather if we intend to be married, to set a good example for him. She told me when she asked me. We may need to come up with something soon."

She nods. "I know."

When we get back to the house, Emi lingers at the passenger door of my Volvo, holding onto the handle, waiting for me to unlock it... waiting for me to take her to her loft.

"Emi," I say to her, go to her, taking her into my arms and kissing her. Her eyes squeeze tight, tears finding their way out. "I'm going crazy without you."

"I know." Her kiss is desperate.

"I need you."

"I know," she repeats, her fingers entwined in my hair.

"Stay with me tonight. Please."

"I don't know what to do," she cries again. "I don't want to give you false hope."

"Are you really thinking you can walk away from this?" My hands cradle her face, lips touch hers once more.

"I don't know if I have a choice."

"You do. Emi, you do. Don't you love me?"

"You know I do."

"Then stay. Stay tonight. Stay forever."

"I can't."

"I don't think I can take you home," I tell her.

"I'll take the subway," she says. "But I can't stay. I would hope you'd respect that decision... and take me home."

"I won't." I shake my head, standing my ground.

"You can't control me," she whispers. "It's my life."

"It's *our* life," I correct her.

"No," she swallows. "It's mine." She turns toward the street and walks away, toward the subway.

I should have stopped her. I should have offered her a ride home. I should have done a million things in that moment to appease her, but as she inched further away from me, physically and emotionally, I realize it might be time I start to let her go.

She could have ripped my heart out with her bare hands, and it would have hurt less.

~ * ~

One evening a week and a half later, Chris stops by to drop off a few DVDs he had borrowed. I invite him in for a beer and a game of pool. Of course, I had ulterior motives. I hadn't seen Emi in over a week. It was like Europe all over again, with sparse text messages a few times a day. The only difference this time is that I was clued into the seemingly-impending breakup.

"So, what are Anna and Eli doing today without you?"

"You mean with Emi?"

"Yeah," I feign awareness.

"I think they were going to run some errands. Try to take Eli out in public for a test run," he laughs. "He's still crying when anyone other than me or Anna tries to get close to him. Emi's trying to break him of that."

"How is she doing today?" I ask. "With Eli, I mean."

"He was awake for a good 15 minutes before he realized she was holding him. Then he just wailed. Anna had to calm him down, but he finally fell asleep. Emi was rocking him when I left this morning."

How could she think God didn't want her to have children? It still seems unfathomable that she could believe such a thing.

"Is she okay?" Chris asks me. "I thought she seemed... I don't know... something... when she stopped by a few days ago. I didn't think anything of it, but Anna mentioned it to me after she left. That she thought something was wrong."

I was sure my attempt at a smile gave me away. "I think she's fine. We're just going through some things. It's fine."

"What's up?"

"Really, it's nothing," I lie. In one of the few texts she sent me, she had asked me to keep this between us. I had given her my word. I had already said too much.

"You know now I'm just going to ask her."

"Well, that would probably be best." My smile has faded by now, the stress of the fight, of our distance, wearing on me. "And then you can let me know," I murmur, shaking my head. "Just ignore me. Of course I don't want you in the middle of this."

"Middle of what? Come on, I'm in it now."

"She's gotten it in her head that God doesn't want her to be a mother," I scoff. "So she's written off any future of children."

"What?"

"Yeah."

"That's the craziest thing I've ever heard." I nod in agreement.

"Your sister is not always practical, and she's not always open to listening to reason," I tell him, knowing he recognizes this. "This could be it," I add with a sigh, defeated, shrugging my shoulders, unable to keep my eyes from watering. "She's put out this ultimatum... I have to be willing to let go of my hopes for kids if I want to stay with her. It's... just... bullshit. I can't do that. I won't."

"Man, Jack, I'm sorry. I had no idea. You've got to talk some sense into her. You can't let her walk away. You're the best thing that's happened to her in... well, maybe ever."

"I know. She's not listening... and she asked me not to say anything. But I honestly just can't keep this to myself any longer. It's killing me."

"What are you going to do?"

"It's not up to me," I tell him. "I told her I wouldn't leave her... but that I wasn't going to give up on building a family of our own, either. I told her this choice had to be hers."

"Let me try to talk to her," he offers.

"No. I don't want her to feel pressured. I need to know that this is her decision, and her decision alone."

"What, did you two divide and conquer today?" Emi asks Chris, startling us in the basement. "The door was unlocked," she says to me. She walks over to her brother and hugs him lightly.

"Jack," she forces a smile.

"Emi," I smile back. "We were just–"

"Talking about me, I know," she says.

"I'm sorry," I tell her.

"Chris, can you excuse us? Anna mentioned you were going to bring her dinner." Her tone is direct and commanding, her posture confident.

"Of course, Emi," he says, waving briefly at me on his way out. "But listen, you were great with Eli... you're great with kids, Emi."

"Chris, don't." He nods and walks upstairs.

Her presence demands my full attention. She pushes the billiard balls to the other side of the table and pulls herself up on it, crossing her legs and clasping her hands under her chin.

"They were working us, you know," she says. "Chris and Anna. She sent him over to talk to you. I came as soon as I found out."

"He already knew?"

"Yeah. I told Anna in confidence... but she told him."

"And what was her take?"

"I don't know," she says. "Like you, I wanted this to be my decision. I need it to be."

"So you've made it?"

"I don't know. That's why I'm here."

"Okay," I say, sitting down on a folding chair in the corner. "What can I do?"

"There has to be a middle ground," she says. "You're going to have to meet me half-way on this."

"And where exactly is half-way on an issue of kids or no kids? It seems pretty black and white to me."

237

"I need you to work with me here. I'm going to need a little faith. I don't have a decision yet... but I'm trying desperately. What's stopping me is that I know what I want the decision to be... and I can't reconcile everything to get there yet."

"What do you want it to be?"

"Of course, I want us to stay together."

I let out a loud sigh of relief. "What do I have to do?"

"It's simple really."

"Okay."

"I just need for you to explore the possibility of no children."

"And what will you be doing?"

"Exploring the possibility of adopting them."

"I have to be honest, after the past few weeks, I'd much rather explore the possibility of no children then the possibility of no... *you*. But Emi, I just don't think it's reasonable to ask me to do that."

"But can you?"

"I don't guess I have a choice."

"I don't feel like I do, either." She's silent before speaking again, softly. "I went ahead and re-booked the flight to Texas."

"We don't have to do that now, yet..."

"I don't want to put it off."

"Okay, fair enough. What brought all this on?"

"Well, I was with Anna today. And all of a sudden, she had some interior design emergency, and she needed to leave. And thank God, Anni-Emi was already there to watch Eli. She abandoned me with him. It nearly killed her to be away from him, but she did it... she made up this elaborate story... for me..."

"And how did that go?"

"Well, he lived." I laugh lightly and smile at her encouragingly. "And he didn't cry once while Anna was gone. He took a bottle from me. He let me rock him to sleep. I changed him." Her smile is serene as she talks about her day. "I even think I made him smile... maybe I imagined it."

"I doubt it," I assure her. "You do that to people." We stare at each other, sharing a long pause.

She tucks her knees into her body and wraps her arms around her legs, resting her chin on her knees. She cocks her head slightly. "I don't know how this is going to turn out," she admits. "But we have to try."

"Yeah," I agree. Even though nothing is truly resolved, I feel as if a weight has been lifted. I have a modicum of hope for us, at least.

"I know this doesn't fix us," she says, "but I was wondering if we could take a night off from this."

"From what?"

"Our differences. Everything that's been keeping us apart."

"Of course," I tell her, crossing the room to go to her and taking one of her hands into mine. "What did you have in mind?"

"I need to know that you still trust me," she says quietly.

"I do." Our gazes meet, and silently, without words, she communicates to me what she needs. "Okay." I squeeze her hand.

She slides off the pool table and leads me out of the room, up the stairs to my bedroom. "You look so tired," she says as she removes my shirt. Her hand grazes my chin before sliding down my chest.

"Sleeping has been difficult with the uncerta–" She interrupts me, placing her index finger over my mouth. She shakes her head. Her hand grips the back of my neck and she pulls my lips to hers.

I let her set the pace, watch as the balance of power shifts to her, allow her to take control. I don't make any moves without her consent. Never has she been so uninhibited with me, and never have I used such self-restraint with any woman. I surrender myself to her every request and ask for nothing in return; but Emi, never one to be selfish, orchestrates a night that leaves neither of us wanting for anything, except more of each other.

~ * ~

I had hoped that our night together would be exactly what we needed to begin to move forward again. Each day that passed, though, a little more distance– a little more tension– would set in. I was so optimistic that things would change, that she would make up her mind once and for all. We were completely in sync that night, and now, we still seem to be hovering somewhere in between a few paces off and complete discord.

But at least we're trying... and today, Emi's *really* trying.

I knock quietly on her door, my eyes fixed midway down the hallway until she answers. "You could have used your key," she says as she opens the door. The tension is still there, but her smile is genuine.

"I'm sorry," I tell her. "I will next time." *I won't until we get past this.* We had the same greeting the last two times I came over, too. "Come on, kids, let's stop playing with the elevator!" My nieces and youngest nephew squeal and run down the hallway toward me, and eventually into Emi's apartment.

"Clara!" Maddie and Jackie yell when they see their friend. Emi grabs them both for hugs on the way in. Andrew hangs back, clinging to my leg, making it difficult to walk.

Emi's smile grows. "Thank God you got yours to wear sensible clothes," she says, eyeing her niece, wearing shorts and a short-sleeved shirt. "I'm such a horrible role model for this one," she says, turning her back to me.

"No, Emi, you're not."

"I was joking," she says, a little strained.

"Okay," I respond nervously. I can't seem to read her anymore. I don't know when it's okay to laugh and when it's not.

"I don't know why Jen even included this as an option. It's way too chilly for shorts."

"Look, Clara," she says energetically, turning her attention back to her niece. "Maddie and Jackie have on jeans and jackets. Let's go put yours on!" Clara stares at the purple hoodie that her aunt dangles in front of her, her eyes defiant but her smile playful.

"That's pretty," Maddie tells Clara, old enough to know how to get the younger ones to do what you want them to do, having seen my sister plead and bargain with Jackie many times over the years. Clara nods, and I give Emi a thumbs up, patting my oldest niece on the back. Emi takes Clara into the guest room to help her change clothes.

Andrew tugs on my pants and lifts his arms up to me. I often wish that his brother was closer in age to him. Ten years was just too much for them to have a good brotherly relationship at this point in their lives. I just remember how much my brothers and I influenced each other as kids. My youngest nephew spends most of the time with the girls and their friends. He was so shy and so emotional... and utterly sweet.

I pick him up and kiss him on the cheek.

"My god," Emi says when she comes back into the living room. "He looks more and more like you every time." Andrew definitely has a lot of my features, and is often mistaken for my son when we are out together. "How are you, little Andy?" she asks him, her voice lilting. She tickles his stomach and he giggles wildly.

He tucks his head into my neck. "Are you sure you're ready for this?" I ask her, still unsure of her decision to get all the little ones together for a picnic. I knew they'd be a handful. I half-wondered if she was doing this in an attempt to overwhelm *me*, convince *me* that we shouldn't have kids, but I'd had years to get used to four little ones. I was a pro.

"Yep," she says, putting on her own jacket and scarf. I take the picnic basket from her as she carries the blanket out the door.

Emi lays down the ground rules as I spread the blanket down on the lawn. "Okay, see that tree right there? The one by the squirrel? And then that one over there where the flowers are? You guys need to stay between those, okay?"

"Okay," they all say in unison, picking up the balls we had brought along and running to an open space. She sits down next to me.

"How was your day?" I ask her, leaning in for the kiss I never got while we were in her loft. It's a quick peck on the lips.

"Good," she shrugs. "Yours?"

"Good. Maddie's team won her soccer game, so we all went for ice cream to celebrate. And then Thomas and Kelly couldn't wait to pack everything up and hand them off to me. Brandon's camping this weekend, so they'll have a rare night to themselves."

"Oh, they're staying with you?" Emi asks as Andrew comes to sit behind us, playing quietly with his Batman figure.

"Yeah, we're going to have a movie night."

"Oh."

"Why?" I ask her. "Did you want to come over?"

"I don't know. I was thinking about it."

"You can. Don't let them deter you, I'm sure I could use a hand."

"No," she shakes her head.

"Okay." I don't pressure her.

Her eyes dart around the lawn surrounding us. Abruptly, she stands up, going quickly toward the girls. "Shit, where is Andrew?" she calls out to me, frantic.

"He's right here, Em," I tell her loudly. "It's okay. He's just playing back here."

"My god," she sighs. "I thought he..." She walks back to the blanket and sits down, putting her head in her hands.

"Shit," Andrew says with a giggle.

"Shit," Emi mumbles under her breath.

"Andrew," I scold my nephew. "You know that word is bad. We don't say that word."

"Shit!" he repeats, louder.

"Andrew," my voice is more stern and I turn to face him, pick up his chin so he looks me in the eyes. "No."

"Sorry, Uncle Jacks," he says, jutting out his bottom lip.

"It's okay. Emi," I turn my attention to her. "We don't say that word," I tell her with a smile. "That's a bad word."

"Sorry, Uncle Jacks," she copies my nephew. "See, I'm not cut out for this."

I laugh, but realize quickly this was not the right time for laughter after seeing her glare. "Emi. Seriously? You cussed. He's heard that word a hundred times from his dad."

"Not only that," she looks away. "I can't even keep up with one of them." I can't help but roll my eyes.

"Sure you can, Emi, you're keeping up with the other three." It was meant to be a joke.

"That's not enough," she barks at me. "Hey, Kelly," she mock-converses with my sister. "I lost one of them, but the other two made it back safely."

"Emi," I groan. "Don't be so hard on yourself. This whole parenting thing is better done in pairs. And hey," I wave at her, "I'm here. We could do this, together."

"I don't know," she sighs.

"This is not something you learn overnight," I explain. "What did you expect? We were responsible for *no* children yesterday. We just picked up four today. Okay, so I would recommend us not adopting quadruplets right off the bat."

She sighs, her attention fixed on the girls. I move to the space on the blanket behind her and begin to massage her shoulders. "Relax."

"I don't want to talk about it."

"We don't have to. Let's just enjoy the afternoon and give the kids some good memories of their aunt and uncle." She nods and leans back into my arms. I kiss her cheek as Andrew climbs into her lap.

"Hey, little man," she smiles, hugging him close. "You stay where I can see you, okay?" He nods vigorously, then kisses her cheek, the same one he saw me kiss moments before. "Oh," she quietly exclaims. "You are so sweet." She returns the kiss as he turns his attention back to his action figure.

"What about me?" I ask.

Her dimples show up for the first time in weeks as she pulls my face to hers and kisses my cheek. "You're pretty sweet, too," she whispers. "Another trait he must get from you."

After eating our sandwiches and cookies, the kids all collapse on the blanket around us as the sun begins to set. Their energy spent, they wind down by pointing out shapes in the clouds overhead.

"Thanks for this," I tell her.

"You're welcome," she says back to me.

"Alright, kiddos," I announce. "Let's get all your toys together and head home." We gather up our things and begin the walk back to Emi's loft.

"Okay, guys," Emi adds. "Is everyone holding someone's hand?"

"I don't have one," Maddie says, taking Emi's free hand. She looks up and smiles. "Emi?"

"Yes?"

"Are you going to be our aunt someday?"

She leans down and whispers in her ear. I strain to hear her answer. "I really hope so," she says.

"Me, too," Maddie responds. Emi smiles the rest of the way home, skipping with our nieces through the lobby of her building.

After helping to put everything away, I peek in to the guest bedroom and tell the girls it's time to go. I hug Clara goodbye before retrieving my nephew from Emi's bed, where he had fallen asleep seconds after we got home. He doesn't even wake up, just lays his head on my shoulder.

"I don't think he'll make it through the movie," Emi says.

"He rarely does," I tell her in a hushed voice. "I had a great time today, Emi. And for the record, I think you were great with them."

Her smile is small, but it's a smile nonetheless. "I did figure out one thing today."

"What is that?"

"I think four is too many."

I nod my head. "Fair enough."

"Bye, girls," Emi says softly, kissing them each on the forehead. "Bye, boys." She tenderly squeezes Andrew's limp arm, then touches my jaw, pulling me in for a proper kiss. Brush of the lips, deeper. I lose my breath, having missed the familiar exchange.

"Goodbye, love. Pick you up Sunday morning at eight?"

"Chris and Anna said we needed to be there at eight, right?"

"Right. Seven-thirty, then?"

"Seven-thirty. Love you."

"Love you, too, Poppet," I tell her, brushing her nose lightly with the tip of my finger.

~ * ~

After the christening ceremony, Emi touches her nephew's pink cheek softly. "You did so well," she whispers to Eli. He's bundled up in her arms, wrapped tightly in a white blanket. His lashes are still matted together from crying, but he is sound asleep, comforted by the sound of her voice. "Wanna hold him?"

"He seems pretty content there. I don't want to wake him." I hope she can't hear the frustration in my voice.

"Okay," she smiles. "I'll keep him."

Chris and Anna bounce around, talking to all the family members and friends who came to Eli's ceremony. Chris eventually comes to us with Donna following closely behind.

"Emi, sweetie, how are you doing?"

"I'm great," Emi says. "Would you like to hold Eli?"

"Would you mind?" she asks.

"Elliott Nathaniel," she whispers to the baby, "this is Nate's mom." Donna extends her arms to take the baby. It was important to Chris and Emi for Eli to learn about Nate, his namesake.

"He is so beautiful," Donna says. Emi strokes his face, and Donna sees Emi's engagement ring for the first time. She quickly glances up at Emi, eyebrows raised, a smile breaking across her face. "Emi?"

Emi's face flushes red, her eyes a little uncertain. "We're engaged," she tells Donna. "Jack proposed at the end of May."

"Oh," Donna says, her eyes filling with tears. "We've talked many times since May, Emily. Why didn't you mention it?"

"I, uh..." She hesitates as I look at her curiously, my heart falling. "I didn't know how..."

"Oh, Emi," she laughs. "Don't be silly! I'm so happy for you. Jack," she addresses me, "congratulations. You are a lucky man."

"I already know," I tell her. "Thank you. That means a lot." My eyes wander around the room.

"I'd hug you," she adds, "but I don't want to let go of this precious little boy." Eli opens his weary eyes and wrinkles his face up, a loud wail escaping his lips. "On second thought, it's been awhile since I've dealt with this," Donna says, handing the baby back to Emi. "I'm very out of practice."

"I'll be right back. I think he's probably hungry... I think." She smiles and shrugs, leaving Donna and I alone. She holds out her arms for a hug. I smile wearily, suddenly uneasy.

"You know," she begins, "I think of Emi as a daughter. I always have... even before she and Nate began dating."

"I will take care of her," I assure Nate's mother.

"I'm sure you will," she says. "You have always been such a gentleman, and she seems so taken with you. So happy with you. I worried about her, that she'd never recover... but she's come so far."

"She has. But he'll always be a part of her life. I could never take his place."

"No," she smiles. "He was my baby. But I think you're wonderful for her. You compliment one another. You know, Nate and Em were so alike. They both made bad decisions... both lacked a little common sense. Both so creative. They had a different relationship. They were such good... friends. Their relationship was based on that... I mean, don't get me wrong, I know they loved each other...

"But what I see between you, it's just different. I know you're friends, you have to be, but I see such adoration in her eyes, in your eyes... it's clear that love is your foundation. It's a beautiful thing."

"Thank you," I tell her. "Like you said, I'm very lucky."

"Not to be nosy," Donna hedges, "but have you two moved in together yet?"

"No," I answer, nervous of any questions that may follow and the answers I don't really have. At least four of Emi's family members had already started in on this line of questioning today, which only heightened my anxiety about our ambiguous future. "I don't think she's ready to give up the loft yet."

"Really?"

"Really. I have a comfortable townhouse that I've asked her to move into with me. I told her we could make any changes she needed, add a studio, whatever, but she's insistent on staying there for now, until we get married. I mean, eventually, I hope we'll make my house our home... when she's ready."

"You know," Donna interrupts my contemplative silence, "the loft is Emi's, to do with it what she wants... but I'd like to know if she is going to sell it. I might know a good buyer."

"Of course," I assure her, as an uncomfortable pause spreads between us.

Breaking the silence, Donna asks, "So, when is the happy day?"

"Oh, um," I look at her questioningly. "Oh, the wedding date?" I feel my face heat up.

"Yes, the wedding date," she laughs.

"Um..." I stall. "We haven't decided on one yet."

Maybe never? Truth be told, Emi's answer when I approached the subject before our current struggle was simply that she would ponder it and get back to me. She always said it, playfulness coating every word, and it never occurred to me– until the past month– that she might be procrastinating for other reasons entirely. We *have* been engaged for three months now, and no decisions have been made. Everything's been put on hold. And now, talking to Nate's mom, I grow even more insecure. Seeing her helps me put two and two together. It seems obvious now.

"What's keeping you? If you don't mind me asking."

"Oh, no, I don't mind at all." My brows furrow as I clear my throat. *Well, this month, it's the fact that she doesn't want to have children anymore. Before that...*

"We're still debating the pros and cons of a big wedding versus something simple... private. There's a lot to consider, I guess."

What was it before she admitted her feelings to me? *Maybe Emi doesn't want to let go of your son just yet.* I sigh audibly, the weight of that realization crushing my lungs.

"Well if you decide on a big wedding, I hope you wouldn't feel uncomfortable inviting me," she suggests.

"Of course we would invite you," I assure her.

"Well, Jackson," she says, adjusting her handbag and smiling warmly. "It was good to see you. And congratulations to you both. Please keep me posted about the loft."

"I will, Donna, you have my word."

"Have a good night."

"Thank you, you too." *I think any hopes for a good night just ended about two minutes ago.*

Across the room, Emi and Chris are playing a game of keep-away with Clara's stuffed animal. Jen stands close by and reprimands her daughter when her squeals get too loud, but Emi and her brother can't stop laughing.

My hands in my pockets, I quietly make my way to the exit of the church foyer and go outside. The air is crisp, the onset of autumn obvious with the beautiful orange and red leaves in the trees.

Could she really be stalling for other reasons, too? From day one, she wouldn't nail anything down. Is she really not... *over him?*

I hate that I'm doubting her... but how can I not? She refuses to move in with me. She won't commit to a date. She doesn't want to raise children with me. *Is* this marriage going to happen? Or am I really just a placeholder for someone else... someone that she possibly did– does– love more? Someone that she was "meant to" have children with?

I walk over to the church playground and climb a few steps up the dome-shaped jungle gym. The sun burns brightly without a cloud in the sky, prompting me to remove my jacket and roll up my sleeves a little. I take out my wallet and look closely at the picture that we took of ourselves in Colorado... the second shot, the shot where Emi surprised me with a kiss on the cheek.

I was so certain of her feelings for me back then. I defended them vehemently to my doubting brother, and now, I'm not so certain she wants to marry me after all. Maybe she just needs a little time to adjust to the idea. I can give her more time. I always do.

A cousin of Emi's comes out with his son, probably around three-years-old. I remember meeting him at Chris's wedding, but I'm not certain he remembers me. If he does, he gives me no sign that he does. He puts the young child at the top of the slide, and, standing to the side, carefully pulls him all the way down, picking him up and swinging him around when they reach the bottom. The little boy giggles wildly every time his dad lifts him into the air. He repeats this multiple times, and although I try to distract myself, I can't pry my eyes away. *I want that.*

I'm so caught up in their merriment that I don't even realize Emi has joined me outside. She kicks her shoes off before climbing up to me. She settles herself on my jacket, facing inward, looking up curiously at me.

"Hey, Godfather," she smiles, taking my left hand and kissing my knuckle. "You just need a ring."

I struggle to laugh. "I'm working on that," I mumble.

"What's wrong?" she asks, her head propped on her fists, elbows resting on the bar in front of her. The glare from the setting sun makes her squint, makes her pale green eyes look even paler, more beautiful.

"Not feeling well," I lie. "I think it must be something I ate."

"Really? Can I get you something?"

"No, I think I'm just going to go home."

"Would you like me to come with you?" she smiles, concerned. "I'll take care of you."

"Actually, Em," I begin, "I'd rather go alone, if that's alright."

"Oh," she says, looking surprised. "Okay. I can get a ride to my place with Chris and Anna, that's fine."

"You don't mind?"

"No... are you sure I can't do anything for you?"

Agree to adoption. Move in with me. Set a date. Commit to me already! Erase my doubts. Tell me you love me more than you loved him. "I'm sure."

"Okay," she smiles. "Let me at least help you to the car."

"I'm fine, Emi," I tell her. "Just go back inside with your family."

I climb off the metal bars and help her down and back into her shoes.

"Are you sure you're just not feeling well, Jack?" she asks, confused.

"Yes," I say, sounding a little annoyed. She crinkles her eyebrows together and looks at me thoughtfully.

"I love you," she says. Staring into her eyes, I search for truth, or doubt. I'm not sure what I see. "Will you call me later and let me know how you're feeling?"

"Sure thing, Em," I sigh. "Talk to you later." I kiss her on the forehead before walking to my car. Before I drive off, I notice she's still standing at the jungle gym, watching me. She barely lifts her hand to wave goodbye.

An unfamiliar car sits in the street in front of my house when I get home. I pull into the driveway and try to see who is sitting in the driver's seat. Not recognizing the woman, I step out of the car and make my way to the front door.

"Jack," a voice calls out from behind me. I stop dead in my tracks as I recognize the voice, confident and feminine.

"Caroline?" I ask, turning around. My ex-fiancée, dressed in tailored pants and a fitted blouse, walks toward me, closing her car door tentatively. She looks more attractive than I remember her, her hair perfectly styled in neat curls, her lipstick blood-red. "What are you doing here?"

"So you do still live here," she smiles. "How are you, Jack?"

"I'm good," I tell her, surprised. "What brings you over here?"

"I was just in the neighborhood," she says, "and I thought I'd see how the house looked. I didn't expect you to still be living here. It looks great."

"Yeah," I say, running my hand through my hair nervously. "Not much has changed," I laugh. We stand awkwardly on the front steps. "Um, did you want to come in?"

"I wouldn't be intruding?" she asks.

"No," I tell her, unlocking the door and holding it open for her. "Come in." She pauses in the foyer as I close and lock the door. I remove my jacket and lay it casually on the back of the couch.

"It really hasn't changed," she laughs, looking around. She walks over to the bookshelf that holds all of my family's pictures. "Wow, look how the kids have grown, though," she says, picking up a group shot of me and Kelly's children from last winter. She either misses or ignores a shot of Emi and me taken at Chris's wedding.

"Yeah, they have," I agree.

"Where were you coming from?" she asks. "You look nice."

"I was at a christening. I'm a godfather," I smile.

"Well, congratulations," she laughs.

"Thanks... do you want to sit down?" I ask her, offering her a seat on the couch.

"Sure, thank you, Jacks." *Jacks.* Her voice is sweet, almost too sweet.

"So, how have you been? What are you doing these days?"

"I still work for the same company," she says, smiling. "I made partner last year."

"That's great, do you still enjoy it?"

"I guess," she says with hesitation. "It's not as fulfilling as it once was,"

251

she adds. "But it's a pretty good job, I guess."

"That's good, I'm glad to hear it."

"You?"

"Still consulting. I spent three weeks in Europe with a new client this spring."

"And how is your family?"

"They're great."

"Do they still hate me?"

"They never hated you, Caroline," I correct her. "Break-ups are just part of life. We had different wants. They understood." I have no doubt that if Emi makes the same decision Caroline did, they would never forgive her. They know how Emi completes my life; how she is my whole world.

"That's a relief," she says. "I always worried about that."

"Well, there was no need."

"I'm a little parched," Caroline says, clutching her throat.

"Oh, excuse me, I'm sorry," I laugh, embarrassed. "Of course, would you like something to drink?"

"A glass of water would be fine," she answers. As I get up to go into the kitchen, she adds, "or maybe a glass of wine, do you have any on hand?"

"Sure," I tell her. "Just a second." While I'm in the kitchen, I hear her turn on my stereo and tune it to a jazz station.

Why is she here? Just in the neighborhood? Really?

I glance at the wine rack and notice it's empty.

"I need to go get some wine from the basement," I tell her on my way through the room. "Just make yourself at home. White or red?"

"Red," she says.

I always wondered how I would react when I saw her again. It had been about three years since we last saw each other. We met at a coffee shop to exchange the last of our personal belongings. It was awkward, at best.

At the time, I was just angry with her. I still had feelings for her, still loved her, but felt as if she had strung me along for years, making me believe we wanted the same things. I was disappointed– no, crushed– when she decided to leave.

It took a long time for me to really see the light, for me to accept that we really weren't meant to be together. Emi was always just a fantasy. Caroline was real. Caroline was who I was ready to settle down with... to *settle* with. Even before I met her, I had long ago accepted that romantic love was just a fabrication made for children's books. We had an arrangement, an agreement of sorts. I cared about her. Loved her. But maybe I wasn't *in love* with her. It would have worked, somehow. At least that's what I had convinced myself to believe.

It's definitely strange to see her, to have her here in my house– *our* house. The memories rush back, flood me with feelings I hadn't remembered for years... the fight we had in the girl's room, still decorated the same way it was when I first showed it to her... the passionate tears she wept as she ran up the stairs to the main level... the make-up sex we had later that night on the couch, the very couch she sits on upstairs, waiting for me. I sit down for a few minutes to catch my breath and clear my head.

Why *today*, of all days?

I find a bottle of Emi's favorite wine downstairs. It's the only red I have on hand... I debate telling Caroline I'm out of red, and offering her a white, but it's just wine. It's not like I'm betraying Emi.

"Everything okay?" she asks as I ascend the stairs from the basement and walk into the kitchen.

"Fine, yes," I tell her, grabbing a corkscrew and two glasses and heading back into the living room. I open the bottle and pour the wine into the glasses, then set the bottle next to my phone on the coffee table at the exact moment a text message from Emi pops up. I shove the phone into my shirt pocket without checking it.

"To old friends," Caroline says, lifting her glass.

"Old friends," I agree, taking a sip. "So, what brought you to the old neighborhood?"

She laughs nervously, taking a drink. "Okay, you got me. I was hoping to see you," she admits.

"What for?" I ask.

"Well, Jacks," she says, brushing my hand lightly with hers. "My priorities have changed."

I swallow audibly, nearly choking out the wine I had just sipped. "Meaning?"

"I wasn't ready then, Jacks," she says, looking deeply into my eyes for encouragement. "I didn't think I would ever want children. That's why I left."

"You don't need to remind me," I explain.

"I know, but if I had ever thought that someday I would want to be a mother, I would have stayed with you. You're going to make a great father... and husband."

"Yes, I know," I tell her, short, feeling my nostrils flare.

"I want that now. I'm ready. And I'm so sorry, Jacks, for not realizing this years ago." I set down my glass, folding my hands in my lap and looking down at the carpet. *Why now?*

"Caroline, I–"

"Just hear me out, Jacks, sweetie, okay?" *Sweetie?* "I never stopped loving you, Jacks. All these years, I haven't even dated anyone. I know you're the perfect man for me, you are. I've always known that... you were always who I wanted, but I know I wasn't what you wanted back then. I know you wanted someone to be the mother to your children, and I can be that now."

"Caroline," I attempt again.

"Wait, Jacks. I am ready to give you everything you ever wanted. I love you, still. We can pick up where we left off, or if you want to start fresh, we can do that, too. We can do this on your terms... if you want."

"But–" This time, she cuts me off by crushing my lips with hers. As she grips onto my neck, I push her back gently, not wanting to hurt her ego.

"Jacks," she continues, not willing to give up. "Remember that night, on this sofa? Wasn't that the most amazing night? You made love to me right here," she says, patting the cushion, leaning back, looking at me through hooded eyes. "You said it was the best sex of your life. Remember?"

The sex that night had been fueled by our fight, by our hurt feelings, by our mutual desires of wanting to be loved for who we were, for what we could give each other then, and nothing more. It was passionate, unthinking, instinctive... good... but it couldn't compare to *any* night I had spent with Emi. Not a single one. "Of course I remember," I tell her, thankful that she let me get an entire sentence out.

"Don't you want that again?"

I stare at her in silence, not sure where to even begin, disbelieving that she's back here, in my house, wanting me, wanting to marry me, wanting to have children with me.

"I'm ready now," she says as her hand caresses my jaw, attempting to pull my face toward hers for another kiss. Her other hand finds itself in my lap. I take both of them quickly into my own, holding them tightly, restricting her movement.

"Caroline," I say stunned, "I am flattered... umm..."

"I'm too late, aren't I?" she asks. My eyes answer her question.

"Yes, Caroline. I'd say you're about eleven years too late."

"What do you mean?" she asks. "We only broke up three and a half years ago."

"Honestly, Caroline," I tell her. "I met the woman of my dreams in college. We're together now."

"Pale Green Eyes?" she asks, knowing the story by heart. I can remember the night I told her about Emi, and how insecure she had felt for weeks after that, telling me she'd never seen the fire in my eyes like she had when I told her the story of how I met her at the party.

"Emi," I correct her.

"But you're not married, are you?"

"Not yet," I answer. "But I hope to be soon."

"Hmmm," she hedges. "Where there's no ring, there's a way."

"No," I argue. "I don't think that's true in our case. Plus, she has the ring."

"Oh," she says, surprised. "Well, how long have you two been together?" she asks.

"Almost a year," I tell her, being vague on purpose.

"Well, it's still early in your relationship, then. We were together three years... look how we ended up."

"Apart, yes," I remind her.

"Don't you regret it? Do you ever miss me?"

"Well–"

"Don't answer," she says. "Do you ever miss this?" Again, her hand settles on my crotch, her fingers kneading gently before I realize what's happening. I quickly stand up, my phone flying across the room and landing roughly on the brick floor around the fireplace, breaking apart into three pieces.

"Caroline," I state sternly, my face feverishly hot at this point. "I'm afraid I'm going to have to ask you to leave."

"Oh, Jacks, it was just getting fun," she pleads. "I'll give you everything... anything you want. Just name it, I'll do it."

"Please leave," I repeat. "You can't give me anything I want. *She* is it. *She* is everything." Even if I'm not sure I'm *her* everything, I can't deny what she is to me.

"Wow," she says, her anger evident in her tone and expression. "Well, I hope you have fun explaining *this*." She smiles and raises her eyebrows, a certain smugness spreading across her face.

"Explaining what? There's nothing to explain," I argue, walking to the front door and opening it for her. "You're my past. Just because you're here today doesn't change that... and she already knows about you. It's history. Period."

"Well, good luck anyway. Something tells me you're going to need it, Jacks." She thrusts the contents of her nearly-full glass of wine at me and hands me the glass before walking out the door.

"Goodbye, Caroline," I spit out the words, hoping to never have to say them again, to see her again. After shutting the door, I strip off my shirts, heading straight toward the laundry room to attempt to remove the wine stains from my dress shirts. *I don't need this today.*

The nerve of her coming here, after three years. This is not her home, it's mine. Someday it will be Emi's, I hope. Caroline had no right coming here, and it was a mistake for me to even invite her in. How was I to know she would end up throwing herself at me?

But at least she knows what she wants. At least she's ready to commit to me now...

I shake those thoughts out of my head. *Who cares if she knows? She's not who I want.*

But who I want– Emi– she's not even certain of what *she* wants. This could easily turn out to be another situation like mine and Caroline's. Any day now, Emi could realize that I'm not who she wants... and choose to leave, just like Caroline did.

Why is it so hard for the woman that I love to... to choose to love me back? To decide to move forward with her life? With our life together?

After starting the washing machine, I go back upstairs to find the pieces of my phone. Emi had sent me a text message, and I wanted to know what she said.

Phone. Battery. Back plate. Doesn't seem so bad. I put the pieces back together, and for a moment, the text on the screen flashes briefly before I can read it all... before it fades away permanently.

"Who was th..."

My heart stops. *Who was that?* Is that what it said? Who was *who?* I take the phone to the wall charger and plug it in. Still nothing. I unplug it and disassemble the phone again before reassembling it more carefully this time. The display still remains dark after I plug it in a second time. I pat it forcefully in the palm of my hand. *Damn it, not now!*

Who was th... What did it say? I look outside the front door to see if Emi might be there... did she see Caroline come in? Surely I'm reading it wrong. Surely my guilty conscience is getting the best of me. Emi was probably asking me about someone at the christening today. That must be it. And if it was urgent, she would have called.

I take a deep breath and sit back down on the couch to have the rest of my wine in an attempt to relax. Before I get too comfortable, I remember the spilled wine by the front door and grab a wet rag from the kitchen to clean it up.

A loud rap on the door jolts me, bringing me quickly to my feet. *I told her to leave... can she not take a hint?*

Throwing open the door, I don't give her a chance to speak. "I told you to–"

"Fuck you!" Emi screams as my breathing halts. Her cheeks are stained with mascara, eyes wild, red from crying. "And fuck that bitch that you're with!" She takes the ring off her finger and throws it hard at my bare chest, the metal clanking on the concrete patio. Without thinking, I grab her arm and yank her toward me until she is inside the house. She struggles, and another voice startles me before I can close the door.

"Get your hands off her, Jack." I hadn't noticed her brother's car in the driveway... hadn't noticed he was standing next to his car... hadn't noticed his wife looking at me from the backseat, disappointment written all over her face.

"I'm not going to hurt her." I don't heed Chris's advice. "Would one of you mind telling me what the hell is going on?" I demand, dismayed.

"That's what we'd like to know," he adds, stepping cautiously toward me.

"Look at you!" Emi continues to yell, surveying the room. "And let go of me!"

"Emi," I state firmly but calmly, trying to pull her face to mine so our eyes meet. "Emi, breathe."

Before I know what's happening, she pulls her hand back and punches me, hard. I let go of her, shocked, touching my face in disbelief. Chris holds

Emi's arms down before she can hit me again, which I can tell she wants to do.

"God, Emi," Chris says, shocked at her physical outrage.

"Fuck, Emi, what the hell are you doing?" I say loudly, turning to walk away from this angry woman shooting daggers at me with her eyes. As soon as I say the words, though, I turn back around to see her expression change from anger to worry to confusion... and I realize I've never used such harsh language with her. I honestly don't even know where it came from.

"Watch it, Jack," Chris warns me. "She came to talk."

"Well then I suggest you let us do that," I tell him.

"I don't want to talk to him," Emi says adamantly, turning into an embrace with her brother. As I sit down on the edge of the club chair, touching my jaw, Chris and I stare at each other from across the room. Without words, I plead with him to let Emi and I work this out, whatever *this* is.

"You need to talk to him, Emi. I'm sure he can explain."

"I can."

"The wine glasses?" she yells, turning away from her brother and walking toward me aggressively. "The lipstick?" *What?* "The fact that you're half-naked? Jazz music? The fact that a *woman* answered your phone and said you were too busy to talk to *me*, your fucking *fiancée*?"

Shit. When did that happen? "Let me explain."

Chris backs out the door, shutting it behind him, an obvious move to get Emi's attention. She groans loudly in frustration. "I don't want to hear your fucking explanation!"

I sit quietly and look around the room, seeing it how she must see it. I raise my hand to my lips and rub the spot where Caroline had kissed me, red staining my finger.

Shit.

It doesn't look good.

"Who is she?" Emi asks, pacing back and forth in front of me in my living room. "Oh, god, is she still *here*?"

"Are we back at square one, here, Emi? Is there no trust between us at all?"

"Apparently not!" she says.

"What in the world have I done to you to earn this sort of treatment?"

"Let's start with the woman who was here with you today!"

"Alright, it was Caroline."

"Your ex."

"Exactly. My ex. As in ex-girlfriend. As in I'm not seeing her anymore. As in I haven't seen her nor spoken to her in years."

"Ex-*fiancée*," she corrects me. "I guess she and I will have something in common."

"What is that supposed to mean?"

"Draw your own conclusions!" she yells.

"Whatever," I say, not wanting to dignify her comment, hoping it is the anger that's making her say such nonsense.

"So you're saying nothing happened with Caroline?"

"I am."

"Then explain the lipstick."

"She tried to kiss me. I pushed her away."

"What's with the wine?"

"We were thirsty, and she asked for wine. I thought I would be a good host and offer her some."

"And why aren't you wearing a shirt?"

"Because she ended up throwing the wine at me when I asked her to leave, Emi, that's why. My shirts are in the washer, I can prove it if you like." She shakes her head in disbelief. "Why do you think I'm lying to you? Damn it, Emi, who do you think I am?"

"I don't guess I know you at all anymore," she says.

"Sure you do," I stand up, taking her by the shoulders and stopping her pacing. I look directly into her eyes, holding her face in my hands so she can't look away. "I'm a good man, Emi, who loves you and would do anything for you. I'm the man who's been there for you through the worst year of your life.

I'm the man who has waited, patiently, *every day*, for you to love me... *enough*. I am the man who thought he could make you happy, the happiest woman in the world.

"You think you don't know me, but I think you're just *afraid* to really know me... to really *feel* for me."

"Oh, really?" she asks.

"Yeah, really, Emi. You know what I think? You want me to draw my own conclusions? Well how's this? I conclude that you will come up with any story you create, any excuse, as long as it means you don't have to move in with me, or marry me, or commit to me in any way. That's my conclusion."

"That's bullshit."

"Is it, Em?"

"It is... and stop turning this on me! *You're* the one who had another woman in your home today!"

"Right. Come on, Emi, it's not as if I was unfaithful to you. I mean, what do you think happened here today?"

"I. Don't. Fucking. Know. Why was she here?"

"You want to know why? Here's why. She's changed her mind about me. She, for one, knows what she wants and is ready to commit herself to me, today. She wants it all, my love, the house, the children... finally, she came around," I say sarcastically. "And I could give a shit because I don't want any of that... not with her."

"That's not what it looks like to me."

"Well, then, you may want to look closer. You're seeing what you want to see. You're not seeing how it really is."

Emi stares at me, speechless, as I challenge her, unblinking. She sits down on the sofa and holds her left hand gingerly in the palm of her right one. "I hurt my hand," she states, her tone still angry.

"You hurt my jaw," I tell her, going into the kitchen and preparing a bag of ice for her. I hold her hand in mine, examining it carefully and noticing the swelling of her knuckles and her thumb. "You shouldn't tuck your thumb in when you punch someone," I tell her, setting the ice down on her hand and conforming it to the swollen spots. "It could be broken, can you move it?"

"It hurts, I don't know."

"Fine," I say, leaving her to sulk. I assume my position again on the chair. "Emi, why don't you trust me? Why don't you believe me?"

"You know, you're one to talk," she says. "You act like it's just me that's lacking trust in this relationship... but in the end, isn't it *you*, doubting *me*?"

"I have *every reason* to doubt you. Without even knowing the facts, you throw the ring back at me. Throw around the commitment *I've made to you* like it means nothing at all. You're so quick to just assume that I messed this up. Are you looking for an out? Looking for me to screw this up so you have a good reason to walk away?"

"Where is this coming from?"

"I'm tired of fielding questions only *you* have the answers to. 'Why won't Emi move in with you? Have you picked a date? Why not?'" I say mockingly.

"Emi won't move in with me because she feels the *spirit* of *Nate* in her apartment. And the date? Oh, she's going to get back to me when she decides whether or not *I'm* the one she wants to be with and not the *ghost* she's currently living with." My words shock even myself, truth laden in every syllable.

"Jack..." she pleads, surprised.

"Just stop, Emi. You know it's true."

"It's not true," she argues softly, but I can tell that she, herself, is not convinced. Her eyes are unsure.

"Isn't it?"

"No," she whispers. "Why are you bringing him into this?"

"In my eyes, Emi, he's always been here. In some capacity, he never left you. Or *you* never left *him* behind."

"I'm committed to you," she vows, on the verge of tears again. "I said I'd marry you, I want to."

"They're all words, Emi. Just meaningless words if there's no action to back them up. And need I remind you, you still haven't made up your mind if you want to marry me *now*. That ultimatum's still floating around out there..."

"No, I do..."

"I want a family, Emi. I'm not giving that up."

"I know, but–"

"Shut *up*, Emi! No buts, not anymore! You either love me or you don't! I need a decision. I can't continue down this path. Every day, you hurt me a little bit more. Every day you can't decide–"

"I'm sorry," she says, first looking down then angling her entire head to the floor. "I love you, Jack."

"You have a strange way of showing it sometimes." Her head snaps back up as I touch my face where she hit me.

"Oh, god, Jack. I'm sorry. Where is the ring? I *do* want to be with you. Maybe I overreacted..."

"Maybe? I've done nothing wrong here," I tell her.

"Okay. I see that now. Look, I'm sorry if you think I treated our relationship carelessly. I *obviously* overreacted. Where's the ring?" she asks again, her eyes now focused on the foyer.

"You threw it at me, Emi. I guess it's still on the front porch." She gets up quickly, setting the ice pack aside as she opens the front door and begins to search the ground for it. I put the ice on my jaw, waiting for her to return. In truth, my ego hurts more than any physical pain.

When she doesn't come back after a couple of minutes, I stand in the doorway and inspect the ground. Chris's car is no longer in the driveway. Emi has now moved her search to the flower bed on the side of the porch. Her tears have returned, her sobs audible. She barely uses her swollen left hand. I can tell it's really hurting her.

"Come inside, Emi. Take the ice, I'll look."

"It's not here," she cries. "I can't find it."

"Just come in and put the ice back on your hand. Let me get my keys, we're going to the emergency room."

"No, I'm fine, just let me find it."

"Emi," I start, waiting for her to look up at me. She mouths the words 'I'm sorry' when her eyes meet mine. I walk around the porch and help her up. "Don't worry about it, Emi. We have bigger things to worry about."

"We have to find it. It's important."

"No, Emi. It obviously wasn't important to you when you threw it at me." She cries harder, and I feel bad letting those words escape. I bring her inside and sit her down on the couch, putting the ice pack back on her thumb.

I go upstairs to put on a shirt and some jeans, and take a quick glance at myself in the mirror, wiping off the rest of the lipstick left there by Caroline. My jaw still red, I realize I don't have to worry about whether or not she can take care of herself... without me...

"I'm sorry about hitting you," she says as she sees me coming back down the stairs. "And I'm sorry about the ring."

"Do you love me enough, Emi?" I ask abruptly. She barely nods. "I mean, what's really holding you back here? What is this really about? Is it kids? Do you really think you're not meant to be a mother? Is it because I'm controlling? Because I try to make good decisions for us? Or is it really that you can't let *him* go, completely?"

"Jack, I love you," she asserts.

"But do you love me more than him?" She looks down at her hand and repositions the ice. "If you can say yes, then I'll buy you another ring... ten more rings... but if *you* can't... then... *I* can't..."

"That's like comparing apples and or–"

"No, Emi, it's not." I cut off her rationalization. "It's comparing two men, two lovers... and you can't have us both. You can't have it both ways. Do you love him more than you love me? Just answer that."

I pick up my keys and wallet, shoving them both into my pockets, standing in front of the door, ready to leave as soon as she tells me she loves me more.

"I love him *different* than you," she states.

"That's not fair, Emi," I tell her, frustrated.

"It's not fair for you to ask me that, either. It's not fair because *he's not here. He can never be here.*"

"Fine, then. If he was still here, who would you choose? That's a fair question to ask, isn't it?"

"No," she says, mad. "It's not."

"That's it," I tell her. "It really shouldn't take you this long to answer. I'm taking you to the ER. I'll call your brother and tell him to pick you up there."

"Jack, don't..."

"Emi, let's go. I'm sure your thumb is broken. We'll talk about this later."

"Do you promise?" she begs.

"If I promised, would it mean anything to you anyway?" I swallow hard, watching her wide eyes pool with tears. I turn away quickly toward the door. "Let's go."

My response just makes her cry more.

"Alright, Chris is on his way," I tell Emi in the waiting room, carrying a clip board to her so she can fill out her information. After putting her phone back in her purse, I hand her the paperwork, but she waves her swollen hand at me. Of course she hurt her left hand, the one she writes with. I just want to go home. "Fine."

Emily Clara Hennigan. *5/18/78.* I fill in her address, recalling the street number from the awning over the entrance to her building.

"What's your zip?"

"10128."

Self-employed.

"Who's your insurance?"

"I don't have any."

"You don't have– of course not. Too bad we're not married," I say sarcastically, wondering if she has the money to pay for her own medical bills. *Can I walk away from her? From this?*

None. Chris Hennigan. 212-555-3552. Brother.

"You're not my emergency contact?" she asks.

"I'm leaving as soon as he gets here. Might as well be a relative."

"Jack..." I continue to ignore her pleas to engage me in conversation, focusing on the paperwork in front of me.

"Any known drug allergies?"

"No," she says, swiping at a tear. After we go over the list of pre-existing conditions, I take the clip board back up to the reception area.

"I think I do," Emi says quietly when I sit back down, my knees bouncing in nervous anticipation.

"You think you do *what*?" I can't even look at her, the sad expression making it difficult for me to remain strong, detached, angry... and I have every right to be angry, for once.

"Love you more than him." I exhale sharply, wanting to laugh but failing to see any humor in her answer.

"You have to *know* it, Emi. You can't just *think* it." I stand up as I see Chris walking toward us down the long hallway. "I've got to go."

"Jack, please don't leave."

"Emi, I still have to pack. I have to go."

"Are we still going to Texas tomorrow?" she asks, hopeful. I take a deep breath, a million thoughts racing through my mind.

"I'll tell you what, Emi. If you decide that you *know* that you love me more than him in the next eighteen hours, you can just meet me at the airport. I'll have your ticket with me. The flight leaves at twelve-thirty.

"And if you don't come... then I guess we'll have a lot to discuss when I get back next week."

"Hey, man, you okay?" Chris asks me as I square off with his sister.

"I'm pretty sure her thumb is broken." I ignore Chris's concern and Emi's cries for attention.

"But, Jack, I love you," Emi pleads as I turn toward the exit. "Jack, don't!" she yells. "I'm sorry, please don't leave me..." I continue through the automatic doors, afraid to turn back. Afraid to see her pale green watering eyes, red with tears. Afraid to see her pained expression. But I'm most afraid that something she'll say or do may actually convince me to stay... and I won't allow myself to be hurt by her anymore.

I still hear her crying, even after the doors shut behind me.

After packing for my trip, I lie restlessly in bed, unable to sleep, wondering if I did the right thing by leaving her with Chris in the hospital. I can't continue to be strung along if she can't commit to me. But I can't imagine my life without her, either. She was my future from the first moment I saw her.

She had only gotten more beautiful since that night in college. I had seen her across the room when she walked in, alone. She seemed out of place, her eyes scanning the room. While all the other girls were dressed in tight sweaters and short denim skirts, she was wearing overalls that swallowed her small frame whole, a long-sleeved concert t-shirt and her hair... my god, her beautiful red hair... in short, spiky pigtails. She reminded me instantly of a cherished doll my sister used to play with, her skin so fair and smooth. Yes, she was out-of-place, but by far the most natural looking girl there. One of my fraternity brothers immediately handed her a beer, and she whispered something to him.

Her smile grew wide, her expression relaxed as he pointed to someone behind me. Her grin was quick, was radiant, and I actually felt disappointed when she waved to Chris and started approaching my friend. She walked right past me, and her green eyes, as vast as the sea, met mine for the briefest of moments. Her soft, porcelain cheeks turned pink as I smiled back at her. My body angled toward her, watched her as she passed, as she made her way to

Chris. He finally saw her... and rolled his eyes at her.

She drank the first beer quickly as I heard him ask her why she was there. It was too loud to hear her quiet answer. He told her she shouldn't be there, suggested that she leave. I couldn't imagine why Chris, a friend who was always fairly civil to people, would be talking to this beautiful girl in such a way. I was drawn to her. I wanted to stand up for her. I approached them, angry with my fraternity brother, at the disrespectful way he was talking to her. Was this an ex-girlfriend? I had to know the story here.

"Everything okay?" I had asked Chris, suddenly nervous to be in her presence as she turned to face me, her eyes curious. My heart sped up when our eyes met again.

"It would be better if she would leave," he answered.

"Shut the fuck up, Chris," she fired back, her beautiful eyes impassioned and angry. *Feisty one.* "It's a free country."

"Just get the hell out of here!" Chris yelled back.

"Hey," I said sternly to him, grabbing his arm. He shook me off.

"Butt out, Jack," he said.

"I'm Emi," she said, a smirk on her face as she held her hand out to mine. "Chris's little sister."

"Chris's sister," I repeated her, sighing, my throat dry. "Of course, I see the resemblance now."

"Jack, was it?"

"Yes, Jack Holland."

"It's nice to meet you." She fluttered her lashes, her smile causing her dimples to grow deeper. "Can you get me another drink?" she asked, handing her empty cup to me.

"Emi, come on..." Chris argued.

"Chris, it's okay. I've got this." He looked at me, hard, but eventually relaxed his shoulders and nodded. He trusted me implicitly, even back then. "Sure, the keg's out back," I told her, nodding in the direction of the patio, inviting her to follow me, hoping that she would... nervous that she would. I knew immediately she wasn't old enough to drink– her brother wasn't either, after all– but my conscience wasn't going to win this fight. I would have done anything for her in that moment.

My hand was shaking when I handed the cup back to her.

"Thank you," she said.

"You're welcome." I expected her to walk away at that point, but she hung around me, looked at me, waited for me to talk. She raised her eyebrows at the silence between us. Normally confident and self-assured, I was stunned to find myself completely speechless.

"You're sweet," she had said. "Is there somewhere we can go that's a little more private?" I looked at her sideways, my jaw dropping, completely unsure what she was suggesting. This wasn't my first fraternity party. I knew the game, even if I wasn't one to play it. She picked up on my bewildered expression and turned an adorable shade of red. "To talk," she laughed. "Just to talk."

"Of course," I swallowed, leading her back through the house to the front yard. We walked just far enough down the street to escape the loud music and sat down on the curb. She sat about a foot away, but angled her knees toward me.

"Any pesky little sisters, Jack?" she asked, playfully pushing my arm like any annoying sibling would do to irritate another.

"Actually, yes. Kelly's six minutes younger than me."

"A twin? That's cool," she smiled. "Do you have twin superpowers?" she asked, taking a drink of her beer. Her casual demeanor immediately began to relax me.

"Superpowers?" I laughed. "I wouldn't call them superpowers... but we have a pretty close relationship. There may be a sixth sense there sometimes."

"Chris and I are typically much nicer to one another," she explained. "We got into a fight earlier. I wanted him to drive me to Mom's for the weekend, but he wouldn't because of this party." She rolled her eyes, punctuating her sentence.

"Oh," I responded, surprised that she was still with me.

"I warned him I'd come when he told me not to. He didn't believe me. I mean, asking me *not* to come was like an open invitation, right?"

"To a pesky little sister," I said, nudging her shoulder, "yes. But as a good older brother, I probably would worry about Kelly being at one of these parties, too."

"I can take care of myself," she said, but her eyes didn't convey the same confidence as her words did. She looked so cute, so young, so innocent.

I nodded at her, smiling. "I'm sure you can." I agreed– to placate her– and hoped what I said didn't come across as patronizing.

"I can!" she repeated.

"Okay, you can," I laughed. Her lips formed a lustrous pout and she crossed her arms as she glared at me flirtatiously. "Typical little sister."

"So is it just you and... Kelly?"

"No, I also have two younger brothers."

"So you're the oldest." She nodded, thoughtful. "I'm the youngest."

"I know," I told her. "Your brother is my little brother in the fraternity. He's mentioned you and your older sister before."

"What has he told you?" she asked.

"Just your typical family fare. What confounds me is what he *hasn't* told me."

"What's that?" she questioned me, curious.

"He didn't tell me how adorable you are." My confidence was coming back.

Even in the moonlight, I could see the pink rise to her cheeks. She raised her eyebrows and looked up at me, fluttering her eyelashes, laughing off my compliment quietly. "Um, what year are you?" she changed the subject, averting her eyes to the ground.

"Mmmm..." I hesitated. "It's my fourth year, but by credits, I'm only a junior."

"Too many parties?" she teased.

"No," I laughed. "I've got a full-time job, too. Just busy."

"Oh," she said, more silence following. "So, in freshman orientation, why don't they tell you to stay away from the dining hall?"

"No, you misunderstood. The food in the dining hall *is* freshman orientation. Our cruel way of hazing the fish," I joked with her. "Seriously, though, yeah, I'm pretty sure the disgusting mildew smell in there poisons all the food..."

"I know, right?" she laughed. "I got sick both times I ate there. Now I'm resigned to eating microwaveable noodles."

"There's a great sandwich shop just off campus," I had told her. "Really inexpensive. I eat there a few times a week."

"Cool," she said. "Maybe you can take me there sometime." She nudged my shoe with hers.

"I would be happy to." She was now gaining confidence, too, as my eyes got lost in her gaze.

"Cool," she repeated, her eyes locked onto mine, lips slightly parted. Everything around us went silent, faded into the night. I was completely caught off guard, absorbed by her, desperate to kiss her, but I couldn't move. "So," she said nervously, shifting slightly, "do we really have to completely evacuate the on-campus apartments every time some idiot pulls the fire alarm?"

"The joy of living on campus," I contemplated, mentally berating myself for letting the moment pass me by. "I don't miss those days. My friend and I got an apartment after our freshman year. We're still scraping by, but it's so much better for my sanity... and sleep."

"I can't wait to live on my own," she said.

"You have a roommate?"

"Three," she groaned. "Four girls in one tiny, two-bedroom apartment. Who, in their right mind, would think that's a good idea? Four girls. I mean, come on. I'm pretty easy-going," she said, "but even I'm having a hard time with it."

"Not getting along with them?"

"Well, two of them are science majors– I'm an art major, by the way– and it's like we speak completely different languages. The other one, Teresa, she's cool. She's a journalism major. She's rarely there, though. In fact, I'm surprised she's not here. She constantly goes out."

"You don't?"

"Honestly," she smiled, "this isn't my scene."

"And what's your scene, Poppet?" *Poppet?*

She laughed quietly, a little surprised at how I had addressed her. "Poppet?" she asked with a wide smile.

"Yeah. Poppet," I answered, not exactly certain why I actually allowed the word to slip from my mouth. "Like, a little doll." Her cheeks again turned a bright shade of pink as she looked at me questioningly. "It's an old British term of endearment. My grandfather used to call Kelly that. I don't know, it just came out," I tell her apologetically.

"No, it's okay," she assures me. "I like it. So, um, what's my scene? I like art shows. Live music in small clubs. Museums. Places I can get lost in my own head." She shrugged shyly. "Not lost in a crowd. Tonight, I'm just here to piss off Chris. Speaking of which, I'm not doing a good job of that if he can't even see me. Wanna go get a refill?"

"Sure," I said, helping her up. I couldn't help but smile as I followed her back into the house, through the living area and back on the patio near the keg. The most beautiful girl I had ever met had chosen to spend her time with me. She was funny, too, and our conversation was comfortable, easy. I couldn't wait to take her to lunch someday in the near future. She wanted to go, she had suggested it herself. And I couldn't wait to kiss her. I ruefully wished I could have those seconds back.

"I'll be right back," I told her, my hand on the small of her back, my lips close to her ear so she could hear me over the music.

"Okay." She bit her bottom lip, blinked her green eyes quickly. I went in search for her brother. I had to talk to him. I knew there was an unspoken "guy code" about dating someone's sister. I wanted to let him know that I was interested. I didn't think he would mind.

After ten minutes of searching the house, both inside and out, I gave up, wanting to get back to Emi. She wasn't where I left her, so my search shifted from Chris to his little sister. I eventually found her, sucking down a jello shot and playing a game of quarters in the living room with more of my fraternity brothers. As they explained the rules to her, I noticed they were being quite liberal with them, making the game impossible for Emi to "win." Her mind, already a little foggy, wasn't catching on to the fact that she would be the one taking most of the shots. I rolled my eyes at my friends, a term I used loosely to describe them that night as I watched them take advantage of the vulnerabilities of the girl who had singled *me* out... or at least I thought she had.

She looked up at me, smiled briefly, but continued with the game, taking shot after shot. Frustrated, confused and angry, I went into the kitchen and started trying to clean up some of the mess that had been made. I watched her out of the corner of my eye, watched the crowd around her grow. Realizing my efforts of cleaning were fruitless and not wanting to watch the scene in front of me, I grabbed a bottle of water and started to go upstairs.

I met Chris on the stairway.

"Russell said you were looking for me?" he slurred.

"Yeah, uh," I stammered, "I was going to talk to you about your sister, Emi."

"She still here?" he asked.

"Playing quarters downstairs..."

"Shit," he muttered. "You left her alone?" I followed him as he rushed back downstairs into the living area. "That's it, Emi," he said, pulling her up by her arm. "This is my sister, assholes," he said to our friends. She just giggled at him, a self-satisfied look on her face. She had achieved her goal of pissing Chris off. "I should have just taken you home. Come on." He took her out the front door. I watched closely from the window, making sure he didn't try to drive in his condition. He took out his phone and made a call, then told her to stay at the picnic table near the front door.

"He's on his way," I heard him say to her as he came back into the house, immediately joining the crowd. I couldn't stand to see her alone, now crying, on that bench. I took some water to her and decided to keep her company while she waited for her ride.

I remember how I felt when Nate showed up and ushered her into his car. I can remember the physical pain I felt when she walked away from me that night. As much as our recent conversations have hurt me, it's all tolerable if, in the end, she's with me forever.

Surely she'll meet me at the airport in the morning. Surely, she will... and even as I make these assurances to myself, a pang of doubt rests in the pit of my stomach, and keeps me awake for the rest of the night.

CHAPTER 9

"Time for another round," I tell the obliging Dallas bartender. "Another top shelf scotch, if you don't mind." He gives me an empathetic smile as he pours the drink for me.

Emi was the reason I was driven to drink the last time I had isolated myself in a hotel bar. That was the night she came back into my life. This could be the day she walked out for good.

Still in shock by the fact that she didn't show up at the airport, I take a slow and deliberate drink, savoring the flavor and the numbness the beverage brings. "Can I borrow the phone again?"

I had planned to stop by the cell phone store before heading to the airport this morning to get a replacement, but I wanted to be there to greet Emi when she showed up. I had stopped by a florist shop instead, still making it to the airport with nearly three hours to spare. I had watched the concourse all morning, wishing I had a phone the whole time. I gave the daisies to the woman at the terminal before I got on the plane. She said I had made her day... how that moment ruined mine.

Now, I was glad I didn't have a phone. I'd never been one to drunk dial–
or for that matter, I'd never been one to allow myself to get drunk anymore–
but today was an exception. If I had my cell phone, I'm certain I would have
called her multiple times today voicing every emotion that I'd experienced at
the time it happened: sadness, disappointment, anger, shock... things would
have been said that I would definitely regret later.

The bartender hands me a cordless phone, and I pull my brother's card out
of my wallet for the second time today, dialing his number.

"Hello?"

"Yeah, Stevie," I say, concentrating hard on the words in an effort to avoid
slurring them. "It's Jack."

"Jacks, when are you coming over? We've been waiting."

"Yeah, I know. You know, I checked into the hotel, and I don't know, I'm
just not feeling well... I think I'll just stay here for the day and come by
tomorrow."

"But, Jacks–"

"No, man, really, I'll call you in the morning. I gotta run." I hang up the
phone before he can convince me to come over... or coerce any information
out of me. When I spoke to him earlier, I didn't have the guts to tell him that
Emi didn't make the trip. This was not a conversation I was looking forward
to having with my youngest brother, the one who had questioned Emi's
feelings for me from the first time he met her.

I wonder what she's doing right now... is she upset at all? Is she at peace
with her decision? What will she do with herself? She chose him over me...
she chose the memory of a man... even the real thing wasn't good enough for
her.

Will another man suit her better, later in life? I had believed I was the
best thing for her, all these months. What a fool I had been. An arrogant fool.
I believed that everything happened for a reason... I believed that we were
meant to be together. *We were meant to be together.* I allow the thought to

linger in my head for a few minutes. I still have a hard time believing that we aren't.

Is this it? Maybe she just needs more time. Maybe she'll come around... but in all honestly, shouldn't her answer have come quickly, been ready to be spoken aloud as soon as the question was asked?

Him or me?

Had it been the other way around, Caroline or Emi or *any other woman* for that matter, I knew the answer from the moment I met her. Emi. It was always Emi. It always would be Emi. But now what? The thought of my life without her now is too painful to even consider. Sure, life goes on, but how happy can that life be?

Suddenly, I begin to feel such immense loss, and I can only compare it to what Emi went through when she lost Nate. It's not the same, I know, but the situation still just seems beyond repair. She had lost him forever, with no hope of returning. I'm beginning to feel the same about her... and she was hopeless for so long.

But she went on to love again... *just... apparently not enough.*

Was there hope that I could even love another woman? And if I could, could I ever love *her* enough? Love *her* more than Emi? *I have to talk to her.*

"Where's the nearest cell phone store?" I ask the bartender, feeling my brain not functioning at its full capacity. I just want to talk to her in private, beg her, convince her to stay with me, even though I know I should let her go. I can't be without her. Does she really have to love me more? Was it fair to ask? Can I be second best? Is that good enough for me?

A part of me believes I'm not that guy... who would settle to be that man, the consolation prize. But if it means I end up with her, with the love of *my* life– even if I wasn't hers– I would do that, wouldn't I?

And then would that be fair to her?

"It's about six blocks south on this main road," the bartender tells me. I pull out the keys to my rental car and begin to walk off. "Did you want to close out your tab?" he calls out after me.

"Oh, yeah, I'm sorry. Yeah..." I shake my head in an attempt to clear it.

"Why don't you get a bite to eat first?" he suggests. "Maybe offset some of those drinks..."

I laugh quietly to myself, recognizing that I've had too much to drink and am not likely making good decisions. Getting on the road would *not* be a good decision. It would be the absolute worst.

"Sure," I tell him, sitting back down. "Thanks."

"No problem. The burgers are good here."

"Sounds fine," I say, uncaring. "And some water, please."

The things I would do for her; had done for her. The sacrifices I was willing to make, all for her. Ending up with Emi was always the only thing that mattered to me.

I rub my forehead, feeling the headache coming on already. I'd been drinking since we took off from JFK. I'd only had two drinks on the plane, but made up for lost time in this bar. I would be hurting tomorrow, for sure... just not sure if it would be the headache or heartache that would hurt me more.

After a few minutes the waiter stops by and sets the plate of food in front of me. I'm not hungry in the slightest, but I know I'll feel better if I eat something. I take slow bites of the savory bar food and drink a few glasses of water before pushing the plate away.

From behind me, a hand appears. Not any hand. One delicately wrapped in a white fiberglass cast. Before I realize who it is, before I get my hopes up, a ring– *the* ring– is carefully set down onto the bar in front of me.

She came.

She came to Texas.

She came to Texas to give me back the ring.

I pick up the ring that I had selected for her and only her, examining it carefully, and I notice her sitting down beside me in my peripheral vision. I can't even look at her. *I guess I won't forever be known as the man with the most expensive lawn ornament in Manhattan...*

"Where was it?" I ask, unable to hide the disappointment.

"Chris had it all along," she says, the sound of her voice making my pulse quicken. I nod quietly, taking it in. "Can I have a french fry?" she casually asks. I push the plate toward her, still staring at the piece of jewelry that was to symbolize my undying love for her. "You didn't mention we would be staying in a hotel," she says.

"It was supposed to be a surprise. I thought it would be nice to have some time alone, outside our element, away from it all, after yesterday..."

"It's really nice," she says. "You don't seem happy to see me."

"I'm overjoyed," I say sarcastically. "How could I be hap–"

"Are you two doing okay over here?" the bartender asks.

"Another water here, and a glass of red wine for her," I tell him, abandoning our conversation.

"Diet soda, actually," she corrects me. "I just took some pain killers," she mumbles. "I tried to call you this morning, and text you... but you wouldn't answer." I simply nod. "Look at me," she says, grabbing my arm with her good hand, forcing me to look into her pale green eyes. Her stare begins to chip away at my defenses. "Why didn't you answer?"

"My phone broke yesterday, Em. I had planned on getting it replaced this morning, but I decided to go straight to the airport... so I could be there, waiting with open arms, when you decided to show up... but you never did."

"I overslept," she says, her eyes dropping to the gaping expanse between us. "They gave me pain killers last night, and I didn't set my alarm... and I tried to call you... I caught the next plane out."

"Why did you come here, Emi?" I ask, impatient, focusing my attention again to the glass of water in front of me.

"You asked me a question, and I needed to answer it."

I don't really want to know her answer. I can't bear to hear it vocalized. She already answered– without words– when she gave the ring back to me.

"Seems pretty obvious," I say, picking up the piece of jewelry. "Emi, I don't want this back. I bought it for you. You should keep it." I open the palm of her right hand, place the ring in it and close her fingers around it.

"Just listen to me, okay? You asked me who I would choose if he was still here, you or him..."

"I know what I asked, Emi, I've been replaying the conversation in my head for the better part of a day." The alcohol has removed any filter between my brain and my mouth.

"Okay, Jack, yes, it would be him," she says as she sets the ring back down on the bar. Her words and actions sting even more than I thought they would.

"Another scotch, please," I tell the bartender when he brings Emi's soda. "Make it a double."

"You don't normally drink like this," Emi says, her voice thick with disapproval.

"I don't normally get dumped by the love of my life, either, so give me this, alright?"

"Jack, will you listen to me? And look at me?"

"What more can you say, Emi? I've heard all I need to hear."

"No, you haven't," she says, touching my chin gingerly and angling my face toward hers. I purposely didn't shave this morning to hide the small bruise she left on my skin. "Does it still hurt?"

"I imagine your punch hurt you far more than it hurt me," I tell her, gently removing her hand from my jaw. "I'm fine."

"Well, I'm still sorry," she says, her voice confident and determined. "Please let me talk, though, okay? I didn't come all this way for it to end like this."

"Fine, remind me who you chose: him or me..."

"Him, Jack... but it's because I would never have known the great love I'd have been missing out on with you. You and I only had a chance at love in his absence, so you asking me this hypothetical question isn't fair... not at all.

"You know, it's actually the other way around, Jack," she whispers, leaning into me and combing her fingers through my hair. "I only loved *him* enough. I loved him enough to forego that crazy tingling that I felt when I kissed you back in college. I didn't feel that connection, that soulmate-feeling with him, but I felt enough love for him that I knew I would be happy with him, always. I knew he would take care of me like no one else could...

"Except you... but I didn't know how important you would be to me until he was gone."

I stare deeply into her eyes, wanting to believe this will somehow turn out in my favor, but fearing the worse nonetheless.

"You gave me life again, Jack. I was barely surviving... and you saved me. And I'm grateful to you for that."

"So, I'm like your hero, but I somehow don't get the girl?" I laugh.

"Jack, if everything disappeared tomorrow, and all that was left was me and you," she says with passion, "you would be all I would ever need. I would never want for anything more, or anyone else."

"Em–"

"I'm not finished," she says, putting her index finger over my mouth. I hold her hand there and kiss her finger, softly. She smiles and takes a deep breath before continuing. "I love that you anticipate my every need. I love that you let me mess up your hair when we fool around, and I love that you'll leave it that way because you know I like it. I love that you know my favorite drink, my favorite color, my favorite music, my favorite flower... I love that you wear the jeans that I like on you, even though I know you're more comfortable in dress clothes," She allows her knee to nudge mine. "I love that you surprise me with trips and nice hotel rooms, even when I've been a total bitch to you. I love that you gave me space to figure everything out for myself. To figure out what you already knew, that you and I were made for each other. I love that you're considerate of me and patient with me. I love that you forgive me. I love that you defend me. I love that you *love* me. I love that you allow me to love you the best I know how... and Jack, I'm sorry if you've ever felt like you were second best..."

She swallows and takes a deep breath before continuing.

"I love you more than I've loved any man, ever, in my life. I've known it for quite some time, but I've never been able to say it. And you know what? It is such a relief to say it. I love you with all my heart, Jack. All of it. Not just most of it, not with what he left... all of it. To the point that it physically hurt to watch you walk out on me in the waiting room last night."

"I know that feeling well," I tell her, holding her hand in mine tightly.

"I am so sorry, Jack. I'm sorry for doing that to you, and for threatening to do it again. I'm sorry I caused you such pain... I didn't know... I mean, you've never walked out on me before. You've never *not* taken care of me. I thought you had given up on me. It was in that moment that I knew I had to give you everything, all of me, or it would all be gone. And it felt right, I wasn't afraid, I wasn't feeling like I was betraying anyone... I just felt like I was finally being honest with myself, with you... even with him..."

I blot newly emerging tears in her eyes with my napkin, holding her head in my hand.

"So, Jack, yes, I want to marry you. I want to pick a date. I want to move in with you. I don't ever want to be without you. I want to love you until death do us part. And I hope it's a long time away, because I have a lot of love to give you."

"But kids..." I interject, noticing her obvious omission.

"Jack, what scares me the most," she says, "is that– for whatever reason– we won't get a child. Either they'll interview me and think I'm unfit–"

"Emi, don't start with that again," I cut her off.

"Let me finish. It's not just that. That's just one thing that could go wrong. What if we never find the right child? Or something falls through? I mean, just because we want to adopt doesn't mean we'll end up with children."

"Why wouldn't we end up with children?" I ask.

"I don't know. But it's a possibility. And Jack, I can't bear to see that disappointment on your face again. Especially over and over again, if we're rejected for whatever reasons, or if the mother changes her mind... whatever happens... That would crush me. And I'm most afraid of..." She hesitates, swallows hard. "I'm afraid you'd leave if it didn't happen for us."

"I wouldn't leave you," I promise her.

"You don't know that."

"No, Emi, I *do* know that. I need *you* to know that." She stares at me intently as I shake my head. "I wouldn't," I whisper to her. "I wouldn't."

"I just want to be enough..."

"God, Emi," I tell her before kissing her deeply. I stand up from my chair to hold her body closer to mine in a tight embrace. "I promise, I won't leave you."

"Can you forgive me?" she whispers in my ear.

"Of course I can, Emi. I do." I continue to wipe the tears from her face with my thumbs, but more fall in their place. I kiss both of her cheeks, tasting the warm saline, hoping to take away any remaining sadness that she might feel. I pull her close again and breathe her in, still numb from the liquor but feeling alive all over again. My lips find hers again, hungry for her kiss, ravishing them. My hand travels down her back, then underneath her shirt and back up again. My eyes open with curiosity as she laughs softly.

In the moment, I had forgotten we weren't alone, but immediately I want to be alone with her.

"I'd like to close my tab now," I tell the bartender, my eyes never leaving hers.

"No way, man," he says smiling, handing me back my card. "It's on the house." I pull my wallet out to put the card away, and take out the largest bill I have, leaving it on the counter with him as a tip.

"Don't forget this," he says, handing me the ring. I nearly trip over Emi's luggage– one suitcase– not realizing she brought it with her. She steadies me, giving me a reproachful look, as I take the handle and drag it behind me.

"I'm fine, Emi," I tell her. "One bag? That's it?"

"I was in a hurry. They have stores here, right?"

"Of course," I laugh, kissing her once more.

"So why did you give the ring back to me, Em?" I ask as we leave the bar.

"It doesn't really fit right now," she frowns, holding up her cast.

"How bad is it?"

"Broken thumb, hairline fracture on my knuckle."

"I'm sorry," I tell her through a small smile. "Does it hurt?"

"A little... listen, Jack, *I'm* sorry."

"Just next time, don't tuck your thumb, alright?"

"I promise, I'll never hit you again."

"I promise, Emi," I tell her, "I'll never give you a reason to."

Once in the room, I lie down on the bed while Emi begins to unpack her suitcase, my head in a daze of alcohol and pure bliss. "How did you know where to find me?" I ask her.

"I called Kelly this morning– by the way, she's been trying to call you all day. Anyway, she gave me Steven's address. So from the airport, I just took a cab there... and he was surprised to see me there, assuming we were together. He told me you were here."

"When did your flight get in?"

"Probably about thirty minutes after yours did. I watched your plane leave the terminal and then frantically ran to get the next flight."

"How was Stevie, towards you?"

"Gracious. Very nice. Very concerned that we weren't together. I just told him I missed the flight... but your phone call made him suspicious that something was going on. He said you sounded drunk."

"Nice," I say. "Did they ask about the cast?"

"Of course," she smiles. "I told them I fell... I guess if you want to make a liar out of me, that would be okay. I deserve it."

"No, I like your story better."

Her eyes stare at me warmly, and she takes a break from hanging her clothes to inspect my jaw closer, pressing her lips gently against it.

"It's really fine," I whisper. "My lips ache for you more." She runs her fingers through my hair as her mouth softly touches mine, her eyes piercing into mine. "I want you," I tell her, holding on to her as she pulls away.

"You can have me... just a little later." She walks back to her suitcase, and I smile at her as she struggles with the hangers with her one good hand. "I could help you with that."

"No, you just stay there. Sober up. You do know your parents are here, don't you?" she asks, her tone saying that she knows I had no idea.

As the silence spreads between us, I immediately regret that I haven't told them about our situation. Even though I asked him not to, I hope that Steven filled them in... but when I look into Emi's eyes, I get the feeling that he did not.

"No, I wasn't aware of that."

She sits down next to me and holds my hand after handing me a bottle of water.

"Yeah, Matty's here, too. Lucas couldn't make it, though... It's a surprise birthday party for you. It was supposed to be today, apparently, but they're rescheduling for tomorrow. Act surprised."

"Damn," I mutter, regretting the afternoon spent drinking away my sorrows... sorrows that would have gone away immediately if I had gone straight to Steven's house after the flight.

"So, my parents," I begin cautiously, "did they... say anything to you?"

"As a matter of fact, they did."

I squint slightly at her and she nods her head.

"They asked me why we came down here for a visit," she begins. I close my eyes and sigh, disappointed in myself as I see what's coming. "I told them we had wanted to talk to Renee about adoption.

"They were thrilled, and asked me if that was something I'd always wanted to pursue... and I told them I had never considered it until we found out that I couldn't have children."

"Emi, I just wanted to tell them in person..."

"So, needless to say, they were shocked," she continues as if she doesn't hear my excuse. "They had tons of questions... most just like yours: was I sure, what happened, did we get a second opinion, yadda yadda yadda," she says, still smiling. "Your mom cried a little, but she went in the other room to try to hide her tears from me. Renee went with her. Your dad did just what my dad would do. He changed the subject. Steven stayed next to me, holding my hand under the table through the whole thing."

"I'm sorry, Emi, I had every intention of telling them. And I had no idea that they were here. None whatsoever. I never wanted you to have to tell them... especially alone."

"It's okay," she says, patting my leg. "It was fine. They seemed disappointed at first, but then your mom came back in... refreshed, her makeup touched up... and she congratulated me... on our engagement and then on our decision to adopt. She thought it was very noble, charitable... very *Jacks*, she said. She said it with such pride.

"She said she can't wait for us to start our lives together."

I run my fingers through her hair, studying every facial feature to see if she is angry with me, or disappointed... I can see nothing but love. "Are you okay?"

"I'm fine, Jack," she says. "I can't wait to start my life with you, either." I struggle to sit up, to kiss her, but she pushes me back into the pillows and leans in, presses her lips against mine. "Why don't you try to sleep for awhile?"

"I just want to look at you," I tell her, squinting again, the headache beginning to pulse.

"You can do that any time," she says. "But right now, I think sleep would do you some good. There was a drug store within walking distance. I'll go get something for the hangover you're going to have... I forgot my toothbrush, anyway."

"I can go with you," I offer, but struggle to keep my eyes open.

"No, you can stay here. Just sleep." She sweeps the hair from my forehead, then kisses it. "Let's get your shoes off." She pulls them off herself, then unbuttons my pants and slides them down my legs. "If you need anything, the phone's right next to the bed," she says softly. "I'll write down my number–"

"212-555-9374," I rattle off.

"Still, just in case," she adds.

Hearing her set the pen and paper down, I reach out blindly for her arm, and tug her to the bed.

"Jack," she laughs. "I'll be right back."

"Stay with me. Make love to me," I plead.

"When I get back, I promise," she says. "Get some sleep. I'll be back in just a few minutes."

"Promise?"

"Promise." Suddenly, her lips are pressed hard against mine, and I feel our tongues tangle together again. She resists me when I try to pull her on top of me. "There's a preview. Now let me go. The sooner I go, the sooner I'll be back."

"Okay, go," I tell her, smiling, dreaming of her with me already.

The room is pitch black when I feel Emi crawl into bed behind me. She forms her body around mine, hitching her leg over my thighs. She places her arm across my chest, her cast laying on the bed in front of me.

"What time is it?" I whisper to her.

"Two-thirty," she answers in a hushed voice.

"Are you just now coming to bed?"

"Yes."

"Why were you up so late?" I put my hand on her bare knee, and trace my fingers up her leg.

"Your brothers and Renee took me dancing." Steven dancing... this doesn't make sense.

"What are you wearing?" I ask, wondering if I'm still asleep, dreaming.

"Nothing," she says coyly. Her answer awakens me, and I turn over to face her. "How are you?" she asks.

"Not bad," I answer, feeling only a lingering, dull headache. "Pretty good, actually. You smell good." I inhale deeply, taking in her clean scent. I run my fingers through her wet hair. "Did you just take a shower?"

"I did."

"You're beautiful," I tell her.

"You can't even see me. You haven't even opened your eyes."

"I don't have to see you to know that." I move my hand to her mouth, feeling her smile. She kisses it, then takes one of my fingers and closes her lips around it. "I can feel you," I add as my other hand travels the length of her naked body, goosebumps rising on her skin along the way. She begins to unbutton the dress shirt I never took off.

"Have you been sleeping all this time?" she asks. "I kept thinking you'd call me, wondering where I was."

"I guess I was. I didn't sleep at all last night... did you have fun tonight? Did you really go dancing?"

"We had a blast... It was Matty's idea... Renee and I had to twist Steven's arm to go, but he finally gave in. We went to Ghost Bar. Matthew was my date, I didn't think you'd mind."

"Your date, huh?" I gently massage her breast, my eyelids still heavy with sleep, my body feeling as if it's on auto-pilot, just doing what it wants to do– has to do– when she is with me. "I'm a little jealous, I think."

"Well, you kiss better, if that means anything," she says. My eyes open wide, and I can barely make out the smug look on her face as my vision adjusts to the darkness of the room.

"I *kiss* better?" I ask. "My brother *kissed* you?"

"Mmm-hmm," she says nonchalantly.

"My *gay* brother... kissed... *you*?" Maybe I'm not awake.

"Yep," she says again.

"Tell me how he kissed you."

"Well, we were out on the balcony, overlooking the city, and there was this awesome breeze, and this driving beat coming from the dance floor inside... and I said, 'This is just one of those moments when you want to kiss someone, you know?' And before I knew it, he kissed me."

"Just like that?"

"Just like that."   She stops me as I try to roll over onto my back, struggling to understand what's going on.

"Am I really awake? Are you really here?"

"You are touching me... you wouldn't be able to do that if I wasn't here. And I wouldn't be able to do this to you," she says, her right hand finding its way down the front of my boxers. I stop her hand, wanting the rest of the story before I allow my desire for her to take over.

"Wait... now, *show* me how he kissed you..."

"You really want to know?"

"You said I was better..."

"You are... alright, I'll show you. You be me. I'm Matty. Just lie there." I start laughing at her request.

"Just lie here? I guess I'm not too worried."

"Shhh... okay, so say my line," she says excitedly.

"What?"

"Say what I said..."

"Ummm... it's... something like, 'hey, it's pretty out here. I need to be kissed.'" Immediately she presses her lips to mine and holds them there for a few seconds before making a smacking sound as she pulls away.

"You're marginally better than that," she teases me playfully.

"So he didn't kiss you like this?" I hold her head in my hand as I brush her lips lightly first, then kiss her deeper. My other hand pressed to her breast, I can feel her heart rate rising, quickly.

"No," she says, breathless.

"What about this?" I ask, my tongue parting her lips and tasting her breath on mine.

"God, no," she says with a gasp.

"And he didn't do this, did he?" My hand travels down her body, in between her legs, feeling her reaction to my touch, her response setting off sparks in every part of my body. I pull my hand away quickly to shrug out of my shirts, wanting to feel her warm skin against mine.

She moans quietly. "I'm not sure, can you do that again?" Her good hand grips at my boxer shorts and pushes them down. I pull them the rest of the way, kicking them off.

"He better not have," I warn humorously as I lift her leg, draping it over my body, and touching her again, slowly, methodically. Her breathing comes faster. "Come here," I whisper, pulling her closer. Her hard cast bumps my elbow, the nerve endings shooting fire up my arm.

"This thing gets in the way," she whispers apologetically, waving her bandaged arm.

"Here..." I tell her, pushing her back into the bed, setting her arm gently by her side and settling my body in between her smooth legs. "Just lie there." We laugh together at her earlier command to me. "I'll take it from here."

I wake up before Emi the next morning feeling great, refreshed, not hungover at all. Quietly, I take a shower and get ready. I leave a note for Emi on the nightstand before taking her cell phone and heading out to run a few errands.

She is ready by the time I return two hours later.

"I was just about to call you to see if you could bring me something to eat..." she says when I walk in.

"Well... I got you some breakfast," I tell her, handing her a container of fruit that I picked up from a local market.

"Perfect, thank you," she smiles as she sits, cross-legged, on the unmade bed.

"Water or Diet soda?" I ask, offering her either.

"Diet soda," she says after biting off a piece of a strawberry. She holds the rest of it, feeding me the fruit.

"Thank you," I say, kissing her.

"Thank *you*. Where'd you go?"

"The market, obviously... and I got a cell phone so I can check the seven messages that have been left for me. I've already read the twenty-eight texts..."

"Sorry," she says as her cheeks turn pink. "You don't have to listen to the voicemails."

"Are you kidding? I can't wait. Your texts were incredible. I'm never deleting them." She rolls her eyes.

"And I got some wine for Steven and Renee... and I got you this." I throw the ubiquitous turquoise box in front of her.

"Seriously?" she says.

"It's nothing, really."

"Tiffany's is *never* nothing," she argues.

"Will you just open it, or do I have to do it for you?" She drops her fork and grabs the box, carefully pulling on the ribbon and lifting the lid. She pulls out the silver chain and studies the pendants, a silver "e" charm partnered with a gold open heart charm.

"You have my heart, Em," I tell her.

"You are far too good for me. I don't deserve any of this."

"Yes, you do, Emi... but I thought you could just put those charms aside and put this on the chain for now..." I pull the engagement ring out of my pocket and hold it out for her. "You know, if you still want to go through with this..."

"Oh, Jack," she smiles, crawling off the bed to claim her ring.

"I'd really like you to wear it."

"I want to wear it. I will wear it!" She fumbles with the necklace, but can't open it with her hand in the cast. She hands it to me, watches me unclasp the chain and pull the other charms off of it, replacing them with her ring. I place the other pendants in the box and tie it back up. "Can I put it on you?"

"Of course." She pulls up her hair and turns around as I fasten it around her neck, kissing the clasp as I set it down.

"I love you," I whisper in her ear. She abruptly turns around to kiss me.

"I love you." She smiles, wide. "More than anything."

"Alright, finish your breakfast so we can go over to Stevie's."

"I'll take it with me, let's go," she says as she grabs her purse, fruit and soda. "Remember, act surprised."

"I've already called them," I tell her. "They know I know."

"But they made me promise..."

"Emi, they're just happy we're together and not fighting. They don't care that I know."

She pouts briefly, then shrugs and follows me out the door.

As soon as we enter Steven's house, Emi finds Renee and pulls her off to the side, whispering something in her ear. My parents embrace me, holding on a little longer than necessary. My mother's eyes greet me with sympathy. I just kiss her on the cheek and smile.

"Jackson, honey, we're so sorry," she says quietly so no one else can hear.

"Don't be, Mom," I tell her. "We're here to figure all that out, and we're fine. It'll all work out fine. Just trust that."

"Are you sure you're okay?" she asks.

"I couldn't be better. Emi and I are getting married, and that's all I need. Anything beyond that is just icing on the cake. I'm just sorry I didn't tell you sooner." She nods. "If anything, congratulations are in order."

"Jacks!" Matty and Steven call out to me in unison, rescuing me from the unnecessary sorrow my mother feels the need to convey. "We're going golfing, tee time's in an hour," Steven says. "Let's go, men." I glance briefly at Emi.

"Shopping," she states, still huddled in secrecy with Renee. "I need to get some things, so Renee's going to take me and your mom to the mall. Go golf your heart out."

"Is this the surprise party?" I ask.

"Party's tonight, honey," my mom says. "We're just going out to dinner...

reservations are at eight."

"Alright, then," I say, walking toward Emi. "Kiss for luck?"

She holds on tightly to my shirt, pulls me to her and kisses me softly. "I don't need luck for shopping," she smiles.

"Of course not. Do you need any money?" I whisper in her ear.

She rolls her eyes at me. "I make my own, remember."

"I was just offering," I tell her, throwing my hands up. "Have fun today."

"You, too."

"So," Steven begins as we walk leisurely on the fairway, "what the hell happened yesterday?"

"I don't know what you're talking about," I lie.

"Fuck you, Jacks, don't lie," Matty says.

"Matthew," my father lectures as he walks past us to the tee. "Language, please." My brother rolls his eyes.

"Very mature, Matty," I add. He backhands my arm. "It was a little misunderstanding, that's it. Everything's fine."

"Were you drunk yesterday?" my younger brother asks.

"I had a few drinks."

"Were you fighting?"

"A little."

"She says you gave her an ultimatum... she was so upset when she missed her flight. She called Kelly in tears..."

"Well, I was pretty upset she didn't meet me at the airport, as well. I thought she *chose* not to, though. Hence the drinking..."

"Jacks," Matthew says. "She loves you more than anything. Every time she mentioned your name last night, her face just lit up."

"So she told you what the ultimatum was?" I ask him.

"She told me," Matty says as Steven walks to the next hole with my father. "She's chatty when she drinks," he laughs. "She understood why you were upset... and she felt bad for dragging her feet. But she loves you, and she wants you to marry her... soon..."

"Good to know," I smile. "I want the same thing. I just wish it were that easy."

"It is that easy. It's gonna happen. And you're going to need a best man," my brother states.

"I hope I will," I laugh, musing over the options. I'd only considered this briefly before.

"Is it Chris?"

"It's a toss-up," I explain. "But in the end, man, it's you. I would love for you to be my best man– if there's a wedding."

"I thought we just established there would be."

"Sorry, you're right. Of course we'll get married." *Of course I can convince her that we can– and will– have children.* "I mean a big wedding. I don't know what we'll do."

"Well, I'll be there, big or small ceremony."

"Alright."

"And more than anything, I want to plan the bachelor party!"

"Yeah, maybe you should get with Chris on that one..." I say with mocking unease, but truly a little uncomfortable with what my brother's idea of fun might be.

"You jackass," he says, "a little trust here, okay?"

"You're right, you're right, I'm sorry."

"Hey, guys!" Steven yells. "Matty, you're up!"

"Coming!" he yells as he walks to the tee.

Later that night, after dinner with my parents, brothers, and Renee, Emi is quiet as we walk toward the rental car.

"So you've just always been this way?" she asks as soon as I close my door.

"What way?"

"What Matty said at dinner tonight..." I remember back to the toast my

brother had made to me for my birthday... and for our engagement. My
brothers had been telling stories about our youth.

"Okay," Matthew began, "so growing up, Jacks was always the good one.
He never got into trouble, excelled in school and sports, and was always
involved in the community.

"Even with all of his activities, he always had time for Kelly, Stevie and
me. Only two years separate us in age, but he was always years beyond me in
wisdom. I don't know how he got that way, but it's just how he's always been.

"Jacks was the first person I came out to. We were actually on our way
home from a double date. I had just graduated from high school, and we had
seen 'While You Were Sleeping' with a few girls from Jacks's school. After
the movie, we stopped at a restaurant for dessert.

"I'd known I was gay for years, was even teased about it on occasion, but
high school is hard enough as a 'straight' kid. I wasn't brave enough to live it
as myself.

"Anyway, after we dropped the girls off, my brother pulled over on the
side of the road before taking me back home. He asked me if I had noticed
what our waiter at the restaurant had been wearing. I listed everything, in
explicit detail– the guy was hot, I'm not gonna lie– down to the brand of
sunglasses he had peeking out of his shirt pocket. They were Oakleys, by the
way. Jacks then simply said, 'And what was your date wearing?'

"I had no idea. I stammered around an answer... I couldn't even get the
color of her blouse right. He didn't make me say it, though. He said the
words for me. 'So, you're gay.' It wasn't a question. It was hardly a
statement. He shrugged his shoulders and started the car, turning it around and
taking me back to his apartment. We talked all night, came up with a game
plan to tell Mom and Dad...

"Anyway, long story short, the evening after I told my parents, Jacks came
home with some laundry. I had called him an hour before, told him that it
wasn't going well. My parents were both in shock a little, didn't really know

what to say... So, our mom, being helpful as always and wanting a distraction from the heavy news, offered to wash his clothes for him.

"All of a sudden we hear this screech from the laundry room: 'Jack!' she yelled to my father. 'We have a bigger problem on our hands!' She comes into the living room where we're all sitting around watching TV and she throws down a baggie of pot on the coffee table."

My siblings and parents were all giggling, having heard this story many times over the years.

"'That was in Jackson's pants!' she yelled, pointing to the drugs. Mom and Dad were so pissed!"

"And Jacks just sat there and took it... owned up to it. I couldn't count how many times they told him they were disappointed in him. And he apologized, acknowledged it was stupid, but strung them along, telling them it wasn't hurting anyone..."

Emi had looked at me, surprised and laughing. I shook my head and rolled my eyes.

"That just made them more angry... and he carried on the charade for weeks. Over that time, my parents got more and more used to the idea of me being gay... realized it wasn't a problem at all, was nothing compared to their good son's drug use.

"Of course, it was oregano," Matty said. "But my point is... yes, there's a point... that Jacks was always the one to protect us all. He would do anything for us, even if it meant tarnishing his own reputation to save ours. He is the most generous person I have ever met.

"Emi," he ended with a special message for her, his eyes warm, "you are the sweetest, most beautiful, most precious woman to walk into his life. He recognizes how fragile you are, and he thrives on taking care of people... so let him take care of you when you need him. Lean on him. Don't ever be afraid to ask him for anything, because you give him purpose. You give him life."

I allow my thoughts to linger on his last statement before returning to her question. "What way?" I ask Emi again in the car.

"Have you always been the one who does everything? Or do you take care of me because you think I'm fragile?"

"I don't think you're fragile... maybe delicate is a better word?" I smile at her, run my thumb along her cheek.

"Please watch the road," she says to me, her voice concerned.

"Of course," I say, putting my hand back on the steering wheel and turning my eyes to the highway. "I'm sorry."

"I don't need you to protect me. I don't need you to feel sorry for me. You know, I *can* take care of myself."

"Of course you can, Emi. No one ever said you couldn't."

"It was implied," she counters.

"No..."

"It's always implied. You do everything for me."

I take the next ramp off the highway.

"This isn't our exit, is it?" she asks.

"Emi, honey," I start slowly, "I want to talk to you about something, but I don't want to be driving while I have this conversation with you. Plus, I saw this park earlier..."

"But it's dark."

"It's perfect," I tell her, finding a parking spot near the grouping of trees I had discovered this afternoon. "Come with me... please." I take the bag I had prepared earlier from the backseat and walk to meet her on the other side of the car. She takes my hand and lets me lead the way to a picnic table.

"Hold on, just a second," I stall, leaving her by one of the trees. "And close your eyes."

"Jack..."

"Just... wait." I take out the contents of the bag and arrange everything on the table. Once all of the items are in place, I press the play button on my iPod and walk over to her, putting my hand on the small of her back. "Go sit down."

She smiles as she sees the familiar scene in front of her, and assumes her seat on top of the picnic table. "I was here, right?" she asks, the strain of our earlier conversation dissolving into a bright smile. She looks even more beautiful than she did that first night.

I had hoped for tonight to play out just like it did those many years ago in college, but I can't wait for her to kiss me. My one regret from that night was not kissing her sooner. I walk over to her, on a mission, take her head in my hands, my fingers toying with her long hair, and I kiss her, ardently and passionately. She wraps her arms around my waist and pulls my body into hers.

"That was nice," she whispers. I nod my head in agreement.

"Do you recognize the song?"

"It was playing in the background when I kissed you that night."

"I wasn't sure you'd remember it."

"And the water," she adds, picking up the cups and the bottle, "just like you brought it to me that night. I always thought it was cool that you were going to split it with me, instead of just bringing two bottles. I don't know why."

"Honestly, it was the only one I could find. But it seemed appropriate. I wanted to share *something* with you that night. I had given up on the kiss, so why not a bottle of water?" I laugh.

"What's with the gum?"

"You were chewing cinnamon gum."

"Was I?"

"You were."

"And you remember that?" she asks me, unwrapping a stick of gum and placing it in her mouth.

"I remember everything. Every second that passed, every sight, smell, sound... touch..." My thumb rubs her cheek. "Taste..." I whisper in her ear as I move in to kiss her once more, my gaze unfaltering. My mouth brushes her lips, then presses against them harder. I feel her soft tongue on mine, tentative and sweet, tasting the spicy flavor of her gum. "This is where it all began for us, Em," I tell her quietly. "A picnic table just like this one... this is where my life, with you, started. And from that point on, I wanted to be with you, forever."

"Jack," she says, her eyes becoming moist with tears.

"I still want that, Emi. But I am so tired of fighting with you. I don't want to do it anymore."

"Okay," she says plainly, "but I still want to *talk* about tonight... not fight, okay? I'm not fragile, not anymore."

"Alright, if this is really a concern, let's just get it all out there... yes, you were once fragile– you were extremely fragile when we met last year, up to the point when we started dating and even a little beyond that. I felt like I had to take care of you.

"But since then, Emi, you have lived through something unimaginable, and you've come out of it victorious. You didn't let it take your spirit... your fire. You became this amazing, strong woman that I love even more.

"I'm sorry if you think I've been overbearing. I'm sorry for making *all* the decisions. But I know you can take care of yourself... and for awhile, yes, I was actually afraid of that. I was afraid that you wouldn't need me anymore.

"So has it been difficult for me to let go? To let loose every now and then? Yes, and I'm sorry you're mistaking my intentions. But the truth is, in all of my life, I have been the one that other people relied on. I have been there to take care of the people I love.

"If you take anything away from what Matty said tonight, it should be this: that maybe this isn't about how I see you. Maybe this is just who I am."

"I do see that now," she whispers. "I'm worried that... I won't give you purpose anymore if I don't need you like I once did."

"I have moved so far beyond that at this point, Emi. I don't do this for you alone anymore. Right now, I'm doing this for us. *We* need help. *We* need to be nurtured, and that's where all of my focus will be until *we* are strong again.

"And once that's done, Emi, I'm just going to put all of my energy into enjoying this life that we are making together. I'm going to share this immense responsibility with you... and you're going to help. Together, we will take care of us, and whatever more life throws our way. I know we are stronger as a couple."

"But even stronger as a family," she mumbles.

"What?"

"Having children will let you take care of people. It's, like, a need for you, isn't it?"

"It's really important to me," I tell her. "But I'm trying to adjust to this idea of it being the two of us. There are definite advantages," I smile at her as I lean in to kiss her again.

"Don't," she stops me.

"Don't what?" I ask, leaning away, trying to read her eyes. "What now?" I sigh, exasperated.

"No," she laughs. "It's just... you don't need to adjust to that idea. Maybe I *can* do this."

"Emi, you *can*. And by no means do we have to do this right away. You know," I say, sweeping her hair behind her ear, "we missed out on a lot of each other's lives because of the outcome of that one night in college, Emi. Between the alcohol, the misread signals and the miscommunications, my inability to man up and... just... *kiss* you... everything became so complicated, and it should have been so simple. I fell completely in love with you that night. It was just about a man and a woman. Me and you. And a picnic table. And the most unexpected kiss. It should have been so simple.

"And really, that's all it's about now. A man and a woman in love. We're overcomplicating things again. Let's start over, Emi. Here on this picnic table, let's commit to making this simple, like it should be. Just let me love you like I need to. That's all I want. And for you to love me in return."

"I *do* love you," she confirms.

"Whatever fears you have, Emi, or doubts... just hand them over. Let me find a permanent home for them, far away. Let me give you hope and confidence... and life... in their place. Let go of the 'what ifs'... and let's just let life happen."

"Okay," she sighs.

"And let's not give up on our dreams to have a family, Emi. *Please.* You want that. We both do, we've talked about it at length. Yes, it will be challenging, and yes, we may face disappointment, but as long as I know you're with me, *I* can handle anything. Don't you think you could, too, if you knew I would always be there?

"I do," she answers, nodding with happy tears in her eyes.

"I will always be there."

"Okay then," she smiles after a moment of brief contemplation. "Let's do it." Her knees bounce with excitement on the bench.

"You're in?" I laugh.

"Yeah," she laughs. "I'm in."

"Seriously? Just so I'm not misunderstanding, we can try to have a family together?"

"I *want* to raise a family with you, Jack. I want to see you become a wonderful father to our children, and I know that we can do this together."

"Thank you," I sigh, grateful, pulling her into a tight embrace, never wanting to let her go.

We finish the bottle of water and listen to a few more grunge songs from our college days before heading back to the hotel.

"I need to get something out of the back of the SUV," Emi says before I hand the keys to the valet. I press the button to open the back door and reach for the black bag spread out in the rear-facing seat.

"I got it," Emi says, stepping in front of me.

"What is it?" I ask.

"It's a hanging bag." She struggles to pull the heavy bag up by the hanger, hugging it close to her body.

"And what's *in* the hanging bag?"

"I bought a dress today," she says.

"Mmmm," I smile coyly at her. "Can I see it?"

"Absolutely...... *not*." Puzzled, I ask her why. "It's the kind of dress you're not allowed to see... yet." My heart stops for a second.

"Wait... as in a wedding dress?" She looks up at me with the faintest smile on her face. "Seriously?"

"I know, Anna's going to kill me. She wanted to help me find one... but oh, my god, Jack, it's so beautiful. Renee had an appointment at this bridal boutique, and I was just going to help her... but they had this one dress... and I saw it... and I knew it was mine.

"And when it fit... I *really* knew."

"So, tell me about it," I request, trying to take the bag from her.

"No!" she squeals, but releases the dress from her grasp and into my waiting hands. I'm surprised by how heavy it is.

"How many dresses did you buy?" I laugh.

"Just one!" she slaps me on the arm.

"It's heavy. Is this a fancy formal-wedding kind of dress?"

"I don't want to tell you!"

"What kind of wedding will it require?"

"Just a romantic one," she says. "That could be anywhere, really."

"How will I know what I need to buy?"

"I'll help you pick out a tux, don't worry."

"Such a double standard," I joke.

"But..." she begins.

"But what?"

"I may be coming over to eat at your place a lot... I probably won't be able to pay my bills for the next few months," she laughs.

"That much?"

"I spread it out over both my credit cards," she explains. "I kind of maxed them both... but I couldn't *not* buy it."

"Well... you know if you sell the loft..." I tease.

"That's actually what I was thinking," she says. I can't contain my smile when I look into her eyes as we step onto the elevator. "So maybe you can help me with that when we get back home."

"Poppet, it's okay. I know this is all going to happen. You can take your time moving in... you don't have to prove anything to me."

"No, I'm ready. Really."

"Whatever you want me to do, Emi, I'd be happy to."

"I've never owned any real estate, so I don't know the first thing about selling that place."

"Well, I can certainly teach you. I have had a little practice over the years."

"I would really appreciate that."

"So, what else did you get today?" I ask, eyeing more bags that are draped over her shoulder.

"Just some clothes since I didn't pack enough... and a present for you... and some shoes."

"Wait, a present for me? I thought you said at dinner that it was in New York."

"Well, one of them is. Your big one is in New York. This is just something silly... you'll probably hate it."

"Yeah, probably," I roll my eyes. "When do I get to see it?"

"When we get back to the room."

"Are you wearing it now?"

"No, it's not anything I can wear. And I only got you half of it, really. You bought yourself the other half."

"Okay, I'm utterly confused now. Thanks."

"Good."

As we make our way down the hall to our room, I eye the bag in my hands. "You know, Em, all it would take is one little slip of this tiny zipper here, and I'd see everything," I taunt her. "It's definitely long..."

"Please, don't, Jack, you know it's bad luck."

"I don't believe in that," I tell her.

"Well, I do. I've had enough bad luck, so I'd rather not tempt fate. Humor me," she says.

"For you... I won't look... but just know that I can't wait to see you in it," I sigh, opening the door for her.

"And I can't wait to wear it."

"Is it white?"

"Would you be upset if it wasn't? Not that it's not..."

"Well, then everyone will know you're not a virgin," I joke with her as I lock the door behind us. "You haven't always dreamed of a white dress?"

"I have," she says. "But I always dreamed of the perfect dress, too. And this is the perfect dress."

"So it's not white?"

"I didn't say that," she says, flustered, as I hang the bag in the closet.

"Okay," I say. "Emi, just know that you will look beautiful in any color. I'd marry you in anything."

"It's fluorescent yellow," she tells me. "And I want you to get a neon orange tux, will that be okay?"

"As long as I get the top hat and cane, my love, I will be happy." She laughs as she sets the rest of the bags on the bed. "What did you get for hangover medicine last night?"

"Just some ibuprofen... and some aspirin, too. I forget which one is good for that."

"Where's the ibuprofen? My muscles are a little tight from golfing."

"I set them on the minibar, by the bottled water. Why don't you take a hot bath while I put all this stuff away, and then I'll give you a massage before bed. It'll be a one-handed massage, but I'll make it good, I promise."

"You don't have to do that..."

"I want to," she insists.

"I'm not going to turn that down," I smile, opening the water and taking the pills. "Care to join me?"

"I need to hang this stuff up... I'll meet you in bed."

"That works," I smile.

Soaking in the hot water, my body begins to relax but my head is swimming with a million random thoughts... the dress, the massage, the loft, the wedding, children, an art studio... I can barely focus on any one thing. She wants to get married soon, as do I. With the dress, feeling its substance, its heft, I think an elopement is probably out. I wonder what she's thinking. Anything big will take a long time to plan.

And the loft... I want her to have a nice space to work, so I ponder which room to redo at home. I think major renovations would need to happen. The basement would not do, the lack of windows made it seem closed and dark. The upper two floors would be the only options... possibly make my office into her studio? I could have an office anywhere. Still, there was only one window, and the view of the street wasn't particularly inspiring. Maybe getting her a studio near the house would be the best solution. I decided to make some calls when we get back. And I'll need to get in touch with Donna about selling the loft, first and foremost.

Emi is lying in bed watching TV when I get out of the bath. Dressed in my boxers, I climb under the covers with her.

"Here, turn over," she instructs me.

"No, I'm feeling better, Em. I just want to lie here with you." I kiss her before wrapping my arm across her stomach, laying my head on her breast, listening to her rhythmic heartbeat. She lays her cast on my side, and starts running her fingers through my hair with her good hand.

"So, tell me, Emi," I begin, "what do you have in mind for the wedding? Have you thought any more about how big, or small... or where?"

"I think I would like our families there," she says. "After hanging out with your brothers last night, I know it's important for them to be there. And I really want Chris and Jen there, too. And I think our parents would kill us both if they weren't there."

"I think you're right," I agree. "Matty is going to be the best man."

"You asked him?" she asks.

"I did. I mean, it can be in title only. If you don't want a formal wedding like that–"

"No, Jack, this is *our* wedding, not mine. From now on, we make decisions together, so you need an opinion, too. So we're having attendants, that's good. What do you envision?"

"I don't know. A small, intimate venue, maybe. Families, definitely... I honestly couldn't imagine getting married without my sister and brothers there. And a few select friends?"

"I just don't want to wait long," Emi says. "Let's start trying to find a place. Maybe sometime around the beginning of the year?"

"That soon? That's not a whole lot of time to plan."

"I can't wait," she says.

"Well, I don't want it to stress you out."

"Let's just say as long as everyone's there, and I have my dress, and you have your suit... and maybe there's a cake and some rings... then that will be enough."

"You say that..." I argue.

"No, really. I don't want a big ordeal. I just want to marry you. Maybe we can do it at your house? In the back yard?"

"That would be easy," I tell her. "Let's think about it. If we do it at the beginning of the year, it may be too cold for that."

"Oh, yeah. I will likely need your sensible thinking for this," she laughs.

"I can provide that."

"Thank you," she says, kissing the top of my head.

"Hey, do you mind if I call Donna and talk to her about the loft when we get back? She mentioned at the christening that she might know a buyer for it."

"Is she going to buy it? I wouldn't feel right selling it to her. It was her son's, after all."

"But he left it to you," I remind her. "You own it, and she recognizes that.

I think she wants you to do with it what you want. And I didn't get the impression that she wanted it. Just that she might know someone."

"Oh..."

"Would you feel okay with me talking to her about it?"

"Sure," she assures me. "All I ask is that you don't make any final decisions without me."

"Of course I wouldn't do that. It's yours."

"Ours," she corrects me.

"No, this one's yours... you'll make the decision, and you'll get the profit from selling it. I imagine you'll get a pretty penny for it."

"How much do you think it'll go for?" she asks.

"I would imagine... in that location... I bet you'll get at least nine something... probably more."

"Nine hundred thousand something?"

I laugh. "Have you ever priced out apartments in Manhattan, Em?"

"Not anywhere near the loft. I knew I could never afford anything off 5th Avenue."

"That's obvious. Nine *million* something... at least."

She is silent for a few minutes. "Nine *million*?"

"Mmm-hmmm."

"I wouldn't even know what to do with that kind of money."

"I can help you with that, too."

She giggles to herself, then asks, "Will I be richer than you?"

I laugh back at her. "Emi, honey, if we're getting married, there is something you should know about me... I've got a couple hundred million in investments."

"Shut up," she mutters.

"And the awesome part of this is that, when we do get married, you'll have that, too."

"Maybe we should sign a pre-nup?" she asks.

"Absolutely not, Emi."

307

"But..."

"First and foremost, I know we are going to last. I love you and I know you love me. Secondly," I add, "there's no way a single man like me can spend that much money in a lifetime."

"Well, then," Emi says, "we'll just add the loft money to what you already have. Maybe you can teach me about investments or charities or something."

"Of course, I'd be happy to."

"Maybe we could set up a foundation or a scholarship in Nate's name... since it was his loft. We could do something to memorialize him."

"I think that's a great idea. We can talk to Donna about that, too."

"Okay," she says, and I can tell she's smiling by the tone of her voice. "Hey, do you want your present?"

"I have to say, if it involves any sort of physical activity, I may have to wait a night. I don't think I can move."

"None whatsoever," she says. "Here." She sets down a turquoise box on her stomach, seemingly the same box I had given her earlier today. I hold the box between my fingers as she pulls the ribbon off of it. She lifts the lid for me as I watch, my head still resting on her chest.

"What is it?" I ask her.

"Well," she whispers softly. "You told me earlier that I have your heart... and I do. I'm wearing the heart with the ring," she tells me. I glance up at the jewelry around her neck to confirm what she has just told me.

"Yes?" I answer.

She pulls a silver keychain from the box and dangles it in front of me. The "e" charm that I had given to her earlier hangs from it. "You gave me your heart, but I'm giving you... me. All of me."

I hold the keepsake over her stomach.

"I was going to say something about having the key to my heart, but I realize how incredibly cheesy that sounds."

"Yes, Em, it does. But it's sweet, anyway. Thank you. I love it."

"I love you, Jack."

"I love you, too." She leans to meet my lips and kisses me, softly.

"Happy early birthday."

"Thank you, Poppet." I lay my head back down and close my eyes, sleep coming easily as I finally feel like things are moving ahead in the right direction.

CHAPTER 10

"Thanks for meeting me, Donna."

"It's my pleasure, Jackson, but I apologize, I won't be able to have dinner tonight. Something came up, so I thought we could just do this over a drink," Nate's mother says to me at the French restaurant where she suggested we meet. "How are you doing?"

"I'm great. Emi and I just got back from a trip to Texas."

"Any special occasion?" she asks.

"Actually, yes. We went to visit my brother and his fiancée... to get a little information about adoption."

"Adoption, of course," she says with a sad smile. "I am so sorry, Jackson. It broke her heart, and mine."

"It's alright," I tell her, squeezing her hand once and letting it go, straightening my tie and swallowing hard to compose myself. "We'll have children. As many as she wants."

"She'll be a great mother," Donna says with an assured smile. "Speaking of which, where is Emily?"

"She was supposed to meet us, but she had some last-minute revisions on a project. She says she's sorry she can't make it... but in all honesty, I'm not."

"I'm sorry?" she asks.

"I wanted to talk to you about something, and I want it to be a surprise to her."

"Oh," she smiles, then laughs to herself. "You're really good together." I smile back, thanking her. "Is it about the loft?"

"Not exactly, but I would like to discuss a few things with you about that. She is planning to move in with me over the next few weeks, so we would like to put her apartment on the market."

"Okay," she says, breathing in deeply before sighing heavily, still putting on a brave smile. "I don't know why this saddens me," she adds. "I rarely spent any time there. I have no real attachment to it. I just... I guess I just knew how much he loved that place."

"Well, Emi isn't entirely comfortable with selling it. She feels a little bit like it still isn't hers to sell," I inform Donna.

"Legally, it is, though," Donna assures me. "She owns the deed. I signed it over to her, and I knew she wouldn't stay forever."

"Oh, I know. Still... it doesn't sit right with her, making money off of it."

"Well, I wouldn't want anything for it, if that's what she's worried about. He would have wanted her to have it."

"I think she had something else in mind. She was thinking of setting up a foundation or scholarship in Nate's name with some of the money."

A smile grows on her face, the corners of her lips reaching her eyes, becoming moist with tears. "I would love that... but of course it's not necessary."

"Of course," I assure her. "But actually, I have something else in mind."

"Okay. What are you thinking?"

After explaining my ideas with Donna, she offered any assistance she could provide. She was sure that Emi would love what we were planning. Confident with the arrangement that we'd made, and wondering how I would keep it all a secret, I walk into the house.

"Emi?" I call out. I peek into the dark office to look for her before going upstairs to the bedroom, the room she has chosen to use as her temporary workspace when she's here. That room is dark, as well, and she is not sitting, legs curled under her body working on her computer, like she so often has been the past few days. Strangely, the stuffed dog from the fair has found a new home in the middle of my bed. "Poppet?" I glance at the patio and start to leave the room before something in the yard catches my attention.

A dog. A *real* dog. A small furry white, black and brown dog. Squeals erupt as our nieces and nephews scurry in the grass, trying to catch it. Quickly I head downstairs to see what is going on.

Food is arranged in the kitchen as I pass through. Lots of it.

A chorus of "happy birthday" greetings meet me when I open the door to the backyard. Everyone local is here: Kelly, Thomas, their kids; Chris, Anna and Eli; Jen and Clara, and Jen's boyfriend Brian; and of course, Emi, sitting in the wooden swing across the lawn in a short, white dress and pink heels. As she walks toward me, the puppy follows her up the steps on the deck.

"Some freelance job," I joke with her. "I'm starting to wonder if you really are a graphic designer or just a pathological liar."

"Oh, Donna was in on it... you made it too easy," she laughs, throwing her arms around my neck. I pick her up to kiss her, then set her down gently. My nieces and nephews shower me with hugs next.

"Uncle Jacks?" Andrew asks, jumping up and down. I kneel down to meet with him on his level. "Did you see your birthday present?"

"No, what is it?"

"Ruby!" he shouts. Madeleine carries the squirming dog to me.

"And we made her a dog house," Jackie adds, pointing to a colorful, pink wooden house in the corner of the patio. "We painted it and everything!"

"I tried to put a bow on her," Emi says, "but she would have none of that.

313

I think she's a little bit of a free spirt."

"A dog?" I ask.

"Is that bad?" she returns.

"Not at all," I laugh. "It's a fox terrier..."

"It is," she smiles. "I remember you saying you loved yours when you were a kid."

"I did. Let me see her," I say, reaching my arm out. Madeleine carefully places the puppy in my hands. "Ruby, you say?"

"That's what we've been calling her," Emi says. "I guess you can name her anything you want."

"Well, why Ruby?"

"She just seems a little fiery, that's all."

"I think Ruby's perfect." I stand, holding the dog between us.

"Since it's going to take awhile before we'll have children, I thought it would be nice to have a dog."

"It's a wonderful idea."

"And so I can help you take care of it, I'll be moving in officially tomorrow. They've all agreed to help," she says, motioning to our siblings. "And I've been packing all week... and it hasn't been easy," she adds, waving her cast at me.

"Now, that's the best birthday present." I put the dog down and all the children resume their game of chase, the dog easily outrunning all of them. "Thank you, Emi."

"You're welcome." I pull her close to kiss her, brushing her lips with mine before they press deeper. As my hand holds on to her neck, my thumb resting just below her ear, I can feel her pulse quicken. I love the effect I have on her. "How did your meeting with Donna go?" she asks quietly when we finally separate.

I smile broadly, remembering our conversation. "It was great. We're putting the loft on the market this week. She knows an agent who can help."

"Why that smile?" she asks.

"I'm just excited about you moving in, Em." It's not a lie, it's just another reason to be happy. "Just makes this all feel more... real... We just need to pick a date now."

"I have an idea for that, too."

"Really?"

"Yeah, we can talk about it later. Right now, everyone's starving and ready to eat."

After fixing our plates and sitting down, I notice Jen and Chris go back into my house. "We forgot drinks. What would you like?"

"Water's fine," she answers. I follow Emi's siblings into the kitchen.

"Hey, can I talk to you two for a second?"

"Of course, Jacks," Jen says.

"I have an idea for a place to get married... but I want it to be a surprise to Emi... do you think there's any possibility that we could make that happen?"

"Depends. Where is it?"

I describe the place in detail– my vision of it anyway– and tell them why I would like it to remain a surprise, why it's necessary for the time being. Jen, emotional like her sister, wipes away the tears that begin to form in the corners of her eyes. Chris's expression shows his consent. They exchange a glance with one another before nodding to each other, then to me. We quickly brainstorm on how I can convince Emi to allow me to be in charge of the venue... and we all hope she has enough trust in us to handle this.

~ * ~

The next night, feeling exhausted after we spent the day moving all of Emi's boxes to my place and cleaning up her loft, I struggle to get the puppy to abandon her playtime in the backyard.

"Come, Ruby... Come... Come on, Ruby," I urge the puppy to come in the house. "I'm tired," I try to reason with the dog. Ruby just rolls in the grass, belly up.

"It's really nice out here," Emi says as she comes out the back door carrying a blanket. She flicks on the lights, a string of lanterns still hanging from last night's party, illuminating the yard with soft, colorful radiance. "I think Ruby might have the right idea. Come on."

I take the comforter from her hands and spread it out below one of the large trees in the back yard. Emi sets down her iPod and a small speaker, pressing the play button. We both lie down on the blanket, looking up at the sky where only the brightest of stars are visible from the city. I pull Emi's head onto my shoulder as I put my arm around her. Ruby is struck with a sudden burst of energy and jumps on my stomach, her little tail wagging quickly.

"Sure, *now* you want to come to me," I comment, rubbing her behind the ears. Emi rolls to her side and strokes the dog's back.

"You think she's jealous of me?" Emi asks.

"She should be."

"Well, you never scratch *me* behind the ears like that," she adds. I move Ruby to the side and lean up, pulling Emi's face toward mine to kiss me as I gently massage behind her ear with my thumb.

"Sure I do," I mumble into her mouth. Ruby hops in between us, nuzzling her head under my arm, separating us. Emi giggles and wrestles with the puppy. "So cute," I comment, watching them play.

"I know she is," Emi says. "I knew you'd love her."

"I was talking about you," I tell her, tucking a strand of hair behind her ear. "But I really do like both of my presents... Ruby and you... Things are really starting to feel... official."

"Speaking of official... let's talk about a date."

"You talk about a date, I'll talk about a location. How's that?"

"You have an idea for a place? Oooo, do tell!"

"No, you first. It'll all hinge on your date."

"Okay," she begins as Ruby wriggles free of Emi's grasp and saunters to her dog house where she sniffs around. "I want to do it relatively soon."

"That makes two of us... but how soon are you thinking?"

"January first." I roll over on my side and study her eyes as she gazes into the stars.

"Are you sure?"

"Positive. I mean, if New Year's Eve always brings sadness... and I think it's safe to say it will always be tainted by what happened... it would be nice to know that it's immediately followed by happiness the next day, you know? It would be, like, a fresh start, every year."

"Isn't that what January first is all about anyway?"

"But we'd have something to really celebrate. Do you not like that date?" she asks, finally looking at me, her eyes unsure.

"I think we could do January first," I tell her, "if you're sure about it. I think that gives me enough time..."

"What, to mentally prepare? I thought you were gung-ho about this already." She props herself up on her elbow, mirroring my position.

"Oh, no, I'm ready. Enough time to get the venue..."

"Oh, yes, now what were you thinking? A church with our families? On a beach in Tenerife? Or maybe back in Vail?"

"None of the above. Not a church, but here, in Manhattan, for sure. Close by. With our families."

"Okay, but is there a specific location?"

"Yes, there is a specific location."

"Care to enlighten me?"

"No." I lean in to kiss her, smiling.

"No?" she asks, surprised.

"Nope," I tell her. "Do you trust me, Emi?"

"Of course I do... but trust you with what?"

"I have an idea for the venue... and I really think you'll like it... but I want it to be a surprise... because it's part of your gift..."

"My gift?"

"You know, a wedding gift."

"Oh, like this house was for Caroline?"

"Great correlation, Em," I tell her as I roll onto my back, only slightly annoyed with her reference to my ex-fiancée that caused so much turbulence just last week. "Can we just never, *ever* talk about her again?"

"Of course, I'm sorry," she smiles, then leans in to kiss me. "But I don't want to move, Jack. You know that, right? I love this house. It's ours... right?"

"We aren't moving. I'm relieved you like the house because I've become quite attached to it... and I'm not lugging around your insane amount of belongings again anytime soon... but what about the venue? Would you trust me to handle that part of the ceremony?"

"I don't know," Emi says. "What about, like, decorations and stuff? Or what if I hate it?" She sits up and crosses her legs, scratching my chest lightly with her fingernails.

"You can pick any decorations... maybe work with Anna... I know she can keep a secret." As for her second question... I just can't imagine that she would hate it. Be a little apprehensive, maybe, but I know she'd like it... eventually... "And I talked to Chris and Jen today, and they like the idea."

"They know the place?"

"No... but I'll show it to them if that will ease your mind. It needs a little work right now."

"A little work? How much 'a little work?'" she asks.

"We have time, Emi, and I know plenty of people who can get it done," I assure her. "That's nothing you would need to worry about."

"It would be inside, though, right, because you know the weather could be really bad..."

"Yes, Emi. You should know by now that I'm nothing if not sensible. I've considered everything. We could probably even get there in a blizzard, if we had to."

"Will it fit our families? And do you want to do extended families? Any friends? I'd kind of like a few friends to come..."

"It is large enough to accommodate our extended families– within reason– and as many friends as you want to invite."

"Can I have measurements?"

I laugh at her oddly practical question, feeling that I'm winning her over. "Yes." I sit up to meet her eye-level, again tucking her hair behind her ears. The light cast by the lanterns makes her hair look even redder, her eyes more translucent. "You're beautiful, Emi."

"Stop distracting me," she laughs.

"I can't help it, you're breathtaking." She pushes my shoulder with her bandaged hand. I take her arm and pull her into my lap, her back pressed against my chest.

"Will you give me a general idea of the space... you know windows, walls, that sort of thing?"

"Whatever you need, Emi. Just as long as you let me surprise you with it." I kiss her neck, slowly.

"But what if I hate it?"

I sigh into her ear before answering. "You won't... but I will make sure Anna gives her seal of approval first. I know you trust her the most. Is that enough of an assurance?"

"And if *she* hates it?"

"Then we scrap the whole thing and elope to Tenerife."

"Is it wrong that I kind of hope that she hates it?" She cranes her neck to look into my eyes, a look of mischief spreading across her face.

"Yes," I tell her. "It is. For the record, though, we can honeymoon anywhere in the world you like... Tenerife, the south of France... anywhere."

"Okay..." She is still unsure.

"Because I happen to know she's going to love the place."

"How can you know?"

"Didn't I ask if you trust me? Hey, how's this? Have you ever been unhappy with any gift I've ever given you?"

"No," she says simply. "You're a great gift-giver."

"I always try to find things that mean something... that I know you'll love. This is the same way, I promise."

"Okay, then," she finally agrees with a loud sigh. "You get the venue. I get to pick the colors."

"Oh?"

"You said..."

"Okay, what colors?"

"Pink and silver," she smiles.

"Pink suits you," I tell her. She smiles back. "But I'm not wearing a pink tux."

"I get to pick," she argues.

"Absolutely not," I laugh, knowing she's not serious.

"Dark grey," she says. "You've done the black tux enough... and that suit you wore that one evening in Vail... I couldn't keep my eyes off of you that night... and maybe a pink tie."

"I'll agree to that."

She shifts slightly, touching her lips to mine, her eyes gazing into mine. Her good hand brushes my unshaven chin.

"We have a lot of work to do, you know... decorations, flowers, invitations... what about the invitations? If I can't know where we're getting married, how am I going to do the invitations?"

"That's what you have bridesmaids for."

"But I have to design it..." she whines.

"Details, my love. No one is going to stop you from designing the invitation. Someone else is just going to have to put the finishing touches on it."

"But..."

"No 'but'... let go..." I encourage her soothingly. "Remember you said as long as it was me, you, the dress, rings and... a cake... that would be all you need."

"I know," she smiles. "I meant that. You may have to remind me sometimes... but I promise to be a good little bride and not get all OCD."

"I'll hold you to it... where's Ruby?" I ask, missing our furry pet.

We both scan the yard, until I see her head poking out of the dog house. "She is actually sleeping. I wasn't sure she would ever do that."

"I think she's just getting used to the new place. I'm too excited to sleep, too," Emi says.

"Really, now?" She gets up on her knees and turns around to face me, sitting closely in my lap and putting her hand and cast behind my neck.

"Really," she smiles broadly. I pick her up and lay her down on the blanket, kissing her quietly under the stars.

"Me, too," I tell her, quirking a brow.

~ * ~

It's been six weeks since Emi has moved in, and the newness still hasn't worn off. Every few days, something else of hers shows up around the house, and I love discovering the subtle changes that she makes. It truly feels more like *our* home as each day passes.

After a jog around lower Manhattan, I come into the house and am overwhelmed by delicious smells coming from the kitchen. I still just can't help but smile when I see her doing things around the house, our house. I peek into the kitchen to see her cleaning dishes as she dances to music coming from her iPod. Ruby paces around Emi's feet, waiting for a morsel of food.

"What are you doing, Em?" I ask from the doorway, startling her.

"Oh, hey," she jumps before turning around and smiling, adjusting the volume on the speaker before walking in my direction. "I made breakfast casserole. It's in the oven, but it should be done in about ten minutes." She leans up to kiss me as Ruby jumps up and down, begging for attention.

"Hey, girl," I lean down to the dog, scratching her behind the ears. Something catches her attention, and she darts upstairs. "Do I have time to shower?"

"You do."

"Hey, is that your phone ringing?" I ask her, recognizing her ringtone.

"Is it? My phone's upstairs." I jog to the bedroom to grab her phone, just as it stops ringing. Ruby is sitting on the bed next to Emi's purse, her head cocked at the sound.

Looking at the caller ID, I call down to her. "It was your old apartment building." The phone begins to ring again. "They're calling back..."

"Can you see what they want?" she yells back to me.

"Hello?"

"May I please speak with Emi? This is Marcus."

"Hey, Marcus, she's tied up at the moment... this is Jack, is there something I can help you with?"

"Um, yes..." he hesitates. "I just wanted to let Emi know that she forgot to take the things in the downstairs storage closet."

"Oh, okay. I didn't realize there was another storage space," I tell him. "One of us will be by later today to get the stuff. Do you know what's in there, if I need a truck?"

"I don't think that will be necessary," he says. "It should all fit in your car."

"Thanks, Marcus. I appreciate the call." I shower and get dressed before going back downstairs. I get some plates and silverware and set the table for us while Emi pours some coffee.

"What did they want?" Emi asks.

"Marcus says that you forgot to clean out the storage closet downstairs. I didn't know there was one," I laugh.

"Wow, I didn't either," Emi says. "That wouldn't be my stuff."

"Nate's?"

"Yeah, I guess so." She carries over the casserole dish and sets it on the table. "That's weird."

"I can stop by there after my meetings this morning, if you'd like. Or if you want to come with me, we can go later this afternoon after your errands."

"Ummm..." she thinks to herself. "If you don't mind picking them up... I guess we may need to call Donna. I wonder if she knew about it."

"I don't mind at all. We can call her this evening after we see what's in there."

"Sounds good," she says, seemingly unworried about the contents of the closet. In truth, I'm nervous, but I feel like we need to put him behind us, put him to rest, before the wedding. I think this will be a good test.

"Marcus," I greet Emi's doorman with a handshake. "Thanks for the call."

"How is she doing?" he asks.

"She's great, thanks for asking. How are you?"

"I'm wonderful, sir. I have to say, though, it's just not the same without her." He smiles warmly. "These tenants become your family."

"I'm sure. But honestly, I like having her home with me."

"I'm sure she's happy, too." I nod. "Are you ready?" he asks.

"Well, honestly, Marcus, Emi wasn't aware there was a storage closet, either, so I don't have a key or anything."

"Oh," he says. "I guess all the stuff in there is probably Nate's then..."

"We're assuming."

"Should I call his mother instead?" he asks.

"I guess you could, if you felt more comfortable relinquishing the things to her, but Emi sent me here to do this. And we're planning to call Donna this evening. I promise that everything will go to its rightful owner."

"Oh, Jack, that's not what I meant. I just didn't know if Emi wanted to, you know..."

"I see. Do you know what's in there?"

"A few boxes," he says. "And it looks like some paintings. They're all wrapped up."

"Oh, okay. Well, let's take a look." He leads me down a long hallway, grabbing a large rolling cart and taking it with us into a service elevator. We

323

go into the basement together, and he walks me to the door with the corresponding unit number to Emi's old apartment. He takes his keys, finding the right one, and opens the door for me.

It's a thin, long closet space with dim lighting. There are about ten wrapped canvases, some medium-sized, some small, and a few boxes set off to the side. Together, we load the dusty contents onto the cart. A part of me feels sad, guilty, knowing that these things belong to a dead man. I know that I really have no right to even be touching them. I am very careful and deliberate with every single piece, making sure that I treat them with the respect they deserve.

Marcus helps to load the paintings into the front and back seats of my Volvo. The boxes fit neatly in the trunk.

On the drive back to my house, I wonder if these paintings are ones that Emi has seen before, or if these will be a complete surprise to her. I wonder why he had wrapped them up and hidden them away. I wonder just what we will be faced with when we unwrap them... what kind of reaction to expect from Emi, who has said she's put him behind her.

Once at the house, I carefully unload his things, bring them into our home, and set them neatly in the basement.

When Emi gets back to the house in the evening, I greet her with a glass of wine and a kiss. She sets her things down and looks up at me, her eyes curious. I have no doubt the contents of that closet have been on her mind all day.

"What was it?" she asks.

"It looks like some paintings and a few boxes. The paintings are all wrapped up. I put everything in the basement, if you wanted to go see what's there."

"Paintings? His agent supposedly keeps all of his paintings... she has them inventoried and stored somewhere. That's odd. Okay, I guess I'll go take a look," she sighs, heading toward the basement with Ruby right on her heels. She turns around and looks at me as I stand in the hallway. "You're not coming with me?"

"Are you sure you want me there? Maybe we should invite Donna over first?"

"No," she says. "I'd really like you to be there with me, if you don't feel too uncomfortable. Grab a beer or something," she encourages me. "But I'm sure this isn't going to be as weird as we think it will be."

"I hope you're right," I tell her, returning to the bar in the kitchen briefly to fix myself a stiff drink. I find a bone for the puppy and carry it downstairs with me.

"Come sit next to me," Emi says, patting the floor beside her. I take off my tie and unbutton the top couple of buttons of my dress shirt. "Let's make quick work of this," she adds, seeming upbeat, possibly a little detached.

"What first, the paintings or the boxes?"

"Ummm, I'll tackle the boxes," she says. "Why don't you start unwrapping the canvases."

"Emi, are you sure?"

"I'm sure, silly. Nothing in here is going to change the way I feel about you, Jack. Please, just know that. *I* know that."

"But these are his personal things..."

"Really, we're probably just fretting over paint supplies or old newspapers or something. I can't imagine he'd be hiding away anything really important to him."

"You're probably right. Alright..."

I take my keys out of my pocket, produce a small Swiss Army knife and carefully slice through the paper on the back of the first canvas.

"A t-shirt," I say. "A t-shirt on the floor... nothing too spectacular about that."

"That's mine," Emi laughs. "But I haven't had that shirt since college." I notice underneath the shirt in question is what looks like a pair of overalls. My heart sputters in my chest as I recognize the outfit.

"Wait, did you... *before?*"

"No," she laughs. "Never. I mean, at one point in college... well, it was actually *that* night in college..." She looks at me soberly and I realize she remembers those clothes too, and she's talking about the night we met. Even then, she thought Nate had been the one to stir up those intense feelings in her. "I think I tried to seduce him. But it didn't work out."

"Who stopped it from happening?" I ask her curiously.

"I think we both did," she says with a shrug. "I knew something wasn't right about the kiss we shared in my bed that night. It didn't feel the same. And he knew I was wasted. He may have wanted things to go further than they did, but I don't think he would have been able to live with himself after that.

"Who would have thought that such a pivotal night in my life would also be such an important one for him? I mean, he painted about it..."

"I remember with perfect clarity every time you shut me down," I tell her with a wistful smile.

"Well that really doesn't happen anymore, now, does it?"

I shake my head and lean over to kiss her. "Thankfully, no. So Nate wasn't your first, obviously... so who was?"

She blushes and laughs.

"This guy in one of my sophomore journalism classes. He wanted to be a screenwriter. He was cute, in a nerdy kind of way... I thought he was really deep, writing poems for me... until I realized they were all song lyrics. I felt duped," she smiles. "But he wanted to pursue his career, and I was too much of a time-suck for him."

"Idiot," I mutter and smile. "But wait, you were a virgin when I met you?"

"I was..." she smiles. "If it hadn't been for you watching over me, one of your frat brothers could have had his way with me."

"Thank God," I laugh. "Wow, but think. I could have been your one-and-only." She blushes before kissing me.

"You *are* my one-and-only," she says sweetly.

I start in on the second painting, pausing to cut open the tape on both of the boxes to make it easier for Emi to get into. Her left hand is still a little frail after having her cast removed earlier in the week.

"Hmmm... is this you? Yeah, that's your hat." Emi scoots toward me and eyes the painting. The image is of Emi's back, neck, head and shoulder, a bare shoulder left exposed when her shirt had slipped off of it. Her head is tilted, her red hair barely peeking out from under her pink winter cap. I outline the slope of her neck on the painting, a shape that I am intimately familiar with. "It's very pretty. I thought he just did abstract art... these are kind of unexpected."

"Wow... I have no idea when he did that... it looks like Central Park in the background..." As her eyes examine the painting, I unwrap the next one.

"Look at your pretty feet. Where were you there?"

"No clue," she answers. "Wait, how do you know those are my feet?" she asks.

"Those two freckles, there and there," I tell her, pointing out two marks on her left foot's second toe. "I love those freckles."

"Wow," she blushes. She moves back over to the box, pulling out a framed photo. "Oh," she says, sounding surprised.

"What?" She hands me the frame. "That is beautiful, Emi." I clear my throat, a little uncomfortable. "Did he take that?"

"No, it's, um, a photo I had sent him when he was in Vegas. Teresa took it... um, Jack," she says, pulling a bra out of the box next. "I think maybe I should open the paintings."

"Of course," I say, eyeing the lingerie in her hand. "Is that yours?"

"Yes," she blushes.

"Is that blood?" I ask, noticing a dab of red on the fabric. I wonder if this is the undergarment she had been wearing at the time of the accident... but then wonder who would have kept it in a storage closet.

"The paint is still on it..." I barely understand her mumbling. She rubs her thumb over the red smear.

"Would you like me to leave you alone?"

"No, but... one of these paintings may be a little... well, he painted a picture of me one day... it was Christmas Eve, just before he died... and if the bra is in here, I bet the painting is one of these."

"I can handle it, Emi. I'm an adult... an adult who finds particular beauty in everything about you, Em. Something he and I both obviously had in common."

"Okay, then proceed," she encourages me, pulling out more items from the box. An old headband, a few receipts and ticket stubs, a ring. "I thought I had lost this years ago... wonder why he kept it.

"It's weird," she continues. "Most of this is from way before the time that we started dating. He told me he had always loved me... and I guess I always believed him, but there was a part of me that thought he might just be saying that, to make me feel more special than the rest... but I guess he really did."

"Another thing we both had in common. I hope you don't think that I just said that to lure you in."

"Jack," she says. "Baby," she adds, a term she only uses when she really wants to convince me of something, her eyes soft and sincere. "I felt the same thing you did, remember? I knew it was 'us' from the start... I was just too drunk to realize it until 10 years later." We both laugh and kiss, then continue with our discoveries.

"Oh, wow, Em... I think I found it... and it's spectacular..." It's Emi, lying on a blanket in front of the fireplace in the old apartment. She's wearing only a pair of jeans, unbuttoned and unzipped, resting on her elbow, looking into the fire. Her eyes are intense, lips slightly parted, cheeks rosy. "You are so beautiful. He captured you perfectly."

"I don't even think I ever saw the finished product," she says, kneeling behind me, rubbing my shoulders. We both sigh at the same time. "He was truly an artist." She wraps her arms around me, rests her head on my shoulder.

"How are you not bored with me, Emi? I have no talents like that. I can't even draw stick figures. I don't write. I can't sing... I mean... do you miss those things?"

"Not for a second, Jack. You ground me... I feel... I don't know, I guess I feel balanced with you. Like with Nate, when it was bad, when we weren't best-of-friends, our future was shaky. It was a little unpredictable. I wasn't always certain of any outcome.

"With you, though... you know, I had doubts about you... but they weren't really about *you*. I had doubts because the biggest relationship of my life taught me to be cautious and uncertain...

"But now, I know you are here to stay. I will never doubt you again. You are my constant. You're my stability. You're my life and my future. You have loved me like no one else– no one– ever has."

"Were you talking to me?" I ask her, touching the painting.

She slaps my chest, hard. "You get to see that anytime you want."

"I know," I smile. I turn around and look at her, and we kiss again. "But are there any more like this one?" I ask.

"Not that I posed for," she answers. "But who knows? He had a great imagination. Those other ones weren't posed for."

I pull another canvas toward me and unwrap it. It's a painting of Emi and Clara, playing in the fall leaves.

"I should give that to Jen... she'd love that," Emi says. "Just look at her smile," Emi says. "Wow, that was almost three years ago already."

"She's grown so much," I notice. "And she looks like you."

"It's just the hair," she shrugs it off.

"No, it's that smile, too. See, she has the same dimples."

"Maybe we favor each other a bit."

"I think so." I start in on the next canvas. "What do you think is in the other box?"

"I don't know... but we're about to find out." She peeks in.

"Oh," she whispers as if the wind had just been knocked out of her. She stares into the box, her gaze fixed intently on the contents.

"Emi?"

She doesn't answer me immediately.

"Emi, are you okay?"

Quickly, two tears fall into the box. She reaches in slowly, pulling out a shattered and crumpled iPhone and setting it on the ground next to her. As Ruby comes over to sniff it, I put it on the table, tiny shards of glass sticking to my hand. I rub the flecks off of my palm and take Emi's into mine, examining it for glass, picking off a few tiny pieces.

She pulls out a set of keys next, and after that, a tiny velvet pouch. She opens it and pulls out two platinum cufflinks. "He wore these that night." She puts them back in the pouch and hands it to me.

"I didn't think she would have saved this stuff," Emi says. She holds up a book, its pages ragged, the cover bent. *The Pregnancy Book*. This item, she tosses across the room. "Won't be needing that," she murmurs in a daze.

"Emi, stop," I tell her, taking the box from her with no struggle. Ruby jumps into her empty lap, and she holds the puppy tight, petting her softly, her eyes averted to the space in front of her. Inside are a few presents wrapped in colorful Christmas paper. I take them out, see that the tags on both of them simply say, *Love ya, Em.* I pull the last item out, a stuffed giraffe. It looks used, worn, dirty, but still has the tags. I attempt to distract her, to pull her out of her trance with the little plush animal. "Was this his toy, from when he was younger?" I ask, waving the giraffe in front of her vacant stare. As soon as her eyes focus on it, Emi lunges to grab it as I pull the string, waiting to hear a soft lullaby... surprised to hear a voice, *his* voice.

"Thirteen years. One night."

I try to stifle the sound with my hands, but it's too late.

"Nine months. One small baby will deliver true love. I can't wait to see you."

"My god," I sigh. "I am so sorry." I crawl to her on my knees, move Ruby aside and hold Emi tightly.

"Don't be," she says, the lump in her throat audible. "He bought that for the baby the night of the accident," she tells me softly, a faint smile spreading across her face. "He played it for me while we sat at the red light. He was watching my reaction when the light changed."

She had never spoken of the details of the accident. I had never asked. I didn't know if she remembered, or if she just wanted to forget.

"I saw the other car coming. I yelled out to him, but it was too late. He didn't have time to react. Didn't even have time to look scared... I can remember he was still smiling, proudly, when the impact hit the car." She begins to shake her head, slowly first but growing more rapid. Her face crumples in pain as I press her head to my chest.

"Shhh," I rock her steadily, let her cry against me. I sit back down and pull her into my lap.

"The way he was looking at me," she sobs quietly, her eyes shut tight. "I can't stand it. It scares me, Jack, it scares me..."

"It's okay," I tell her. "It's going to be okay, Emi, sweetie."

"I don't want to see him like that..." She seems lost in her thoughts.

"Em, open your eyes," I urge her. "Emi, look at me. It's all right." Finally, she pries her eyes open to meet mine, a look of relief spreading across her face as soon as she focuses on me. She reaches up and touches my face, outlines my lips with her finger. I take her hand and kiss her palm slowly. She pulls away to unbutton two more buttons on my shirt, and slips her hand inside, covering my heart. She presses her ear to my chest.

"I'm here, Em. You're safe here." Her tears subside as we sit quietly for a few more minutes before she responds. Her breathing slows with a few heavy sighs. Eventually, she looks up at me, her eyes a little red, but pleading... wanting... needing...

"I know, Jack," she says, smiling as her muscles relax in my arms. "I'm so—"

I interrupt her apology with a deep kiss, breaking away to make a request. "Please don't ever apologize for sharing these moments with me. Your feelings and your memories are not things to be sorry for. They're beautiful pieces to this great and intricate puzzle that is... *you*. So uniquely you." I smooth her hair down.

"And I love finding new pieces, finding the right place for them, each one making you a little more... more *visible* to me. There are so many facets to you, Emi. And each one... each and every one... reveals something completely new about you. Every time I learn something new, I realize there is so much more I don't know. And I thirst to know everything... understanding that I never can... that I never will... that you will always surprise me.

"See, where you need stability, I need a little unpredictability. It keeps me on my toes... and it keeps me completely enthralled with you. That's why we're so good together."

She nods, still smiling. "Can we go upstairs?" she asks.

"Of course." I assume she wants to get away from the memories, but am surprised as I follow her path through the house.

She leads the way to the second floor and continues on to the third, to our bedroom. She lets go of my hand, leaving me in the doorway as she crosses the room to look out the balcony window. Ruby paws at the glass, and Emi opens the door so our dog can explore the patio.

"Do you think he's happy for me?" she says quietly.

"I do. I really do. As long as you're happy, I know he is." I follow her to the window and rub her arms slowly. She takes my hands in hers and pulls them across her body.

"Sometimes I feel guilty," she admits.

"About?"

"How happy I am. You know, is it fair? Is it right?"

I kiss the top of her head. "You deserve this. It's more than fair. It's more than right. You should never feel guilty with what life has given you... nor with any of the choices you've made." She nods slowly.

"I made the best choice when I picked you." I can hear a smile.

"Picked *me? I* picked *you*, are you kidding? This whole thing was my choice!"

She turns around in my arms laughing, pushing me away playfully against my chest. "Who kissed who that night in college?"

"You were drunk, you didn't know what you're doing," I tease.

"Like hell I didn't."

"Alright then, Poppet, I'll concede to that, but then who kissed who after Chris's rehearsal dinner?"

"I wanted it," she whispers, coming back into my arms.

"I'm glad I could give you what you wanted. I hope I always can," I tell her in earnest. Our lips meet for a kiss, one that starts slowly but develops into something urgent quickly.

"I just want to feel close to you," she says, her words desperate. "I want to feel as close as I possibly can. I want to feel like nothing will ever come between us."

"Nothing can, Emi. Nothing ever will."

She finishes unbuttoning my shirt and taking it off. I remove my undershirt as she takes off her blouse. I put my arms around her, unhooking her bra and pulling it from her shoulders before I bring her in tightly, embracing her. She kisses my chest slowly. She runs her fingers down my stomach, tracing my abs, until her hands reach the waistband of my pants.

"Mmmm..." she says, smiling. "You are so good to me, Jack. You're good *for* me." She kneels on the bed, still facing me, pulling me toward her for another kiss. Eventually, I guide her down to the pillows and lie down next to her. She moves on top of me, pulling one of her legs over mine, sitting up. She holds one of my hands as we stare at one another, saying nothing but saying everything.

"Come here, you," I urge her quietly and pull her gently down on top of me. She kisses me, sweeping her lips over mine briefly. "I love you," I sigh. She returns the sentiment. I wrap my arms tightly around her, run my fingers up and down her back until, after a bit, she falls asleep.

After about an hour, I move her as carefully as I can to the pillows.

"Don't go," she whispers, still not entirely awake.

"I'll be right back," I assure her, covering her with a blanket. I first head to the kitchen for a drink, waiting for her to follow me but hoping she'll go back to sleep. I take Ruby outside, peering back at the house for any sign of Emi. The bedroom light doesn't come on. She doesn't come down.

I return to the basement with some tape and carefully cover the paintings back up. I put all the items she had removed from the boxes back into them neatly, securely, and seal them tightly. I move everything into the empty closet of one of the bedrooms, turning the light off and softly closing the door.

CHAPTER 11

"How am I going to enjoy this holiday when the wedding is in eight days?" she says as her legs bounce anxiously in the car. "Eight days, Jack. We're getting married in eight days!"

"It can't get here fast enough," I tell her.

"Are you kidding? There's so much to do!"

"There's nothing to do, Emi. It's all done. Whatever isn't done isn't that important."

"Whatever," she scoffs. "I don't have my something old *or* my something blue," she states, matter-of-fact.

"I could take care of both of those for you," I suggest, secretly knowing that I already have done one, and she will find out in a matter of hours when she opens the presents I got her for Christmas.

"No," she hedges. "You still have tons to do, too. You've got to pick up your brothers this week, get the tuxes... did you think of a gift for Matty?" she asks.

"He doesn't need a gift," I remind her.

"It's customary," she says. "You have to get him something."

"Fine, I'll figure it out, but I'm not going to stress over this... no matter how much you try to suck me in to your world of anxiety." She playfully slaps my forearm. "Come over to my side," I suggest. "It's calm and hassle-free over here."

"I don't know how you do it," she comments as I park the car in front of her father's house. "But I'm glad you do." I walk to the passenger's side, where she steps out of the car and immediately embraces me in a tight hug. "It does feel good on your side."

"Stay, then."

"Hey, guys!" Anna calls from the front step, holding Eli, bundled in a bright blue coat and matching knitted cap.

"Oh, look how cute he is!" Emi exclaims.

"Go say hi to your godson," I encourage her. "I'll grab the gifts." She doesn't even let me finish my sentence before bounding up the sidewalk. She takes the baby from Anna's hands and smothers him in kisses as she carries him inside.

"Hey, man," Chris says as he comes down the sidewalk. "Merry Christmas."

"Merry Christmas to you, too."

"Need help?"

"I could use a hand," I tell him, giving him a few large boxes from the backseat. We carry the gifts into Emi's dad's house and place them under the tree.

"Jack," Emi's dad says from across the dining room table after lunch. "Do you think you could help me with the Christmas lights? I could use your height. One of the bulbs is out and I can't quite reach it, and we don't want Santa to miss the house because of it." He winks at Clara.

"Of course," I tell him, pushing away from the table and following him outside. A ladder is already set up, leaning against the side of the house. He points out the broken light and I climb the ladder with a replacement in hand.

"How's work going, Jack? You staying busy?"

"Yes, sir," I tell him. "But I'm looking forward to the wedding and the honeymoon so I can get away from the business for a little bit."

"Do you think you'll be traveling overseas again next year?"

"I imagine so," I tell him, unscrewing the faulty bulb. "That will probably be a biannual thing for me. But of course I hope Emi will join me for the full trip this time. And if you and Elaine would ever like to travel with us, the invitation is always there."

"That's a very nice offer, Jack," her father says. "Listen, I wanted to get a little time with you today."

"Well, you have a captive audience," I say from the top of the ladder. "What can I do for you, Robert?"

"It's not what you can do," he says. "It's what you've done."

"Is something wrong?" I ask him, looking down at him.

"No, son," he says. I smile to myself. "Jack, what you've done for my daughter over the past few years... it's impressed the hell out of me."

"Wow," I say, taken aback and installing the replacement bulb. "Thank you. That means a lot."

"My Emi needed a good man like you."

"That's very kind," I tell him. "I think we're a pretty good fit for one another. Are they all lit?" I ask, motioning to the string of lights.

"That looks good," he says, holding on to the ladder as I descend the steps. "Thank you."

"No problem."

"I have to admit, I thought I knew what was best for her. When you told me you were going to ask her to marry you, I thought it was too soon. I honestly didn't believe she was ready to leave him behind. *We* still weren't ready."

"It's fine," I tell him. "I respect that."

"No, it's not fine. You knew better. You know her better. You helped her better than we could, in ways we never knew how. You are the best thing that could have happened to her. And she needed the best."

"I feel the same way about her," I admit.

"Well, I just want to thank you. On behalf of her mother and her step-parents. Thank you for giving her hope again. You wouldn't let her be a victim of her past. You have such patience, and such compassion. And you believe in her."

"I do. I believe in her and I love her. And I hope I've proven that I would do anything for her. I'll keep her safe. I'll make her happy, just as she makes me happy."

Emi's father's eyes begin to water. "Congratulations, Jack. And welcome to the family. I'll be proud to call you my son."

"Thank you, Robert."

"You can call me 'Dad.'"

"Thank you, Dad," I respond, extending my hand to shake his. He pulls me in for a hug.

Once we get inside, Clara is begging Jen to open her presents under the tree. Emi and her stepmother pass out hot chocolate for everyone as they get comfortable in the living room. Jen, Clara, Anna and Eli all sit on the floor closest to the tree.

Emi finally joins me on the couch with a glass of wine in hand. I set down my mug and nudge her to sit up so I can rub her tense shoulders. She doesn't argue. When I'm finished, she pulls her feet up on the couch and leans back against me, my arms holding her tightly. Periodically, someone will hand us presents to open.

Brian and Jen got Clara a bike with training wheels, so the three of them go outside to play with the new toy. Anna watches as Chris tries to assemble a play mat for Eli, who is sleeping peacefully in his mother's arms. Emi and I help her parents clean up the paper and boxes before excusing ourselves later that evening.

"I can't wait for you to open your present," she says on the way to the hospital.

"I can't wait for you to open yours, either. Do you want to do it tonight when we get home?"

"No. Let's save it so we have something to look forward to tomorrow."

"Alright. I really appreciate you coming with me today."

"Are you kidding? I think we should make it a new tradition."

"It always used to be," I explain. "Last year was the first year I didn't do it. And although I had the perfect Christmas with you, I did miss spending it with these kids. It's a pretty neat experience to see how excited they get on Christmas Eve."

"So you read them 'Twas the Night Before Christmas?' And then what do you do?"

"We help pass out gifts that were donated. A lot of the parents spend all their money on medical bills, so providing them with presents isn't always in their budgets."

Donna greets Emi and me in the lobby, hugging us both tightly. We exchange holiday greetings before she takes us to the playroom. About thirty children of all ages are seated in the room, some with their parents, some with new toys, all with expectant smiles.

"I'm so glad you agreed to do this again," she tells me. "It just wasn't the same last year. You just tell the story better than I can."

"I'm happy to do it. I'm glad you invited me back."

Emi and Donna sit in a corner and talk to one another while I read the story to the kids. The younger ones always have such beautiful expressions of wonder and curiosity. It really warms my heart.

After the reading, the children are given two cookies: one as a treat to themselves and one to leave for Santa.

While the parents and nurses help tuck them all into bed, the rest of the volunteers and some of the hospital staff sort through the donations. After all the children are in their rooms, small piles of gifts will be placed outside each child's room, waiting for them to fall asleep. Nurses check on the children throughout the evening, moving the presents to their rooms once they know they're sound asleep.

I've heard that Christmas morning is one of the most rewarding days at the hospital, as the children wake up to the gifts that Santa left.

"Mister?" one little girl says to me as I begin to meet up with Emi. Her big brown eyes stare up at me through long lashes. I had noticed her during the reading, sitting alone in a chair and playing with a well-loved teddy bear. Her dark brown hair, pushed back by a small plastic tiara, cascades over her shoulders, framing her olive-skinned face. She looks like a little Italian princess. I would guess her age to be about three years old, maybe a little younger than Andrew.

"Yes?" I answer, kneeling down to her level.

"Do you know Santa Claus?" she asks. She puts her tiny hand around the end of my necktie, pulling it lightly as if she is trying to get my full attention. Little does she know she already has it.

"I sure do," I tell her.

"I never got to tell him what I wanted this year," she frowns.

"Oh, no?" She shakes her head slowly. "Well, what did you want for Christmas?"

"Teddy's sick," she says, handing her stuffed animal to me. The bear is missing one of its button eyes and is coming apart at one of the seams. Stuffing is also bursting out of a hole in one of its arms.

"Did you want Santa to bring you a new one?" I ask her.

"No," she says hurriedly, taking the bear back from me. "I just want Teddy to be better again." She frowns as little tears form in her eyes. She sniffles quietly as her lip trembles. "My mommy gave me Teddy."

"Oh, okay. Well I bet we can make him better. Can I see him one more time? I promise you can have him back."

She slowly holds the bear out again and hands it to me.

"Hmmm..." I tell her. "I'm no doctor, but I think Santa can fix him. I think his elves have just the medicine he needs."

"Really?" Her big smile brightens the room as her little fingers trace the snowflakes on my silk tie.

"Really," I tell her. "But I'm afraid I might have to take Teddy with me tonight, so they can do the surgery."

"No," she whines quietly, dropping my neckwear and reaching for her toy. "I don't want him to go."

"What's your name?" Emi asks the little girl as she holds her hands behind her back.

"Olivia Sophia DeLuca," she says, nodding her head with each word, as if she's practiced it a million times.

"She goes by Livvy," a nurse standing nearby says.

"Livvy," Emi repeats. "That's such a beautiful name!"

"Thank you," the little girl says. "What's yours?"

"I'm Emi. And this is Jack."

"Hi, Memi and Jack," she says shyly as Emi and I both laugh softly.

"Livvy, can I take a look at your bear?" She nods and hands the teddy bear to Emi.

"Oh, that'll be easy for the elves to fix," she says. "I just talked to Santa, though," Emi tells her, "and he said we need to take him for just a few hours. He'll be back before you wake up in the morning. And in the meantime, he wants you to take care of this little dog." Emi touches the stuffed dog's nose to Livvy's. Her giggle is loud and contagious, garnering the attention of Donna and a few of the other volunteers. "This little dog can't find its owner, so Santa wants you to keep an eye on him tonight while the elves are busy fixing Teddy."

"What's his name?" Livvy asks, taking the dog from Emi.

"Um... Kitty," I tell her, as Emi laughs quietly under her breath.

"Kitty?" Livvy asks, scrunching her nose at me. "But it's a puppy!"

"I know, what a funny name, right?" I lean into her, smiling.

"It is funny," Livvy agrees with a squeal and a laugh.

"So, Livvy, can you watch Kitty while we take Teddy to the workshop?

So the elves can make him better for you?"

"When will he be back?" she asks, her eyes wide with worry.

"He'll be back in the morning. If you sleep all night, he'll be right next to you when you wake up," I tell her, pushing a few stray hairs out of her eyes. "So is that okay?"

"And Kitty gets to spend the night?"

"Kitty gets to spend the night," I assure her. "And if Kitty has fun and gets a good night's sleep, maybe he would like to stay with you."

"And Teddy, too?"

"Of course. Teddy, too."

"Okay," she agrees.

"It's a deal?" I ask, holding my hand out to her.

"Deal!" she exclaims with a nod of her head, grabbing one of my fingers with her tiny hand and shaking it.

"Do you want to give Teddy a kiss goodnight before we take him to the elves?" Emi asks.

Livvy puckers her lips and closes her eyes, making a loud smacking noise as Emi touches the bear to her mouth. "Bye, Teddy."

"You know, Santa's already on his way here," a nurse tells Livvy. "You know he can't stop by until you're asleep. Are you ready to go to bed?"

Livvy smiles another huge grin and nods. Emi and I watch as the nurse takes the little girl's hand into hers and begins to lead her down the hallway. Livvy stops suddenly, pulling on the nurse's scrubs. The nurse leans down as Livvy whispers something in the nurse's ear.

"Sure you can," she says, letting go of Livvy's hand. The little girl turns back around and walks toward us. Emi and I both stoop once more to her level. She hugs Emi first, giving her bear one last kiss, then pulls on my tie a few times, her eyes blinking, curious. Her tiny finger extended, she signals for me to move closer.

I lean in, and as she wraps her arms around my neck and squeezes tightly, she whispers in my ear. "Merry Christmas, Jack." Her voice is so tiny and quiet, I almost mistake my own name for another word. It almost sounded as if she said "dad."

"Merry Christmas, Livvy," I tell her, returning her sweet embrace. "Sleep well, little Contessa," I whisper softly. She kisses me on the cheek, then runs quickly back to the nurse. Emi and I both stare after her, making sure she makes it to her room.

"God, I hope you can sew, Em," I laugh.

"It's been fifteen years since Home Ec, but I think I can manage okay. I have a little sewing kit at home that Mom put in my stocking about five years ago. Never even been used, but I found it in the move."

"Perfect," I say as I take her hand. "Well, Donna, I guess we will be back in a little bit."

"I can have one of the other volunteers take care of that," she offers. "You two probably have a lot going on."

"I wouldn't dream of it, Donna," Emi says. "I made the promise, I'm going to make sure it gets done. She was precious, just–"

"What is she in the hospital for?" I interrupt.

"She's just getting over a bout of pneumonia," a nurse answers.

"She's in the foster system," Donna adds, her eyebrows raised. "Her mom died a few months ago of cancer."

"Really," I consider. "That's awful. Poor little Livvy." I purposely avoid Emi's eyes. My mind is already churning, but I know it's too soon. We aren't even married yet. "Well, we will have Teddy back before Santa comes, I promise," I tell her.

"Just find one of the nurses. They'll make sure it gets to her."

"Penny for your thoughts," Emi says on our drive home.

"I don't need a penny," I tell her.

"Can you pull over for a second?" she asks.

"We've got a deadline, Em," I remind her. "Livvy needs this bear before she wakes up."

"It will take me thirty minutes, tops, to sew up Teddy."

"Still, I would hate for her to wake up and him not be there."

"I want to talk about her."

"Please, let's wait until we get home. Okay?" I ask, putting my hand on her knee. "Don't worry, I want to talk about her, too."

"Okay."

"I know what you're thinking," she says as she settles into the couch and begins to mend the stuffed animal.

"I don't think that you do," I tell her. "I'm more practical than you're giving me credit for."

"But it crossed your mind, didn't it?"

"Of course it did. I mean, what are the chances?"

"Exactly," Emi says. "I don't really know what to think. I mean, think about it. Out of all the children's hospitals, she's in the one we go to. She singles you out. Coincidentally, she is an orphan. And she's the sweetest little girl... and so cute. Is it a sign?"

"There are a lot of things to consider, Em," I tell her. "You know, we don't know her history. We don't know the first thing about foster care or adoption in New York. Maybe someone's already working on that. We're not even married yet. You weren't sure you were cut out to be a mom a few months ago. The signs could point either way."

"If there is anything I'm certain of, right now, Jack," she begins, "it's how much I want you to be the father of my children. However we get them. Seeing you with her tonight... you were so gentle, so caring, so reassuring. You knew all the right things to say. You have never looked so... sexy... as you were tonight."

"That's weird," I laugh.

"I'm completely serious. Jack, I would do anything to be able to give you your own children," she says, her voice quivering and eyes watering.

"Poppet, we've been over this," I tell her, sitting on the couch next to her.

"I don't care how we become parents... just as long as we do."

"I know," she says, taking a deep breath as she sews a patch on the bear's arm.

"And I don't care what the doctors say, I will enjoy trying to prove them wrong," I suggest.

"Well, Jacks, we've been over that. It's not going to happen," she says with a wistful smile, "but I am certainly not opposed to trying, either... often..."

"I know. Another reason I love you," I kiss her forehead and wipe away her tears.

"How does he look?" she asks, holding up the stuffed bear.

"I think Livvy will be amazed at how quickly he recovered."

When we return to the hospital, Emi makes a request of the head nurse. "We made a promise to this little girl that we would get her bear back to her before she woke up," she explains, "and I just want to make sure it happens. It's not that we don't trust you, but would you mind if we went to her room with you?"

"Actually, Donna gave us instructions, that you two should be the ones to take her the bear. And what Donna says, we do. She has done so much for this hospital."

In the back of my mind, I begin to think that Donna may be behind this chance meeting. Emi and I exchange smiles, knowing glances. We both lean in, and I brush her lips lightly with mine. "Let's go," she whispers.

"Let me take you to her room," the nurse offers.

"How much longer will she be in here?" I ask on the way.

"I think she's set to be released to her foster parents on Monday."

"Good," I sigh. "It must be hard for her, being in here, alone, on Christmas."

"We make sure it's a special day for all the kids. There are quite a few children here her age that she's already made friends with. She'll have fun."

The nurse peeks through her door before allowing us to enter. A musical night light casts colorful shadows along all four walls. Livvy is sound asleep with Kitty tucked under her arm. She seems cold, curled up in a little ball under the covers. Her ear is cool to the touch as I tuck her bangs behind it.

"Is there another blanket?" I softly ask the nurse.

"Yes, in the dresser," she points to the furniture next to me. I quietly pull open the drawer and find a soft afghan, placing it over her body. Emi tucks part of it over her ear, smoothing her hair down.

"Goodnight, Contessa," I say softly, tucking the bear under the blanket next to her, where she is certain to see it as soon as she opens her eyes in the morning. Emi clings to my arm as we watch her sleep for a few minutes.

Once in the elevator to the parking garage, she wraps her arms around me. As it reaches our floor, she looks up at me, her eyes pleading.

"Jack..." I smile and take her hand, walking next to her to my car. "You already have a nickname for her."

"I'm calling my lawyer first thing in the morning." She entwines her fingers with mine and squeezes tightly.

"But it's Christmas," she reminds me as we get into the car.

"This can't wait." *We have to try.*

It was a relatively sleepless night for both of us. When we got home, we immediately started researching the foster system and adoption in New York, just so we could be informed and a little prepared. The process would not be easy... and the odds were certainly not in our favor. But we both felt it was worth a try... that *Livvy* was worth a try. And eventually, we realized that any child we could take in and provide a loving home to was worth our efforts. If not Livvy, the child meant for us would come along.

Of course we both fell in love with Livvy at first sight. Anyone would. It's difficult to not get our hopes up. When we finally went to bed, emotions were still high, and through our love making, we healed old wounds. We assured each other of our commitments. We eased one another's fears. We quelled insecurities and encouraged strengths. We proved that the love we share would get us through anything. And it would.

In the end, we make a decision, the only one that makes sense: that we will do everything in our power to help Livvy find a good home– even if it isn't ours. It's the only thing that gives us peace of mind.

The following morning, after a shower and a lengthy conversation with my lawyer, I meet Emi in the living room where she has started a fire and lay down on the couch. The last two Christmas presents sit in the middle of the coffee table. I bypass them both and lie down on top of Emi, kissing her deeply. Her familiar moans tell me what I want to hear.

"I love you," I tell her, my lips traveling to her neck.

"You are amazing," she responds, her fingers tangled in my hair. "What did the lawyer say?" she whispers breathily as I unbutton her blouse and kiss her just below her collarbone.

"He said," I kiss her breast, "to keep our options open," her taut stomach, "and to keep exploring all avenues." I unbutton her jeans, pull them down just slightly and kiss each hip. "So that's what I intend to do." Her hands cling desperately to my shirt, pulling it over my head. My lips find hers again as her hands unfasten the button and zipper of my pants. She pushes at the waistline, but I take over, removing the rest of my clothes and hers as well.

"*This* avenue takes us nowhere," she says, her tone playful, not a hint of sadness. I pull away from her, cock one of my eyebrows at her and smile.

"Really? I beg to differ. This avenue has taken us to many, many," I shift slightly, teasing her, "many incredible places."

"Oh, yes," she sighs. "I remember now. I like those places." She pulls my mouth back to hers.

"I know you do," I whisper between kisses.

"Take me... now... please..." Her hands grab my waist, and I exhale slowly at the sound of her gasp.

I wake up to Emi kissing me, her naked body lying on top of mine.

"Did I fall asleep?" I ask.

"I think you're exhausted," she answers. "Can I make a proposition?"

"Of course," I answer.

"Why don't we open our presents– because I can't wait to give you yours– and then we can go back to bed for the rest of the day."

"I think that's a great idea." She climbs off of me and begins to dress herself again. I pull my pants back on and add another log to the fire before assuming my place next to her on the couch.

"You first," Emi encourages me.

"No, you go," I yawn.

"Nuh-uh. You first," she argues. "And wake up." She pokes me in the side and I tickle her in retaliation. She takes my hands into hers, holding them still.

"Alright," I concede, picking up the small box addressed to me.

"I made you immortal," she says excitedly as I unwrap the gift. After lifting the lid and moving the tissue paper aside, the title of a small book stares back at me. *Our Father, Who Art in Brooklyn.* "Okay, let me explain," she chimes in as I pick up the book curiously. "So, this is the result of my late-night freelance work. I've been illustrating for a friend of mine who's writing some children's books. And her series is about a single dad raising his two children alone."

I flip through the pages, recognizing myself in the illustration of the father. The two children look strikingly like Clara and Andrew.

"This is incredible, Emi," I laugh. "Wow. I'm in a book!"

"Yeah, do you like it?"

"I think it's... incredible," I repeat. "But I have to ask. Why is he single?" I ask nervously.

"Okay, I didn't write the books. And I'm not sure why he's single. I don't think that was ever mentioned. I don't think it's relevant to the story."

"So this isn't your fun and creative way of telling me you're leaving me?"

She slaps my arm. "No, and it's not my way of telling you that you have two children, either. But..."

"But?"

"He gets a girlfriend in the third book of the series," she smiles. "The first one, this is the only one that's finished printing, though. Want a sneak peek of book three?"

"Of course."

She digs further into the box under the tissue paper and pulls out a piece of card stock with a drawing of a woman, who coincidentally looks quite similar to Emi.

"Very nice," I laugh. "She's beautiful. I think he would be quite attracted to her. God, I hope she's the one..."

"Well... want *another* sneak peek?" she teases me.

"Yes..."

She takes another card from underneath and shows me a drawing of illustrated "us" in wedding clothes. "They get married in the fifth book." She bites her bottom lip as her cheeks flush red.

"That is awesome, Emi," I laugh. "How did you convince the author to allow the characters to look like us?"

"She happens to think we're the perfect couple."

"You told her about us?"

"Not really." She closes the book and points to the author's name on the cover. "Teresa wrote them. Her brother is single, raising a son on his own, and she'd noticed a lack of books that addressed that issue. So she set out to write the series."

"That's a departure from her normal work, isn't it?"

"Uh, yes. Let's just say that the kids will have to wait about twenty years before reading any more of her work."

"Right. Well, Em, this is... wow. I'm in a book!" I repeat. "I don't think I could have ever guessed such a thing. This is really cool."

"I know it's not something useful or anything you'll go bragging to your friends about," she says, "but I hoped you'd like it."

"I do, Em. It's... something no one else could ever get me. And think how much our nieces and nephews are going to like this. It means a lot."

"Well, Merry Christmas." I lean in to kiss her.

"Merry Christmas to you. Now open yours."

She sighs heavily. "You always spend too much."

"Not this time."

"Alright." She unwraps the paper carefully, then opens the small box slowly. "See?" she huffs, frustrated, as she looks at the delicate bracelet inside. It's silver, feminine, etched with flowers and leaves on both sides of a small metal plate. Small emeralds dot both sides of it, with the letters "E" and "H" engraved in the center.

"I spent no money on it," I tell her.

"Right... you just whittled it with your own two hands."

"No, I didn't do that either," I say, taking the bracelet out of the box. "This," I say, clasping it on the wrist of her right hand, "was my grandmother's. My grandfather bought it for her as a wedding present." As she holds her hand out in front of her, her smile slowly grows.

"What was her name?"

"Elizabeth."

"And did you search all your life for a woman with a name that started with 'E?'" she asks. "Is that why we're meant to be together?" she laughs.

"Exactly," I admit in jest.

"It's beautiful. It looks brand new."

"She only wore it on special occasions. It was a very extravagant gift to her. They didn't have much money. But she cherished it."

"I love it, Jack," she says. "Are you sure you want to give this to me? It shouldn't go to someone in your family?"

"You will be 'in my family' in seven days, remember?"

"I know, but... you know what I mean."

"Actually," I begin, "I didn't even know about this piece until about a month ago. My father called me one night and told me that Grandma had this bracelet... and he talked to his sisters and brother, and they all agreed that I should give it to you. My aunt had it sitting in her jewelry box all these years. It doesn't hurt that you're the first woman since her with the right initials," I tell her.

"Lucky me," she smiles. "God, thank you, Jack. It's gorgeous."

"And now you have your something old..."

"I do..."

"And I can help you pick out something blue. I have some ideas," I whisper in her ear before kissing it.

"Let's go back to bed," she says, taking my hand and leading the way upstairs.

CHAPTER 12

I set the spray of flowers next to the headstone as Emi touches the letters in his name, silent. She takes my hand as she sits down on the bench next to his gravesite. I think back to last year when we visited the cemetery together. It was the first time I'd come here with her, but it wasn't my first visit to the Nate's final resting place.

The other time was a few days after Emi had told me about losing their baby in the accident. I didn't know why I had been drawn to visit the site at the time, but I had been. I knew how sad it made her, but I believed that Nate and their child were together, somewhere. I had taken a small bouquet of pink daisies to honor the little girl that Emi believed they would have had. At the time, I had not known that this child would be the only one Emi would ever be able to conceive.

As Emi sits quietly, her thoughts kept to herself, I wonder what her life would have been like had the child lived. Would she have devoted all of her love to her daughter? Would she have been open to loving me? I still feel confident we would have been together. I would have raised the little girl as my own. A pang of sadness runs through my chest, making it tight. I squeeze Emi's hand involuntarily. She looks up at me, a faint smile on her face.

"Love you," she says. I lean in to kiss her on the cheek. She holds my face to hers, though, and brushes her lips to mine. Slowly, the touch of her soft lips spreads warmth throughout my body on this cold, winter day, the second anniversary of his death.

"How do you feel?" I ask her.

"I feel okay," she says. "I feel like we're doing the right thing."

"Good," I smile, kissing her a little deeper. "I can't wait until tomorrow."

"Me neither," she says. "But I don't want to go stay with Anna tonight," she whines. "I just want to be with you."

"You're the one who said it would be bad luck... I'm pretty sure this was your idea."

"It was, I know," she concedes. "I'll get you for the rest of my life." She smiles dreamily.

"Fancy meeting you here," a voice greets us from behind. Emi stands and blushes, letting go of my hand to meet Donna a few feet away. Nate's mother carries a bouquet of exotic, mixed flowers.

"How are you, Donna?" she asks, her voice sympathetic.

"I'm good, Emi. That arrangement is beautiful," she adds, setting her bouquet next to the one Emi had selected this morning. I stand to hug her, her embrace lingering. "How are you, Jackson?"

"I'm fine, Donna, thank you." We exchange a glance, her presence not a surprise to me. "James didn't come?" I ask.

"He thought this was something we should do together, just the three of us," she answers. I try to inconspicuously shake my head, an effort to let her know that Emi was not aware of our plans.

"What is?" Emi asks, hearing what was intended to be a private conversation.

"Um, coming here," Donna says, catching on too late. "Just remembering him today."

"Oh," Emi says, confused.

"No, Em," I admit. "When I said I had something to show you today... it's really something we both have to show you. It's something we've been working on."

"Oh!" Emi repeats, this time with more enthusiasm, but then her confused expression once again comes across her face.

"I'll give you two a moment alone while I go heat up the car." Emi looks back to see that my Volvo is the only car there. "Take as much time as you need."

"Okay."

I take a deep breath as I start the car. I'm more nervous about this day than I am about the day I proposed– or about tomorrow, the day we are supposed to get married. If she doesn't like the venue, it will surely put a cloud over what is meant to be the happiest day of our lives.

A few minutes later, I help Donna and Emi into the warm car.

"Are you ready?" I ask her.

"I guess," she smiles tentatively. "I can't even begin to imagine what's going on."

"Don't worry," Donna assures Emi. "You'll love it."

I wish I had as much confidence as she does. A short time later, just before we pull up in front of the building two blocks away from our home, I ask Emi to close her eyes. She shoots me a sideways glance before complying. "I'll help you out of the car."

Donna and I both take an arm and lead Emi into the front door of the first floor of the two story building.

"Where are we?" Emi asks.

"We're at the venue for the reception," I tell her. "And just so you know, it's okay to cry."

"Jack..." she whines. "Am I not going to like it?"

"No, that won't be it... go ahead and open your eyes."

I watch Emi's face carefully as she slowly peels her eyes open. Her head is still as her eyes survey the room slowly, cautiously. She inspects the large open space, the carefully chosen lighting in the room, the colorful illustrations on the wall, once again looking confused.

"It's not finished yet," I tell her.

"Okay..." she says, unsure. "Where is this place?"

"Come look around."

She turns to glance at another wall, her face perking up when she sees a set of familiar drawings. "Those are mine!" she exclaims, seeing the illustrations she had done for an article last summer. "Why are my illustrations on the wall?" *She seems happy...*

"Come look at this one..." I encourage her, taking her by the hand and leading her to Nate's mom. Donna stands next to a framed print centered in a six-foot space on another wall. The picture is a colorful abstract painting of a boy and his father.

"I don't recognize it..." Emi says, her eyes examining it, "but it's colors are so rich. It's beautiful... it reminds me of..." She gasps quietly, both hands lifting to cover her mouth. "Nathaniel J. Wilson, 1984," she says, touching the glass that covers the child-version of his signature. Tears begin to stream quickly as she smiles in awe. "Was that his dad?"

"It was," Donna says, taking Emi's hand in her own. "He painted that when he was six from a picture I took of them. I locked it away a long time ago, when his father died. I couldn't look at it, seeing them together in the painting, but knowing the loneliness Nathan felt when he died. It brings me comfort now, though. They're together."

"You should keep it," Emi encourages Nate's mother.

"It belongs here now," she answers.

"Where is this place?" Emi repeats her original question. "What have you guys done?"

"Well, Em, since you gave up the loft, your space... I wanted to give you one back. This is just part of it, by the way."

"Well, what is it, exactly?"

"It's Nate's Art Room," I smile. "This is a non-profit that we founded, in his name. We used some of the money you put aside from the sale of the loft for it."

"Nate's Art Room," Emi repeats, backing away from Nate's artwork and looking at the rest of the room. In the corner, a small child's table is set up with four chairs, the only furniture in the room.

"Yes," Donna says. "It's a place where school-aged kids can come to be creative... it will be staffed like a day care, but it will have enrollment criteria for underprivileged kids who are artistically gifted."

"We'll supply all the tools, and a safe and quiet place to go... so they can just create," I add.

She looks at me, eyes wide.

"There's a secluded outdoor space down that hallway, too. We'll start landscaping it as it gets closer to spring, but it already has a huge oak tree in one corner."

"What a beautiful idea..."

"We're working with other local artists," I tell her. "In fact, they helped decorate the place. And they'll be coming down monthly to volunteer their time with the kids."

"He would really like this." Emi's voice is quiet.

"Yes, he would," Donna confirms. "But do you like it?"

"I do!" Emi exclaims. "And this is my space?" she asks us.

"Well, technically, yes, it's all yours... but you have your own space upstairs to work. We'll get to that."

"There's an upstairs?" She looks around for a stairway, peeking down the hallway.

"The stairs are outside. Did you want to go up and see?"

"In just a second," she says, pulling me to the corner with the kids table. "I love this, I do... but um... what does this have to do with the reception?" she asks, a little nervous, as I thought she might be.

"We're having the reception here," I explain. "Don't worry, there are decorators coming tonight to hang fabric around the walls, and install some additional lighting. Anna's been very involved, making your ideas come to life. The drawings will be hidden for the ceremony."

"And this table?" she asks.

"Well, there will be kids at the reception, so it will likely stay. But we'll have adult tables, just like the ones you wanted."

"Okay," she sighs, relieved. "So are we getting married outside then?" she asks.

"No. Come with me." I open the front door for her, where Donna had exited a few minutes before us. Emi walks toward the car. "Over here, Em." I motion toward an iron staircase on the side of the building, hoping she doesn't glance up to notice the lettering– NATHANIEL J. WILSON GALLERY– that was installed above the windows.

"Second floor?"

"After you..."

Emi gasps and stumbles back into my waiting arms when she opens the door. "That's his painting... from LA... on that wall..."

"It's on loan from the restaurant owner," I tell her. "Does it bother you that it's here?"

She walks in slowly, approaching the large mural. "Wow, it matches your hair," I say, feeling as if the wind had been knocked out of me at the realization.

"It makes me sad," she admits. "It made me sad when I first saw it. I know his style. I knew the emotions he put into his paintings."

She's quiet as she touches the paint.

"It matches my hair because it was painted for me," she explains. "He told me he was imagining what his life would be like without me in it... when he painted it." Emi tries to hide her tears from me, but I immediately walk to her, taking her into my arms and holding her. She grips me tightly.

"Why is it here?" she whispers. The large mural had been such a distraction, she didn't even see the other paintings and prints that hung on the walls and display spaces.

"Well... the artwork you and Donna have shouldn't be hidden away in some basement... or in Kate's warehouse... or even in our homes. This is a gallery we opened, to showcase his work... and it will host shows for other artists, too." I hand her the handkerchief I had brought with me, knowing I would need it at some point today.

"We're getting married here?" she asks.

"I hope so."

She begins to walk away from me, looking around the gallery, still sniffling, her heels clicking lightly on the hardwood floor. She finally begins to see the other pieces of art around the room.

"It is very pretty here... and probably just the right size..."

"So..." I wait for her consent.

"Where did these come from?" she asks, continuing her discovery of the large room.

"On loan from other galleries and artists, for the wedding. Anna, Jen and Kelly scoured the city and found the most beautiful pieces around... and we made arrangements to have shows for them in return."

"They are gorgeous. This one is spectacular," she says, eyeing a large painting secured to a wall all by itself, a bold close-up of three daisies.

"Now, that one," I tell her, walking up behind her, "I had commissioned for you. That's for you." I put my arms around her and kiss her temple, glancing at her reaction. A smile returns to her face. "It fits perfectly over the bed," I continue.

"You give me too much," she admonishes.

"You deserve so much more," I argue. She shakes her head. "So, right there," I say, pointing to the corner between her painting and the window, "that's where we'll exchange our vows. And outside that window, you see that park?"

She nods.

"It will create a beautiful backdrop for our wedding."

"It doesn't look like much right now," she says, her eyes a little distant, but pointed in the direction of the barren trees.

"Just trust," I urge her. "Anna has planned every detail to make this a perfect wedding. She's listened to everything you've asked for, and I know it will be the wedding of your dreams."

"As long as you're there," she says, "that's all I need."

"Thank you," I tell her. "So you'll still marry me? Here?" I smile, hopeful, my eyes pleading.

"Of course," she replies as relief washes over me. "And thank *you*," she replies, following it with a kiss. "Where did Donna go?"

"I think she's probably outside in the yard. She wanted to give us some time alone to see that," I say, pointing to a door in the opposite direction. "That... is your workspace."

Her smile broadens as she walks toward the tall wooden door.

"Go on," I encourage her as her hand rests on the knob.

"Holy shit, Jack," she murmurs. "It's like an apartment."

"A small one, yes," I say. "I wanted to make sure you'd have everything you need here."

She sits down on a moss green daybed, leaning against the pillow on one side. "This is awesome," she says. "Have you sat on it?"

"I thought it was comfortable... and if you're ever here so late you just want to crash, there are blankets and pillows in the closet over there next to the bathroom. But so you'll know, I will always be ready to come by and walk you home. Anytime. It's just two blocks from the house."

"I promise to always come home," she says, standing up and walking to the mini kitchen, the refrigerator stocked with water and diet soda. "Did Anna design this place?" she asks.

"Of course she did."

"She did an amazing job. I'm pretty sure we saw this desk somewhere last spring... I told her I loved it... and now I have it..." She sits at her desk as I perch on the edge of the daybed. "Did you get me a new computer?"

"Well, I thought you'd need one here so you don't have to lug that old laptop around all the time." She hits the power button and grins at the familiar start-up chime.

"Jack, this is too much." She stands, walking across the room, pulling back the tapestry curtains and looking out the window overlooking the park.

"Emi, it was the least I could do after encouraging you to sell the loft. I know how much that place inspired you."

"Is that a dog bed?" she asks, laughing.

"We thought you might want company some times."

"I'd want *you*," she says, walking back to me. "Will you visit?"

"Of course," I say, kissing her. "I was hoping you wouldn't get too comfortable here. And you can always work from the bedroom, like you do now. I love waking up to the warm glow of the computer screen highlighting your beautiful face."

A soft knock interrupts us. "What's the verdict?" Donna asks.

"The wedding is on," I tell her.

"Do you like it, Emi?" she asks.

"I love it. And Nate would have loved it, too. I know he dreamed of having a gallery one day."

"Will it do for your wedding?"

"It's beautiful. Of course."

"I told you that you didn't need to worry, Jack," Donna gloats.

"You were worried?" Emi asks me.

"Yeah," I sigh. "Just a little."

"You. Me. Dress. Rings. Cake." Her hand caresses my face. "That's all I need, right?"

"That's what you said."

"That's all I need. Thank you... for all of it. For everything. For you... for loving me."

"You're most welcome, Emi."

~ * ~

We stare across the restaurant, watching our families interact at the rehearsal dinner. "Looks like your mom is getting an earful from Elaine," Emi whispers to me. "She just doesn't know when to shut up sometimes. God love her, but man! Can she talk!"

"I think they probably make perfect dinner companions then," I tell her. "My mom is just too polite to turn away. She's a great listener."

"Your dad looks uncomfortable."

"He's not big on social gatherings," I tell her.

"I'm going to go talk to him," she says. She smiles wide and squeezes my thigh before walking over to my father. She pulls a chair close to him and sits down, leaning into him to talk. My father laughs at something she whispers to him, and his shoulders seem to relax immediately. She just *does* that to people.

She did that to me on the night we first met.

I walk to the bar and order a scotch, taking it outside on the patio, feeling reflective and remembering that night in college. I watch her through the window as she invites my shy niece into their conversation. Jackie crawls into my father's lap as Andrew runs over, tugging on Emi's sleeve. She picks him up and bounces him on her knee, causing him to giggle loudly. Contemplative, I scan the room to see the rest of our families and friends enjoying one another's company.

Lost in my own thoughts, I'm startled when Emi joins me on the restaurant's patio.

"What are you doing out here?" Emi asks, pulling on her coat.

"I was just thinking about the night we met," I tell her, snapping out of my daze.

"What about it?" she asks.

"I just remember how comfortable you made me feel. I had never felt as

362

nervous as I had once you started talking to me... but within seconds, you put me completely at ease. Just like you did with my dad."

"Awww..." she says. "You got it backwards, though."

"No," I shake my head. "You don't remember it clearly."

"I remember a lot," she says. "I told you, once you kissed me last year, most of the night came back to me. I remember how cute you looked as I walked past you. As soon as I saw you, I decided I was going to try to get up the nerve to talk to you.

"And then, you came over to make sure I was okay. Right away, you presented the opportunity... and right away, I knew I was safe with you. I was completely at ease from that moment on."

"So, if you remember that night," I say as we put our arms around each other, "what were you thinking on that picnic table... when you were so quiet for so long?"

"I kept asking myself over and over again, 'Why didn't he kiss me?' and 'Why wasn't he the one to pull me away from the other guys?'"

"You were not."

"I totally was!" she says. "After you didn't kiss me on the curb, I was confused. I had convinced myself that you weren't interested... but I thought we had shared a moment there... so I decided to test you by playing drinking games with your brothers. But you didn't 'rescue' me that time."

"You were testing me..."

"I was. You failed miserably," she jokes. "Then, when you just sat there on the bench and did nothing, I just got more frustrated. I thought I misread you... that is, until, I tripped into your arms and saw that look in your eyes again. And I was drunk enough to take advantage of the situation... and I kissed you.

"And that's about all I remember... of you, anyway. Then things got kinda confusing with Nate."

"Right... damn," I say, smiling. "I failed miserably."

"You've made up for it," she assures me. "You've never failed me since."

"I hope I never do."

"I don't think you ever could," she says. "Anyway, I think they're ready to serve dinner, and there are a few people who have some things to say..."

"Well, what are we waiting for?" As she begins to walk in, I pull her back to me. "One more thing..." I tuck her hair behind her ears and pull her in for a kiss. "That's for the curb."

"You're forgiven." She kisses me again.

"Dear Emi," Chris begins as the waitstaff brings out the food. He clears his throat and swallows hard before continuing, reading his toast from a folded piece of paper. Anna rubs his arm for encouragement. "I remember the night that Jack told me that the two of you kissed in college. I was so angry, I hit him. Gave him a black eye. Even after that, he still had the nerve to talk to me about you. Kept asking me to find out if you liked him...

"I never did... and eventually he dropped it.

"I never asked you because all of my fraternity brothers wanted to go out with you after that one party. How was I supposed to know that this one– that Jack here– would be someone special to you?

"Of course, I feel bad about this now... knowing you could have been with him all this time... and thinking of the heartache it may have saved you over the years, with break-ups, incompatible boyfriends and bad dates..."

Emi squeezes my hand tightly. I watch as she looks up at the ceiling, willing the tears to abstain from falling to her cheeks.

"But that's all in the past... and we can't live with regrets. So, I apologize for keeping the love of your life from you all those years. I find comfort in knowing, though, that the years you spent apart helped to sculpt you into the beautiful person you are today, Em. Those years made you the person that Jack, my best friend, fell truly in love with. He was a little infatuated in college. If he knew how silly you were back then– if he had gotten to know you then– I don't know that he would have stuck around. I would never have put College Emi and College Jack together. Not in a million years. You were creative, confused and flighty, changing your mind and opinions daily, living in a fantasy world... an idealist to a fault. And then there was Jack, driven, completely grounded, knowing what he wanted in life, sometimes a little too smart for his own good... a total realist.

"But that just goes to prove my point. You were different people then. Over the years, you've both drifted into this space in the middle where the idealist and the realist fall in love.

"And now, I can't imagine two people better suited for one another. Well, maybe my beautiful wife and I..." he mutters.

"Anyway, to my amazing sister and my best friend," he says, raising his glass. "I hope you find support, happiness and above all, love, in each other, every moment of every day that you're together."

"Thanks, Chris," I tell him, smiling.

"Love ya, Chris," Emi smiles.

"Okay, my turn," my sister says, addressing Emi and me. "I have been fortunate to know my brother all of my life. And I can tell you– all of you Hennigans– that there are definite advantages to having Jacks in your family."

"First, he's got mad grill-skills," she smiles. "I've heard that there is a little competition in your family with Chris, but I'd put my money on my brother. And when you're ready to fight it out, please invite me. I'd be a great judge. I like my steak medium rare.

"Secondly, he is amazing with kids. Doesn't matter whose they are, he's a natural with them. I guess he can thank me and our brothers for that, since he spent quite a lot of time keeping us entertained and out of trouble when we were growing up.

"He is an amazing listener. And he'll keep his mouth shut when he needs to, or give great advice if asked. He's *really* good with financial advice." She winks at me.

"And on that note, he makes a pretty good living," she shrugs. "He gets by, at least." Our families laugh.

"He is selfless and caring... like no one I've ever met. He will always put others in front of himself. And he never asks for anything in return. He is humble and kind, and always the first to lend a hand. He's a great problem-solver, and he knows how to compromise. He's very methodical, reasonable... and he makes sound decisions. And he'll admit when he's wrong... but he rarely is.

"He can fix cars, among other things," she states. "Maybe something you didn't know, but Jacks got the highest grade in his junior-level shop class. We all thought we had a car mechanic on our hands... but he surprised us with this whole computer nonsense in college.

"One more thing, he plans awesome vacations," Kelly adds. "And I have been informed that this year we will be having a combined Holland/Hennigan spring break, so let the madness ensue!"

Everyone claps as Emi leans in and kisses me. "You're asking for trouble," she laughs.

"But most importantly..." Kelly says as she lifts her champagne glass, "the most important thing that he brings to the table... Jacks apparently makes someone in your family very happy. And Emi," she concludes, "I can honestly say that he found someone that really deserves him... someone that appreciates him and gives him purpose. I often worried that there wasn't anyone good enough for my big brother... but you've surpassed all of our expectations, and you've made him happier than we've ever seen him. I will be honored to call you my sister."

"Thank you," we say together to Kelly. Emi blots a tear from her eye and leans into me.

"Yeah, on that same note," Jen chimes in, "I just want to say that I think you two were made for one another. I just wish you both all the happiness in the world." She gets choked up and smiles. "Happy tears," she says, wiping them away from her cheeks.

Stevie, Matthew, Anna and both of our fathers toast us before the night is through. Over drinks, our parents have become quite comfortable with each other, and our siblings have spent most of the night comparing stories.

"This feels right," I whisper to Emi, kissing her ear shortly after eleven. "I'm going to miss you tonight."

"I'll miss you, too," she returns. "But just think. In less than twenty-four hours, I'll be your wife."

"I can't wait."

"Kiss her goodnight, Jacks," Matthew says. "We've got places to go... Emi, we get him tonight. You can have him the rest of your life."

"No strippers tonight," she smiles. "Matty, I mean it."

"You don't get a vote, sweetie," he teases her. "He only gets one wedding, which means one bachelor party– so we have to make it count!"

"Chris!" she calls out to her brother.

"Yeah," he says, Anna clinging to his side.

"No strippers, right?"

"This is Jack's last night as a single man. We do what he wants." She looks at me, her eyes pleading, yet playful.

"I love you," I tell her. "You know me. Sleep well knowing that."

She looks at me, suspicious, and sighs heavily. "I know you. I know your brothers and mine, though, too." She gives me a stern look that eventually melts into a smile. "I love you."

"You girls have fun... try to sleep."

"Can we have our midnight kiss early?"

"Of course." I kiss her deeply, putting all the assurance I have into the loving gesture. "Happy New Year, Em. May this be our best year yet... and may all the years that follow be even better."

"Happy New Year, Jack. I have no doubt they will be."

CHAPTER 13

"Damn it," I mutter under my breath, checking my watch after staring at myself for far too long in the full-length mirror. "Darn it!" I correct myself, remembering my vow to Jack to clean up my language. I smooth out the folds in the dress and shift on my heels, calling to Anna through the bathroom door.

"Hair up or down?"

"You still haven't decided?" she responds, frantic. "We don't have any more time!"

"I'm aware of that, and you're not helping to speed things up. Up or down!?!"

"Down!" she exclaims. *I knew she'd say that.* I start to pull the clips out of my hair, turning the curling iron back on, knowing I'm going to need to fix a few strands. "No wait!" she adds. "Whichever way it's already done! I thought we decided, either way looks beautiful!"

"Too late!" I respond after brushing my hair out. I tilt my head to the side, pulling a few locks in front to frame my face and smile. Picking up the hairspray, I commit to the look and turn the curling iron off. I can't be late. Not today. The butterflies in my stomach flutter wildly as the smile on my face grows. *I can't wait!*

Much to Anna's relief, I rush by her on my way to the closet, listening to her whispering updates to Chris into her cell phone on my readiness. After switching shoes– only twice– I go to my dresser and look over the jewelry I had set out the night before. I hold up the ornate diamond necklace Jack had given to me as a gift for the wedding and run my fingers over the stones. Even though I know he'd like to see me in it, it's too extravagant, too much for even today, what is likely to be the most important day of our lives. I set it back in its black velvet case and put it in the safe in the closet and lock it up. When I get back to the dresser, I hear my phone vibrate. Glancing across the room, I see his picture on the display and run to answer it.

"Jacks," I sigh into the phone giddily.

"At what point of undress are you right now, Poppet?"

"I'll have you know, I'm dressed."

"Anna tells Chris you're having hair problems?"

"Anna lies." She glares at me as I stick my tongue out at her. "I'm ready. I'm just putting on my jewelry and then we'll be on our way."

"I knew it wasn't a good idea to leave you two alone today," he laughs into the phone. "Jen would have made sure you were here by now."

"What, are you anxious to see me?"

"More than you know. You won't be late?"

"I promise, I won't. I want to look perfect, that's all," I plead. "They're all going to be judging us."

"You are beautiful, Emi, and no one is judging us. That's all behind us. This is just a formality today."

"Right," I breathe heavily. "Just a formality. I can't believe this is happening. Jacks... thank you. Thank you for everything."

"No, Emi. Thank you. You have given me everything I've ever wanted. I have to admit, though, I'm anxious to get this behind us, and I just want you here with me."

"I'll be there as soon as I can."

"Okay," he says, obviously smiling. "Don't forget the flowers."

"I won't, they're in water by the door."

"Tell Anna to drive carefully. Don't speed, these things always start late anyway."

"She won't speed, and we won't be late. Promise."

"Thank you. I love you. I'll see you soon."

"Love you," I tell him before hanging up. I put on the engraved emerald bracelet and the delicate necklace with the floating heart, touching the new, O-shaped charm we had bought together a few days ago. *Just a few more hours, and this will all be official.*

I reapply some powder and lipstick and smile once more in the mirror. Anna follows me out of the bedroom, gathering things I've left along the way and stuffing them in a bag.

In the office– or what *used* to be the office– I make sure everything is in its place. Ruby looks at home on the new pillow.

"Silly pup, let's get off of that," I tell her playfully, rubbing her belly as she stretches out and yawns. "Want a treat?" She bounds off the bed and out of the room, clearing the way for me to turn off the lights and close the door. We'd worked hard on the renovations, and I wanted everything to be just... *so.*

After giving the dog a snack, I pet her on the head and grab my purse and the small bouquet of pink carnations I had clipped from the backyard garden earlier today. I hand Anna the keys to the Volvo and she juggles those, both of our bags and her purse. I straighten the pink and white bow around the stems as I carry everything out to the car. Anna puts all of our things on the floorboard as I set the flowers in the seat, checking it one last time before heading out.

Before getting out of the car, I look at myself in the passenger seat mirror one last time. *This is it.*

Chris, holding Eli tightly, meets us halfway as we ascend the steps.

"You look beautiful, Em."

"Thanks," I say, exhaling nervously. "How's my big boy?" I ask my nephew, tugging on his little ball cap and pinching his rosy cheek lightly. He giggles before ducking his head into his daddy's shoulder. "He's getting so big!"

"I know, he's a good eater," Anna says.

"Let's get you inside. I think all the families are here," Chris informs me.

"Teresa?"

"She's here, camera in hand." I sigh in relief. She had been on a publicity tour with her book series, and she wasn't sure she'd be back in town.

"Cool... and did Matthew make it?"

"He said a little headache wouldn't keep him from this."

"How's Jack?" I ask.

"He's Jack, what do you expect? He's completely calm and collected. And blissfully happy. He's so excited. But we need to get going."

"Okay. Should I be this nervous?" I ask my brother and sister-in-law, fidgeting with the bow on the flowers, wanting it to be perfect.

Anna sighs, having repeated the phrase about seventeen times today. "There's nothing at all to be nervous about. It's just a–"

"Formality, I know," I finish her sentence as we walk down the hallway.

"Here we are," Chris says, waiting in front of the large wooden doors.

"You guys go ahead," I encourage them. "I'm just going to check myself one last time." Anna groans but takes Eli into her arms as Chris leads them into the adjoining room, leaving me in the vast hallway. I glance both ways, wondering where the ladies room is. Not seeing any signs, I pilfer through my bag and find my compact. *Okay, this is it.*

I bounce on my toes briefly before pulling open the heavy door. The room is surprisingly bright as sunlight filters through skylights I hadn't remembered from the last time I was here. I had remembered it being grey and sterile and so cold and impersonal, but maybe it was cloudy that day. My eyes scan the room and land on the faces of various family members spread out in the front benches. They're all talking amongst themselves, all in high spirits and dressed in bright colors. That was my only request of them. I wanted us all to remember this day as a vibrant, happy day, full of life and hope.

Finally, I see Jack, at the same moment he sees me. We both smile, and I feel immediate relief at the mere sight of him. I see his shoulders relax, too, in his pressed white dress shirt and a new tie I've never seen him wear before. It's deep red with different colored dots in yellow and pink and a pale green that he would say reminds him of my eyes, I'm sure. He takes a step out into the aisle, holding his hand out for me. The gesture reminds me of our wedding day.

As I amble down the walkway, I think back to the day that Jack and I were married a little over ten months ago. I had eventually decided to ignore the superstition about seeing the groom before the wedding. That morning, after a sleepless night, Anna and I snuck into his house where he and his groomsmen slept, and I made breakfast for them.

When he finally came down the stairs on that morning, exhausted from a late night out with his brothers and mine, he smiled broadly when he saw Ruby jumping at my feet in the kitchen. Slowly, he walked in to meet me.

"This isn't bad luck," he had stated simply, knowing by then how my mind worked and easing my fears before I even had time to think them, before I had any additional doubt about my choice to go to his house that morning. He anticipated my every thought. *God how I love him.* I couldn't wait to be in his awaiting arms. "Good morning, my bride," he said, his voice deep and scratchy and utterly sexy.

My stomach fluttered wildly. "Hello, my groom."

"You're making breakfast for me?"

"I wanted to make sure you had a good start to the day. It's an important day, you know..."

"The most important day." He kissed me again. "I'm glad you're here.

Ruby hogs the bed when you're not here... I didn't sleep well."

"Emi hasn't slept at all," Anna reported from the living room.

"Good morning, Anna," Jack called out to her.

"Hey, Jack. Sorry about the crazy one. She couldn't wait to see you... before the freaking sun even came up."

"Are you kidding?" he said. "Thanks for indulging her."

He kissed me once more, my constant smile making it difficult to form my lips around his, but he seemed to be having the same problem.

"Have you really not slept?" he asked, his thumbs rubbing my face below my eyes.

"I couldn't. I missed you. And I'm just so excited."

"Not nervous?" he asked. He tapped my bare feet with his toes. "They don't feel cold."

"No cold feet. I've never been more certain of anyone."

"Me neither," he agreed. "What can I do to help?"

I pulled out a bottle of champagne and orange juice. "Mimosas?"

"Mimosas it is... Chris, Anna?"

"Mmmm," they both answered.

"Will you be joining us for breakfast?"

"I'm going to sleep," Anna said as I peeked into the living room to check on my brother and my maid of honor.

"It's your favorite, Chris," I told my brother. "Mom's breakfast casserole..."

"I'm going to eat," Chris said, stretching. "It's breakfast casserole, Anna. You know you want it."

"Not more than sleep."

"Whatever. Yes, we'll both be eating." Anna covered her head with the sheet and rolled away from Chris. He climbed back out of bed and joined Jack and I in the kitchen. "I'll start the coffee."

While the casserole baked in the oven, Jack took me outside with Ruby to watch the sun rise. He wrapped his arms around me tight, trying to keep me warm, even though he was only dressed in sweatpants and a t-shirt.

"Where are Matty and Lucas?" I asked.

"Sleeping on the pull-out in the media room. We didn't get home until four, so I'm going to wait until the last possible minute to wake them up."

"Yikes. You didn't fare much better than me. Aren't you exhausted?"

"No, I'm pretty excited, too." He kissed the top of my head.

"Are you cold?" I asked him.

"Not too much," he said. "Not with you here... look how clear it is this morning. Not a cloud in the sky. So beautiful."

"It is..." I agreed. "But it's supposed to snow again tonight."

"That will be perfect," he said. "Absolutely perfect."

I turned around to face him, wrapping my robe around his bare arms. His cold hands brought goosebumps to my back and a shiver to my body. Ruby raced to the back door, pawing at it in an attempt to open it. Chris opened the door to let the dog in, closing it quietly, leaving us alone on the patio.

"Are your vows ready?" I asked him.

"I've had them memorized for months," he said.

"Emi," I mocked his voice. "Thank you for getting really drunk at that party in college..."

"Wait, did you go through my things? Did you find my notes?" he joked. "That's exactly how my vows start..."

"That's how mine start, too," I told him, testing him. "A bonus to not having a church wedding." He laughed quietly in my ear before nibbling on it.

"Mmmmm..." I mumbled, my head suddenly in a fog.

"Should I just kiss you there when they pronounce us husband and wife?" He kissed my neck next. "Or here?" I hummed quietly again as he pulled my tank top down just a little, kissing the top of my breast. "Here, maybe?"

"Only if you are willing to drop trow in front of our guests... and the preacher..." I pulled his lips to mine and kissed him gently. "I want you to kiss me exactly like you did that night."

"I had every intention of that," he told me. We practiced the kiss.

"Mmmmm, perfect," he mumbled, coming back for a second attempt. "Thank you," he said. His body trembled from the cold as my teeth began to chatter.

"I have cold feet now," I whispered to him through my gritted teeth as I stepped onto his cold bare feet.

"Yeah, me, too," he said, lifting me up and carrying me into the house. "But, again, not about you."

"Same here," I concurred. "Definitely not about you."

It had been the perfect start to the perfect day. And it truly was. It was a whirlwind of nerves and excitement and family and friends. I was glad we'd had a good photographer and videographer, because it all happened so fast, I didn't think I'd be able to commit everything to memory. There would have been no way for me to remember it all, but I had watched the video many times, just to see the way Jack had looked at me, and to hear the beautiful words he had said to me. My heartbeat still quickens at the thought of it all.

Anna had turned around to me before making her trip down the aisle. She hugged me one last time. "Just smile pretty," she had said, "and enjoy every second of this night. I love you."

"You, too, Anna," I said, the tears making their way to the surface. I watched as she turned around the corner, out of my view. My dad wiped the moisture from my eyes with his handkerchief.

"Happy tears?" he asked.

"Definitely," I choked out.

"Baby," he said... "my sweet little Emi..." He sighed. "I can't believe it's finally here." The music changed to the song I chose to walk down the aisle to. "Where's the Wedding March?" my dad asked.

"Too cliché," I shook my head.

"Of course. We can't have anything traditional for my sweet little Emi. You always had to be different," he whispered in my ear as we turned the corner. "You have always been so special to me," he added... and anything else he said was pointless because I saw Jack. I saw the man I was going to marry, and the vision of him consumed me. I didn't even see anyone else. I didn't see any *thing* else.

His eyes, full of confidence and adoration, locked on to mine. He made me feel stronger just by looking at me. I felt the heat in my cheeks rise with the corners of my lips. He mouthed the words *I love you* to me. I noticed his foot tapping quickly, as if he couldn't wait for me to meet him in front of the crowd. His hands were clasped loosely in front of him, and as my father and I approached, he stepped forward to us.

I looked into his eyes intensely, feeling nothing but jubilation. He stared back at me, then brushed my cheek with the back of his hand. Ignoring typical wedding customs, I took his hand into mine and kissed his palm, then brought it down and held it tightly.

"Who gives this woman to be married to this man?" the preacher asked of the room.

"Her mother and I do," my father answered, kissing my cheek before sitting down. Jack lead me forward to the alter and stood facing me, still holding my hand in his. Anna peeked over my shoulder and took the bouquet from me... I'd already forgotten everything we rehearsed the night before. I blushed, and Jack smiled, squeezing my hand.

Beside Jack, Matthew stood anxiously in front of Steven and Chris. He kept shifting from side to side and rubbing his knuckles, even as he smiled at me and mouthed "gorgeous." Behind the groomsmen, outside the windows, I noticed just how beautiful the park across the street was. From where I stood, I couldn't even see the cars below or the buildings down the street... just the most beautiful grouping of pink and white lights I'd ever seen.

"You look beautiful," he said, my attention coming back to him, his eyes sparkling.

"So do you," I whispered back, choking out the words. "And this is beautiful." The preacher talked, said things that I should have been listening to but couldn't focus on. I was definitely suffering from sensory overload, just hoping I would recognize the queues to say my vows... or to exchange rings... or to kiss my husband. I knew Anna would prompt me at the right moments.

I was just lost in his eyes, feeling that they were speaking to me in their own language. He told me how much he loved me... how much he needed me... how much he had loved getting to know me...

"Emily Clara Hennigan," he said, startling me with the sound of his voice. When he began speaking to me, I'd realized we'd reached the part where we exchange vows. I was completely focused on him.

He sighed deeply.

"Emi..." he continued. My heart rate soared. "Every day I've known you has been a new opportunity for me to know myself. I didn't know my full potential, not just as a man but as a human, until you shared your love with me." He cleared his throat, swallowing a lump. He looked at the floor briefly before bringing his eyes back to mine.

"I've been a good son. A supportive brother. An attentive uncle. A loyal friend. An honest businessman. An adoring boyfriend, and a devoted fiancé.

"And now, because of you, I have the opportunity to become a faithful and caring husband... and possibly a doting father."

I smiled warmly at him, weaving my fingers in between his.

"And you," he continued, "have been an exceptional daughter. A kind sister. A thoughtful aunt. A steadfast friend. A talented artist. A passionate girlfriend, and an affectionate fiancée."

A tear dropped from my eye. "Thank you," I mouthed to him.

"And it is my honor, Emi, to be the person who watches you become a loving and constant wife... and hopefully someday, the most amazing mother." I wiped a tear from his cheek.

"I love you, Emi. I love the silly girl you were when we first met, and I love the woman you are today. And I can't wait to find out who you'll become tomorrow, next year, even fifty years from now. But two things I know for certain. You will always surprise me. And I will always love you."

Unable to contain myself, I leaned in to kiss him. Fortunately, he met me halfway and lightly touched his lips to mine.

"Not yet!" Matthew whispered, at which point we both started laughing.

"I love you," I said quietly to him.

"Emi?" the preacher urged. "Your vows?" I nodded.

"Jackson Andrew Holland... the second..." I glanced at his proud mother and father, suddenly rethinking my opening sentence, but proceeding as planned. "I first just want to say that I'm really glad I got drunk at that party in college." The entire wedding party started laughing, including Jack. "I warned you," I said innocently.

"You did," he encouraged me by squeezing my hands.

I took a deep breath before continuing. "Jack... I knew when I met you that you were just the type of man I needed. You were grounded to my flighty. You were rational to my emotional. Your were polite to my rude. You were sensible to my stubborn. You were patient to my restless. You were reserved to my uninhibited. You were trustworthy to my unreliable. You were practical to my absurd.

"You are the strengths to my weaknesses.

"And over time, you've brought out the best in me. With you, I am more responsible, more stable, more composed, more amenable, more tolerant, more controlled, more dependable, and more reasonable. I am better with you, and that makes me happy."

He shook his head at me.

"But the best thing about you... is that you fell in love with me when I was much weaker. Unconditionally. You never once asked me to change. And I know you never would. And I know that, on those days that I am flighty-emotional-rude-stubborn-restless-uninhibited-unreliable-absurd," I took a deep breath, "that you will still love me."

"I will," he confirmed. "I do."

"And that makes me the happiest.

"Thank you, Jack, for being the grounded, rational, polite, sensible, patient, reserved, trustworthy, practical and, above all, the strong one in this relationship. Your strength has carried us here, to where we stand today, to this alter.

"Becoming your wife, though, means I get half of everything." Our friends and family members laughed. "So with your shared strength, I promise you, that I will help carry us wherever our lives may take us, together."

"You're the strongest woman I know, Emi," he told me.

"Thanks to you," I smiled. He shook off the compliment. "I love you, Jack, and I can't wait to tackle whatever life throws our way... because I know that we're strong enough, together, to handle anything."

"We are." Again we kissed, and again the audience laughed as I saw Matthew flinch out of the corner of my eye.

"The rings?" the preacher asked. Matty and Anna handed us the rings. The preacher nodded to Jack, signaling him to continue.

"With this ring," he said, taking my hand into his and sliding the circle on my finger, "I promise to be attentive, understanding, faithful, loving and kind, for all the days of our lives."

The preacher then nodded at me.

"With this ring," I repeated the vows we had agreed upon, putting the ring on his finger and holding it in place, my eyes confirming my devotion, "I promise to be attentive, understanding, faithful, loving and kind, for all the days of our lives."

"And with that," the officiant said, "I now pronounce you husband and wife." He turned to the audience and announced, "May I now introduce to you Mr. and Mrs. Jackson and Emily Holland."

Our guests applauded loudly, almost drowning out the most important part of the ceremony.

"Jack," he said, "you may *now* kiss your wife."

"Come here, you," he says softly when I reach him in the front of the courtroom. I smile at his invitation. It was the same one he had murmured quietly before we exchanged our first kiss as husband and wife. He takes my head in his hands as my heart flutters in excitement, grabbing hold of his arms, barely hanging on to the carnations. He looks at me tentatively, just like he had that night in college, just like he had on our wedding night, measuring my reaction.

As his lips brush lightly against me, he closes his eyes just before I shut mine. We'd kissed this way hundreds of times, felt this electricity every time, but today, it feels different.

We part briefly to look into one another's eyes, his deep blue into my pale green, then meet again for the deeper kiss. The chaotic room seems to go silent, the world around us disappearing as it always tends to do when he kisses me this way. A familiar little voice suddenly echoes in the cavernous hallway, just outside the courtroom, interrupting the quietness, but thankfully so. *It's almost time.* Our smiles force the kiss to end, and he takes my hand in his and we both turn to the back of the room.

"Just a few more minutes..." he says as the door opens.

Our lawyer follows one of Livvy's social workers into the courtroom. As Jack greets the lawyer, I turn my attention to the large crowd of our families that has gathered to witness this special occasion.

"Have you heard from Kelly?" I ask Jack's parents.

"We just talked to her," his mother confirms.

"Is Andrew feeling better?"

"He's fine. It was just a sprained ankle, but Kell said he's been in good spirits all morning."

"Good."

"I guess she should be meeting with the caterer right about now."

"Sh...*oot*, Jack?" I interrupt his discussion with a tap on his shoulder. He turns and raises his eyebrows, his smile still warm. "I didn't leave a key for your sister."

"She came by the house yesterday, Poppet. I forgot to tell you, I had a spare made for her."

"Of course," I sigh. *Always a step ahead of me.* "Thanks." He nods and continues his earlier conversation, weaving his fingers between mine. I turn to the front of the room, anxious for this legal stuff to be behind us once and for all. Chris comes to sit on the other side of me, Anna and Eli in tow. After he kisses me on the cheek, the bailiff announces the judge's arrival.

As the proceedings begin, my wandering mind takes me back to the evening that Livvy moved into our home. It's hard to believe three months have already passed since we began the supervisory period.

Up until that point, we had been granted visitations with the sweet little girl we met last Christmas. Our compulsive endeavor to help find her a good home worked in our favor. Her foster family– a loving, big family– was only providing temporary guardianship, so there was no one contesting our petition to adopt her.

Olivia had cried the first couple of nights she stayed with us. Even though the three of us had spent significant time together in previous months, it was hard for her little four-year-old mind to grasp the concept of parents and families and homes. Olivia had never known her father, and we found out quickly that her young mother had spent a significant amount of time in the hospital, being treated for leukemia, before she died. Livvy knew what a mommy was, but didn't even know her own mother very well.

She exchanged a tearful goodbye when "Mr. John" and "Mrs. Charlie" brought her to our home. We had prepared all of her favorite foods, and the five of us had dinner together. John and Charlie Shaw had five grown children of their own, but hated having an empty house when they all eventually moved out. Becoming foster parents was a natural choice for them, and their home had been open to these children in need of good parents for the past ten years.

It was obvious that Livvy held a special place in their heart. Anyone who met her fell immediately in love with her, just as we had. It was difficult for her foster parents to say goodbye, especially when the alligator tears streamed from Livvy's big brown eyes. It broke my heart, and Jack's, as well. I remembered how he had turned away briefly to wipe a tear from his cheek.

He hated to see her cry.

From the day we met her, even though we had committed to simply finding her a good home, I knew that Jack would do everything in his power to make sure it was *our* home, and he did. I didn't know all the details, but I knew that he and Donna used quite a few of their contacts to get us in the system. It helped that Jack was very well known in the city for his philanthropic endeavors– and that he had never made an enemy in all of his life.

"Mr. Jack?" Livvy had said when the Shaws left, wiping her nose with the sleeve of her t-shirt. She always went to him first. She would be *his* little girl, a thought that made my heart swell with joy. I never thought I could love him any more, until I saw him with her.

"Yes, Contessa?" She was his little princess, and she had so quickly become our whole world. Jack helped to blot her tears with a tissue as he drew her into his lap on the couch. I cuddled up next to them, releasing her hair from the short pigtails and combing my fingers through the fine locks. She started to pull on his tie, something she had done since the first day we met, as her head fell on his shoulder.

"Do I have to call you 'Daddy' now?" His mouth fell open, only slightly, before he closed his lips together and swallowed hard. He closed his eyes and inhaled slowly.

"Livvy, you can still call us 'Mr. Jack' and 'Mrs. Emi,' if that makes you happy," I answered for him in a soothing tone. We had talked about it before.

Of course we would never demand her to call us her mom and dad. In fact, I was reluctant to accept the possibility until everything was legal. I still feared that something would occur to keep the adoption from happening, even though everything had gone our way up to that point. Jack's disappointment was something I didn't want to ever see again, but I always knew that it was a possibility. Losing her would be devastating, and I knew getting so attached was dangerous. I wouldn't allow myself to consider the consequences anymore.

"We do hope to be your mommy and daddy someday, though, remember? And when it starts to feel like we're doing a good job of that, then you can call us that."

"How will I know if you're doing good?" she had asked.

"I think you'll just... know," Jack answered.

"I *want* you to do good," she said with conviction well beyond her years.

"*We* want to do a good job," I had told her, but when we tried to put her to bed that night, we both felt we were failing miserably as she squealed loudly when we turned the light off to her bedroom. She was deathly afraid to be alone in the basement at night, something we had only briefly considered. Our nieces and nephews often stayed down there, but we had realized they were never alone.

And, in all honesty, we hadn't wanted to be so far away from her, either, even with the remote monitor we had installed in her room so we could hear her from our bedroom two stories away.

Until she moved in, neither Jack nor I were prepared to make any permanent changes. I didn't want to jinx things, and even though Jack was never one to be superstitious, I think he felt the same. One night was all it took, though. She slept soundly in between us that night, curled up with Teddy, as Jack and I whispered quietly until early morning.

The next day, an architect and a contractor were hired, and until the room was complete, we set up a temporary sleeping space for her in the living room. Jack and I would curl up on the couch to watch her, making sure she and Ruby were comfortable and fast asleep on the pull-out bed before returning to our own bedroom.

Even then, we would often wake up to Livvy climbing into bed beside us, with the dog always following a few minutes later. She would chatter with us about her dreams– she had a very active imagination– and Jack would always lull her back to sleep by reciting by heart one of the many children's books he had memorized over the years. Sometimes he would carry her back downstairs, but more often than not, we would both curl up around her, listening to her deep-breathing and entertaining sleep-talking until we, too, fell asleep.

We finally fell into a pretty good routine, and day by day, things began to feel more permanent. Twice a week, Donna would take Livvy down to Nate's Art Room, allowing her to explore her burgeoning creativity while making new friends, which also gave Jack and I some alone time. We never once regretted our decision to adopt so quickly, but the fact still remained that we were newlyweds and our attraction to one another hadn't even begun to wane. I doubted it ever would.

As the weeks went on, I eventually stopped allowing myself to think about the irrational what-ifs because I knew Jack and I were both irrevocably attached to *our* little girl. Losing her wasn't an option. We were already a family, maybe not on paper, but in our hearts we were. Jack made it easy for me to focus on the present day, and Livvy always kept us on our toes.

We ditched our routine last night, though. We didn't try to make Livvy sleep on the sofa-bed. The bedroom renovation had been complete for a few days, but we had kept it all a secret and wanted to reveal it to her after the proceedings today. The decor was inspired by the Corduroy mural that Nate had drawn. After all, it was a well-loved bear that brought us all together in the first place. When we finished dinner, we had taken a long walk with Ruby through Central Park. As soon as we returned home, the three of us settled into bed with frozen yogurt with fruit and a double feature of two of Livvy's favorite movies. I had planned the night. I needed a distraction from the doubts that came creeping up at the last minute, and I knew that hearing Livvy's giggle would take my mind off of anything negative. It did temporarily. She and Jack had both dozed off near the middle of the second movie. After it ended, I watched them both sleep, their faces both restful and content, for at least a couple of hours. I may have quietly cried a little out of fear, but I was careful not to disturb them. I wanted to remember them in that moment forever, just in case something completely unexpected happened today.

Jack had planned a morning meeting with the lawyer, and Livvy was to stay with her caseworker and Donna until the hearing was over, so they left early, allowing me to go back to sleep for an hour after I helped get Livvy ready. I didn't think my nerves would allow me any rest after I tearfully kissed her goodbye.

"Miss Emi, why are you crying?" she asked, her bottom lip beginning to quiver. Jack gave me a concerned yet loving look, and I knew he was worried I'd upset her.

He leaned in and whispered so only I could hear, "There's nothing to worry about, Poppet. You're being silly." He kissed my temple and wiped away the tears, then swept Livvy into his arms and started bouncing her on his hip.

"She's just sleepy," Jack answered. "You know how sometimes you get cranky when you don't get a nap?"

"You need a nap?" she asked inquisitively. "You just woke up!"

"You'd be tired, too, if you stayed up to watch all of Wall-E like I did. I had to know how it ended!" I fibbed.

"Wall-E and Eva live happily ever after!"

"Just like us..." Jack said, a smile spreading across his face. I rolled my eyes, but couldn't help but smile back. "Speaking of which, Contessa, we need to get going. You get to go have breakfast with Miss LaVonne and Miss Donna this morning, remember?"

"Pancakes!" she cheered.

"Eat some fruit for me, too, okay, Livvy?" I requested.

"Okay," she sighed.

The judge clears his voice, bringing me out of my reverie.

"In regards to the child custody case of Olivia Sophia DeLuca, the municipal court of New York awards sole custody of the minor in question to Jackson Andrew Holland the second and Emily Clara Holland."

As I listen to the judge's final determination of Livvy's future, I get goosebumps in anticipation of seeing her again, but this time, for the first time, she is legally our daughter. She's been our daughter for months, but it's finally official. No one can take her away from us now. I involuntarily squeeze Jack's hand. He turns to look at me and places his arm across my shoulders and rubs my bare arm.

"Are you ready?" he whispers.

I nod my head. "*So* excited." His smile grows bigger and he pulls my body into his, kissing the top of my head.

When the proceeding has ended, we thank our lawyer and one of Livvy's case workers. Jack pulls on his suit jacket before hugging his parents, and then mine.

"So where is she?" my mother asks.

"They've got her in another room. They said they would take us to her," he answers.

"What are we waiting for?" Jen asks. I shrug and start to make my way to the back of the courtroom. We all congregate in the hallway, and our families make arrangements for the afternoon, talking about who's going in whose car back to our house.

I hold Jack's arms around me as he stands behind me and whispers in my ear. "You're the most beautiful mother I have ever met." I blush and thank him while he kisses my temple.

"And you are... the perfect fa–"

"Daddy!" a tiny voice calls out from down the hallway. Jack's breathing stops and his body stills as his arms tighten around me. I crane my neck to see his bewildered expression as my eyes start to water. He releases his arms as we both turn around to meet the light clicking sounds of Livvy's white flower eyelet sandals on the tiled floor as she runs toward us.

All attention is focused on the little brown-haired girl, carrying her stuffed dog in one hand and her stuffed bear in the other.

"My little Contessa," Jack says as he bends down on one knee, his arms outstretched. I put my hands on his shoulders and watch as her eyes connect with his, and her toothy grin spreads from ear-to-ear.

I can't stop the happy tears from dropping from my eyes at her pronouncement. Donna and LaVonne walk slowly behind her, both smiling, as Teresa takes out her camera and starts taking pictures. Jack picks her up and swings her around twice, kissing her cheek and smoothing out her windswept bangs. The addition of two bright pink bows– undoubtedly Donna's doing– accentuates the hair I had pulled up earlier into little top-knots on her head.

"It's okay if I call you Daddy today, right?" she whispers to him, her eyes wide as his eyes water. When she sees me, she drops her bear and holds her arm out for me to take her. After handing her the carnations– her favorite flowers– I hug her tightly as she throws her arms around my neck and squeezes. "Miss Donna and Miss LaVonne and me had pancakes and fruit like you said and Miss Donna said that the judge said that you're my Mommy and Daddy today. So, Miss Emi, I can call you Mommy now?" she looks at me with curious eyes and takes a deep breath from her run-on sentence.

"It's official today, baby," Jack confirms, picking up her stuffed animal and placing it in my bag. He takes her back into his arms, and as she hugs his neck, Jack and I exchange a reassured look before he puts his hand on my cheek and kisses me, full on the lips. "I love you," he breathes.

"I love you," I sigh back, my fingers ruffling his hair before he pulls me into an embrace with them both. When we finally let go, Livvy has buried her finger in the knot of his tie, trying to loosen it, repeating an action she had seen me do many times before.

"Your tie is pretty," she says.

"It is really nice, Jacks, where'd you get it?" I ask him.

"Anna actually bought it for me. She thought it would look nice with your dresses. It does," he smiles. "But that's not the best part," he adds, loosening the tie when her little fingers can't seem to do it. He flips the tie over to reveal an embroidered tag on the back of it.

"*Olivia Sophia Holland*," he reads the tag to her. "And then that's today's date beneath it. This is *your* tie. Whenever I wear it, I'll be thinking about you, and remembering how special this day is."

"But, Daddy, it's on the back. No one will even see it," she complains softly with the cutest furrowed brow I have ever seen.

"That way, you'll be closer to my heart," he says. I sigh at the sweet gesture and quietly thank Anna.

"Oh!" Livvy exclaims, as if to say '*of course!*' "Okay." He kisses her forehead again, hugs her again. "Where are all my friends?" she asks as she pulls the flowers to her nose to take a sniff. We had told her about the celebration we were having at the house, and she was excited to see everyone again.

"Your friends– and your *cousins*– are already at our house waiting for us to come home."

"Come here, Little Liv," Matthew says, whisking her away from Jack. She laughs loudly as his strong arms fly her through the air, her white, green and pink ribbon dress ballooning out underneath her textured white coat. "What else do we have to do in this cold, drab building? It's a beautiful day, don't we have a soiree to go to?" Matty bounces our daughter– holy... *our daughter*– on his hip as she continues to giggle.

"Yeah, don't we have a saw-ree to go to?" she repeats him.

"What are we waiting for?" Jack laughs, gesturing for them to go ahead of us. He puts his arm around my shoulder and kisses my temple gently as we watch his brother follow the rest of our families, carrying Livvy down the hallway. "Who knew this is where we'd be a year ago?"

"A lot can happen in a year. Think about it. In less than a year, we'll be taking her to her first day of school." I sigh audibly. "I already feel like we've lost so much time with her, Jack," I tell him, my eyes tearing on what I knew would be an emotional day. He pulls me into a hug and nuzzles his head to mine, holding me tight, his slow and calm breathing in my ear settling my nerves as I think about what the future holds for us.

Will our little girl cry on her first day of school, like I did when I watched my mommy leave me, alone in a room with a bunch of strange kids? Or will she be like Jack, the strong one, sitting at her tiny desk, waving me away as I watch her from the door, wistful tears pooling in my eyes?

Will Livvy believe that there really is a pixie that flies around, giving children silver dollars when they lose their teeth? I could remember the excitement that came the night before, and the wonder I would wake up to as I held the coin in my hand the next morning. Jack told me he only pretended to sleep on the night he lost his second tooth, just waiting to see this so called "fairy," who looked remarkably similar to his mother. He kept the secret, didn't spoil it for his siblings.

She was already so curious *and* creative, I wasn't sure she'd end up spending her summers with her nose buried in books, or outside, committing the beauties of nature to memory so she could paint them quietly in her room at night.

Would she excel in the arts? Or academics? Or sports?

And how would she handle her first crush? Her first heartbreak? How would *we* handle it? Would it ever get easier, seeing her cry?

What about her first love? Or second? Or the love that would walk with her through life, always there to make her worries disappear with a single kiss. I could see Jack, sitting across the table from an eager boy, asking all the right questions to determine whether or not this *kid* was good enough for his little Contessa.

Hopefully, she'll be lucky enough to eventually find someone just like her father. Her father, my partner. I look up at him and smile.

"What are you thinking about, Poppet?" he says as we start to walk together toward the exit, now just the two of us, alone.

"Her wedding day."

"Hold it, my little girl isn't getting married." I laugh at his expected response. "Didn't you just say you felt like we'd already missed too much of her life? Why are you jumping decades into the future?" He looks down at me, his blue eyes sparkling as a ray of sunshine peeks through the door that someone has pushed back open.

"I just wonder who she'll take after," I tell him.

"I hope a little of both of us," he says. "Only time will tell."

"Going forward, I just want to make every single day count."

"I promise to make every single day count," Jack vows. "I promise."

"I promise," I whisper back to him.

"Daddy, are you coming?" Livvy's little figure silhouettes in the doorway, the bright sunshine obscuring any details.

"Yes, baby, we're coming," he answers her, walking toward her. Jack's long stride beats me to her and he sweeps her up, carrying her out of the building and leading our families down the steps.

From the shadowy hallway, the bright afternoon sun beckons me as I watch them from the great doorway of the courthouse. I admire Jack as he listens to Livvy's chatter, completely captivated by every word. I can't hear the conversation, but every time I hear his voice, she laughs heartily, kicking her feet playfully.

Nearing the crosswalk that leads to the parking garage, Jack stops suddenly, adjusting Livvy on his hip and looking around slowly. Our eyes meet from across the courtyard. He nods his head slightly, signaling for me to join them before they cross the street. I've never seen him so happy, so content, so... *complete*... as I do in that moment. I recognize the same feelings in myself, and know that this is the way my life is supposed to be. I smile broadly, take a deep breath, and step out into the noonday radiance, toward my family, my daughter, my husband, my true love... and I never look back.

BOOKS BY LORI L. OTTO

Lost and Found

Book One of the Emi Lost & Found series

Time Stands Still

Book Two of the Emi Lost & Found series

Never Look Back

Book Three of the Emi Lost & Found series

SPECIAL THANKS TO

John T. Perry

Shirley Otto

Clarinda Alcalen

Trisha Duke

Melissa Dean

Kristina Bradshaw Evans

Trina Robinson

Mitzi Clark

Jeff Daniel

Stephanie Barone

Summer Ortiz

Des Grosshuesch

Angela Pritchett Meyer

Linda Shasberger

CPSIA information can be obtained at www.ICGtesting.com
Printed in the USA
LVOW011612130513

333556LV00019B/1022/P

9 781453 755440